ILSA

ILSA

A Novel

MADELEINE L'ENGLE

NEW YORK

Cover design by Connie Gabbert

ISBN: 978-1-5040-4944-3

This edition published in 2018 by Open Road Integrated Media, Inc.
180 Maiden Lane
New York, NY 10038
www.openroadmedia.com

TO MY MOTHER

ILSA

PART ONE

1

I watched the little girl for a long time. She sat on a rickety wooden fence that had never been painted any color. Now it had the look of the burned, parched-out brown-gray of the August grasses at her feet—or again of the cracked palm leaves that sounded like paper rattling in the sultry devil's breath of wind—or the dead hair of Spanish moss smothering the live oaks.

She was talking to some men from a chain gang. They were very big and very black, and their muscles moved with a smooth, liquid beauty under their bare, sweat-streaked backs. Their black-and-white-striped trousers were cut off or rolled to their knees and so dirty that the stripes were blurred to a uniform gray.

"Why are you here?" the little girl was asking. "Did you kill your wife with a hatchet?"

Standing with their weight on one lazy leg, their picks swung loosely over their shoulders, the colored men were telling her how they got on the chain gang—some for petty thievery, some for meaningless murder, some for rape, some because they beat their wives when they felt good.

I crouched very still behind a clump of palmettos because I was scared. Mamma had told my sister and me time and again that if we were bad the chain gang would come at night with their fetters clanking, and the overseer, too, with his long black whip like a snake and his gun in a leather holster on his hip; then we would have iron bracelets soldered onto our ankles and become part of the gang, with the chains dragging as we walked. I was especially frightened because I'd just been very bad, and my being hidden there behind the palmetto clump, with the hot, dry sand burning through my trousers and through the calluses on my feet, was bad in itself.

The men didn't see me and neither did the little girl. She was far too busy with her conversation, sitting there on her burned-out fence. Her huge straw hat had slipped back on her head and was hanging by a pair of frayed scarlet ribbons. Her wild, sun-bleached hair was exposed to the intense heat of the afternoon. Her faded blue cotton dress was tight against a body that, almost imperceptibly, was beginning to lose its childish straightness and take shape. The dress was so tight, indeed, that there was a great rent down the back, and though some of the men eyed her in a way I didn't understand and didn't like, the biggest buck of all kept wishing plaintively that he hadn't broken his wife's neck so she could be there to sew up the tear, or put in a patch, because the little girl had said she didn't have a mother.

After a while the overseer moved out of the small shade of the live oak tree where he had been standing, wiping his forehead and the back of his neck with a red cotton handkerchief. He cracked his whip against boots that were laced to his knees. I looked at him and thought that he was dressed exactly the way Mamma described the overseer of a chain gang; but his face wasn't a bit frightening. He simply looked tired and bored.

When they heard the crack of the whip the colored men said good-bye to the little girl and shuffled off through the gray sand of the road while she waved good-bye to them until they rounded the bend and were lost to sight in the pine woods. She sat kicking her heels against the fence for a few moments longer; then she jumped down and caught sight of my pony where I had tethered him to a palm tree a few yards down the road in the opposite direction from which the chain gang had gone.

I got up from the shade of my palmetto clump and followed her. She didn't hear me because she was so intent on the pony, who was nuzzling into her empty palm.

"Hey," I said.

"Is he yours?" she asked, turning around.

I slapped Billy's rump in the way that he liked. "Yes. He's mine."

We were silent. I hoped she would speak again. I liked her clear, cool voice. After a while she said, "What do you call him?"

"Billy."

I wondered where she lived. She seemed very much at home out here in the wilderness in her faded dress and bare feet and sun-bleached hair. Her strong, straight legs and arms were covered with mosquito bites and she began to scratch her ankle now, saying, "My father has a horse. Her name is Calypso. What's your name?"

"Henry Randolph Porcher. You spell it P-o-r-c-h-e-r but you pronounce it *Puhshay*," I said pompously. "What's yours?"

I thought she smiled a little oddly as she answered, "Ilsa Brandes."

"How old are you?" I asked.

"Thirteen. How old are you?"

"Ten. Almost ten and a half. But I'm taller than you are." And I was; by a full inch. She didn't say anything; she just shrugged slightly, and we stood looking at each other, one on either side of Billy, until we saw a tall, stooped man in a shabby Palm Beach suit and a panama hat walk slowly down the path toward us.

He had an extraordinarily fine head, blue flamelike eyes that were duplicated in the little girl, a broad high forehead from which thick light hair was brushed back proudly under the hat, a patrician nose that was delicate and strong at the same time, and a sweet, sensuous mouth.

I didn't notice any of this at the time. I only knew that the little girl was no longer paying any mind to Billy or to me but was looking with adoration at the man. She stood still and tense in the middle of the road until he came up to her, put his hands on her shoulders, and looked with his blue eyes into hers.

"Well, Ilsa?"

"Father—"

"You have made a friend?"

She nodded.

"Suppose you introduce us?"

She turned to me. "This is Henry Randolph Porcher. My father, Dr. John Brandes."

"How do you do, sir?" I held out my hand.

He frowned when he heard my name; nevertheless, he smiled as he took my hand in his and said, "So you are one of the famous Porchers." He pronounced it properly, the French way, not the soft, slurred "Puhshay" I usually heard it called.

"Yes, sir."

"I am delighted to make your acquaintance, Henry, and I would like to ask you to stay and take supper with Ilsa and me, but I think your father would not like to have you enter my house. Do you live in that big place on the river? Are you one of those Porchers?"

"Yes, sir."

"You have a good two hours' ride ahead of you. I think you had better start now if you are to get back before dark."

"I'm not going back," I said.

"What?"

"I'm not going back."

"Never?"

"Never."

"I'm afraid your father will have something to say about that."

"Please let me stay to supper," I begged.

Dr. Brandes hesitated for a moment before he answered. "I really do not see how Ilsa or I could contaminate you, but the Porchers are such rare creatures that they are very afraid of contagion."

"It's so hot," I said.

Dr. Brandes looked down at my flushed face. "Yes. You are right there, my boy. It is very hot. And, since you rode out here in the heat of the day, you'd probably do better not to go back while the sun is still full. Both of you come along to the house with me."

"May I ride the pony?" the little girl asked quickly.

"Ilsa," Dr. Brandes said.

"Oh, she can ride him," I answered, and in a flash she had vaulted into the saddle and was off like the wind.

"Ilsa!" Dr. Brandes called after her. "Don't ride the pony too hard! Remember he feels the heat, too!"

She pulled the pony up immediately, and they trotted on, while Dr. Brandes and I followed behind.

2

I hadn't realized how near we were to the ocean until the unmistakable sound of waves was suddenly distinguishable from the sound of the hot land wind in the pines. But even when we got up to the house we couldn't see the water because we went in the back way. It was a long, low house, made half of coquina, half of cypress wood. It was set quite far back from the beach, and was surrounded by palmettos, scrub oak, myrtles, and palms. Ilex bushes grew closely around it and by the door was a chinaberry tree. As we came up to it there was a flash of red from ilex bush to tree, and Dr. Brandes pointed out to me a redbird's nest. The heavy smell of four o'clocks burdened the air, and we could hear the sea gulls mewing like cats.

Ilsa had taken Billy to a low barn that was off to one side. Now she came running to meet us, then hurried ahead into the house, slamming the screen door in our faces. We followed her into a big room paneled in pine. The walls were lined with books, many of them in Latin and German, and most of them heavy and dark and learned-looking. In one wall was a huge fireplace with a bright tapestry above it; a skylight faced north, and under it was a long pine table covered with books and papers and specimens of plants and insects in jars. Under the staircase was a piano; the lid was up and a lighted lamp had been placed by it to keep out the damp. From the two front windows and the front door you could see the great stretch of ocean and sand, with a long cement ramp leading down over the scrub and the dunes, culminating in a little bulkhead to keep the tide from eating the sand away up to the house.

Ilsa was sitting on a low stool, scratching her mosquito bites; but she stopped quickly as we came in.

"I saw you," Dr. Brandes said, and they both laughed in a way that made me dreadfully homesick—but I guess it was for something I'd never had.

"They itch so!" Ilsa said.

"Do you want your foot infected again?"

"Unh unh."

"Well."

"All right, Father. I'll try not to scratch. Do you want to go swimming, Henry?"

I nodded. "But I haven't got a bathing suit."

"Oh, we don't need bathing suits. We can go in just in ourselves, can't we, Father?"

He looked from Ilsa to me, nodding his head slowly. "You can undress in my room, child. Ilsa, you will please hang your dress over your chair and not roll it up in a ball on the bed. Turn around." He looked at the rent in the back of her dress. "Ilsa! How did you do that?"

She looked down at her feet that were firmly planted on the rough pine floor. "Climbing a tree. For scientific purposes."

"Explain."

"I wanted to see how far back from the beach you could still see the ocean."

"Did you?"

"Yes."

"How far?"

"Tomorrow I will measure it. I got in a conversation. Father, please take Henry up to your room so we can go swimming."

"All right, ladybird." He turned to me. "Come along, child."

I followed him up the stairs. His bedroom was bare and light and immaculate. A narrow bed, with a mosquito net rolled above it; a chest of drawers; a straight chair, all made of unpainted pine. The curtainless windows looked out on the beach; it was like being in a cabin on a ship. Dr. Brandes gave me a large towel and left me. I undressed. In a moment I heard Ilsa's impatient voice. "Henry! Hurry up!"

I ran downstairs, and she burst out laughing. "Father, look at him!"

"Ilsa, that is not polite."

"But he's brown only where he hasn't worn a bathing suit! It makes him look skinny!"

"Ilsa, you will apologize or you will go upstairs and lie on the bed with your eyes closed for an hour."

She looked at me and held out her hand. "If I've said anything rude, or anything that would hurt you, I'm very sorry."

I took her hand. "Oh, it's all right."

"Father, he's younger than I am," she said. "I thought it was only in front of grown-up people that I couldn't say what I thought."

"When what you think is unkind, you don't say it to anyone."

"I see."

He pushed her short wild hair back from her face. "Child, some day you are going to find it very hard to forgive me for the life I've given you."

She flung herself at him. "Don't be silly. . . . Come on, Hen, I'll race you to the water."

She tore out of the room, slowed up, and stumbled a little as she got into the soft loose sand, then leaped like some wild animal across the great stretch of beach packed firm by the tide, scattering a group of sea gulls, who rose into the air screeching and swirling over our heads as she splashed into the water. I followed her, a good distance behind.

"You didn't do too badly for someone who's never been here before," she said kindly.

The water was very quiet. We were only shoulder deep when we got beyond the breaking waves and could relax in the quiet swells. Ilsa rolled over on her back and floated, and the sea gulls gathered on the beach again.

My sister and I were never allowed in the water unless a grown person was with us. Ilsa said, "Father taught me to swim in all sorts of water, so if I go swimming alone I won't get caught in the undertow or change of tide. But I'm not allowed to go out above my head; so if you do, I assume no responsibility for you. Father says if you ever see anything that looks as though it might be a shark or a barracuda, just float. Don't move a finger. Sharks are very nearsighted and they're not apt to see you unless you get excited and move. You're a pretty good swimmer. You live on the river, don't you?"

"Yes."

"Aren't there moccasins in the river?"

"Yes. Papa keeps antivenom in his bathroom," I said, "and we always have to have a grownup when we go swimming."

"Who's we?"

"My sister and I."

"How old is your sister?"

"Twelve."

"Everyone's younger than I am," Ilsa said. "What's her name?"

"Anna Silverton Porcher."

"I like the name Anna."

"We call her Silver."

"Well, I like that, too. Why aren't you going home?"

"Because I cut Monty's head open."

"Who's Monty?"

"Montgomery Woolf. Our cousin. I hate him. But he's older than you. He's fifteen. Almost."

"Did you kill him?"

"I don't think so. But maybe he'll die."

"Why did you cut his head open?"

"Because of Silver's rocking horse. She never lets me ride it. And then when Monty and Eddie and Violetta—our cousins—came over this morning to spend the day, she let Monty play with my violin I was making."

"Making?"

"Yes. Out of cypress wood. And using rubber bands for strings. And he broke one of the strings and he laughed and then Silver got on the rocking horse. She's much too big for a rocking horse. Twelve years old. And she said I couldn't ride it, but Monty could. She just sat there and rocked and rocked and smiled and smiled and looked at Monty, and then I hit him on the head with the violin. I wish one of the nails had gone right through his head."

"What do you want with a rocking horse when you've got a pony?" Ilsa asked me, then ducked under the salt water and began blowing bubbles. She came up and said, "You're too old for a rocking horse, anyhow."

"It's a very *big* rocking horse," I said, as she went down again. I watched the bubbles rising to the surface of the water and remembered the hurt when Mamma rapped me on the head with her thimble and said I was a wicked boy and she was astonished at me, and I would have to pray very hard that night if I didn't want the chain gang after me; and Papa called me into the library, pulled down my trousers and switched me, and told me all about gentlemen respecting their sisters and not striking their cousins, even though Monty was almost fifteen.

I knew I would always hate my cousin Monty Woolf and his twin sister Violetta, though I sometimes liked going over to their house to play, and I was fond of their younger brother, Edwin, who was just a few months older than my sister. There was a large grove of magnolia trees near their boathouse where we used to play, and there were oak trees, too, and great grape vines hanging from them that made wonderful swings.

On Sunday, after Sunday school, we often went over for dinner, and afterward we played the Bible Game, a kind of combination of conundrums and Old Maid, that was not considered playing cards and that taught us all the stories about the Bible so that I remember them to this day. Tobias and the Angel was always my favorite, and somehow or other I learned that Alborak was the white mule Mohammed went to heaven on, though I'm sure that's not in the Bible and wasn't in the game.

"I suppose you go to school," Ilsa said, rather wistfully.

"Of course. Don't you?"

"No. Father has me read things, though. Do you like school?"

"Not much. But I like our teacher. She really teaches the big ones English, but she has us this year because our own teacher is sick. Her name is Miss Myra Turnbull. She took us on a picnic and we sang a song about me."

"About you?"

"Yes." I sang loudly:

O, where have you been wandering, King Henry, my son?
O, where have you been wandering, my pretty one?

King *Henry*, see? She said it was about me."

"It's a nice song," Ilsa said politely. "I think I'd like to go to school." Then she turned a somersault in the water. "In the water backward somersaults are easier than forward ones. Have you ever looked at faces upside down?"

"What?"

"Looked at faces as though they went the other way around? Float. Now, see, if I cover your nose and mouth with this hand, and look at you as though your nose and mouth go where your hair goes—upside down, you see. . . . Oh, Henny! You look awful! You look like a ghoul. Do you want to try me?"

She floated and I covered her face with my hands so that only her eyes showed. When I tried to imagine her face with her eyes upside down, it was awful, terrifying! "I don't like it!" I wailed.

She turned over and laughed. "Oh, Henny, I didn't mean to scare you. Come on. Let's go home. Father ought to have dinner ready. Look, Henny, see how small the waves are? I can float all the way into shore on one. Father showed me how to hit it just right no matter how small they are. Look!"

She disappeared into the crest of a wave. I could see her naked tan body as it flashed in to shore. She tumbled onto the beach and shouted at me, but even though the wind was blowing hot from the land the sound was diffused and I couldn't hear. I tried to throw myself into a wave as she had done, but it passed on without me. I knew she was laughing. I stayed for a minute in the cool salt water, letting it lap gently against my neck and shoulders. I wondered what it must feel like to be part of the beach and have the water caressing you daily. I thought a mother should caress the way the ocean did. But when Mamma tried to be affectionate it was like the touch of the dried-out rose leaves she kept in her bureau drawers.

Ilsa stood on the shore and waved her arms at me. I waded in to her. "I wasn't laughing at you," she said, reading my thoughts. "It took me an awful long time to learn to come in on small waves like these. I was just laughing because I felt good. You act as though you keep expecting people to laugh at you. You ought to just laugh at them. I'll bet they're funnier than you are. I'm hungry. Come on. It's going to be night soon."

At the beach the evenings are longer than anywhere else at home because the whiteness of the sand holds the light as long as it can. But even at the beach it comes as a surprise. One minute it's bright daylight and the next minute you can't see two feet in front of you. When we climbed up the ramp to the house, the beach and the quiet pools of water in the shallow sloughs at the ocean's edge held all the gentle luminous colors of the mother-of-pearl shells that were washed up after a storm. But when we crossed the long room and looked out the back door where the ilex bushes, the myrtles, and the palmettos went into the pines, night was already coiled there, lying behind the house like a languid black snake. The chinaberry tree was a dark shadow from which Dr. Brandes emerged.

"Did you have a good swim?" he asked, as he came into the room. We nodded. From one of the shelves he took two candles in blue-and-white china holders, which he gave us. We went upstairs to dress. I could feel the soft dry grains of sand under my feet as I climbed the stairs. I put the candle on the chest and went over to the window. There were still a few faint stains of day left on the water, and as these began to go, from the very edge of the horizon came a clear arm of light that swept over the sea, flickered and went out, then swung over the dark water again, and again, and again.

Mamma had told us about the lightship. To be sent to the lightship was a threat even worse than the chain gang. Three men were out on that lightship, and they were there for six-month stretches with nothing to do but tend that light. Sometimes a boat would go out to bring them supplies. One night, long before I was born, the light had failed to go on, and a large sailing vessel had gone to the bottom. When the investigators went out to the lightship the following morning they found what was left of all three men lying on the deck in pools of blood. Around and around the ship sharks were swimming, their teeth and their white bellies gleaming, while buzzards were already at the bloody carcasses, occasionally dropping from their too-eager beaks something which the sharks would snatch up. It was because of this dreadful event, Mamma told my sister Silver and me, that the sharks still circled the boat, day and night, waiting for three more men to get in a fatal brawl, or perhaps for one of them to fall overboard. And a buzzard was always perched on the highest mast, the wind blowing his black, scraggly neck feathers, so that the livid flesh showed through. If Silver or I were especially wicked (only, of course, it would be me—Silver was never wicked, according to Mamma), we were told we would be taken out to the lightship and fed to the ancient witch of a buzzard and the avaricious, anticipating sharks.

I was still standing naked by the window watching the lightship when Ilsa came in carrying her candle. She put it next to mine on the chest and came over to the window.

"Father's going to take me out to the lightship some day," she said, as its finger appeared on the edge of the horizon and pointed across the ocean.

"You mean you'd like to go?"

"Oh, more than anything! Wouldn't you?"

"I—I don't know," I stammered, thinking of Mamma and the sharks, but nevertheless calmed by the bright strength of the light as it traveled across the water.

"Hurry up and get your clothes on," Ilsa said. "I'm hungry and I know Father won't let me begin without you." She took her candle and vanished.

I stood by the window for a moment longer. I was comfortably cool for the first time in weeks. I was so cool, indeed, that I felt goose flesh come up in little ridges on my arms. As I turned from the window, the smell of dinner from downstairs fogged out the smell of salt and sea, and my stomach reminded me of how hungry I was. I pulled on my trousers and my blue cotton shirt, which were still damp from the perspiration of the afternoon, and remembered that I had left my sandals behind the palmetto clump where I had hidden while I watched Ilsa and the chain gang. I knew I would be punished for this, but on top of all my other naughtinesses it wouldn't make my punishment much bigger, and, anyhow, I knew they would all be surprised by my sudden burst of independence, so I was glad, because I hated wearing shoes in summer. I wondered if Ilsa ever had to wear shoes in summer, and somehow I didn't think she did.

3

When I went downstairs, Dr. Brandes no longer had on his shabby Palm Beach suit; he wore a pair of dark riding breeches. They were made of a handsome material I didn't know, and had evidently once been very fine. The candlelight was reflected in the polish of his boots; his shirt was of silk, and, though it was frayed around the collar and the cuffs, he looked wonderfully rich and handsome. His goatee hid the fact that his chin was a little too small for the rest of his face. The odd thing at the moment about his costume was that instead of his riding jacket, which was folded over a chair, he wore a white chef's apron. A small table was set for supper. Steam came from silver dishes. Hominy. Mullet. A bowl full of salad. Ilsa and I didn't talk during supper. We ate. Then Ilsa cleared the table and we went out into the kitchen to wash up.

Ilsa got a clean dish towel off the rack and handed it to me. "I'll wash and you dry," she said. "So you are one of the famous Porcher-Silverton-Woolf tribe." Her lips curled scornfully.

"What's wrong with us?" I asked. People didn't usually speak about our family that way. People kowtowed to us. We were important, partly because we had money, and partly because of our name.

Our town was rather odd that way—too far south to be really southern in the old tradition, and yet not far south enough to be a resort. The residential section was roughly divided into two zones, the Southerners mostly on our side of the river. Although a few lived on some of the beautiful water-front property on the south side, it was mainly the hangout of the Northerners who had come down; and we looked askance at anyone who lived there whom we had not known always.

Papa was the most looked-up-to man in town, and we were considered Southerners because, although Grandpa was born in Colorado, his people had emigrated from Kentucky, and Grandma came from Missouri.

"Father says," Ilsa went on, "that we're still too close to the Civil War for you to have so much money, if your father and your grandfather were honest."

"Ilsa!"

She swung around. Dr. Brandes was standing in the doorway.

"What is it, Father?"

"I am ashamed of you."

"I'm sorry, Father."

I could tell that she was indeed very sorry, but her voice did not falter as she looked at him. His eyes burned like very cold blue flames; they were like the inside of a flame that is never hot.

"I will accept any punishment you say, Father. I will try not to be rude again. I don't mean to keep being rude to Henry. I like him. I wish I could see him again, even if he is only ten and a half. How are you going to punish me, Father?"

"I won't punish you this time. I like you to learn without punishment," he said, adding bitterly, "if it is possible for anybody to learn anything without punishment. . . . Hurry up with the dishes. We must take Henry Randolph Porcher home."

He left.

"I don't want to go home," I said.

"If Father has decided you are to go home, you will go. Don't you like the town?"

"I suppose so. I don't know. I've never lived anywhere else. Do you like it?"

"I've never been there."

"You haven't!"

"No."

"Have you always lived here at the beach?"

"Yes."

"Just with your father?"

"Yes."

"Is your mother dead?"

"Yes."

"When did she die?"

"When I was born. Now who's being rude?"

"Was I?"

"Father says that asking personal questions is rude. Here, you're awfully slow. I've all finished washing and you haven't nearly finished drying. I'll help you." She took another dish towel. When Dr. Brandes looked in the door again she was folding the dish towels over the rack.

"Have you finished?" he asked.

"Yes, Father."

"You may go out and saddle Calypso. Saddle Henry's pony, too."

I followed him from the kitchen. Ilsa banged happily out of the back door. I sat down on her magnolia-wood stool and watched Dr. Brandes as he took one of the candles and went upstairs. Then I fixed my gaze on the candle nearest me. It burned with a steady, warm flame; the sultry land breeze didn't waver it as a sea breeze would have done. The tallow was fragrant and dripped down onto glass *bobèches* that protected the candlesticks. As I watched the candle flame, my eyes began to sting; I put my head on my knees and my mind seemed to merge with the sound of waves caressing the sand. I wasn't sure which were my thoughts and which were the waves. I didn't hear Dr. Brandes come downstairs. He put his hand on my shoulder and said, "Sleepy, child?"

I raised my head and nodded. My eyes were so blurred with sleep that I didn't see him clearly; he looked as he might have looked seen under water or through fog.

Ilsa came in and stood in the doorway. "The horses are ready, Father." She looked at him eagerly, silently, begging not to be left behind.

"You had better ride the pony, Ilsa. Henry's too sleepy to stay on. I'll take him up with me."

I staggered to my feet.

"Fill my pipe, Ilsa," Dr. Brandes said. "I'll have to use it to keep away mosquitoes. Rub lavender oil over your arms and legs and face."

"It'll make me all shiny!"

"You'll look better all shiny than you would all covered with bites. Hurry up, now."

While she filled the pipe he put on his riding coat; then, as she began to smear herself with the heavy-scented lavender oil, he turned to me. "You, Henry, are the first, and probably the last, of the Porchers or any of their ilk to have crossed this threshold for over fifteen years. Do you feel sullied?"

"No, sir."

"If your father tells you what dreadful creatures we are, perhaps you will remember what you have seen for yourself. I would like it if you and Ilsa could meet again."

"Yes, sir. Won't we, *please*!"

"I hope so." He frowned a little and the straight up-and-down lines furrowed between his eyes were as clear-cut and definite as the rest of him. There wasn't anything indefinite about his bone structure or the flesh which covered it. This was true of Ilsa, too. Looking at her firm tan body, you felt that the skeleton beneath it would be clean and exquisite, and that it was satisfied with its covering. But if you looked at my cousin Violetta Woolf, Monty's twin sister, who was already a belle at not quite fifteen, with her soft plump body and her lustrous dark red hair, you had no idea what she would be like devoid of her outward trappings. As for me, I didn't care. Edwin was the only one of the Woolfs I could bear.

Dr. Brandes took the bottle of lavender oil and rubbed some over me. Then we went out. The night was black and heavy. You could almost put your hand out and feel it, warm and clinging like velvet. The low murmur of sea breaking on sand, of sea breathing quietly from shore to horizon, was augmented by the steady hum of insects. Frogs from back in the swamp. Mosquitoes. Locusts. Crickets. In spite of the lavender oil and Dr. Brandes' pipe, insects swarmed around my ankles. Remembering what he had said to Ilsa, I didn't dare bend down to scratch the bites, but concentrated on following with my eye the flashings of a firefly, until Dr. Brandes lifted me up on the saddle in front of him. Then I managed to scratch my itching legs against the horse.

While the path was narrow, Ilsa and Billy rode behind Calypso. We rode this way for about an hour. Gradually I became accustomed to the insects that swirled constantly about us like smoke, and, leaning against Dr. Brandes, I slept. When I woke up we were on the beach road. Billy and Calypso were side by side. Dr. Brandes and Ilsa were looking intently at a hot red glare that stained the sky in the direction of town.

"Is it a forest fire?" Ilsa asked.

"I don't know," he said.

"If it's a forest fire, we might have to turn back, mightn't we?"

"Yes, ladybird."

"Do you think it could be as far off as the town?" she asked.

"I can't tell yet. You live in the biggest house on the river, don't you, boy?"

"Yes, sir."

The closer we got to town the greater the red glare on the horizon became. When Dr. Brandes said, "I'm afraid it's the town. And it's not a small fire," I began to tremble. I remembered the time Randolph Silverton's house burned down. The flames shinnied up the water pipes like snakes, and when the roof shivered and collapsed it seemed that none of the houses near by were what they seemed, but had become perishable paper things that could vanish in a moment. Cousin Anna Silverton, after whom my sister Silver was named, was dreadfully burned saving one of the colored girls who was trapped in the servant's quarters; and I remembered the terrified wailing that my cousin Dolph let out when she was carried away on a stretcher to the Woolfs' house; and I remembered the look on old Cousin Randolph's face as he stood there by Cousin Anna's huge gold harp, clutching two silver candlesticks to him like a crucifix, listening to his wife moan as they carried her down the driveway, while he tried to quiet the animal terror of the boy.

Dr. Brandes felt my trembling and his arm tightened around me. "It's in the center of town," he said. "If you're on the river your house should be all right."

We rode for a long time in silence. When we had crossed the long wooden bridge we could see actual flames in the bloody glow ahead of us, and could feel the heat from the fire thrown like a heavy blanket over the already stifling night. The air was full of hot particles of dust, the way I imagined the air must feel after an earthquake or the eruption of a volcano. The roaring of the fire, although we could not as yet see what was burning, made the roar of the ocean during the mightiest storm seem like a whisper.

As we got into town, and the horses' hoofs began to clop on the pavement with the night sound they have, which is so different from the clopping they make by day, a group of Negroes came running past us. They were draped in sheets and their faces were distorted with terror. They were screaming, "Jedgment day, jedgment day, jedgment day," in a kind of mad wail. Every once in a while they would flop to their knees, crying and sobbing, "Lord Jesus, wash me clean; Marse Jesus, wash me in the blood of the Lamb; Marse Jesus, forgive us, for we done sinned." Then they would stumble to their feet again and run down the street, wailing ceaselessly, "Jedgment day, jedgment day!"

Calypso reared, pawing the air frantically as she caught their fear. Billy whinnied nervously, but Ilsa bent close to him and petted him, whispering soothingly into his ear. Dr. Brandes held me firmly while he quieted Calypso; then he looked to see that Ilsa and Billy were all right.

"Is it, Father?" Ilsa asked.

"Is it what?"

"Judgment day."

"I doubt it."

When we reached home it was almost like waking from a nightmare to see the house still standing, untouched by actual flame. But it was like a fragment of clear sleep set in the midst of horrible dreams, because the air surrounding it was a dirty, dusty red. I looked at Dr. Brandes and Ilsa, and their faces were covered with soot, although we had not yet actually seen the fire.

Dr. Brandes hitched the horses to the post, and we ran up the broad white steps. Mamma met us at the door. In her hand she brandished a carving knife. I thought, for a moment, that she had gone stark, staring mad, that she must have set fire to the town.

"Henry," she said. "Get the silver and bury it under the big live Oak at the foot of the drive. Hurry, boy, or I'll whip you." She turned to Dr. Brandes without seeing him. "Who are you?"

He bowed slightly. "John Brandes, at your service, Madam."

The excitement fled from her face. It became cold and icy, like marble, as her eyes suddenly focused on him. "Get out of this house," she said quietly. "And take that—that unfortunate child beside you, with you."

Papa appeared behind her. "Cecilia, this is no time for words like these. I don't know who you are, sir, but your help is desperately needed. . . ." Then he looked at Dr. Brandes and his face became as rigid as Mamma's. But he went on talking, in a voice that was so calm that it was more frightening than hysteria. "The whole town is going. The water supply has run dry. There is no use trying to draw buckets from the river. The land breeze is carrying flaming brands for blocks, and dropping them like matches from house to house. One may fall here at any time. Cecilia, finish with the portraits and load them in the carriage. Brandes, if you will help me with my books. Child, if you will help Henry with the silver. There is no time to lose."

He hurried into the library, followed by Dr. Brandes. Ilsa came after me through the rice portieres and into the dining room. My sister Silver was in there, wrapping the china in linen and packing it in buckets she had brought from the stable. Mamma climbed onto a chair, and with the carving knife slashed the portrait of her sister Elizabeth out of its heavy gold frame.

"Give me a tablecloth," I said to my sister.

Into the tablecloth I put as much silver as I could carry. Ilsa filled another, and we staggered out, while Mamma dashed madly around brandishing her carving knife and cutting the portraits out of their frames.

We dumped two loads of silver by the tree and went back for two more. My sister was still wrapping china in linen and packing it in buckets. By the time we had dumped our last load under the live oak tree, she had the eight buckets packed, and we helped her tote them out and load them onto an old wagon that was used to carry muck from swamp to garden. Then we got two spades from the tool shed and went back to the live oak. The shovels were gone and we saw Papa and Dr. Brandes digging by the magnolia tree nearest the river, surrounded by Papa's rare and precious books.

We dug until we were black as devils and pouring with sweat. Once Ilsa blew on her hands, which were covered with blisters and bleeding with splinters. Silver was somewhere in the house helping Mamma. There wasn't a servant to be seen, and I guessed they had all joined the white-sheeted crowd of judgment-dayers.

Then, over the trees, flew a living piece of fire. It flew through the tops of the trees, so that they became umbrellas of flame, and landed on the roof of the house. Papa said, "It's time to go."

Most of the room in the carriage was taken up by the portraits. Aunt Elizabeth's pale face, with its darks brows like Silver's, stared at us with a strange expression as it lay sideways on the seat. Papa got on the driver's seat, with Silver beside him; Mamma climbed into the carriage, surrounded by portraits and boxes containing her jewelry; Dr. Brandes and I climbed onto the seat of the wagon; Ilsa rode Calypso and led Billy. Just before we started off, Papa climbed down from the driver's seat and let the other horses out of the stable, smacking them sharply with his whip so that they tore down the street away from the fire. He had harnessed his favorite horse, Lafitte, to the carriage.

Flames were already coming from the house as we started down the driveway. Ours was the farthest house out to have caught fire. As we drove toward the bridge, we could see other families frantically trying to save what they could, as we had done. When we passed the Woolfs' house, Violetta, Monty, and Edwin, my cousins, were all carrying portraits which had been cut out of the frames, and packing them in their motorcar. That was something great-grandmother Porcher had taught all her children, and she knew about it because that was the way many of her family portraits had been saved during the French Revolution.

I thought with pain of the Silverton house. It was in the center of town, and I knew it must have burned again, because Cousin Randolph, in spite of Cousin Anna's pleading for stone, had insisted on building another white, wooden home, with a neo-Grecian façade like all the Silverton, Woolf, and Porcher houses. I was sure that another fire would kill Cousin Anna.

We overtook more families fleeing the fire. When we came in sight of the bridge there was a long line of all kinds of conveyances waiting to cross. The wind on our backs was like a tongue of flame. We were a long way from the bridge, and other carriages, goat carts, wagons, a string of impotent automobiles, unable to pass, were piling up behind us. One riderless horse, crazy with fear, reins hanging and flapping against its flanks, tore up beside us. Ilsa struggled to control Calypso and Billy, and I could see that Dr. Brandes was afraid she would be thrown. Our horse shied violently, and four of the eight buckets slid off the wagon onto the road. I could hear the crash of breaking china.

When the mad horse had passed on, and our horses had quieted down, showing their fear only by a nervous whinnying, twitching of the ears, and an occasional tremor through their bodies, Dr. Brandes handed the reins to me and climbed down from the wagon. I didn't dare turn around in case the horse should rear again, but I knew he was talking to Papa. In a few minutes he came back with my sister Silver, and drew the wagon to the side of the road, away from the line. Ilsa, Calypso, and Billy followed him.

He said to us, "Unless the wind changes, the fire will overtake us before we reach the bridge. We are going to try to swim across with the horses. I will take the little girl with me on Calypso. Ilsa, you and Henry will ride the pony. Your father tells me, Henry, you have had the pony in the river before."

"Yes, sir, but not at night, sir. Not when we were afraid of anything."

"You must not be afraid now," he said. "If you are not afraid it will be all right. Ilsa, I trust you."

"Yes, Father," she said.

I climbed onto Billy behind her and clung tightly to her waist. Her body was firm and strong, not wavery with terror like mine. Dr. Brandes held Silver in his arms. I couldn't tell whether or not she was afraid. The more Silver felt anything, the more composed and quiet her face got, and her dark eyebrows seemed all the more startling against the blondness of the rest of her. When her face became cold and composed like marble, I was afraid she might grow up to be like Mamma.

Dr. Brandes urged Calypso down the river bank and into the water. Ilsa dug her bare heels into Billy and made him follow. In comparison to the horrible hell-heat of the night, the water of the river was icy as it lapped at our feet. My toes curled in rejection, but soon it was over my ankles and then over my knees, and my trousers were wet against my thighs. Billy swam desperately, stretching his neck out to its furthest limit in order to keep his head above water. We kept our eyes glued to Dr. Brandes and Silver ahead of us on Calypso. He did not turn around, but every once in a while he would call, "Ilsa!" and she would answer, "Yes, Father!"

The darkness of the river water lapping against us was nothing like the water of the ocean as it had lapped so gently at my neck and shoulders in the afternoon. I knew that if this murky river water, black from cypress, came up to my neck and shoulders, it would claim me forever, I didn't know which was more horrible, the harsh breath of flame or the insidious licking of water.

"Ilsa!" Dr. Brandes called.

"Yes, Father!"

We were halfway across the river.

"Do you suppose snakes—" I whispered suddenly.

"Don't be silly," Ilsa said. "The snakes have gone down the river to get away from the fire."

I felt something long and slimy twine itself about my ankle and waited for the stinging prick of a moccasin's fang, but in a moment my ankle was free again, so I supposed it must have been a tendril from one of the water grasses, and Ilsa was right about the snakes.

Dr. Brandes, Silver, and Calypso clambered onto the bank. Five minutes more and Ilsa and I on Billy were beside them.

"Now pay careful attention," Dr. Brandes said. "Ilsa."

"Yes, Father."

"You will take Henry and his sister home on Calypso."

"Where are you going?"

"Back to town. They need everyone they can get."

"But, Father—"

"Ilsa, don't argue with me. Do as I say."

"Yes, Father."

"You will walk Calypso. When you put her in the shed, see that she is comfortable."

"Yes, Father. Of course."

"When you get home, the first thing you will do is to run up the flag for Ira."

"But when will you be back, Father?"

"As soon as I can. I want you all to go down to the ocean and wash your hands and feet in the salt water. Don't go in above your knees. The water will sting your blisters, but I want you to stay in it until you have counted five hundred, slowly."

"Yes, Father."

"Then go back to the house and get ready for bed. Ilsa, take Henry's sister with you in your bed. What is your name, child?" He looked at Silver for a long time, searchingly, and, raising one smoke-blackened finger, traced the line of her dark eyebrows.

"Anna Silverton Porcher. And I don't want to sleep in her bed."

"You will do as I say."

"I won't." Silver spoke in the same quiet, controlled voice that Mamma had used when she tried to throw Dr. Brandes out of the house.

"There are only two beds," Dr. Brandes said. "Ilsa, you will see that Miss Porcher shares yours."

"Yes, Father."

"Henry can have mine. You can give him a pair of my pajamas. I want you to stay in bed until Ira or I come to you. Do you understand?"

"Yes, Father."

"I expect your complete obedience."

"You will have it, Father."

Dr. Brandes lifted us onto Calypso. Ilsa took the reins. Silver sat in front of her; I was behind. Dr. Brandes watched us while we went down the road.

"If the wind doesn't change, what will happen?" I asked.

"Everybody in town who didn't get across the river will be burned," Silver said. "Papa will be burned and Mamma and all the Silvertons and Woolfs and Porchers. Cousin Anna Silverton will really be burned this time. And your father will be burned to death, too," she said to Ilsa.

Ilsa's fingers tightened on the reins, but all she said was, "The wind will change."

4

When we had gone down the beach road about a mile, it did change. All of a sudden Ilsa put her index finger into her mouth, drew it out, and held it up to the night, announcing, "The wind is coming from the ocean."

Silver started to cry. It was the first time I had seen her cry in over a year. Now her face became all contorted, and tears forced themselves out of her tightly closed eyes.

"Why are you crying?" Ilsa asked.

"Because the wind changed."

"Did you want everyone to burn up so badly?"

"No," Silver wailed. "I was so afraid they would! Mamma and Papa and everybody. I was so scared!"

"They'll be all right now," Ilsa said.

Silver cried for a few minutes longer. Then she fell asleep, and Ilsa had to steady her with one arm.

Calypso walked very slowly. She was tired from the long ride into town and from the hard swim across the river. I knew that Ilsa, swaying to the slow rhythm of Calypso's exhausted hoof beats, was wondering if her father had made it back across the river on poor little old Billy.

The sun was coming up over the ocean when we got back to the beach. The sky over the horizon was flooded with deep reds that were so calm and quiet that they couldn't remind you of the stain the fire had made against the sky. The revolving bar of light from the lightship flickered and went out.

Ilsa took a flag down from above the kitchen table and ran it up a rough flagpole behind the house that I hadn't noticed before. Under the chinaberry tree and the ilex bushes, hidden behind the corners of the house and the shed, night still lay hidden like black sand drifts. We went into the house and undressed, and followed Ilsa down to the ocean. Silver refused to take off her underclothes. She was very shocked, and wanted me to keep my shirt and trousers on because I wasn't wearing any underclothes, but I wouldn't. Our colored nurse gave me my bath at home because I was a boy, but often Mamma would give Silver hers, not trusting the old woman's ability to get her really clean. And Silver told me that Mamma made her wash in her chemise, and that Mamma had never seen a naked body, not even her own. Mamma had every sympathy with Papa's sister, our overly refined Aunt Violetta (after whom Violetta Woolf was named). Aunt Violetta was so delicate and so refined that she died of embarrassment in childbirth.

"You said you thought it was silly about Mamma, and wearing your chemise in the bath," I said. "Why are you being like Mamma now?"

"I'm not being like Mamma. When I take my bath there's nobody there but family or Nursie. Going in bathing in front of strangers is different."

"Oh, let her wear all that stuff if she wants to," Ilsa said impatiently. "Come on, let's hurry." And her brown nude body flashed out the screen door, down the ramp and onto the sand. I tore after her; Silver followed slowly, lifting her bare feet high like a disdainful pony. The early morning wind, coming cool and beautiful from the ocean, blew her beach-colored hair back from her face, blew her white cotton underclothes tight against her body, that, like Ilsa's, was just beginning to take shape. Ilsa and I waited for her at the ocean's edge. When we went in and the salt water touched our filthy, blistered hands, I started to jump up and down and yell with pain, but Ilsa and Silver stood with their hands plunged in the ocean and glared, each daring the other to wince. I knew that Ilsa's hands were more torn and cut than Silver's. She had worked as hard as Papa and Dr. Brandes, digging and burying, while my sister had mostly followed Mamma about, and her hands were only a little blistered from the buckets of china.

When Ilsa had finished counting five hundred, we walked back to the house, slowly, reluctant to go to bed just as morning was coming. The sky was no longer flame red against smoke gray; pale pink clouds on a soft blue sky were like illustrations from one of Silver's books of fairy stories. The sand was silver and gold, and the froth from the waves blowing along it in the wind felt comforting against the fevered palms of our hands. When you walk along the damp sand in your bare feet just as morning breaks, I think, no matter who you are or how old you are, you feel ten years younger. Since I was only ten and a half, I felt practically unborn and deliriously, wildly happy, like a sea gull bursting from its shell. I began to run up and down, back and forth, kicking and digging with my toes in the sand, waving my arms about, tearing, shrieking, toward a troupe of sandpipers that strutted superciliously away, driving the sea gulls scolding aloft, singing and shouting to the sun that was leaping over the water's edge.

When Ilsa and Silver got to the ramp they called me. The cement of the ramp still held cool and wet from the night, although the sun had reached it. We went into the house and climbed the stairs.

Silver said, "Henry, I'm going to stay with you."

"Dr. Brandes said you were to sleep with Ilsa."

"Well, I won't."

"I'm sorry," Ilsa said, "but you will."

"I won't."

"Father told me that I was to see to it that you shared my bed. I don't like it any more than you do. Stop making it difficult and come along. This is my room."

"I won't!" Silver's voice rose as much as it ever did. "Mamma said—"

Ilsa took Silver's wrist and began to twist it, not with anger, just with great determination. After a moment Silver screamed, and tears rushed to her eyes.

"Will you go in the room?" Ilsa asked.

For a moment Silver stood still in the hall, her wet, white underclothes clinging forlornly to her body. Ilsa reached out as though she would twist her wrist again, and Silver turned and went into the bedroom.

"But I won't undress in front of you," she said.

"You needn't. Just let me get you a nightgown." Ilsa went to her small chest of drawers, which was painted a blue green, the color of the sea, and took out a cotton nightgown which she thrust at Silver. "Here," she said. "Come on, Henry. I'll give you a pair of Father's pajamas."

She slammed the door on Silver, and we went across the small hall to Dr. Brandes' room. There were only those two rooms on the floor.

The rest of it was used as a kind of attic storeroom, packed neatly with wooden crates, huge wicker boxes, and a couple of big black trunks.

Ilsa took down the mosquito netting, tucking it in around the bed; then she took out a pair of her father's pajamas and held them against her. "I wish Father'd come home," she said, in the softest voice I'd heard her use. "I wish Ira'd come."

"Who's Ira?" I asked.

"Ira's from Georgia. He helps Father find specimens, and he stays with me when Father goes off on field trips or up North to meetings. He sings wonderful songs. I wish he'd come. Oh, well!" She suddenly threw back her head and braced her feet wide apart on the floor. "I guess he'll be here in a little while and Father'll be back as soon as he can. You go right to sleep. If you get to sleep your hands'll stop hurting. I guess your sister Silver's had time enough to undress. Good night, Henry."

"Good night, Ilsa."

She went out and shut the door, and I put on Dr. Brandes' pajamas and got into bed. I slept, except for short intervals, all day. When at last I really woke up, I knew that it must be after six, although the sky was still bright and the sun had not abated its blazing against the house. I dressed and went downstairs. The living room was empty, but a good smell of cooking came from the kitchen. I went out and a tall man with thick, dark red hair, that looked as though it had been cut with a hunting knife, was stirring something in a big iron pot on the stove.

"Hey," he said. "You Henry Porcher?"

"Yes, sir."

"Ilsa and your sister been up this past hour. They've gone for a swim. Hurry and join 'em before the sun sets down. I'm Ira."

"How do you do, Ira?" I said.

"Hey, Henry Porcher," he said. "Pleased to make your acquaintance, Ilsa says you're a right fine boy. Good for Ilsa to have a young friend. What's the matter with your sister?"

"Silver?"

"I reckon."

"Nothing."

"She sure mighty stuck up about something. You go on and swim up a appetite for supper. Rabbit stew. Lemme see your hands."

I spread my palms out to him.

"Kinda sore?"

"Kind of."

"When you come back I'll put some salve on them and fix you all up. Skeedaddle, now."

Ilsa and Silver were just coming out of the ocean when I got down to the beach, but they went back in the water with me. The salt stung my hands, but it wasn't as bad as it had been. I wanted to cry when Ira cleaned the broken blisters with alcohol, but again Ilsa and Silver stood with stony faces, so I controlled myself. My disinfected hands hurt so that at first I couldn't eat, but had to concentrate on staring down at my plate in order to keep the tears back. But after a while the stinging subsided, and I had three helpings of stew.

After supper we went for a walk on the beach. It wasn't much fun because Silver wouldn't talk to Ilsa, saying that Mamma wouldn't want her to. I said, thinking of Dr. Brandes, that Papa would think it very rude of her.

She walked back to the house in silence. When she clambered up on the dunes to get away from us, and headed toward the scrub, Ilsa called her back, saying sharply:

"Don't go there. You'll get covered with red bugs. And they're horrid to get out. You have to dig them out with a pin."

Without acknowledging Ilsa's warning, Silver crossed the beach and walked by the ocean's edge, looking down at her feet and pulling her toes away fastidiously when the long waves lapped up the sand, reaching for them.

Ilsa and I found a big shell that we took turns kicking along the beach. We tried to kick it all the way back to the house, but we lost it off the edge of the ramp into a clump of Spanish bayonettes. Ilsa laughed a lot.

5

When we got back to the house Ilsa took out a book and sat down on her magnolia-wood stool. Ira was nowhere to be seen.

"I guess it would be best if we all read awhile," Ilsa said. "Just pick yourselves a book you like. Maybe when Ira comes in from taking care of Calypso and the cows he'll sing us a song."

I picked out a book with wonderful colored pictures of plants. Silver found a book about insects. After a while Ira came in and lit the candles and the lamps. Ilsa begged him to sing to us, but he wouldn't.

Although I had slept so soundly all day, my eyes began to close around eleven o'clock, and, in spite of the fact that they were older, Ilsa and Silver looked sleepy, too. We all sat, looking at our books, not reading. Ira was doing something to a bottle of specimens on Dr. Brandes' table.

After a while I noticed a strange sound, a steady monotonous buzz, almost as though someone underneath the house were sawing away at the foundations. It wouldn't have been difficult for someone to get under the house if he wanted to, because it was on a slope of dune, and the front, facing the beach, was built up off the scrub on heavy coquina legs. I realized that no one could be sawing through those, and that filing them away would be quite a proposition, but, added to the strangeness of the evening, the noise filled me with fear. I was, oddly, almost more frightened than I had been during the fire the night before. I glanced over at Ilsa to see if she had noticed the noise, but she was looking down at her book, half asleep. Then I looked at

Ira; he was intent on his work. But Silver's eyes were black with terror, staring into nowhere at the invisible something that was making a persistent, hideous rumble, her head a little to one side, her fingers clenching and unclenching as she listened and listened.

"Ilsa!" she said suddenly, her voice sharp and thin. "What is it? Is it a ghost?"

"Is what a ghost?" Ilsa asked, her voice blurred with sleep.

"That noise!"

"What noise?"

"Can't you hear it? Listen!"

Ilsa tried to wake up and listen; then she started to laugh. Silver's eyes stopped staring with fear and became dark with fury.

"It's the cows!" Ilsa said, laughing. "They can't help getting covered with ticks, poor things, and at night they get under the house and rub their backs against the joists. It's the only way they have of scratching. I'd be ashamed to be afraid of that. I think it's sort of a sweet sound. Friendly."

Silver didn't say anything. She began to turn the pages of her insect book much too quickly.

"Ira," Ilsa said after a while in a soft low voice like a bee in the honeysuckle. "Ira, darling—"

"No."

"Please, Ira, darlingest Ira, please sing us a song."

"No," Ira said again. He sounded angry. "Get upstairs, all of you, and go to sleep. I don't want to hear another squawk out of you."

I thought he was one of the most disagreeable men I had ever seen. We went upstairs.

During the night Silver had her terrible dream. I knew, because I woke up when she screamed. It woke me up all the way, so that I couldn't go back to sleep. I heard Silver crying, and then I heard Ilsa's voice, and then I heard Ira's voice.

Lying there in the dark, in Dr. Brandes' strange, bare room, with the beach and the ocean stretching to infinity outside, I felt so small and so alone that instinctively I climbed out of bed and went to Ilsa's room, like a lost moth heading for the light.

Ira was sitting in the wooden rocking chair by the window, with Silver on his lap. His voice was no longer cross, but soft and slurred with sleep, like the night ocean.

"Tell Ira about your dream, baby," he said.

Through her sobs Silver managed to say, "Oh, it's a face, Ira, a perfectly ordinary face, and then it looks at me and I look at it and suddenly it begins to open its mouth in a smile, the most horrible wicked smile, and the mouth goes on opening and opening, and the face splits wider and wider apart, all the teeth and the horrible twisting lips, it opens and opens—it makes me so afraid—it's so awful—it makes me so afraid."

Silver had never told her dream before. No one had asked her to. It didn't seem to me anything awful enough to make her scream and tremble the way she did every time she had it, but Ira soothed and comforted her as though it was the most terrible thing in the world.

Ilsa lay on the bed, looking at them with bright, wide-awake eyes. When she saw me come in she moved over, and I crawled under the mosquito netting and sat down beside her. After a while, when Silver's sobs had quieted, and she lay limp in Ira's arms, Ilsa begged:

"Ira, Ira darlingest."

"No."

"Please. Please, Ira. Because I'm so wide awake, and I can't get back to sleep, and we don't know where anybody is or anything, and we have to talk and eat; only none of it's real, none of it belongs to anything."

It was the first time she had admitted that she was worried.

Ira rocked back and forth silently for a while. Then he started to sing, in a dreaming sort of voice:

THE GRAVE OF BONAPARTE

On a lone barren isle where the wild roaring billow
Assail the stern rock and the loud tempests rave,
The hero lies still, while the dew-drooping willow
Like fond weeping mourners leaned over the grave.
The lightning may flash and the loud thunders rattle,
He heeds not, he hears not, he's free from all pain;
He sleeps his last sleep, he has fought his last battle,
No sound can awake him to glory again.
No sound can awake him to glory again.

"Who's 'he'?" asked Silver, her voice coming up, up, through leagues of sleep.

Ira looked down at her crossly. "Napoleon Bonaparte. Who else could it be, I'd like to know?"

"Never mind, Ira," Ilsa said. "Go on."

Through her sea-green blur of sleep Silver reached up and pulled gently at the flesh under Ira's chin, as though she expected to feel Mamma's soft white dewlap between her fingers. Ira's eyes stopped glaring, and he began to sing again:

O shade of the mighty, where now are the legions
That rushed but to conquer when thou led'st them on;
Alas! they have perished in far hilly regions,
And all save the fame of their triumph is gone. . . .

Yet, spirit immortal, the tomb cannot bind thee,
For, like thine own eagle that soared to the sun,
Thou springest from bondage and leavest behind thee
A name, which before thee no mortal had won.
A name, which before thee no mortal had won. . . .

Ira paused and looked at Ilsa and me lying sleepily under the mosquito netting. Silver was relaxed peacefully in his arms. I climbed down off the bed and held the mosquito netting open for him, as he picked her up and put her in, saying softly to Ilsa, "You go back to sleep now and not another squawk."

"All right. Thank you, Ira darling."

I followed him out.

"Pretty little thing, your sister," he said.

"Yes."

"Wish I had a lot of kids. Ilsa's as close as I ever come to having a kid. I'm right fond of Ilsa."

"I think she's wonderful," I said.

"Surely is too bad you can't be friends."

"Why can't we? We are friends," I said.

"You kind of remind me of Johnny Brandes at your age." He leaned against the chest of drawers, and a cigarette dangled out of his mouth. "Lots of things about you's like he was when he was a kid. Only you watch out you don't get too sweet on the girls when you grow up. Girls can be a heap of trouble. You get along to sleep, now. Still a long time till morning." He went out.

6

It took me quite a little while to get back to sleep. When I woke up I heard hoof beats and the sound of a carriage coming toward the house. I ran out of the room, crashed into Ilsa, and we half fell down the stairs. She could go more quickly than I could because her nightgown was her own, while Dr. Brandes' pajamas were much too big for me, and I kept tripping over the feet.

They came in the back door, Dr. Brandes and Papa and Mamma. Papa and Dr. Brandes had their hands in bandages. As Ilsa brushed past me to get at Dr. Brandes, I ran toward Papa. Although he embraced me much more warmly than usual, I felt lonely, because I knew he wasn't as glad to see me as Dr. Brandes was to see Ilsa, and even more lonely because I wasn't as glad to see him.

Mamma stood just inside the screen door. She seemed changed. Her face was no longer smooth and cold, like marble. It seemed somehow disintegrated, like a statue built in the sand.

Papa sent me upstairs to get Silver.

When we came down, Papa and Dr. Brandes and Ira were sitting at the table, drinking out of heavy-stemmed glasses, green as the light through trees in early summer. Mamma wasn't there, so I guessed she must have gone out to the carriage rather than sit down at Dr. Brandes' table.

Papa drained his glass as we came down, and rose. "Well, Henry, Anna Silverton," he said, kissing Silver on the cheek. "Thank Dr. Brandes for his kindness and his hospitality, and we must be going."

"But where are we going?" I asked, afraid we would have to go back to town and live in the burned-out ruins of our house.

"We will stay in Charleston for the winter while the house is being rebuilt," Papa said.

"But I want to see Ilsa again!"

"Henry, thank Dr. Brandes for his kindness at once. Your mother is waiting for us in the carriage."

Dr. Brandes took my still sore and blistered hand in his bandaged one. He turned it over and looked at the palm. "You did good work," he said. "I am proud of you. Good-bye."

"Good-bye," I said.

"Henry"—Ilsa still clutched her father, but held out a careless hand to me—"don't you worry. We'll see each other when you get back from Charleston. Good-bye."

"Good-bye," I said again.

"Silver," Papa said.

"Good-bye thank you very much for your hospitality and your kindness please may we go now Papa," Silver said quickly.

Papa said good-bye to Dr. Brandes and Ira, and we went out to the carriage, where Mamma was sitting with her hands lying like little lizards in her lap.

For a while we drove in silence, which Mamma finally broke by saying, "The first thing I shall do is give you both a good hot bath."

"But we're not dirty," I protested. "We washed very thoroughly last night."

"You will need a good deal of washing to get the dust of that house off your feet and the feel of those sheets off your bodies or my name is not Cecilia-Jane Porcher."

"Now, Cecilia," Papa said. "John Brandes was invaluable during the fire. He saved many lives by his ministrations."

"Fortunately," said Mamma, "we do not have a fire every night, so his ministrations are not always so invaluable."

"It was a great kindness on his part to take our children when they were in need of a roof over their heads," Papa continued.

"Kindness!" Mamma gave a small laugh like a sandpiper. "Mark my words, he was only waiting for a chance to get them into his clutches."

"I doubt if he has that much interest in my children," Papa said.

"Interest! If *he* has no interest, who should have?"

"Really, Cecilia-Jane," Papa said. "That's quite absurd. In any event, John Brandes is a fine naturalist. He is highly thought of in the North."

"The North!" Mamma laughed again. "What can you expect?"

"Some people consider Baltimore the South," Papa said.

Mamma's eyes became brighter than I had ever seen them. "If I had known what was going on, those children would never have crossed the river with that man. Rather would I have seen them being carried down the stairs in their coffins."

"I would rather have them alive," Papa said, laying a hand on Silver's knee. "And the stairs are burned to a few charred pieces of wood and a handful of ashes, so you'll never have that pleasure, at any rate."

Mamma looked down at her hands and sulked. Her hands were very small and delicate, and she wore too many rings on her slightly curled fingers. The flesh on the back of her hands was thin and transparent, and the veins showed through in soft raised lines. On summer evenings in the garden Silver loved to sit close to Mamma and move the veins about, or to reach up and pull her soft white dewlap. It seemed strange that with so much softness in her actual construction Mamma gave such a feeling of hardness.

When she went out of doors she always carried gloves, which she never put on her hands except when she cut the roses; then she wore gardeners' gloves. But whenever she was indoors, at home or when she was visiting, she wore white kid gloves, which she gave to her little maid every night to clean. We never knew exactly why she did this, and sometimes, when he had had an extra drink, Papa used to tease her about wearing gloves to serve tea in; but she never offered any explanation, and she never tried to conquer the habit which she had started after I was born.

It was not until we crossed the bridge to town that we began to see the damage done by the fire. There would be groups of houses that were nothing but black skeletons, almost as though the flesh had been burned off them and only the charred bones remained. Then would come a house that had scarcely been touched by the fire, and then a house that had been burned down to its foundations. It was the same way with the trees. Sometimes their blackened bones seemed pressed in agony against the landscape; sometimes the tops were burned off, leaving green beneath; sometimes there would be just a stump as a reminder that there had ever been a tree there at all.

As we drove through the streets, where smoke still lay like evil-smelling fog, we passed many funeral processions.

"See a funeral, hear of a wedding," Mamma said, almost gaily. Papa looked at her, and she sulked down at her ring-heavy hands again.

There was a long funeral procession going by in front of what had once been the Silverton house. I touched Papa on the sleeve and whispered, "Cousin Anna?"

"Your Cousin Anna is at the Woolfs'. They have very kindly offered to take the whole family in until their house is rebuilt. The wind changed before the fire reached your Uncle Montgomery's house."

"But is Cousin Anna all right?" I asked.

"Certainly she's all right," Papa said irritably.

"It was so awful for her last time, I thought . . ." I looked away from Papa's face. I didn't realize it was cross mainly from worry and exhaustion and the pain in his burned hands. I looked away from his face and down at my knees in the torn, soiled knickers that had been ruined by the events of the past—how many days was it? Only two? They seemed at least as long and full as the rest of my days put together.

We stopped off for the night in Savannah.

After dinner at the hotel, during which both Silver and I were too tired to eat, Mamma took Silver up to bathe her, and I went for a walk with Papa.

We didn't have much to say to each other. It was really the first time I had been alone with Papa, except when I was being given a lecture or a switching. Papa was almost as tongue-tied as I was. Every once in a while he would point out to me the various objects of interest, indicating them with his silver-tipped cane. Each time we came to a long stretch of silence, I resolved to ask him about Ilsa, why Silver and I were not to be allowed to see her, why Mamma had brandished the carving knife at Dr. Brandes and tried to keep him from entering our fire-doomed house, why Papa had locked at Ilsa so strangely and curiously. I had my own very definite ideas on the subject.

Several times I opened my mouth to speak and shut it again. Then I decided I would count to ten, and when I had said ten I would ask Papa. When I had reached ten I decided I would count to a hundred.

"Ninety-nine," I said to myself, "one hundred!" and opened my mouth to speak.

"It is too bad," Papa said before I had got a word out, "that your mother insists on going to Charleston for the winter. It would be better if we stayed on here in Savannah, but I cannot persuade her. She is set on Charleston. I hope she will not regret it."

I felt that he was talking to himself rather than to me.

We walked along again in silence. The moon was coming over the rooftops. Again I gathered up courage to speak. Again Papa spoke before me.

"I know I should punish you for your astonishing behavior in running away the other day, Henry, but, in view of all that has happened, we will forget it this once. When you were at the beach, did you talk much to Dr. Brandes and Ilsa?"

I had an idea that he refrained from punishing me, not because of the fire, or because I was usually obedient, but because he wanted to find out something, though I couldn't think what.

"Oh, yes, Papa," I answered.

"Did they say anything to you about the family? About your mother or any of us?"

"No, Papa." I knew I must not tell him that Ilsa had called us biggety, or that Dr. Brandes had used a rather angrily bitter tone whenever he mentioned our name.

"Are you sure?"

"Yes, Papa."

"Dr, Brandes said nothing about anyone in the family?" he insisted.

"No, Papa. Why?"

"No reason. We knew him slightly at one time. Never socially."

"Why not?"

Papa pretended not to hear me. With the silver tip of his cane he pointed to an imposing Civil War monument. I sighed with fatigue.

"Are you tired?" Papa asked.

"I guess so."

"We are all tired and overwrought," Papa said. "Let us turn back."

We returned to the hotel. I stood in the center of the lobby while Papa went over to the desk to get the key.

The lobby was tiled with black and white in octagonal patterns; the only color was from somber pots of palms. It seemed immensely high because it was built like a court, with balconies on four sides, going up for five stories. At the very top was a kind of skylight of stained glass, but it was so far away that the colored design gave no warmth.

Papa came back with the key and we went over to the stairway. As we started up I finally blurted out:

"Papa, is Ilsa a bastard?"

His face turned white with anger. "Henry!" he said. I knew I was in for a whipping anyhow now, so I pressed on.

"Is she?"

"Never let me hear you use that word again."

"But is she, Papa?"

"Henry, you are not to say another word until morning. If I should tell your mother what you have just said, she would Wash your mouth out with soap, but I would not use such a word in the presence of a lady. Where did you pick it up?"

I shut my mouth tightly and looked down at my feet. My cousin Monty often used that word, along with similar words he had picked up from my uncle.

Papa took my hand and pulled me roughly up the stairs, jerking me down the long cream-colored corridor, past innumerable dark brown doors, into his room, where he ordered me to pull down my trousers.

As I fastened my belt again, standing first on one leg, then on the other until the stinging pain subsided, Papa said, "Dr. Brandes and his wife were married by the church, as are any man and wife. Ilsa was born eleven months afterward. She was both conceived and born in wedlock. Her mother died a few hours after she was born."

Papa had given me a talking to about the facts of life the winter before. Monty had told me a good deal more. So that guess about Ilsa had been wrong.

7

I climbed into bed. We were on the second floor, and light from a street lamp outside came in the window and poured over my bed. There were noises. Many more noises than I heard from my bedroom overlooking the river at home. A clock striking the half-hour. People passing on the street below, laughing. Somewhere in the distance a woman singing. The clang of a fire engine.

As I heard its nervous bell I was overwhelmed with fear that perhaps Savannah, too, would be burned; but the fire engine passed into the dark distance, there was no glare in the sky, no horrible smell of burning homes. I lay down again—on my stomach because of the tingling on my bottom. When Papa spanked, he spanked.

And then, suddenly, I was flooded with the most overwhelming waves of homesickness I had ever known. Not homesickness for the destroyed town, or our lost, white-pillared house, or my small mahogany spool bed that was no more; but waves of homesickness for a coquina and cypress house set far back on the dunes, for a bare room furnished in unpainted pine, for Ilsa's authoritative voice, and Dr. Brandes' quiet one, and Ira's cross one. I wanted to weep with an agony of longing for a place and for people I had never seen or known a few short days ago.

I pulled the covers over my head to try and hide even from myself the hot tears that coursed down my cheeks.

8

It was late Saturday afternoon when we got to Charleston. We were to stay in a brick house a block away from the Battery, the home of an ancient cousin of Papa's, a Miss Eustacia Porcher. She was bedridden, and after we had gone up to her room and paid our respects to her as she lay in her huge canopied bed, we were warned that we must always be very quiet so as not to disturb our Cousin Eustacia who had so kindly opened her home to us.

Silver and I were so tired that we were given milk toast and put to bed at once. Papa announced that we were to be allowed to sleep late the next morning and would be excused from church. He clasped his hands behind him as he said this, and stared up at the ceiling in the way he always did when he knew that what he was going to say would get an unpleasant reaction from Mamma, and a reaction that he intended to ignore. Mamma looked odd, but she didn't say anything, and Papa took her out to inspect the garden. I was certain that it wasn't only because he knew Silver and I were tired, and he wanted us to sleep, that he was excusing us from church in the morning.

Whatever the reason was, I was delighted. I hated church. Silver was not so pleased. All her dolls had been burned and she would have nothing to do. And she rather enjoyed being dressed in her best clothes, which had also been burned (perhaps that was why Papa didn't want us to go to church), and sitting beside Mamma in the pew, wearing her own small white kid gloves and holding her own prayer book bound in pale blue leather. Mamma would sing the hymns in her high, thin voice which managed, somehow, to be very piercing and loud, and was the most uninhibited thing about her, and which Silver did her best to imitate:

> *Art thou weary, art thou languid,*
> *Art thou sore distress'd?*

Papa and I would mumble inaudibly while Mamma's and Silver's voices rose in thin high curls of sound up to the cold arches of stone above our heads.

I woke up before Silver the next morning. Mamma and Papa had already left for church when I went downstairs, and a very ancient colored butler, in a white coat so starched that it stood out around him and made him seem twice as large as he was, gave me breakfast. He was so solemn as he hovered over me and served me with waffles and cane syrup that I didn't dare speak to him or eat as much as I would have liked. I left the dining room as quickly as possible, feeling lost at the huge oval table; the room was so dark that the only things visible seemed to be the white coat of the butler and the eyes of the portraits staring down at me from the walls. Their eyes followed me as I slid down from my chair, and it made me uneasy; I felt that I was being pursued, spied on, and the fact that all the eyes belonged to people who were, or had been, my kin, didn't make me feel any better.

I wandered upstairs. It was almost as dark on the stairway as it had been in the dining room, and I kept stumbling as I reached sudden wide stairs and false landings.

From Cousin Eustacia's room came the sound of singing. I edged along the dark, paneled corridor and peered in through the door, which was ajar. Cousin Eustacia was sitting up in bed, propped by dozens of pillows, and she was singing Ira's Napoleon song.

"'For like thine own eagle that soared to the sun,'" she sang, and her voice soared with the eagle and cracked in its flight. I edged into the room, gaining courage from the song.

Although she was turned away from the door, and I had made no noise, she broke off suddenly. "Well, who have we here?"

"It's me," I whispered.

"Who is me? Speak up, child. Don't be a lally gag."

"Henry."

"Henry what?"

"Henry Randolph Porcher. Papa said we were going to be with you till our new house is built and we weren't to disturb you."

"So the first thing you do is disturb me."

"No, I—I didn't mean to disturb you. I just liked the song you were singing. The Napoleon song."

This seemed to please her. "Well, come in, come in," she said. "Have you no backbone? Either come in and disturb me properly, as I can see you want to do, or stay out and leave me in peace."

I took a few steps into the room.

"Now close the door so that we shan't be bothered."

I shut the door and looked around me. It had been too dark the night before to see anything but a huge canopied bed and a thin figure erect against a white mountain of pillows. Now, in the sunlight that filtered through the rattan blinds, I realized that it was the strangest room I had ever seen. The walls were painted with cypress trees growing out of black water. Flamingos gleamed scarlet through the trees; alligators raised their heads and showed half-opened, jeweled eyes; a panther poised, ready to spring. On one wall there was even a sea cow painted with her baby. The ceiling was a continuation of the scene—a dark, star-cluttered sky showing purple between the branches of trees. The floor was covered with a heavy brown-black carpet, the color of water where cypress grows. The curtains of the bed were the dark purple of the sky.

I must have looked very foolish as I stared around me, my mouth hanging open and my eyes protruding; because Cousin Eustacia burst into a discordant squawk of laughter.

"Do you like it, or do you agree with William in thinking it's horrible? Come now, be honest. Tell me the truth. Yes or no?"

"Oh, I think it's wonderful!" I gasped with complete truthfulness.

"Painted it all myself," Cousin Eustacia said.

"*You* did, Cousin Eustacia?" I was completely lost in admiration.

"Every last stroke. Took me ten years. Finished two years, seven months, eleven days ago. Can you imagine? Got into bed the day I finished and haven't been out of it since. Now that you've looked around, come over here and let me look at you."

Although Cousin Eustacia had completely won my respect with her painting, I was afraid of her. I went up to the bed very slowly, trying to down a sudden fantastic idea that she was going to grab me and smother me in those dusty purple hangings.

"Come, come, come," she said. "I don't like to be kept waiting."

I peered around the purple hangings and she reached out and clutched my arm. "Hey! Listen! Do you hear footsteps?"

I strained my ears to hear over the heavy beating of my heart, and it seemed to me that there was a sound of footsteps coming toward us down the long corridor.

"Yes, ma'am, I think so."

"Get up onto the bed," she ordered.

"Ma'am?"

"Get up onto the bed, quick!"

I didn't dare disobey. My heart almost bursting out of me with terror, I clambered up onto the high bed and sank deep and helpless into the feather mattress as Cousin Eustacia pulled a long gold cord and the purple velvet hangings closed noisily about us. We were in unrelieved blackness. Not a speck of light could come through those smothering folds of velvet. I could scarcely hear over the frantic beating of my heart.

"It's my nurse," Cousin Eustacia whispered. "I don't want her to disturb us. She's a dreadful creature. Always wears a white dress and cap and white shoes and stockings. Can you imagine? Born in Ireland, too. Impossible. Can't understand a word she says."

We heard the door being pushed open. "Go away!" Cousin Eustacia shrieked. "It's Sunday, and I'm praying! Leave me alone!"

A soft, not unpleasant voice, called back, "You'll ring, then, if you're wanting me?"

"Yes. Now go away! Go to church and beg God to forgive you your sins."

After a moment we heard the door close and footsteps retreating down the long corridor. Cousin Eustacia leaned over me, pressing her sharp elbow into my stomach, and stuck her head out of the curtains. Then she fell back against the pillows again, reached out and pulled the cord, and the curtains rolled back. I took a great breath.

"There!" Cousin Eustacia said. She reached among the smothering purple folds and brought up a bottle. Pulling out the cork, she put the bottle to her mouth, threw back her head, took a long swallow, and let out a sigh of satisfaction. As she replaced the bottle, she said, "I am very angry at your father. He sent me a telegram, and I dislike telegrams. Wanted me to take a house near here for him. Can you imagine? Naturally, I did no such thing; I told him to come here. Though why I say naturally I'm sure I don't know, because it's most unnatural. But kin is kin, and as I never leave my bed, I don't have to see you if I don't want to. And I like hearing people in a house. Houses resent not being lived in. I hear your mother's gone to church. Can you imagine?"

"Yes," I answered stupidly.

"She's a bigger fool than I thought she was."

"But we always go to church on Sunday," I said, surprised.

"Not to this church. But your mother always liked wearing the hair shirt. No doubt she thinks she's being very noble and forgiving, though I imagine William will see it in a different light. I'm very fond of little old William."

"Who is William?"

"Oh, more kin," Cousin Eustacia said. "So they've never mentioned him to you? Well, you'll probably hear of him soon enough, if I know William. Now tell me all about the family. I'll get more truth from a child than I would from either of your egregious parents. I can't bear your mother. Never could. Your father's a weak fool, but he's all right. I shall leave him my money. Can you imagine? How is your mother's brother? Always detested him."

This cemented my feeling of affection for my cousin. "He's just like he always is," I said. "I don't like Uncle Montgomery, either. But I hate Monty."

"Who's Monty?"

"My cousin."

"Oh, yes. One of Montgomery's twins. You'd think one would be more than enough of him to send into the world at a time. But no. It would have to be twins. Can you imagine? No doubt if his wife had lived he'd have sent nineteen children into the world instead of three. How *is* the girl? Violetta, isn't it?"

"Yes. She's very pretty, but I don't like her."

"Why?"

"She—she sort of smothers people," I said, thinking more of Cousin Eustacia than of my answer. She seemed very unlike the prim old lady I had bowed to the evening before. It never occurred to me to connect the bottle she kept hidden in the draperies, or her heavy exciting breath, with this new personality.

"So Violetta is smothering, hey?" Cousin Eustacia said. "She would be, if she's anything like her mother. Not like your father's sister Violetta, then?"

"I never knew Aunt Violetta," I said.

"Then get down on your knees and thank God," Cousin Eustacia exclaimed. "Violetta was a horror. Always wore violet. Can you imagine? With a name like that. She and your mother were a pair. Your

Aunt Violetta was like your mother, only more so. Can you imagine? You'd have thought they were sisters. How's Montgomery's other boy? Edwin."

"Oh, Eddie's all right. He's smaller than I am, even if he is older than Silver, but he's nice. He never bends your arm back or anything."

She peered forward at me. "Hah. Yes. Can see you're the kind who'd have his arm twisted, rather than do the twisting. But you're a handsome child. Though I never much cottoned to brown eyes and fair hair. See much of your Cousin Anna?"

"Oh, we always see a lot of everybody. I mean, us, and Uncle Montgomery's family, and Cousin Anna and Cousin Randolph, and Dolph. Cousin Anna's my favorite kin."

"You have very good taste for such a pretty little face and such vague big eyes. Does Anna still play her harp?"

"Not often."

"That's a crime," Cousin Eustacia said. "Your sister—what is that heathenish name you call her—Silver?—has more spine than you have. I'm right, aren't I, hey? Though she's not as much like Elizabeth as she looks. Can you imagine your mother and Montgomery Woolf having a sister like Elizabeth?"

"I never knew Aunt Elizabeth, either," I said. I was beginning to be heavy with sleep. The windows were all tight shut and the curtains were stifling. Perspiration trickled down my back. Cousin Eustacia kept leaning forward and breathing her dark restless breath into my face to emphasize her words. I stood by the bed, not daring to take a step away, staring at Cousin Eustacia lying like an animated stick of wood against the pillows, the purple curtains pressing close about us, the cypress trees and the dark water seeming to bear in on us from the walls, the dark branches and the night sky sagging down on us from the ceiling.

"Your Aunt Elizabeth and your Cousin Anna were the only ones I could ever endure, but kin is kin, and that is why you're here," she said. "I'm tired of you now. Go away. Don't come back again unless I send for you."

Without waiting for me to step back from the bed, she pulled the cord and purple velvet swept about her, leaving me to choke in dust. I hurried out of the room.

Silver was looking for me. "Where have you been?" she demanded.

"Oh, nowhere," I said.

We sat on the stairs to wait until Mamma and Papa got back from church.

"Cousin Eustacia reminds me of Miss Turnbull," I said.

"Of whom?"

"My teacher." I began to hum my song, the one Miss Turnbull had sung. "O, where have you been wandering, King Henry, my son?"

Although Silver was much more reserved about her own affairs than I, she was very curious about other people, especially her own family, so I wasn't surprised when she began talking, about Ilsa, first of all asking me if I liked her.

"Of course," I said.

"Mamma doesn't."

"Mama never saw her before she came to our house last night."

"Mamma doesn't like her father."

"What about her father?"

"That's what I wondered. I thought maybe she'd told you something."

"Who, Mamma?"

"No, goosey. That Ilsa. Mamma wouldn't tell *you* anything."

"I don't think Ilsa knows anything about it," I said. "She doesn't think we're as high and mighty as we make everybody think we are, that's all."

"I don't like her. She's a stuck-up pig. And her hair's cut short. I've never seen a girl with her hair short like that, unless she'd been sick or something."

"Well, maybe she has."

"She didn't look to me as though she'd been sick."

"Well, I like her. She's my best friend."

"Pooh. You're only ten and a half. You're too young. She wouldn't be friends with anybody three whole years younger than she was."

"I don't care," I said. "We are friends. You heard her say we'd see each other when we got back from Charleston. The minute we get back I'm going to ride—" and all of a sudden I felt an empty feeling in my stomach, as though everything had dropped out and left me. I had remembered little old Billy. How I could have forgotten him for that long I don't know.

"What's the matter?" Silver asked.

"Billy," I said, and stood up as the doorbell rang. "Mamma and Papa're back," I shouted, and started downstairs as the houseboy came out into the hall and went to the door.

When the houseboy opened the door we saw Papa and the coachman supporting Mamma, who was half fainting, and moaning slightly. Papa looked grimmer than I had ever seen him. Silver and I scuttled off the stairway as Papa carried Mamma up without paying any attention to us.

"She just done fainted," the coachman explained to us as he went down the steps.

Dinner was late, and we ate it in oppressed silence. Papa said that Mamma had been seized with a fainting attack in church. In the middle of dinner he sent for his prayer book, and sat staring at it with a stern expression.

After dinner we went into the parlor. Papa told Silver to play; so she sat down obediently at the piano, and, with her precise cool touch, played a Handel minuet. Just as she finished one of the servants came in and said that Mamma wanted her in the bedroom. After she had left I sat perched on a hard wing chair covered with mustard-colored velvet and stared at Papa, who was still studying his prayer book, not turning the pages, but looking fixedly at one particular place. After a time he got up and I heard him, too, going upstairs. I wandered out into the garden, which was kept cool and fresh-looking in spite of the scorching end-of-summer heat, by hoses and sprinklers set in various places about the lawn and around the flower beds. Since my suit was already as ruined as possible by the events of the past few days, I stood under one of the sprinklers and cooled off, while I tried to figure things out. I was irritated with Mamma for having a fainting fit, because if everybody was attending to her it would make it even more difficult for me to find out anything about Ilsa; and I was determined to see Ilsa again no matter what dreadful thing Dr. Brandes had done, how many banks he had robbed, how many men he had killed, how many carriages he had galloped up to on Calypso, a handkerchief over his mouth, a pistol in his hand, adventure in his heart. I swayed slowly back and forth in the comforting spray of water that threw its quiet drops over me and the Louis Phillipes and Cape jessamines indiscriminately.

Silver's voice came from behind me. "You're getting your clothes wet."

"It doesn't matter," I said, turning around and blinking at her as she stood in the full glare of the sun. "They're ruined anyhow. What've you got there?"

"Papa's prayer book."

"What for?"

"Brother," Silver said mysteriously, "I've got something to tell you. Where can we go?"

"I don't know." I looked vaguely around the strange garden.

Silver took me by the elbow and led me to a small arbor covered with moon vine. Then she opened the prayer book.

"Are you going to read to me out of the prayer book?" I asked disgustedly, thinking that she was trying to make up to God for the fact that we hadn't gone to church.

"Oh, very well, Henry," Silver said. "If you don't want to hear what Papa read to Mamma up in the bedroom, and what made her have the fainting spell in church, I don't care. Mamma said it was all Dr. Brandes' fault, too."

"I want to hear." I turned back quickly.

"I'm not sure you're old enough," she said.

"Oh, please, Sister!"

"I don't think Papa hardly knew I was in the room," she said, then. "He just stalked in and stood by Mamma. It was awful dark in the room. Mamma had the blinds drawn, and I was sitting by her in the corner, where I could keep putting cologne on her head. I don't think Papa even knew I was there at first, and then it was too late."

"What did he say?"

"He went over to the window where the light came in at the edge of the blind and he read her this thing out of the prayer book."

"What thing?"

"I've got to find the place. Don't hurry me." With her usual I cool and maddening deliberation she turned the pages of the Episcopal prayer book. At last she said, "Oh, here it is. I had it before, but I lost the place when you said you didn't want to listen."

"I never said that! I do want to listen."

"All right. Well, *listen*, then." She began to read. "It's from 'The Order for the Administration of the Lord's Supper, or Holy Communion.'"

"Go on," I said.

"I will, if you don't try to rush me. It's the part in the smallest print before it really begins."

"Yes, go on," I said.

"'If, among those who come to be partakers of the Holy Communion,'" Silver read, "'the Minister shall know any to be an open and notorious evil liver, or to have done any wrong to his neighbors by word or deed, so that the congregation be thereby offended; he shall advertise him, that he presume not to come to the Lord's Table, until he have openly declared himself to have truly repented and amended his former evil life, that the Congregation may thereby be satisfied; and that he hath recompensed the parties to whom he hath done wrong; or at least declare himself to be in full purpose so to do, as soon as he conveniently may.'"

"What does that mean?" I asked.

"It means"—Silver lowered her voice and looked around, then put her head very close to mine and whispered—"the minister wouldn't let Mamma take communion."

I felt a strange secret shiver go all through me. "Why?" I asked, peering over her shoulder at the prayer book. "He didn't think Mamma was 'an open and notorious evil liver,' did he?"

"Of course not, goosey," she said. "It's this part here that I haven't read yet."

"Which part?"

"Listen. 'The same order shall the Minister use with those, betwixt whom he perceiveth malice and hatred to reign; not suffering them to be partakers of the Lord's Table, until he know them to be reconciled.'" Her voice was an aweful whisper.

"Oh—"

"Yes," Silver said, "it's awful, isn't it? Mamma said she was disgraced for ever. She wanted Papa to have the minister run out of town and tarred and feathered and all sorts of things, but after Papa read her this thing he said she couldn't."

"Is it because of the way she feels about Dr. Brandes and Ilsa?"

Silver nodded. "Papa said the minister would have to tell all about it to the Ordinary."

"What's the Ordinary?"

"I don't know. But the minister has to tell the Ordinary all about Mamma and not letting her have communion because when he asked her if there was still hate in her heart toward a man and an innocent child, she couldn't say before God that there wasn't. Papa says that the minister'll lose his church because of it. Papa said he didn't do it because of God and Jesus, but because of his own personal feelings, and he'll have to tell the whole story to the Ordinary. When Mamma said, 'Does the whole thing have to be raked up again?' Papa said she ought to have known better than to have gone to that church when she knew he was there, and if she was that stubborn she ought to have read her prayer book more carefully before trying to take communion. Papa said that Mamma was just as willful and headstrong as her sister Elizabeth—you know, Aunt Elizabeth—in her own way, and Mamma got very white and started to faint again even if she was already lying down, and then Papa saw me and he shouted at me so loud I'm surprised you didn't hear it out here, and then he sent me away. He dropped the prayer book when Mamma got all funny again, so I picked it up and came to look for you."

We were called just then, and we didn't have another chance to get away and talk. My clothes had dried out, so I didn't get scolded for standing under the sprinkler. We were given an early supper of milk toast and sent to bed.

9

It must have been about midnight when Mamma woke us and dressed us in our bedraggled clothes. Her voice was angry and nervous. She shook us roughly. "Hurry, Henry; hurry, Anna Silverton; get out of bed quickly and into your clothes," she said sharply, and pulled the covers off us. At home Nursie woke us by singing in her midnight voice:

Wake up,
Jacob,
Day's a-breaking,
Peas' in the pot
And hoe cake's
A-baking.

We were both so heavy with sleep that we hardly knew what was going on. We didn't say good-bye to Cousin Eustacia. I remember leaning against the firmness of Papa in the carriage and suddenly sitting up, wide awake for a moment, demanding to be told where Billy was. Reassured of his safety, I sank against Papa again, the jouncing of the carriage wheels over cobblestones muffled against his well-padded body. Then I remember standing outside the railroad station waiting for the northern train to come round the bend. Light spilled out of the station windows and lay in patches on the ground and glinted on the tracks. A car pulled up and left its headlights on, the light pouring from them like two streams of water across the darkness. I remember the roar of the train and its red glow as it came under the bridge and heaved to a stop. I remember the porter boosting me up onto the train, and then sitting in an empty seat with Silver while the porter made up our berths. The next clear memory is arriving some place just at dawn and driving out to a hotel with a big yellow veranda all the way around it.

We lived in that hotel for the next five years.

PART TWO

10

The Woolfs and the Silvertons came up to the hotel early in July, partly so that the family could be together for the summer and partly to try to persuade Mamma to come home in the autumn to the now-completed house.

When I look back at the five years I lived in that hotel, I always see it as it was that summer—rocking chairs moving lazily like the swells of the ocean, bright summer skirts spreading over the dark green wooden chairs with the woven seats and high backs, the sun warm on the yellow veranda. From the summerhouse you could always hear the heartbroken calling of the doves on the roof. And you could always smell food from the big kitchen and the cream-colored dining room with the round tables covered with white tablecloths, full and spotless, reaching nearly to the ground. When there was watermelon for dessert we children were allowed to take it outside to eat, where we would bend almost double to keep it from dripping down our fronts, and plunge our faces into the cool, fragrant pith, coming up smeared with juice and little black seeds and ecstasy.

During the day the shutters were half pulled at all the windows, so that the light filtered through, losing some of its cruel potency, and lay in dusty lines on the polished parquet floor, on the potted plants, and on the tables stacked with magazines and papers.

In the afternoon we were sent upstairs for an hour to rest. Edwin Woolf and I had a room together next to the one shared by Monty Woolf and Dolph Silverton. Silver and Violetta Woolf were across the hall. All the rooms had tall brass bedsteads, huge mahogany wardrobes, a lowboy, and a washstand with a flowered china pitcher and basin. The windows had screens and the beds no mosquito netting. Edwin and the girls and I were sent to bed in the evening before Monty and Dolph. It wouldn't be dark for quite some time after we were supposed to be asleep, and I always lay restless and wide awake until the small orchestra, that came for eight weeks every summer, started playing dance music and light classics in the summerhouse. I would lie in bed and listen to the music, gradually growing drowsy. When I looked over at Edwin sleeping peacefully on the next bed, lying on the very edge, the covers tumbled off him, one arm and leg flung over the side of the bed, I was grateful that I was sharing the room with him instead of with Monty.

Often, before we went to sleep, Eddie and I used to amuse ourselves by trying to count the family—the Silvertons, the Porchers, and the Woolfs, all the great-aunts and great-uncles, the aunts and uncles, all the cousins; but there were so many that we could never remember them all, and never during the entire summer did we get the same number twice.

Monty and Violetta Woolf were very grownup at sixteen. Violetta had her hair up and her skirts down, and Monty had a new man-of-the-world expression when he looked at Silver. He was wonderful to behold, with his dark red hair and pale complexion, his regular, clear-cut features, and his long, languid limbs. His eyelashes were thick and dark and longer than most girls', but there was nothing effeminate about him. In his dark trousers and white shirt, open at the throat, he caught the adoring attention of all the old ladies at the hotel, and all the young ones worshiped him. When Monty was around, no one paid any attention to me or little Eddie, or to Dolph Silverton, though he was a very nice-looking boy. I remembered that Cousin Eustacia had called me handsome, and I hated Monty for being such a sensation.

I could never talk with Monty or Violetta, they acted so grown-up. Eddie, just a few weeks older than Silver, and Dolph Silverton, though he was almost seventeen, seemed much less changed, and I wasn't shy and uncomfortable with them as I was with the twins, whom I disliked, if possible, more than ever.

Cousin Anna, Dolph's mother, was the one who was truly different. The tragedy of the second fire seemed to have taken away her intense awareness, that had been so important a part of her. She spent most of the time sitting on the veranda, a novel in her lap, rocking back and forth. At the table, or after meals, when the family gathered on the veranda, if she didn't want to talk she would sit in complete silence, ignoring any conversation that was directed toward her. Or, if she felt like talking, she didn't care what she said, and blandly ignored Cousin Randolph's furiously shaking head and raised eyebrows. She was the first person in the family who openly dared say that it was silly of Mamma to wear those white kid gloves all the time.

"It's plain silly, that's all it is," Cousin Anna said one day at dinner. "And just you stop kicking me under the table, Randolph Silverton, because it's not going to do you a piece of good. The trouble with you, Cecilia-Jane, is that you may be a wife and mother but you're a prissy old spinster at heart, and why you didn't go the way of your husband's overly sainted sister Violetta is more than I can see. Why is it you're such an old maid, Cecilia?"

Mamma said nothing, but continued angrily to eat her soup.

"If you persist in wearing the gloves," Cousin Anna said, "why on earth wear so many rings under them? They look so ungainly. You have very pretty little hands, Cecilia. I've noticed when you're out of doors and take the gloves off. If it weren't for your frustrated expression, you'd be a very beautiful woman. What are you frustrated about, Cecilia? God has given you everything most women pray for beside their barren beds at night."

And then, to everyone's infinite relief, she decided that she had done enough talking for one meal and lapsed into silence. I could see that Papa had been about to send us children from the table.

The next day Papa decided that we were to go off for a picnic, instead of coming into the dining room with the grownups. As we gathered on the veranda, ready to leave, each clutching a packet of sandwiches, a hard-boiled egg, and an orange, I went and stood beside Cousin Anna, who was rocking slowly back and forth and pretending to read. She had always been my favorite among all my kin. I knew that for some reason the others scorned her for the way she had rushed into the servants' quarters the first time her house burned down, and dragged out the fear-crazed darky. I admired her for it with an admiration so intense that when I thought about it I felt as though something had kicked like iron into my stomach.

I liked Dolph, too, although he was the oldest of all my cousins and didn't play with us often. He was gentle with his mother, and at table, when he saw that she wasn't eating, simply because she was too apathetic to cut her meat, he would reach over quietly and do it for her. She would accept his attention, smiling slightly at him, patting his hand, and eating her meat obediently. I felt unhappy when

I saw the way he looked at Violetta's glossy auburn hair and creamy complexion.

"Hello, Henry boy," Cousin Anna said, as she saw me detach myself from the others and stand by her. She looked at me through half-closed brown eyes.

"Hello, Cousin Anna," I said.

"Henry"—she turned to me suddenly, speaking with the old concise energy that seemed to have vanished the night of the fire—"don't you be upset by what I say. At the table or out here. I won't say anything that isn't good for you to know."

"I'm not upset," I answered.

"Hey, Henry, come on," Monty called.

"Good-bye, Cousin Anna," I said.

"Good-bye, Henry boy. Bless you. Don't let that Montgomery Woolf bully you."

Dolph came over to kiss his mother good-bye, and we started off.

We climbed until we came to a flat piece of ground among the huge pines that stretched upward high above our heads. There was no grass. No rocks. Only a soft, rust-colored carpet of pine needles. We lay on this, panting and hot, and ate our lunch.

"Monty's hair is just the color of the pine needles," Silver said, "only it's alive."

"Violetta's, too." Dolph looked at her with admiring eyes.

"I saw a friend of yours before we left home, Henry." Monty grinned, cracking his hard-boiled egg on Eddie's head. "She asked to be remembered to you."

"Who?" I asked without much interest, wondering which of the vapid little girls my sister and I occasionally played with had sent me a giggling message by the handsome Monty.

"Ilsa Brandes."

I sat up quickly, and Silver nudged me. If we were careful, we might be able to learn something. Monty and Violetta, somehow or other, managed to learn all the spicy gossip that went about town, but they could be like prima donnas about imparting it if they felt biggety.

"Oh," I said casually. "How did you happen to bump into her?"

"We went down to the beach for the day." Monty rolled over with great elegance and put his head in Silver's lap. She flushed. After a moment she began diffidently to play with his thick, ruddy hair. "Pa had to go over to July Harbour to see somebody about some fishing boats or something, and it was low tide, so we drove on the beach. Pa let me drive," he added with pride, looking around to see that we were suitably impressed.

"Oh, Monty," Silver sighed, "Papa keeps talking about getting a motorcar, but we never do, and I'm just sick and tired of that old carriage."

"Yes, but how did you meet Ilsa?" I persisted.

"There was a patch of sand that was soft," Monty said.

"You mean you drove too near the dunes." Violetta looked over at Randolph and giggled maliciously.

"I did not," Monty said. "There was a bar of soft sand and we got stuck in it. Pa was having forty-seven duck fits, when all of a sudden this girl comes galloping down the beach on a black mare. Lordy, what a horse!"

"Yes," I nodded. "That would be Calypso."

"Uh huh," Monty said. "I think she said it had a funny name like that. We yelled at her like mad, and she wheeled around and came back to us. That girl sure enough can sit a horse pretty. Kind of a violent girl, isn't she, Henry?"

"Is she?"

"For a small girl she's got lots of fire. I'm going to marry her when I'm older." I sat up angrily at that, but he went on imperturbably. "When we told her the trouble, she tore back up the beach a piece, and then she and a funny old character came back with a couple of boards and a shovel and some rope and dug us out. She said she was sorry her father was off on a—a—"

"Field trip," Edwin said. "He plays with plants and bugs and snakes and things in fields."

"Uh huh," Monty said. "So she said she couldn't offer us any hospitality, because there wasn't anything in the house but corn liquor, and not much of that. The man said he was on his way to get them some rabbits or some fowl, and Pa said it was against the law, but the man said, not on their own land it wasn't."

"Pa said it was a crime and a scandal to the community," Violetta announced righteously, "that she should be allowed to live there with that low-down no-' count piece of white trash, with her father away so much of the time, and her not hardly a child any more."

"Mother says her father is a brilliant naturalist." Dolph joined in for the first time. "She's read articles he's written. She said he was the most charming young man she'd ever met."

"You mean Cousin Anna knew him!" Silver exclaimed.

"Well, honey, I guess she couldn't have said that if she didn't," Dolph said. He looked as though he'd like to have put his head down on Violetta's green-skirted lap, as Monty had done with Silver, but he kept sitting, leaning back up against a huge pine. He didn't seem particularly interested in Ilsa or her father.

"Pa says he comes from a po' white family downstate," Monty continued. "And this wealthy northern woman sent him up to Baltimore and abroad to study, so he got himself important and thinks he's right smart and good as other people. But he hasn't got any kin at all. They're all dead as doornails."

Violetta nodded. "People with the right kind of kinfolk don't let them all die just like that."

Dolph looked bored. "The way you and Monty like to gossip is bad as the Tuesday sewing circle. What difference does it make? We don't have anything to do with them. You kids make me sick the way you go on."

"We do so have something to do with them." I said. "Ilsa's my friend. My best friend."

"Shoot." Violetta laughed. "You're too young, Henry."

"Somebody can be your best friend without your being their best friend, can't they?" I rolled over and dug my nose deep into the fragrant pine needles.

"Monty," Silver said softly, ruffling his hair with her curled fingers that were so like Mamma's. "What happened to her mother?"

"She died in childbirth." Monty flaunted the grown-up technical expression.

"But who was she?"

"Blessed if I know. Care less." Monty was through with the subject. He was starting one of his stomach-aches. All three of the Woolfs had weak stomachs. Mamma said they had been fed on Mrs. Winslow's Soothing Syrup to keep them quiet when they were babies, and it ruined their digestions.

"Come on," Monty said crossly, sliding on the slippery pine needles as he got up. "Let's go home."

11

I woke up around midnight that night. The moonlight was pouring through the window onto my bed. Edwin had the sheet over his head and lay with his face buried in the pillow.

I couldn't get back to sleep, so I got out of bed and went to the window. Although all the lights were out downstairs, and the hotel had quieted down for the night, there was someone walking in the garden, pacing restlessly up and down the paths. I leaned out of the window and peered out into the night, trying to see if it was anybody I knew. After a while I made up my mind it was Cousin Anna, so I slipped into my clothes, tiptoed out of the room, down the creaking corridor and stairs, and out one of the side doors into the garden, without stopping to wonder whether I might be unwelcome.

When Cousin Anna saw that someone was walking toward her she stopped and waited. She looked relieved when she saw who it was. She didn't ask me what I was doing, or tell me to go back to bed, but started to walk again, while I fell into step by her side. The night was fragrant and filled with moonlight. It seemed that the fragrance I breathed in with deep cooling breaths came from the moon itself rather than the flowers that, under its strange reflected light, were new flowers, of new color and shape and pattern. In the moonlight, with her scars softened and obscured, Cousin Anna looked very beautiful.

"I don't believe in intermarriage," she said after a while, her voice sounding as luminous and foreign as the night. "It's one reason why we're decaying away to a handful of emberless ashes. But it seems there is nothing I can do about it. Perhaps if I had more energy—but I haven't. I'm perfectly well, you know, strong and healthy; but nothing is worth the effort any more. I simply don't care. Sometimes I think I would rather be dead than have to go through the insufferable boredom of putting on my clothes in the morning and taking them off at night." She was silent for a while; then she said, half smiling, "In insane asylums moonlight like this is a troublesome thing. The ones who are violent only part of the time have to be tied down night and day. And the ones who are allowed to eat in the dining room, the ones who really don't seem crazy most of the time—when the moon is full they are lunatics, too. They have to have their knives and forks taken away, or anything they might be able to use against themselves or each other. They have to be watched twice as carefully." She paused for a moment. "When the moon is full like this, I'm restless, too. I can't sleep. I have to get up and walk, or I feel perhaps I might go mad. No one is without a grain of insanity. On nights like this there's something about to burst inside me, something sobbing and wailing like the doves on the summerhouse, and I have to walk it up and down as though it were a baby, to try and quiet it. I have to defy the moon; I have to walk directly under its glare and prove that I'm stronger and more powerful, because I'm still alive and it's nothing but a poor, dead, burned-out thing, all passion spent."

We walked for a time longer in silence. Then Cousin Anna said, "My husband, your Cousin Randolph, is beyond being touched by the moon. He's lying up there on that hard brass bed, with the moonlight pouring in stripes across him through the blinds and falling into his mouth. Sometimes I wonder what would happen to him if he took a swallow of moonlight by mistake. It might do him a lot of good."

We turned down the cinder path and went up the steps to the summerhouse. Cousin Anna sat down on one of the stone benches, gleaming marble-white. She was wearing a blue-gray Paisley shawl which turned silver in the moonlight, and she wrapped it tightly about herself and shivered.

"Are you cold, Cousin Anna?" I asked.

"Not outside."

"Cousin Anna?"

"What is it, Henry?"

"Did you know a man called Dr. John Brandes when you were young?"

She didn't appear to have heard my question. She turned to me, and I thought perhaps I shouldn't have said "when you were young," because in the moonlight, with her hair loose about her shoulders, she didn't look much older than Violetta. She was three years older than Mamma, so that would make her thirty-six. Of course I didn't know that then, because Mamma would have died rather than admit her age.

"Henry," Cousin Anna Silverton said, "don't you grow up to be biggety. You've got nothing to be biggety about. Nobody in the whole Porcher-Silverton-Woolf contingent has any right to this overpowering sense of superiority they pour on high and low, the way this moonlight's pouring down on us. Sometimes I think maybe pride's as potent as moonlight, or we wouldn't fool people the way we do. Folks with as much money as we have don't have any call to be proud, if they remember how they got it. When I was a little girl in Mississippi we would have considered it a disgrace to have money, or even to have had enough to eat three times a day, seven days a week. We lived on soup and rice for months, so that Papa could have his portrait painted. It was a beautiful portrait in his uniform with his saber. It burned up in the first fire. My brother should have had it, but when he took the cloth he gave it to me. I wish now I hadn't let him give it to me. He didn't want to. And if he'd kept it, it might still be alive. Though if I know Papa, he'd rather be burned to a frazzle than hang on the wall of a house in New Jersey. That's where they sent him last winter. New Jersey. I don't know how he'll stand the cold."

"They sent who to New Jersey?" I asked.

"My brother William," Cousin Anna said. "They took away his church and sent him to New Jersey to some town with an Indian name nobody can say, so nobody goes there, and those who do, don't go to church."

"Where was his church they took away?" Excitement rose in me like the tide to the moon.

"Charleston. Cecilia didn't tell you about it?"

"No, ma'am."

"She wouldn't, of course. William was so pleased when he was sent to Charleston shortly after Elizabeth died. I wish I'd had a chance to tell him that Cecilia was coming, though even I didn't think she'd be such a fool as to go to his church. She might have known what would happen. William has always been a gallant idiot, sticking his neck out for what he thinks is right. William is a nice boy, but he never understood Elizabeth for a minute. His wife's a nice little thing. Mary Huger. He met her in Charleston, and it was the best thing in the world for him. Poor Mary, all this fuss because of William's dark and gory past must be quite a blow to her, although he wrote me that he was perfectly frank with her about the whole thing."

"Oh," I said.

"Shall I tell you something, Henry?" Cousin Anna asked.

"Yes, ma'am," I breathed.

Cousin Anna looked around her carefully and lowered her voice to a whisper. "I hate your mother."

She stood up, flying her Paisley shawl about her, and walked rapidly toward the house. I hurried along behind her. But she didn't say anything more. She went into the house as though I weren't there, slamming the screen door in my face. Then she ran up the stairs, her shawl trailing after her, the back of one hand pressed tightly against her mouth.

12

Toward the end of the winter, when I was thirteen, Cousin Randolph died of a heart attack. This frightened Mamma, because her own heart had been playing tricks on her a good deal, and she began to read the Bible constantly. After Papa had read us Cousin Anna's letter announcing Cousin Randolph's death, a very brief letter, written on paper with only a fine black edge to it, I sat looking at Mamma. Her face had gone very pale; her little lizard's head, on its slender neck, was proud against her fear of mortality; her stiff body was elegant as a fashion plate; her eyes cold, cold; her nose pinched in as though the world had a smell unpleasant to her fastidious soul; her hands always in the impeccable white kid gloves; and I thought of the things Cousin Anna had said about her and wondered why they were so true. God had certainly given Mamma a good deal, but she had apparently enjoyed none of it.

Shortly after Cousin Randolph's death, I read in one of the newspapers in the hotel lounge that the distinguished naturalist, John Brandes, had died of a fever at the beach in his home near July Harbour. It gave a long résumé of his accomplishments and the honors that had been awarded him, and ended up by saying that he was survived by a daughter, Ilsa. This latter part I read without understanding. As soon as I realized that Dr. Brandes was dead, it was as though the world had suddenly become a little darker, and there was no longer as much light for comprehension as there had been.

I showed the paper to Silver, but she didn't give it much mind. She had just received a letter from Monty, away at school, with a snapshot of him and a group of other students enclosed. Monty was in the middle, wearing a striped blazer and holding a banjo. He had an idiotic grin on his handsome face, and I turned away from Silver and the picture in anger, trying instead to see Dr. Brandes—the high forehead, and the strong delicate nose, the firm sensuous mouth, and the slight chin with the goatee. I wondered what Ilsa was doing, how she was bearing it. I had a vision of her with her arms around Calypso, comforting her, and trying wordlessly to explain to the mare why her back would be bare forevermore of the form that gave her meaning. . . . And a vision of Ilsa sitting in the big room at the beach, with one of her father's books lying open on her lap, while Ira cleaned the big table under the skylight, stripping it bare of jars and specimens. . . . And a vision of Ilsa pacing up and down on the sand close to the ocean, with the same restless despair as Cousin Anna pacing in the garden of the hotel.

But I knew that none of these visions was valid, because I still saw Ilsa as the child in the torn blue cotton dress, whereas she must be sixteen now and must have changed as much as I had.

I said nothing to Papa and Mamma about Dr. Brandes' death, but they knew. Everyone in the family had written them. Mamma said that it was about time, and she supposed the girl would stay on down at the beach alone with that uncouth assistant of her father's and sell her soul to the devil forever, and that would be the end of her and good riddance to bad rubbish.

But Cousin Anna put an end to Mamma's smugness on the subject. I knew that Papa had received a letter from her, because I recognized the writing and the fine black-edged envelope when the post was brought in. I was curious all during lessons that morning, because Cousin Anna's letters always seemed to contain gunpowder. This one certainly did.

At lunch time Papa said, "Well, Cecilia-Jane, young Randolph Silverton is going to marry Violetta Woolf."

Mamma nodded approvingly. "A most suitable union. Violetta is a charming young girl, or was when we saw her last, and I'm sure she'll be a most fitting mate for Randolph. I was afraid he might have absorbed some of Anna's peculiar ideas. Or that dreadful uncle of his; that fiend out of the bowels of hell. I believe he still writes Anna occasionally from wherever he is—New Jersey. Can you imagine?"

"After all, Cecilia," Papa said. "He is Anna's brother."

"That makes it even more inexcusable. I think we made a great mistake to name Anna Silverton after her." She had a way of moving her small reptilian head as though the neck which supported it were a great deal longer than it was. Now she arched her neck so that one got an impression of snakelike length, and looked with her cold unblinking eyes at Silver, who flushed. Silver and Mamma were no longer as close as they had been. Silver had come to woman's estate the winter before, and Mamma had felt obliged to tell her that it was a perfectly normal phenomenon and that she was not bleeding to death. Ever since that time there had been a strangled restraint between them. Mamma no longer looked at Silver with mild affection; she looked at her, in fact, as little as possible, and then with a kind of distaste, as though this sudden reminder of the animal facts of life were a deliberate and unforgivable thing on Silver's part.

Papa unfolded the two sheets of Cousin Anna's letter carefully. "'I suppose it is no use asking you and Cecilia to come home for the wedding, so I shall not do so,'" he read. "'In any event it will be a very quiet one to be held in the parlor at the Woolfs'. Montgomery thought it would be more proper to wait until a year had gone by after Randolph's death—only, of course, Montgomery called it "passing" and I am sure you and Cecilia will, too, so forgive my bluntness in speaking of it as what it is. To return to the wedding, if Dolph and Violetta are bound and determined to get married, I suppose they might as well get it over with as soon as possible, no matter how young they are. Dolph will regret it soon enough, but I am not going to try to direct his life for him. I have seen too many unfortunate consequences of that kind of behavior, as I told Montgomery. My son will have to make his own mistakes and abide by them.'" Papa cleared his throat and deliberated whether or not to read the next part, finally deciding against it. Out of the corner of my eye, I read, "No matter what I think of this match, I am not going to run the risk of ruining his life as Cecilia and Montgomery and your pious sister Violetta ruined Elizabeth's. At any rate I hope Dolph and young Violetta will get some enjoyment out of their marriage before it goes on the rocks. I did, and I can assure you that that compensates for a good deal. Though Cecilia, of course, wouldn't understand that. Violetta is an appetizing little morsel, which ought to make up to a certain extent for her deficiencies."

Mamma looked at Papa, who was skimming to the bottom of the page and turning it over. "Well. Go on," she commanded.

"Anna is becoming extremely vulgar," Papa said.

Mamma nodded. "Yes. Purely to shock me. If it gives her pleasure to become cheap and bawdy, who am I to stop her? Go on with the letter."

But Papa had folded the letter and put it back in his pocket. "She is going to take Ilsa Brandes to live with her," he said.

Mamma's face and neck became crimson. Then the color slowly receded, leaving her deadly white except for a persistent flush in the lobes of the tiny ears that lay close against her head. I felt that only the other families in the dining room, and the fear of making a spectacle of herself in public, kept her from flinging back her chair and removing herself from the sound of such treasonous words, leaving Papa and Silver and me at the round table, while water spilled from her overturned goblet, dripping over the white tablecloth onto the floor.

But she did nothing so passionate. The color came and fled, and she sat there, her ringed hands under the gloves clenched, her breath coming sharp and quick.

Satisfied that she wasn't going to faint, Papa took out the letter again, and read. "'Although I'm sure she would infinitely prefer to remain at the beach with that odd assistant of her father's from Georgia, I suppose it would be the topic of much unmerited scandal, and if we don't look out for her, who will? My sense of duty may differ from Cecilia's, but it is no less existent. As for me, it will be a great help to have someone with me in this house. Although I am only thirty-six, too many fires seem to have aged me prematurely. I suppose this house will burn, eventually, like the others. Why Randolph insisted on building a third of those neo-Greek, scion-of-the-old-South affairs, is beyond me. Without age and tradition behind them, they are valueless and seem only pretentious and in poor taste.'" Papa had told us that our new house, which was being rented to some people from Alabama who were taking care of the mill while we were away, was also to be as much like the old one as possible.

"I find it difficult to believe," Mamma said, "that Anna has the heritage she claims. She is coming to sound more and more like poor white."

"Shall I go on with the letter?" Papa asked.

Mamma nodded.

Papa read. "'She is an interesting child, the most alive creature I have ever seen.'" Then he stopped. I managed to read, "The really strange thing is that she reminds me continually of Elizabeth. Perhaps this is a judgment upon Cecilia and Montgomery. I am sure God must find Elizabeth's death and the manner of her dying hard to forgive. I wonder what would have happened if her child had lived? Perhaps this wild creature, so like her, and so desperately no part of her, might be someone quite different, more like her mother, who—"

Papa saw my eye on the letter and realized what I was doing. He sent me up to his room to wait for him, and by and by he thrashed me soundly. But the thrashing wasn't important.

While I sat in the summerhouse to wait until the pain had subsided, I remembered, unaccountably, as it seemed to me then, something that had happened before we left home, when Silver and I went to school instead of having private lessons. Miss Turnbull had given us a composition. It was one of the first real compositions we had done, and all of them were read in class. One little boy wrote a fantastic story about mistaken identity during the Civil War, and we all complained because we said it was too coincidental and strange to be true. I remember that Miss Turnbull looked at us very seriously, and told us that the world was so immense, and yet so minute, that the people in it were scrambled about with such diabolical inspiration that nothing that was about human beings, nothing that took place on the face of the earth, was too strange to be true. Afterward, we found out that the little boy's wild tale was based on actual fact; it was something that had happened to his uncle.

Often, while Silver and I were having our lessons in one of the small reception rooms in the hotel, I would remember Miss Myra Turnbull with regret, and think of the many things she had told us that I was too young to understand. We had simply regarded her as another old-maid teacher, although she was quite young at the time, not more than twenty-two or -three. But she was one of those people who change very little between twenty and sixty. Instead of growing and developing into whatever kind of creatures they are, slowly and consistently, they have three periods of their lives, with sharp lines of demarcation between them: they are children, then grownups, then old men and women.

Suddenly thinking of Miss Myra like that made me miss school dreadfully. The lessons Silver and I were given didn't amount to much, and I was filled again with the desire to learn that Miss Turnbull had given me.

Another thing that made me eager to go home was that I felt that now Ilsa had become one of the family, and I couldn't see that there was any more reason why I shouldn't be allowed to see her as much as I liked.

I would get Silver to beg Mamma and Papa to take us back, but finally I came to realize that we would never go home while Mamma was alive. When Mamma had decided she was disgraced, and was going to retire from the world, she meant it. We knew that her heart, like Uncle Randolph's, was bad, and often I would catch myself looking with guilty hope at the purplish tinge to her fingernails, and the slight swelling that disfigured her elegant ankles when she was tired.

She lived until I was fifteen. I was the one who found her lying on the floor of the summerhouse, her white dress soiled from her struggle against death, her cold open eyes staring accusingly at me, her mouth bleakly open, while horrible strangling sounds still tore from her throat. On the roof the doves wailed unceasingly.

I rushed back to the hotel for help. Papa came running, and Silver. Papa looked stern and angry, as he always did when he was upset, and Silver's face had quickly gone devoid of expression. Her gray eyes under the dark brows were as unfathomable as Mamma's lifeless ones.

One of the colored boys carried Mamma back to the house. All the ladies and gentlemen on the cream-colored veranda rose as we came up the steps. The dark green chairs rocked mockingly by themselves. A group of children in the yard took their dripping faces out of their watermelon rinds, and stared at the limp white figure being carried into the house. From somewhere behind the kitchen came the sound.

PART THREE

13

We went home late in September. I sat in the train staring out the window, trying to drive out of the back of my mind the thought that somehow I had killed Mamma by wanting her to die so that I could go home to Ilsa and Cousin Anna and Miss Myra Turnbull. When I closed my eyes I could see her dreadful ashen face with the open, condemning eyes, and hear the bestial groans coming from her throat. It seemed a strange indignity that Mamma, who had been so fastidious and remote from the physical part of living, should have had to end her life alone in a violent animal struggle against death.

Papa sat sternly reading the paper. Every once in a while he would pull out his white lawn handkerchief and wipe his mustache as though he had been eating something. Her hands folded delicately in her lap, Mamma's diamond and sapphire ring on her little finger, Silver sat looking with cool, uninterested eyes at the other people in the Pullman. I kept turning toward the window, watching the bare rice flats stretching on into the sky, rusty brown and watery, watching a lone tree sticking up, black and burnt-looking, out of place against a sky like a bright ribbon from Violetta's hair, a sky so bright and blatant that after a moment I had to turn and look with Silver at the other people traveling south with us.

It was insufferably hot. The large fans creaking and whirring above us seemed only to blow the heat at us with more force. Silver's face, usually pale and cool in the warmest weather, looked flushed and damp above her black dress. I felt wet to the bone.

Papa fanned himself angrily with his paper. I thought we would never get home.

The train was two hours late.

We took a cab and drove through the night that, at last, after five years, had all the familiar odors of childhood, drove down the wide street where the live oaks arched their locked branches overhead. When we turned down our own drive, I reached out and clasped my sister's hand.

As the house became visible through the trees it looked so like our old place that I caught my breath in amazement, but later on, after we had been greeted with the old wonderful warmth by Nursie, and been admired and exclaimed over, I realized that it was only a cheap imitation. Five years of living in a place can't seep into the panels and walls as centuries can. And though the portraits were hung again in heavy gold frames, though most of Papa's books were back, almost undamaged, in the glassed-in bookcases in the library, there were many things I missed—the rice portieres Great-uncle Henry Randolph had brought from China; Silver's old rocking horse; the big screen made of oil paintings that Grandfather Montgomery Porcher had collected all over the world, that had stood in the dining room; Mamma's Chinese sewing table, inlaid with mother-of-pearl; my mahogany spool bed.

I went into the dining room and stared at the picture of Aunt Elizabeth, grateful that Silver, at seventeen, might have been taken for the original. If Silver looked so much like Aunt Elizabeth, surely she was not going to be like Mamma.

I had never really, with the eyes of my mind, looked at the picture of Aunt Elizabeth before. Now I stood in front of it, looking up at the steady gray eyes, the dark, determined eyebrows. There was an expression about the mouth that made me feel that she must have laughed a great deal, and at the same time that she was laughing lightly, she would be quite cold-bloodedly getting her own way. And there was something about the way the eyes looked at me, the way the mouth was closed, the way the head was proudly held, that did, indeed, remind me more of Ilsa than my sister. I was determined to go over to Cousin Anna's the first thing in the morning.

Silver came in and stood behind me. She, too, looked at the portrait of Aunt Elizabeth.

"She wouldn't look so peculiar if it weren't for those eyebrows. It's crazy to have black eyebrows, and hair this color. I like that dress. I'd adore to have a red velvet dress. I wonder how long we'll have to wear mourning for Mamma?"

"A year, I suppose." I would have liked to wear the black band for longer because of the feeling of guilt I still had about her. But I didn't see why Silver should have to wear mourning at all. She had always been gentle and obedient with Mamma, and up until that strange restraint had come between them, I'm sure she never had any but loving thoughts about her. It seemed criminal to me that she should be forced into unbecoming black when she was seventeen and at last coming home to her family and friends. I knew the way the young men who spent the summers at the hotel had looked at her, and how Mamma had seen to it that there was never an opportunity for her to talk to any of them. I hoped that now, at last, she would have her chance, and that she wouldn't be forced to lose a year because of the forbidding black of mourning.

She must have read my thoughts, because she said, "Brother—"

"Yes?"

"I try to grieve about Mamma, but I can't seem to."

"I know." We both turned our heads toward the library, where Papa had locked himself. We pictured him sitting at his huge desk, head in hands, studying the miniature of Mamma he always kept with him.

"Brother—" Silver said again.

"Yes?"

"Mamma wasn't always the way she was."

"I don't ever remember her any different."

"Well—she would have felt badly if anything had happened to you."

"Only because it was her duty."

"But she did love *me* when we were little, I know she did," Silver persisted. "I suppose it's because I'm a girl. She always talked as though she loved me until after I began to grow up. I don't understand."

"No," I said.

"I suppose you wouldn't remember—I was only about five, so you'd have been too young—but I remember being waked up one night and brought into the parlor, and there were a lot of ladies and gentlemen, and Mamma had on an ivory satin evening dress and diamond and ruby earrings, and she had on those long white kid gloves you wear in the evening, you know, so they looked all right—and, Henry, she looked so beautiful, and I ran to her and she took me in her arms, and Cousin Anna took you on her lap, and you went right back to sleep in your little white nightgown. But what I mean is, Mamma was so wonderful and beautiful and—and *gay* then, and she let me taste her champagne. I don't understand. What was it that Mamma *wanted*? Where did she belong?"

"She didn't belong to be a mother."

"But why?"

"I don't know."

Silver sat down in Mamma's old armchair at the end of the table and looked at the shining polished tea and coffee sets on the dark mahogany sideboard. She sighed. "Oh, well. I'm glad these things got saved, aren't you, Henry?"

I nodded.

"Papa says you're to have our old playroom for your room and I'm to have the bedroom. I suppose our things must be about unpacked by now. I'm tired. Let's go up."

"All right, Sister."

"It seems funny to be home. And I keep missing things," she said. "I used to love those rice portieres and the way you could see such beautiful flowers on them when you stood in the place where the light hit them just right. I suppose the Woolfs still have theirs. Papa says we'll call on them tomorrow evening, and Cousin Anna afterward. And he says you aren't to go over to Cousin Anna's before."

"Oh, he does, does he!" I answered. "Well, he'll have to tell me himself, then."

"Oh, please, Brother." Silver put her hand on my shoulder. "He'll just yell at us both. And Papa feels real bad about Mamma, even if we don't."

"Oh, all right," I said crossly. "Come on up."

At the landing there was a window seat cushioned in brown plush. On either side were glassed-in bookcases of poetry and Victorian novels. From the window you could see down the drive to the wrought-iron gates. We turned to each other, then sat down on the window seat, pressing our faces against the panes and staring out into the dark. The magnolia tree was still there, its leaves smooth and shiny-black. Silver opened the door to one of the glassed-in bookcases and pulled out a small leather-bound volume of Byron's poetry.

"I think I'll stay here and read awhile. You go on up, Henry."

I nodded and left her.

It seemed strange to go into our playroom, and find it quite a different room. Our little chairs and table were gone, and our toy chest. A low mahogany bed was where Silver's rocking horse had been. There were white dotted-swiss curtains at the windows; the wallpaper was white with blue and silver stripes. My night clothes were laid out on the bed, three of my books on the bed table, the rest neatly stacked on the flat-topped desk and on the floor. I would have to ask Papa to give me a bookcase for the books I had managed to collect during the five years we lived at the hotel. Most of them I had sent away for with my pocket money. Cousin Anna always gave me a book at Christmas and on my birthday. These were some of my favorites: *Stalky and Co.*; Browning's poems; an anthology of Elizabethan plays.

At the window the white curtains stirred slightly with the breeze from the river. The fire had left enough live oaks, hung with summer-dried and dusty Spanish moss, so that the river was partly obscured and showed only as a cool glimmer here and there through the trees. I sat down on the bed and pulled off my shoes and socks. My hot, swollen feet were grateful for the cool of the floor under them. I sat still on the edge of the bed with my feet stealing the cool of the floor, and tried to sense the room. It still belonged to whomever had slept in it for the past few years, but I had a feeling that I could make it mine as a hotel room can never be one's own.

14

Early the next evening we went over to the Woolfs. I had forgotten how the atmosphere of that house oppressed me. As we went into the entrance hall I remembered that it was here that Aunt Elizabeth had been living when whatever it was that made Mamma and Aunt Violetta and Uncle Montgomery hate her so had happened. The house always seemed full of hate, and I was only just beginning to realize what a horribly destructive thing hate is, how it destroys inwards as well as outwards. I remembered something that Miss Myra Turnbull had taught us: that nothing in the chemical world vanishes. Everything that is in the world remains in some form or other. Decaying matter turns into mould and gases and is regenerated and becomes living matter again. I had come home from school and realized that that was what must happen to the human body after death. Even if the soul went to heaven, the body would become part of the earth again, of sand and wind and trees and sea.

Standing in Uncle Montgomery's ill-lighted front hall, while the houseboy went to announce us, I thought that it must be the same way with thoughts and emotions. All the powers of evil and good we let loose are freed into the world forever. Every will to hurt, to cause pain—every time we are shaken by anger—that fury, that cruelty, remains forever. I felt that an untold deal of evil thinking had gone on in this dark sunless house, buried in the decadent green of too many trees.

Silver and I nudged each other as we pushed through the rice portieres that still hung between the living room and the hall and that clung tenuously to our hot bodies as we went in. Uncle Montgomery and Edwin were alone. We sat down, and Uncle Montgomery got out the port. He had gone very gray; I hadn't noticed this at the funeral. Silver kept looking around and I knew that she was wondering where Monty was. After a while she asked about Violetta.

"Most suitable, most happy marriage," Uncle Montgomery said. "She and Randolph will expect you to call on them as soon as your father gets his motorcar. Built their house across the river, you know. Some of our water-front property. And how do you like your new home?"

"Oh, it's—it's real nice," Silver said. "How—how's Monty doing?"

"Montgomery is splendid," our uncle said. "Been working with me all summer. Hope to hand the practice over to him whenever he decides to marry and settle down. Delighted to see you and Henry. Always had great family feeling. Can't overestimate the importance of the family. Thankful to say all three of my children have it."

Papa nodded.

"Most sorry," Uncle Montgomery said, "uh, most sorry the boys couldn't get up to the funeral. Sorry none of the children could come. Sent Monty and Ed over to stay with Violetta and Rand. Anna offered to take them, but I didn't want them around that girl."

Papa looked at Uncle Montgomery; then he turned to me. "Why don't you and Edwin take your sister over to your cousin's now, Henry? You can send the carriage back for me in an hour. Your uncle and I have some, ah, business to talk over."

Silver and I were glad enough to escape.

My head began to thump with excitement as we climbed Cousin Anna's low white steps. The palms of my hands were wet with cold sweat. Silver was so preoccupied with wondering where Monty was that she didn't notice my nervousness. She wouldn't have, anyway.

Barbara, the girl Cousin Anna had saved from the fire, led us in. Cousin Anna's new house, like ours, looked much the same as the old. Barbara took us through the living room and opened the French windows wide.

"Miss Anna sitting down by the magnolia tree. I think she expecting you if you care to go out and join her. I don't likes to ask her to come back in."

"Of course," I said. "We'll go out to her. Is—is Miss Ilsa with her?"

"No, sir, Mr. Henry. Miss Ilsa, I think she gone out awhile back with Mr. Montgomery." She sounded troubled.

"Oh," I said. "All right. Thank you, Barbara."

"I could have told you that," Edwin said. "I thought you knew. They drove over to Violetta's with some things. Pa's mad as hops."

We went out the French windows and walked toward the magnolia tree at the foot of the garden. There was a wide wooden bench around it, and Cousin Anna was seated on this, leaning back against the tree, her hands lying loosely in her lap.

"Hello, Cousin Anna," I said. She didn't move.

Panic rose momentarily in my throat. When once you have discovered how indiscriminately and lightly death can strike, you expect to find it everywhere. To a boy of fifteen the knowledge that someone who has been an alive part of his life can disappear and leave no noticeable vacancy in the universe is frightening; and the unimportance of death becomes the most important thing in the world.

"Cousin Anna!" I said again sharply, and her eyes stopped staring into spaces far beyond her garden and focused on us. "Well, Henry and Silver," she said. "So you've come home. 'Evening, Edwin."

This was evidently one of her times when the lightest movement was too much effort. She continued to lean her head back against the tree, her hands in her lap as though they had been dropped and discarded there. "Why don't you sit down?" she said after a while. "Ilsa'll be back soon. I made her promise that, at least, and I've never known her to break a promise."

We sat down, silent; night was suddenly on top of us, but still no one moved and no one spoke. I stared up through the shiny dark leaves of the tree at the stars, blossoming so close it seemed as though they were clinging to the branches. Several times Silver sighed heavily and moved restlessly in her black dress; except for her small pale face and hands she was almost blotted out by the night. Cousin Anna wore a shawl with metallic threads that caught the light and shone faintly. Edwin, in his white linen suit, was the most visible of us all.

After a long time Cousin Anna remarked dispassionately, "Well, I guess I got my come-uppance when I thought I could make things better by taking Ilsa Brandes to live with me."

"Why?" I asked.

She didn't answer my question, but said instead, "I was Elizabeth's best friend, you know."

"No. We didn't know."

She seemed to remember Silver suddenly. "Well, namesake. Are you glad to be home?"

Silver nodded. "Yes, ma'am."

"A little let down?" Cousin Anna asked.

"I guess so."

"It must be startling to come back to the world at your age. If you can call this town the world. Are you aware that there's a war in Europe?"

Again Silver nodded.

"And one we ought to be in," Cousin Anna said; "but that's aside from the point. Do you like your new house?"

"It's not as nice as the old one."

"Of course not. You didn't expect it to be, did you?"

"I guess not."

"How about you, Henry? Do you feel a little lost, too?"

"Maybe."

"You've both grown up since I saw you last, haven't you?"

We nodded, staring back at the house, searching the French windows for a sign of Ilsa or Monty.

"How are Dolph and Violetta?" Silver asked, hoping to lead the conversation around to Monty, completely unaware and careless of Eddie's glance resting lingeringly on her.

"They're both still alive and comparatively healthy," Cousin Anna said. "Violetta had a miscarriage a year after they were married and won't be able to have any children."

"Oh," Silver said, in a small shocked voice. We were not accustomed to conversation like this.

"Perhaps it's just as well," Cousin Anna continued. "*She'll* be perfectly happy and contented with life as it presents itself to her, at any rate."

Silver and I stiffened suddenly, and I turned away from Cousin Anna and back toward the house again. Someone in a light dress was coming out and walking with firm quick steps toward us.

Cousin Anna realized that we weren't listening, and her eyes followed ours. "Ah, here's Ilsa," she said.

While Ilsa approached I felt suffocated with heat and excitement. Looking up at the night through the tree I realized that the stars were obscured, and the sky seemed to be bearing closer and more heavily upon us.

Ilsa came up and kissed Cousin Anna, looking for a moment sharply into her eyes; then stood back and smiled easily at us. I knew that I would have recognized her anywhere at any time, if only by her erect, confident bearing and the ease and conciseness with which she moved. Her hair was long now, like anybody else's, but her head had the old arrogant tilt, her eyes the same frightening clarity. She wore her blue-and-white dotted-swiss dress like a queen's robe. She was the wind and the ocean, the sand and the stars. And for some reason she reminded me of the Swiss flower I had read about, the edelweiss, blooming clear and strong where no other flower dares to grow.

"Henry and Silver," she said, and I had forgotten what a deep voice hers was, what a strange quality it had, reminding me of the smoky fogs that covered the sharp gray of ocean. "There's been great excitement in the family about your return. Hello." She held out both hands. I took one eagerly. After a moment's hesitation Silver took the other. Ilsa looked at us. "Yes, I'd have known you both. Henry, you were a funny baby and now you're grown up; but you, Silver, look much the same. Are you?"

"I don't know," Silver said, resentment coming quickly to her voice.

Ilsa turned to Edwin. "Hello. It's nice to see you."

"Hello," Eddie said shyly. He seemed to respect her and at the same time to be a little afraid of her.

Behind the house sheet lightning was flickering and the air pressed closer and closer about us.

Ilsa drew her hands out of Silver's and mine and bent down to Cousin Anna again. "We'd better go in now, darling," she said gently. "It's going to storm."

I had almost forgotten that almost every afternoon or evening during the summer at home there was a thunderstorm. These storms were extremely localized; you could hear the thunder and see the lightning, but the rain would fall only in certain places. Sometimes we could see the rain pelting in huge, almost hail-like drops on the river, while the house would remain dusty and dry. Often, when the house was actually in the center of a storm, we would be nearly deafened by the shock of the thunder when the lightning was caught by the rod.

"Come now, darling," Ilsa said cajolingly to Cousin Anna, speaking as she might to a child or a lost puppy. "Barbara's making some cold tea for us. Monty went home in Henry's carriage to pick up Mr. Porcher. They'll be back soon." Although she bent so close to Cousin Anna and spoke so persuasively, she never insulted her by touching her or trying in any physical way to get her to throw off her apathy and rise. Thunder began to roll in the distance, sounding almost like the breakers at the beach.

Cousin Anna looked into Ilsa's eyes for a long moment, as though in this way she would be able to get enough spiritual energy to make the trip back to the house. Then she stood up; Ilsa walked beside her, still not touching her; Silver and Edwin and I trailed behind.

Cousin Anna's rooms always had a life and charm that none of the other rooms I knew could approach. As we stepped over the threshold, the air suddenly lightened and the rain began to fall in great heavy drops. Ilsa stood in the window frame for a moment after we had entered the room, the wind blowing the skirts of her light dress about her and spattering her with rain; after a moment she came into the room and pushed the doors of the windows to. Cousin Anna sat in a chair upholstered in silver-gray velvet. I noticed, as she leaned back against it, again tossing her hands uselessly in her lap, that her ash-blonde hair was the color of Silver's, and must have been the color of Aunt Elizabeth's. Ilsa's hair had much more violence to it; it was the tawny color of the sea oats, which waved their wild tassels on the highest dunes above the ocean.

Silver and Eddie sat on a low bench near Cousin Anna. After a moment Ilsa and I seated ourselves on the sofa that faced the fireplace in which stood a copper bucket full of Cape jessamine.

"Well, Henny," Ilsa said to me. "How are you? Are you all right?"

"I guess so. Are you?"

"Oh, yes. I'm always fine."

"Do you like it with Cousin Anna?"

"I like Cousin Anna very much."

"She's wonderful, isn't she?" I said.

Ilsa nodded.

"Do you—do you still have the house at the beach?"

"Yes. Father left it to me. Your Cousin Montgomery has been trying to make me sell it, but your Cousin Anna says it's mine and I'm to do with it as I please. I'd rather sell myself."

"And Calypso?"

It seemed to me that she went a little pale. "Calypso died about a month before Father. It was my fault."

"What do you mean?"

"I was galloping her on the beach. She was tired. I'd been galloping her too long. She put her left foreleg in a hole and went down. It broke her leg. Father had to shoot her." Although as she spoke her voice was quite cool and calm she clenched her hands in her lap so that the bones pressed through at the knuckles and showed white. Then, as her fingers loosened, she said, "I hope your little old Billy is all right."

"Yes. Papa sold him when he sold the rest of the horses, but I went to see him this morning. He's awfully fat and lazy now. And I'm too big to ride him anyhow."

She looked at me. "Yes. You've grown a lot."

Barbara came in then with the tea things. Ilsa got up and served tea quietly. Cousin Anna didn't move, but her eyes followed Ilsa, and they were troubled.

"Your Cousin Anna and I drink tea at all hours of the day and night," Ilsa said, as she handed me mine. "We like tea the way Monty likes gin. Not that I'm averse to gin once in a while. Wouldn't that shock your sister Silver!" She grinned; then went and opened the windows. The rain was still falling, but gently now, no longer driving into the room. Soon it would be gone and the stars would hang heavy about us again while the lightning flickered fitfully somewhere on the horizon.

After the windows were open, and she had taken a quick glance at Cousin Anna, Silver, and Edwin, to see that they had everything they needed, she came over and sat down by me again. "I should have written you when your mother died."

"Why?"

"It would have been the courteous thing to do. What with Father, and now your Cousin Anna, getting after me, I ought to have learned some manners."

"I didn't write you about your father."

"That's different."

"Why?"

"You're a boy, and that was two years ago when you were only thirteen. Did you love your mother very much?"

"No."

"I didn't think you did. Why?"

I said, after a moment, "She didn't like me."

"I guess that's as good a reason as any for not liking a mother. Though it wouldn't be so good for somebody else. I apologize for asking so many personal questions."

"I don't mind. I was—I was awfully sorry about your father."

"Yes. He liked you, you know."

"Did he really?"

"Of course. I wouldn't have said so otherwise."

"I'm awfully glad. Was he—was he ill long?"

"About three weeks. Ira and I nursed him. He told us what to do. But it wasn't any good."

"Didn't you have a doctor?"

"Oh, yes, but he couldn't tell us anything Father hadn't told us already. He might have pulled through if he hadn't been so exhausted. Father had a wonderful constitution. But he'd been away on a long field trip, going after special specimens he needed for some experiment he was working on, and while he was gone he was lost and without food or water for several days. He looked dreadful when he staggered home. And then, less than two weeks after, he woke up with a terrible headache, and that was how it started. Ira cried like a baby. I'd never seen Ira cry before. He's down there now. He's promised to keep the place up, even to leaving a lamp burning by the piano whenever he's in, so the keys won't stick and get out of tune so quickly. . . . Here come Monty and your father." She rose.

Papa and Monty came in. They both kissed Cousin Anna, who had not moved, and then Monty turned to Silver. She stood waiting for him, her eyes shiny and excited, her mouth a little open. Monty kissed her on the cheek, then held her off to look at her. "Well! Hey! You've grown into a regular little beauty. Hasn't she, Cousin Anna?"

Cousin Anna made no response. Papa cleared his throat, shook hands with Eddie, and sat down. Ilsa and I relaxed on the sofa again.

Monty pushed Silver gently back onto the bench and stood looking down at her. His dark red hair was thick and polished-looking; his brown eyes were fringed with heavy lashes that softened the otherwise harsh lines of his face, and made you forget the sudden flare of his nostrils and the hairline rather too low on his forehead, the neck a little too thick and too short, the voice a little too loud and too jovial. I knew you saw none of these things unless you hated Monty. Mamma had called him Adonis, and Mamma wasn't given to indiscriminate praise.

He sat down by Silver on the bench for a moment, his arm about her. I felt impotently hot and angry. Cousin Anna looked at them, but she didn't move. After a moment she said, "Ilsa, will you ring for the port?"

"Thank you, no, Anna," Papa said. "I had ample refreshment at Montgomery's."

"Tea?" Cousin Anna asked.

"Thank you, no, Anna," Papa said again. "We can only stay a moment. The children are still tired from the journey and I must take them home."

Monty moved away from Silver and came over to Ilsa and me on the couch, sitting down on the other side of Ilsa. "Are you really the reason Pa tried to keep me away from Cousin Anna's during my vacation?" he asked softly.

"Probably," Ilsa answered, wiping the little beads of moisture from her upper lip. Monty's shirt and mine clung to us wetly. The freshness in the air from the shower had all gone by now.

"I've only seen you three times," Monty said, "and always against Pa's wishes, and I feel as though I'd known you always." He slipped his hand surreptitiously behind her back. She looked down at her small strong hands. I felt miserable and superfluous.

"Henry and I knew each other when we were little," she said, as though to draw me into the conversation.

"Yes, I know," Monty said. "You've told me that before. Henry this, Henry that. He's getting to be quite a big boy."

I hated him; how I hated him.

"Quite tall for only fifteen, aren't you?" he asked.

"Almost sixteen," I said angrily.

"Tall as your old cousin Monty, aren't you?" he went on, unperturbed. "You and Silver surely growing up." He looked over at Ilsa slantwise. I was sure she was desirable to him mainly because she was forbidden. "Think I can get one of the cars tomorrow afternoon," he said. "Want to drive down to the beach with me? Could you slip away?"

"The beach? Could we go home?" she asked quickly.

"You mean the place where you used to live? Sure, honey, any place you like. Sorry not to ask you and your sister, Henry. Another time."

"We couldn't have gone anyway," I said with dignity.

Across the room Papa gave up trying to make conversation with Cousin Anna, and rose. Ilsa showed us to the door. Monty stood behind her, saying loudly that as it was still so early he would stay for a while and visit with Cousin Anna. As we left I saw his arm go around Silver's waist and his fingers slip up toward her breast. I felt sick with anger and distaste.

15

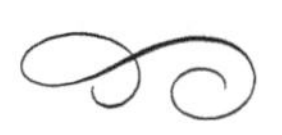

The carriage took us home, then went on with Eddie. When we got in, Papa locked himself in the library again. I had gone in that morning to borrow one of his books and discovered that most of them were unread. Papa, buried in the morning papers, warned me that if the pages were uncut I must by no means tamper with them as he had the mistaken impression that that would lessen their value. It seemed a very peculiar thing to me to collect books if you had no interest in what was in them.

I stood still for a moment as he slammed the door, without looking back at Silver or me; then I followed Silver upstairs. She paused at the landing, and sat down.

"I didn't get a minute to talk to Monty alone," she said, her shoulders drooping. "Eddie stuck to me like glue."

"I like Eddie," I said, thinking of his gentle little face and his long fingers, delicate and kind as a woman's.

"I like Eddie, too"—Silver moved her head restlessly—"but I did want to talk to Monty. It's been years since we've seen him."

"It's been just as long since we've seen Eddie." I was deliberately trying to be irritating.

"Monty and I are grown-up."

"Eddie's older than you are."

"Girls grow up quicker than boys." She looked out the window at the lawn, spotted with camellia and azalea bushes, at the magnolia tree, at the two huge stone dogs on the side terrace. After a while she forgot that she was cross with me. "Monty's awfully handsome."

"And you're very pretty," I said gallantly.

She laughed and blushed. "Oh, shoot, with these big black eyebrows!" She leaned her head against the window glass again.

I sat down beside her and stared out into the night, too, my mind filled with a strange combination of excited happiness and nervous unrest. And as I sat there, with Silver motionless and dark beside me, I drifted into an unquiet, dreamful sleep. I was dead and I went to heaven. Heaven was very white and clean and chill. Mamma sat on an alabaster throne carved all over with delicate white chameleons. Around the throne was a moat of ice, frozen so cold that little whorls and coils of gassy smoke rose from it. Mamma's crown was of ice, too, and pressed close upon her forehead, turning her complexion a transparent frozen green. Her lips and fingernails were stained blue, and above the throne a dove hung suspended, whimpering gently. I stood looking at Mamma and she looked back at me with those glassy, accusing eyes.

Then Violetta came up, carrying a harp. She wore long white robes and wings made out of thousands and thousands of layers of tissue paper. Her silky brown hair hung down her back in the corkscrew curls she wore when she was little. She was smiling with a strange, frigid kind of pleasure. She told me that since I had murdered my mother, of course I wouldn't be allowed in heaven, and I should have known better than to try to come there in the first place. If I liked, she herself would personally conduct me to the gates of hell.

I thanked her, but said I would prefer to find the way myself, and since Ilsa wasn't in heaven, I didn't want to stay anyhow. With a cold, clammy hand Violetta gave me a shove, and I felt myself sliding off the slippery marble platform of heaven that was like the marble top of the washstand in Mamma's room, felt myself sliding off and falling, falling. As I plunged downward, swirling and tumbling, flinging and jerking, until I felt that every bone in my body must be dislocated, I thought that this was how Satan and the fallen angels must have felt.

Then my breath and life were crushed out of me as my body crashed upon what felt like black glass, but as I was already dead this didn't make much difference, and as it was unrelievedly dark I could not see whether or not I had done myself damage.

I had never known such darkness.

Darkness—

Darkness so deep it had no edges, no thin line of light, no shape, no form. Darkness—complete—moving with winds that burned and parched and dried, with winds that chilled in searing damp; darkness that held the echoes of forgotten cries and faded screams undying in its folds; darkness that hid the gates of hell so only touch could tell that they were there.

Darkness filled with the murmur of a thousand wings, wings coming from left, from right, from above, from below; Moloch, Baalim, Ashtaroth, Astoreth, Thammuz, Dagan, Rimmon, Osiris, Orus, Belial; darkness filled with blare of song, inhuman and unknown, that loosed the bars of hell and made the gates roll back with roar of all the waters of the earth raging with one voice.

But once I entered the gates of hell I seemed to wake from my dream. The darkness and madness were gone. I thought, quite calmly, as I looked around at the dim, lost figures in the murky glow, that here I was, dead, and in hell, and it didn't really matter because Mamma and Violetta wouldn't be here, at any rate.

Cousin Anna and Aunt Elizabeth walked by, arm in arm, but they didn't see me. Their eyes were like smouldering coals, and Aunt Elizabeth's dark eyebrows were alive with flame. Then I saw Dr. Brandes and a man in a clerical collar whom I knew to be Cousin William. They were seated at a small table in the middle of a raging furnace, playing chess. The legs of the table were of serpents, coiled and writhing about each other, and the chessmen were continually being devoured by fire. I went over to them and spoke, but realized that they could neither see nor hear me as they sat in their furnace. Then I started to go around from spirit to spirit, asking all of them where Ilsa was, but no one knew. No one had heard of her.

Then it struck me suddenly that she might not be dead; she might not be in either heaven or hell, but on earth.

This thought was so terrible that I was blind from the horror of it.

The next thing I knew, Silver was shaking me, and I was back on the brown-plush window seat on the landing at home.

"Brother, wake up, wake up!" Silver was saying over and over. "Wake up! What's the matter?"

"I—I don't know," I said stupidly.

"You fell asleep. Were you having a nightmare?"

I nodded.

"What was it?"

"Just a nightmare," I said. "It would sound silly if I told it. The really bad dreams are only bad if you're asleep."

"You'd better go on up to bed." She laid her hand in a worried fashion on my knee. "You must still be awful tired if you can fall asleep like this."

"All right," I said, and stood up, stretching. "Good night, Sister."

"Good night, Henry." She watched after me as I went on up the stairs.

16

The next time I saw Ilsa was about a week later. It must have been some time after midnight and I had already been in bed for several hours, but I hadn't been asleep. It was hot with that dreadful final blare of heat that comes in the autumn before the cooler winter weather settles in for its few months of comparative comfort. I lay restlessly on top of my bed in molten misery. A mosquito came in through a crack in the screen and buzzed about me persistently. After a while I turned on the light and went after it with a fly swatter, working myself up into a proper lather before I managed to get it, making a bright red stain on the blue and silver stripes of the wallpaper. The creature had been full to bursting with my blood, and I looked at the spot with fury. When I went back to bed I could sleep less than ever; I selected a book but I couldn't concentrate, and it seemed even hotter with the light on, so I lay there wretchedly in the darkness.

I felt so insufferably alone. I remembered Miss Myra Turnbull telling us once that this desperate need we have to belong to someone goes back to our earliest forebears, the lowest form of animal life, the amoeba, each individual particle of which has to be joined to other particles to make a whole.

Then I heard a low whistle from the garden. At first I thought it was a night bird, but when it was repeated I realized it was a human whistle, so I got up, pushed up the screen rashly, and leaned out the window. Standing below on the edge of a flower bed was a slight straight form. I called down softly: "Ilsa!"

She nodded and beckoned. I turned back into the room, put on my seersucker bathrobe and a pair of slippers, and stole out through the kitchen door.

As I came up to her Ilsa took my hand and held it tightly for a moment, swaying a little unsteadily. "I'm certainly glad it was you who answered my whistle. I hoped you would," she said. Her words were just a little slurred, her voice like smoke from smouldering grass after a forest fire. "I'm a damned fool, Henry," she said, "but I've got to have some black coffee."

"Come on in the kitchen." I took her by the arm and led her in, lighting a candle, thinking it would make less light and be less apt to disturb the rest of the house than the bright ceiling light with its milky glass globe. Then I stopped in despair. "I don't know how to make coffee!"

"I do. Just show me where the stuff is."

"I don't know."

"Well, I'll find it." She walked about the kitchen, her quick, deliberate grace gone a little jerky. In a short while she had a pot of coffee brewing on the stove. Then she leaned against the door, wearily, rubbing her hand against her forehead as though it ached.

"What's the matter?" I asked worriedly. "Don't you feel well? Is something wrong?"

"I've had too much to drink," she said brusquely, "and I'm not going back until I'm sober. I'm causing your Cousin Anna enough worry as it is." She went over to the sink and turned on the cold-water tap full force, holding her hand under it until it had run as cold as it was going to. Then she cupped her hands and dashed water over her face again and again and again. It splashed down the front of her dress, leaving dark streaks. The back of her dress, between the shoulders, had a wet stain from perspiration.

"You've splashed water on your dress," I said.

She shrugged. "It will dry." She went over to the stove and looked at the coffee, but it wasn't ready, so she sat down at the kitchen table "Your crazy Cousin Monty," she said lightly, "had his wallet stolen, so he couldn't buy me any coffee. He was just as eager as I not to have your Cousin Anna fussed up, so he dropped me off here and told me which was your window. I was going to throw gravel up at any minute."

"Where's Monty now?"

"He's gone home. I told him you'd take me back after I'd had some coffee, but it was just to get rid of him so he could go on home to bed where he belonged. I didn't think you'd mind giving me the coffee, but I won't have you going back with me. I'd rather walk by myself, anyhow."

"Of course I shan't allow you to walk home alone," I said indignantly. "A young girl like you all alone on these dark streets at this hour of night!"

She rested her head on her hands. "Don't argue with me, Henry. I can take care of myself." She went over to the stove, then, and looked again at the coffeepot. This time she poured herself out a cup. I noticed, as she came back to the table, that she was walking much more steadily.

"We had a lovely time," she said. "Danced and danced and danced. Monty's a beautiful dancer. Did I wake you?" she asked.

"No. I was awake."

"At this hour?"

"I couldn't sleep."

"Why not?"

"It's too hot, and there was a mosquito, and I couldn't get my mind to stop running around."

Ilsa poured herself another cup of coffee. As she sipped the hot black stuff she looked at me with those disquietingly penetrating eyes of hers. "What are you worried about, Henry?"

"What do you mean?"

"The other night over at Cousin Anna's—and now tonight—you act almost as though you had something on your conscience."

"Maybe I have."

"What is it?"

"Do you believe," I asked her, "if you want anything badly enough, you can get it—just by wanting?"

"Yes," she answered.

"Then I have Mamma's death on my conscience."

"You wanted her to die?"

"Yes."

"Why?"

"I wanted to come home. Silver and I loathed it at that awful yellow hotel. It was like being buried alive. Mamma never let us get acquainted with any of the other guests. And there were things I wanted to come home to."

"What?"

I wanted to say, "You," but I didn't. I just sat silent, hanging my head like the gangling, unattractive adolescent that I was, until Ilsa spoke again.

"But you didn't do anything about your mother's death except want it, did you?"

"No, of course not!"

"Then, for heaven's sake, hold your head up and stop brooding. If everybody somebody wished out of the way lay down and died the world would become completely depopulated in no time at all." She spoke in an even, reasonable voice. I looked at her, relief lightening my face. "Don't have a puny conscience, Henry. You've got what you wanted. Relax and be glad about it."

I shook my head doubtfully.

She went on. "Or don't allow yourself to want something you're not going to have the courage to accept when you get it."

I got up from the table and poured myself a cup of coffee. Remorse slipped off me like a garment, and I wanted to tear off the hypocritical band of mourning.

"Fill my cup, please," Ilsa said, and I poured in the steaming liquid which she gulped down. "I haven't any right to give you advice," she said. "I wouldn't, if I were quite sober, although I'm much better, thanks to this." She waved her coffee cup. "Shall we go walk down by the river for a few minutes? There might be some shooting stars. There usually are this time of year."

"Oh, yes, do let's," I said quickly.

"I'll clean up the evidence first." She took the two coffee cups over to the sink. Silently and efficiently she put everything back in its place so that in the morning no one would know the kitchen had been used during the night. Then we walked down to the river. There was a faint breeze low on the water. We went out on the old dock and sat down, swinging our feet over the edge. The dock was rickety now. Many of the boards were sagging and broken and some of them were gone entirely. I took Ilsa's arm to guide her, though she walked with such firm unafraidness in the unfamiliar night that it seemed as though she were guiding me.

The stars were reflected on the water. When I lay down and looked at the river beneath us, I could see, between the cracks, the faint swell of it rising and falling in black and silver.

"The last time we were at this river was when we rode across on Billy the night of the fire," I said.

She nodded. "I remember." Suddenly she pointed up to the sky. "Look! A falling star! Make a wish."

I looked, too late, but I made my wish, anyhow. "Why is it there're always meteors in August and September and not the rest of the year?" I asked.

"I don't know. At home, at the beach, I always used to lie out on the dunes at night to watch for falling stars. Sometimes, when he wasn't too busy, Father'd come with me and tell me about the stars. It was all wonderful and exciting, the way he told it. We'd sit high on a sand dune and wait for the late moon to rise. And it seemed to me I could watch the long swift curve of planets and the moon swinging up in the sky, turning from blood-red to bone-white, and the stars—down at the beach they really look on fire, as though you could actually see them burning off there, millions of light-years away. And then the golden comets flinging feathered tails of light like heavenly peacocks strutting across the sky." She stopped and laughed. "I thought I was practically sober, but I must have been wrong. Listen at me. This is really only the second time in my life I've been drunk, Henny. The other was with Father. I'd never seen him so furious with himself—or with me, for that matter. He made me drink gallons of coffee. Are you disgusted with me for the way I've behaved tonight, Henry?"

"What do you mean?"

"Nice young ladies do not drink."

"I'm not disgusted," I said. And I knew that nothing Ilsa did could ever disgust me, could ever really be disgusting. And I knew that I belonged to her, as much as the earth to the sun, the moon to the earth.

I think we are all somehow conscious of our destiny even before we can possibly know it. I must always have been aware of Ilsa, known she'd be the most important part of my life. I must have known this from the time I was conceived, the way the seed is conscious of its destiny. "Do you know what I mean?" I asked Ilsa, without speaking. "It's like the awareness in the seed of an iris that makes it grow into an iris and not an Irish potato. And it's like the thing that must make a crocus push its way through the snow up North and in the icy places because it *knows* that spring will come."

Ilsa stood up and stretched. "I'd better be getting along. I'm all right now," she said.

I scrambled clumsily to my feet. "All right. Let's go."

"Really, Henry." She sounded annoyed. "Haven't I made it clear enough that I'd rather be alone? No one's going to attack me, and if they do Father taught me how to defend myself." She went ahead of me, stepping surely on the rotting boards, while I stumbled after.

We walked back to the house in silence. Then she held out her hand. "Thank you for the coffee, Henry, and your company. Good night."

I took her hand, holding its coolness briefly in mine, feeling weak and stupid because I was obeying her instead of seeing her home, as I knew I ought. I stood there and watched her as she walked down the drive and disappeared into the night.

17

Some cousins of ours had an old houseboat which Monty persuaded my uncle to rent for the rest of the summer. We all went down one week end to get away from the heat in town. There was a feeling of storm in the air. At night, lightning hovered over the water and thunder rolled in with the waves on the other side of the long sand bar that made one arm of the inlet where the boat was anchored. And there was a feeling among ourselves that was like the oppressive waiting of the weather.

Cousin Anna sat on the covered deck, leaning back in her canvas chair, not moving, her eyes flickering from one to the other of us. Eddie trotted after Silver like a hound puppy, completely ignored, while Silver kept her eyes on Monty, though she pretended not to. Dolph and Violetta were continually going off into corners and whispering, looking back at Monty and Ilsa, looking back at Cousin Anna and Uncle Montgomery and Papa, Violetta pleased and important, Dolph worried. And Monty and Ilsa kept ignoring the looks and the whispers that were directed toward them, and would climb up the ladder to the upper deck, stand balanced together on the rail, and dive cleanly into the water of the inlet, to swim with strong, precise strokes over to the sand bar and back.

Sunday morning Ilsa and Monty took the outboard motor and went off mulleting with Ira. The rest of us were to go to dig for clams. We left Uncle Montgomery and Papa sitting with Cousin Anna; they were arguing in intense, low voices.

"I don't like it any better than you do," I heard Cousin Anna say as I climbed into the rowboat after the others. "But what we like isn't the important part. I think you had better remember Elizabeth."

"What *is* all this business about Aunt Elizabeth?" I asked.

Violetta raised her eyebrows in a pleased way. "You mean you don't know?"

"I wouldn't ask if I knew," I said.

Violetta settled herself righteously next to Dolph. "I guess if Aunt Cecilia-Jane or your father didn't say anything to you it's none of my affair."

Eddie took the oars; he was almost as strong as Monty in spite of his littleness. "I think it's silly to make a family skeleton of it," he said. "The whole thing was silly in the first place. And if Monty and Ilsa want to get married, that's their business."

A thin tail of smoke on the horizon was all that could be seen of a passing ship, and I longed to be on it, to run away from his words. I had a sudden violent physical desire to jump into the water of the inlet, to swim across to the arm of the beach, run stumbling over the mile of dune and scrub to the ocean, and swim out to the ship. It was the same sort of kinesthetic longing some people get when they are on high places, an almost irresistible instinct to jump, so that they draw back, shuddering. I knew that I would drown if I tried to swim to that thin plume of smoke, but I had to cling to the gunwales to keep myself from jumping overboard.

Silver's voice came jerky and angry. "What do you mean, marry? Monty's not thinking of marrying anybody yet. Certainly not that girl."

"Why not?" Eddie asked reasonably.

Silver's dark brows drew together in fury. "I don't see why Cousin Anna didn't leave her down at the beach where she belongs. She's not one of us and there's no good her trying to be." Her eyes filled with sudden tears, and she turned away, trailing her fingers in the water.

"You watch out, and if you see a turtle, pull your fingers in quick," Eddie said. "They snap a lot faster than we can move."

Silver didn't answer. She turned away from the violent blue of the sky, away from the brilliance of the day, the intense ecstatic colors, blues and greens and yellows and sharp blazing whites. A large tear rolled off the end of her nose to join the salt water of the inlet.

Violetta pulled away from Dolph, and reached out, putting a plump hand on Silver's shoulder. "What's the matter, sugar? What you crying over?"

"I'm unhappy about Mamma!" Silver said fiercely. "Have you no decent respect for—for—" her voice faltered again. Dolph pulled a handkerchief out of his pocket and gave it to her; stifling a sob, she buried her face in it.

With a strong sure pull of the oars, Eddie swung the boat around and grounded her on the beach, the flat bottom scraping softly against the broken shells that lay like a tawny shadow along the edge of the water. He helped Silver out, and the rest of us scrambled after. I was glad that all the attention was on Silver, that no one could see my bleak, miserable face. I was filled with a rank jealousy for Monty off mulleting with Ilsa and Ira.

Eddie put his arm around Silver. "Come along, honey, and I'll show you something."

She blew her nose and nodded.

"Come along," Eddie called to the rest of us. "There's a mess of fiddler crabs just over this dune here." He turned back to Silver. "Watch out you don't cut your foot on broken shells. My feet are so calloused nothing'll go through 'em, not even a snake fang."

We followed him, Silver and I, like strangers, raising our bare feet sharply against the knifelike edges of shell that the others, even Violetta, walked on with easy familiarity. When we had crossed the bar of shell the sand felt warm and soft and I dug my toes deep into it.

As we climbed the dune we saw a swarming mass of little creatures crawling busily and haphazardly about, hundreds and thousands of clean brittle little fiddler crabs, ludicrous as they scampered sideways over the sand. "Watch!" Eddie said, and started to walk around them in large concentric circles. As he went around and the circle became smaller and smaller, the fiddlers seemed obsessed with the idea that they must stay within it. Soon they were scrambling on top of each other, and while Eddie walked around in smaller and smaller circles, they made a little hill of themselves. We watched, fascinated.

Eddie walked back to us. "Just like people." he said. "Come along. Let's go find some clams."

We found a good gray mudbed of clams. The sea grasses grew in the mud, strong and green and sharp as knives. Violetta cut her finger and kept sucking it; it was a good excuse not to dig. But the rest of us plunged our fists into the thick, wet clay until we were smeared all over with it, and the sun was baking it right onto our backs.

After a time Silver came over to me, pushing a strand of fair hair back from her face with her muddy hand, leaving a streak across her forehead. "Brother, you think Monty and Ilsa'll get married?"

"I don't know." I felt that there wasn't much use our talking about it, even though we agreed for once, because she didn't like Ilsa and I didn't like Monty. But after a while I said awkwardly, "I know you're fond of Monty."

"Fond of him!" She flashed me a look of hatred that I knew was meant for Ilsa. "After all, he's my cousin. I'm fond of all my family."

"That's it!" I said, plunging my fingers into the fish-smelling mud and pretending to dig for a clam. "He's our first cousin. It isn't good, really, to be fond of him—that way."

"What way?"

"You know what I mean. It's not good for cousins to marry."

"According to the Bible it's perfectly all right," she said angrily. "You didn't make a fuss about its being wrong when Violetta and Dolph married."

"That's different. They're only fourth or fifth cousins. It was only Cousin Randolph's grandfather and Mamma's and Uncle Montgomery's grandfather who were brothers."

"The number doesn't matter. Kin is kin, if you're going to start being fussy about it. Papa and Mamma were cousins. All the Porchers and Woolfs are cousins of one sort or another."

I dug deeper into the mud and pulled out a grandfather clam that squirted up into my face. Throwing it into the bucket, wiping my face on my rolled-up shirt sleeve, I said, "Well, I hope they'll be happy." My voice sounded flat and ugly.

"Happy! If that girl isn't happy now she's getting what she wanted—though, mind, I won't believe it till it happens—she's even more no'count than I thought." Her little nostrils drew themselves in. Her lips seemed to tighten and become thinner. I was suddenly afraid of her.

"Sister! Stop!" I cried. "You sounded just like Mamma! You look just like Mamma!"

Her face fell back into its own lines again. It became angrily determined. "Don't you worry, Brother," she said. "I won't be like Mamma. I want things Mamma never wanted, and I'm going to have them."

"Hey!" Dolph called, picking up one of the clam-filled buckets with an effort. "We've got enough, now. Let's go back to the boat."

18

I couldn't sleep that night. The deck was hard and uncomfortable beneath me, the cotton blanket was too short, mosquitoes tormented me. I moved away from Dolph, Eddie, and Monty, without disturbing them, and climbed up to the upper deck. Ilsa was there before me, sitting with her back against the railing, looking over the arm of sand dune and scrub to the open sea. She looked up and nodded as she saw me.

"How did you get up here?" I asked.

"I slipped up about an hour ago. You were all sound asleep. It was too hot in that cabin. I couldn't bear it. Anything wrong?"

"No. I just couldn't sleep. Ilsa—"

"What?"

"Are you going to marry Monty?" I held my breath.

In a flash of lightning I saw her wide, spontaneous smile. "I shouldn't be surprised."

I turned away from her, away from the purple sky that seemed to be breathing with stars and the flittering of lightning, away from the ocean that broke on the long beach across the mile of dunes; and stared down at the water below me, the water that seemed to hold all the darkness that flooded my mind. My mind was so dark, indeed, that I no longer could see the reflections of the stars that broke the blackness of the water and made it bright.

After a long time I said, "I guess we should have expected it."

"Should you?"

"So that's what everyone's been whispering about all week end, isn't it?"

She nodded.

"But what's it got to do with Aunt Elizabeth?" I asked. "Cousin Anna keeps telling Uncle Montgomery and Papa not to forget Elizabeth."

"Your Aunt Elizabeth and my father were in love," Ilsa said quietly. "They wanted to marry and your family prevented it."

"Oh—" A great wave of comprehension raised itself from the dark waters, curled over, and spread across my mind. But there was still another question. "Why did they want to stop it—their getting married?" I asked. "Why shouldn't they have married?"

"Father came from a poor family down state. They didn't think he was good enough for the family."

"Oh."

"And Elizabeth was engaged to your Cousin Anna's brother, William, the minister."

"Oh, my golly," I said. "What happened?"

Ilsa sighed. I knew that she had Cousin Anna's capacity to feel the sufferings of others more than her own. What happened to herself she could shrug off; what happened to anyone else she felt deeply. "It was really quite simple," she said after a moment. "Elizabeth and William were engaged. They were very fond of each other, but that's about all. Their marriage seemed an excellent idea and they were both mildly happy about it. It wasn't exactly a marriage of convenience—to them, at any rate—but it certainly wasn't any great passion. Anna knew that. She told me she had been afraid all along that something would happen. Elizabeth was too violent a girl just to marry quietly and settle down to being a good wife to a man she was merely fond of. But even your Cousin Anna didn't expect anything to happen quite so soon. It was only a week after the engagement was announced that Elizabeth met my father and they fell in love and there wasn't anything any of them could do about it. William, who must be an amazing creature, understood the whole situation, and was willing to release her to Father, but then your family stepped in. They didn't know she was pregnant, and when they discovered it, it was too late."

"Why?" I asked, "I should think when they knew Aunt Elizabeth was going to have a baby they would have let her marry your father. Wouldn't that have been the best thing to do under the circumstances?"

"Of course. But they were too late."

"What do you mean?"

"Father wasn't there to marry her."

"Where was he?"

"He got a chance to do some special work abroad with a scientist he admired very much. He wasn't even in America."

"Oh," I said.

"He met my mother while he was in Europe. I don't know anything about her. I'm not even named after her—Father just chose Ilsa. I know he met my mother in Budapest and I think she was English and I think she was a dancer. Father never wanted to talk about her and, of course, I never urged him. I'd like to know more about her. I don't even know how Father felt—whether he loved her—or whether he was just fond of her and knew he couldn't have Elizabeth. . . . You see, when he left, he was angry and furious and hurt and he didn't leave any address. He didn't know that your Aunt Elizabeth was as closely guarded as though she had been a prisoner. He thought she'd betrayed him. That was what hurt her more than anything, that he could believe that of her. But sometimes Father could be awfully weak. I've never understood it, because mostly he seemed so strong. . . . Well, there you are, Hen. . . . I guess it's pretty hard on your family, having me pop up like this to marry Monty. It's not that I have any great desire to become a member of your august tribe, I can assure you."

"I know that," I said. "I know you'd never do anything for that reason."

She looked over at me quickly. "You do, don't you?" she said. "I'm very grateful to you." After a moment she added "Monty is, too."

Under my breath I muttered, "I don't want his thanks."

If she heard me she took no notice. "I think I'll go for a swim. Want to come?"

"Now?"

"Why not? It's a lovely night." Our bathing suits were hanging over the railing. "Go down and put your suit on," she said, handing mine to me. "I'll be ready when you come back." She raised her arms over her head and stretched, a gesture of sheer physical well-being. "Oh, Hen, I'm so terribly happy," she said.

I slithered down the ladder. She was lounging against the rail, waiting for me, when I climbed up again. Without speaking she smiled at me, pulled herself up onto the rail, stood poised for a moment, then plunged into the water. She dove deep and quiet, with hardly a splash. I knew I would wake the others if I tried to dive, so I crept downstairs again, lowered the rope ladder, and slid into the water. A faint disturbance on the dark surface a few yards away I knew must be Ilsa, so I swam toward it. As I came up to her, she rolled over onto her back and floated; I paddled by her side so I could watch her face. The trouble that had darkened it up on deck was gone now; it gleamed peaceful and white out of the dark water like one of the stars that hung low above us.

"I want to die in the sea," she said. "If I know I'm dying, and I'm inland, I'll get myself to the ocean somehow and die there. I wouldn't feel clean dying anywhere else. We buried Father at sea. It was what he wanted."

I remembered Myra Turnbull reading Shakespeare's lines to us:

Full fathom five thy father lies;
Of his bones are coral made:
Those are pearls which were his eyes:
Nothing of him that doth fade,
But doth suffer a sea-change
Into something rich and strange. . . .

For the first time I caught the beauty of the words. I wanted to repeat them to Ilsa, but I was afraid to speak.

"It's the only clean way to die," she repeated. "To become part of the salt water. The most beautiful things in the world belong to the ocean—coral and pearls and wonderful strange breathing plants and gulls and sandpipers and starfish and sand dollars and conch shells. There's no place left in the world that's free, except the ocean."

I nodded. The black night water lapped about me possessively. My teeth began to chatter with cold. Ilsa noticed.

"We'll go now," she said.

We swam back to the boat.

19

During the next weeks I kept thinking of the way Ilsa had stretched up there on the deck, the way she had exclaimed, almost involuntarily, "Oh, Hen, I'm so terribly happy!"

And she was. Happiness seemed to sparkle from her like light on the water. And while she was happy, I was resentful, and Silver was miserable.

We went over to Violetta and Dolph's for a wiener roast.

Wiener roasts were very fashionable, so, of course, Violetta had to be constantly giving them. She had a whole mess of people, most of whom Silver and I hadn't seen since we were little. All the time we were shaking hands and telling people how *glad* we were to see them, we both kept our eyes on the driveway. Last of all, late as usual, the Woolf car drove in, bouncing over the uneven road, with Eddie, Monty, and Ilsa.

"I wish Monty wasn't so beautiful to look at," Silver whispered fiercely.

For once Monty had eyes for none of the girls in their frilly dresses. He kept looking at Ilsa and the lines of his face softened into a tender expression I never remembered seeing before.

I felt lonely and out of things. Somehow I didn't have anything to say to all these people. One couldn't go on reminiscing indefinitely about things that had happened when one was ten; so after a while I walked around to the back of the house and stood looking into the wire pen where Dolph kept his hunting dogs. When they saw me coming they started barking and hurling themselves against the pliable wire of the pen, but when they realized that I hadn't come to take them hunting, they quieted down, all but one who kept flinging himself toward me and yelping in an agony of pleading.

Then all at once, through the sharp sound of barking, came the shrill sound of a scream, echoed by several others, and then the excited raising of voices. I hurried back to the benches set about under the live oaks, forming a rude circle about the fire that was much too hot for the early autumn day.

"What's the matter?" I asked Lee Jackson.

"Violetta got knocked and she spilled a whole pot of boiling water over someone's hand."

"Whose?"

"That girl who lives with Mrs. Silverton. What's her name? Ilsa something."

I pushed my way through the crowd. Monty had grabbed a plate of butter and was spreading the soft yellow grease over Ilsa's hand and wrist. Her face was white with pain, her lips shut in tight control, but the hand she held out to Monty was steady. He bound his handkerchief loosely around it, then put his arm about her waist.

"I'm just going to drive you in to the doctor, honey," he said to Ilsa, and led her to the car. A moment later they drove off, and I heard one of the girls saying to Silver, "Golly, it would be worth getting a little old burn if Monty Woolf looked at you like that."

I turned back to the pen of dogs, sick at heart. They didn't even bark at me this time. They knew I wasn't going to take them out hunting. They knew I was just little old Henry Porcher, so what was there to bark about?

Silver and all the cackling hens Violetta had invited to her wiener roast might be thinking of the way Monty had looked at Ilsa, but I had seen the expression in her eyes as she held her scalded hand out to him, a look of love that had shone even through her pain, and that I knew would never be on her face when she turned to me.

20

Every tongue in town wagged so about Monty and Ilsa before they were married that the actual marriage itself seemed relatively unimportant, and pretty soon it was an accepted thing, except in the family. The family had to accept it on the surface, to save face, but Papa and Uncle Montgomery were pretty grudging about it, and I knew how difficult it must be for Ilsa. It would have been even worse if Cousin Anna hadn't roused herself enough to lash out at them about Elizabeth, bringing it all back to them, and unfortunately, to herself, as vividly as possible. They didn't like Ilsa, but once she was married to Monty even Violetta wasn't going to allow anyone outside the family to say anything about her.

During the weeks that followed I went often to visit Cousin Anna, not only because I knew she must be lonely without Ilsa, or because I myself gained repose by sitting silently with her under the magnolia tree, waiting for night to pounce on us like a lithe amorous cat, but mostly because there was always a chance that Ilsa might come. Usually, she paid her visits to Cousin Anna during the day, while Monty and my Uncle were downtown, but sometimes she would slip away from the dark house in the evening.

The first time she came was less than a week after the wedding. Cousin Anna and I were sitting together, lost in our individual reveries, her face in shadow, her brown eyes half closed, my features stiff and stark with misery. I sat there and cursed God for making me three years younger than Ilsa. For the lack of a few meager years, I felt, my life was wasted, lost. For a moment I thought of willing Monty's death, then thrust the idea away with horror. I am not cut out to be a murderer, and anyhow I felt that the idea was morbid and impractical.

After some time Barbara came toward us from the house. I looked at her questioningly.

"Miss Anna," she said.

Cousin Anna's eyelids moved faintly and Barbara knew that she was listening.

"Miss Ilsa here, Miss Anna," she said, looking down at the motionless figure with loving, grateful eyes. "She say can she come out and sit with you."

"Of course," Cousin Anna said. "Why does she ask?"

"She say maybe she not welcome."

"Tell her to come," Cousin Anna said.

I had somehow expected Ilsa to be changed; but superficially, at any rate, she seemed exactly the same. She smiled at me, then stood gravely looking down at Cousin Anna, who held out both her hands. Ilsa took them in her own and held them for quite a long time. It was the first real physical contact I had seen between them.

"You thought I wouldn't want to see you?" Cousin Anna asked.

"I wasn't sure."

"You should have known better."

"Yes. I know."

"Sit down."

Ilsa seated herself and turned to me. "Evening, Henry. Where's Silver?"

"She and Eddie drove over to see Violetta and Dolph," I said.

"Oh, yes. Eddie mentioned it at supper. Why haven't you been over to see us?"

"I thought maybe you and Monty'd rather be alone."

She laughed at that, a perfectly light, gay, natural laugh. I didn't know what it meant. Cousin Anna looked at her sharply.

"It's a beautiful night," Ilsa said after a while. "It must be lovely at the beach. Monty and I are going down to spend a few days in Father's old house next week."

I said on an impulse, although five minutes earlier nothing had been further from my mind, "I'm driving down to the beach tomorrow. Reuben's going to give me another driving lesson. Can I give Ira any message from you?"

"So your father finally got himself a motorcar," Cousin Anna said.

"Just tell Ira we're coming, would you, Henny? He'll take care of everything, as long as he expects us."

I promised I would. The next afternoon I set off with Reuben, the chauffeur Papa had got to go with the car. I drove most of the way. I found driving easy and enjoyed it.

We stopped the car at the edge of the good road. I didn't dare drive over the two sandy ruts that led to the back of Dr. Brandes' house for fear of getting stuck, even though they were still damp and spotted from the shower that had passed us on our way down.

I walked, stumbling, toward the house, my heart pounding with unreasonable excitement because I was going back to Ilsa's home, where I had spent the most thrilling and, in a way, the happiest hours of my childhood. As I approached the house I half expected to see Dr. Brandes coming toward me in his Palm Beach suit or his beautiful riding habit, that had been torn and ruined by the fire.

A redbird flashed from ilex bush to chinaberry tree, exactly as on the day when I had first come to the house. I saw sunflower seeds in a basket hanging from the tree, and in a moment the redbird was perched on it, pecking at the sunflower seeds and observing me with a circumspect eye.

I called, but got no answer. After a while I pulled open the screen door and went into the house. It was much the same, except that the big table under the skylight was, as I had imagined it, bare and cleared of specimens. I called Ira again as I started up the stairs. Again no answer. Again no changes. I might have been the excited little boy of ten going up to undress for swimming.

I came downstairs and went out the back door again, looking for Ira in the low shed that served as both stable and barn. The stall that had once been Calypso's was clean and bare, but there were three stalls obviously in use that I thought were probably for the cows that had so frightened Silver and me the night we stayed at the beach.

I began to be afraid that Ira must be off somewhere with his gun, or out setting snares. Because I had told Ilsa I would inform him that she and Monty were coming, I felt that the message was as important as any supremely vital political trust. I felt that I could never face her again unless I found Ira. I went back through the house and down the ramp to the beach. And there, to my relief, I found him digging donax.

"Hey, Ira," I called.

He looked up and frowned against the light as he saw me coming toward him.

"I expect you don't remember me," I said. "I'm Henry Porcher."

He looked at me and scowled. "I remember you all right," he said. "You've growed up some, but you're not much changed, I guess."

"I have a message from Ilsa."

His face lighted up. "She all right?"

"She's fine. She asked me to tell you that she and Monty would be coming down sometime next week."

For a moment I thought he would strike me. Then he went back to digging donax, scooping them up out of the wet sand at the ocean's edge with an old tin can and sifting them through his fingers into the bucket. When he spoke his voice surprised me by being quite amiable. "Help me finish this here bucket of donax," he said, "and I'll give you a mess to take home to Ilsa. She loves donax soup."

I squatted down and plunged my fingers into the amorphous gray sand at the water's edge. The tiny shells were every delicate shade imaginable, glistening blues and pinks and lavenders and greens and maize colors, and the beach was full of them, their little holes bubbling and swelling as though they were the pores of some huge sleepy sea beast. In a short time the bucket was filled, and I followed Ira back up the ramp to the house. He took the bucket of donax into the kitchen and came out with a jug of corn liquor.

"You old enough for this?" he asked.

"Sure," I said, sitting on Ilsa's magnolia-wood stool.

Ira hummed as he poured out the powerful stuff, and I recognized the Napoleon song he had sung to Silver, the Napoleon song I had heard Cousin Eustacia singing.

"Sure is lonely here without Johnny Brandes or Ilsa," he said. I nodded. We sat there, drinking our corn, not talking. After a while Ira tipped the jug again and refilled his glass. When he offered me more I shook my head and rose, thanking him for his hospitality and telling him that I must hurry back to town. I still could not realize how much less time it took in the car than by horse.

On my way home I stopped by the Woolfs' house to deliver the donax. Ilsa was in the drawing room, at the piano. She played very well, with a strong, firm touch. I told her about the donax, and she ran delightedly out to the kitchen to see them. As I waited in the drawing room, all the oppression and hate the walls of that house had stored up seemed to descend on me. I thought it was a pity that it hadn't burned in the fire like the others.

21

Silver called me into her room that night. For a while we talked about Ilsa and Monty. Although Silver was jealous and resentful of Ilsa, accusing her of marrying Monty only to get into the family, I could see that Ilsa had a peculiar fascination for her, too. I told her that Ilsa didn't give a damn whether she belonged to the family or not.

Silver shrugged at that, but after a while she said, "Brother, what do you think of Eddie?"

"He's the only one of the Woolfs I've ever been able to bear."

"When he smiles," she said wistfully, "he has a dimple at the corner of his mouth, just like Monty."

"Thank God he's not like Monty in any other way," I said, still feeling a little high from the corn.

"I feel much older than seventeen," Silver said, sighing. "And I feel as though you were older than you are, too."

"It's because we were away from everything and everybody for so long. If Mamma hadn't died when she did, our lives would have been completely wasted—if they're not anyway," I added, with what I hoped was appropriate bitterness.

But it was quite lost on Silver. "I know it's not nice to speak about such things," she said. "But oh, Brother, I do want babies."

22

It was several months before I saw Ilsa again. I knew from Barbara that she was often over during the day, but in the evenings, when I was at Cousin Anna's, she seemed conspicuously absent.

But one evening she did come. It was early in January, and cold. Because of the dampness, it feels much more raw and unpleasant when it is in the fifties at home than it does in drier climates when the mercury is many degrees lower. Cousin Anna and I sat close to the fire. She was wearing a gaudy embroidered scarlet shawl that one of the old gentlemen peering down from the portraits had brought over from Spain, and that somehow did not look incongruous as it lay heavily on her slight, still-erect shoulders.

When Ilsa came in I knew there was something different about her, but what it was I did not at first realize. It was not only that the expression on her face was much older; there seemed to be something blurred and softened about her usually concise contours. It was raining, and her tawny head glistened with moisture; drops clung to her lashes and softened the ice-sharp blue of her eyes. She kissed Cousin Anna, nodded at me, then stood by the fire, holding her hands out to the blaze. She stood there for a long time, perfectly still, every nerve and muscle tense, until the log had crumbled and turned to gray ash. And suddenly I realized, as she dropped her arms to her sides and leaned her head briefly in an uncharacteristic, weary gesture against the mantelpiece, that she was with child.

As though divining my thoughts, she raised her head and turned abruptly from the dead embers.

"I'm going to have a baby," she said quietly.

Cousin Anna responded dispassionately. "That's customary, isn't it?"

"Before I have it," Ilsa said, "I want to make absolutely certain of one thing. Monty told me last night that there was insanity in the family. Is that true?"

"No," Cousin Anna said.

I looked up sharply at Ilsa's words. She was staring intently at Cousin Anna, ignoring me. I might not have been in the room.

That always struck me as a strange thing. All my life the people I have loved—Ilsa, Cousin Anna, Silver, Myra Turnbull, Joshua Tisbury—have accepted me as a friend, have confided in me—but, somehow, there has been no actual contact made. It has been almost as though they could talk to me because I didn't exist.

I think that's because there has been no give and take. I have a pitcher into which the people I love have poured themselves. I have accepted everything and been allowed to give nothing. When they discover that I have passions of my own it seems to jar them.

In this way I have sat in many rooms and walked in many gardens, and it has been as though I were a stick of furniture or a branch of a tree. I seem to have caused no sense of restraint or embarrassment. People have been able to talk freely in front of me, almost as freely as though I weren't there. I suppose some might think this a great compliment; it has given me a curious feeling of nonexistence.

Now Ilsa said, still looking probingly with her cold blue stare at Cousin Anna, "Monty said that Elizabeth died in an insane asylum."

Cousin Anna nodded. "Yes, that is true," she said. Her hands opened and closed gropingly, her eyes widened for a moment, and she looked around the room as though she were looking for a way of escape. It was not, I felt, that she was ashamed of her words, but that she could not bear the idea of having her emotions stirred up once more.

"Well?" Ilsa asked.

Cousin Anna spoke with great weariness. "She tried to bring on a miscarriage," she said. "But Montgomery and Cecilia-Jane followed her out to the stables and dragged her back. It would have been far better if she had been allowed to ride her horse to her child's death." She stopped and looked at the burnt-out fire for a long time, struggling to keep what she was saying a thing of words. At last she went on. "When the time came for the baby to be born the Woolfs and Violetta Porcher had worn her to a frazzle. She was underweight and overwrought and her nerves were torn and raw. Montgomery had practically deafened her with his shouts and threats. Once I saw him strike her. And nothing can be more unendurable than two pious females like Cecilia and Violetta Porcher. Montgomery was easier to endure than they were. The so-called insanity was the result of the treatment of her family and the overdose of a narcotic given her by a stupid quack, because the family pride was too strong to allow Elizabeth to have a recognized doctor or midwife. The first thing she heard when she came out from under the drug was Cecilia-Jane telling her to thank God that the baby had been stillborn. And there was Violetta leering at her over Cecilia's shoulder, and Montgomery pacing up and down, and the doctor keeping me out in the corridor. . . . But any doctor, Ilsa my dear, will tell you that there is no hereditary insanity in the family, that actually there is no insanity at all, though, if you ask me, half the people who are still left wandering around loose in the South are queer as Dick's hatband. Present company not excepted. So have your baby without undue worry, Ilsa. You're young and shouldn't have much difficulty." She stopped and out her hand unsteadily to her eyes. "Please call Barbara, now, Ilsa. I'm tired. I want to go to bed. I don't want to think." She sounded suddenly old and petulant.

As we were saying good night to her she turned with one of her rare quick movements to Ilsa. "Darling," she said, "there's nothing for you to worry about, I promise you. Have your baby and be happy with it. Bless you, my dearest."

Ilsa kissed her gently.

Cousin Anna drew a long shuddering sigh. "You don't know," she whispered, "you don't know what it was like to see a vital beautiful human being turned into an inert lump of clay, into a wild inhuman beast. . . . You don't know. . . ."

Ilsa took her firmly by the arms. "Don't," she said, catching her gaze and holding it with the force of her own. "Don't, darling."

Cousin Anna clung to Ilsa's strength. After a moment she said, "Believe me, Ilsa, I meant it for the best when I took you away from your beach and brought you to town to live with me. But I don't blame you if you reproach me for it."

"Don't be silly," Ilsa said. "You sound like Father. He was always saying I'd find it hard to forgive him for the life he led me at the beach, and now you're going on in exactly the same way about taking me away from it. You're the two people in the world I've loved." She took

Cousin Anna's shawl, which was slipping off her thin shoulders, and arranged it gently.

Barbara looked at us reproachfully, put her arm about Cousin Anna's waist, and led her upstairs.

Ilsa and I went out into the hall. She slipped brusquely into her coat. "I've got to get back now."

I noticed that she never said home except when she referred to the house at the beach.

She opened the door and stood looking out into the rain. "I'd like to go somewhere where there was snow," she said. "And mountains to climb."

"Are you glad about the baby?" I asked.

"I don't know." She held out her hand and let the rain fall on the upturned palm. "What Monty said put any thoughts of gladness or resentment out of my mind. Now that I know it's all right for me to have a child, I suppose I might as well be glad. I shan't make a good mother, though."

"Yes, you will."

She turned to me and smiled. "I'm very fond of you, Henny. Find yourself a *good* wife, will you?"

Her fingers touched mine, briefly. Then she disappeared into the rain.

PART FOUR

23

Time and tide waiteth for no man. Time and tide waiteth for no man. Time and tide. Time and tide. Time and tide. . . . I woke up and stirred from my cramped position on the day-coach seat. Time and tide—my mind ground around with the wheels, and panic ground unreasonably and increasingly in my heart.

If time and tide waiteth not, God knows man waiteth not; man and woman waiteth for no man.

I tried to stretch, but my legs only bumped into the seat in front of me. Vague snores and restless shiftings and twistings sounded muted through the night turning of the wheels and the dark rattling of the coach. I wished I had kept enough of the money Papa had sent me for the trip home to be able to take a Pullman, instead of giving most of it to Telcide, and having to make the long journey south in the day coach.

I peered out the window, but the landscape was bleak and unfamiliar. It would be a long time before we began to pass through pine scrub, through rice flats, over rivers where the water ran dark, by thin rut roads where the sand was as white and fine as ocean sand. It would be a long time before we began to pass the little square cabins, with small black children peering from the doorways, and chickens scrabbling in the yards.

Time and tide waiteth for no man. Man and woman waiteth for no man. I had been gone for eight years, gone from home for eight years, gone for eight years, eight years, eight years. . . .

Everything that came into my mind ground around in my head with the wheels, ground around in my sleep and fatigue-fuddled mind.

Ilsa Brandes, Ilsa Brandes, Ilsa Brandes. . . .

That had gone around in my head, just the disembodied name—when my mind was busy with other things, that name had gone around in my head how many millions of times during the past eight years?

Ilsa Brandes, Ilsa Brandes, Ilsa Brandes. . . . *WOOLF.*

—Did she ever, did she ever wonder—I thought—Did she ever think once during those years: where is Henry, what is Henry Porcher doing now, Henry Randolph Porcher?

How would she think of me, why would she think of me, with a husband and baby, husband and baby, husband and baby. . . .

Silver wrote me about the baby. Silver wrote me about Ilsa's daughter. Silver wrote me about her own marriage to Eddie. Silver wrote me about her own three babies, the three little boys, and one named for me, one named for Henry Porcher. Only you must remember it is not pronounced Porcher, the way it is spelled, it is pronounced *Puhshay*.

"I never write letters, Henny," Ilsa had said—but she did come to the station to see me off; that she did do. "I never write letters, so don't expect to hear from me." But she hadn't known it would be eight years, We hadn't thought it would be that long. Eight years is a long time—and never a word, a word.

"I'll think of you," she had said, "and you must have a good time, Hen, and be happy! For heaven's sake, be happy! You're always so serious—it isn't good."

—I can't help it, I can't help it, I can't help it. . . .

—Oh, why was it so long, why was it eight years! How can she be expected to remember I exist!

—Well—I had thought once—this seriousness is like a venom, this obsession is like a poison. When you are poisoned you take an antidote; you take milk, or brine, or soapy water; anything to make you throw up and wash out the toxin.

Telcide was my antidote, Telcide was my soapy water, but the poison remained to devour me and it was not a poison, it was a burning, searing coal. . . . If only the coal could burst into flame and burn me to ashes—I thought—so that I could be born again. . . . But I knew that this ember could never become a fire.

At first I had wondered rebelliously why Papa kept me away, why he sent me off to school, why he kept me from coming home during vacations. And then I was glad; when the war came I was glad, because I thought that perhaps I would die. But I didn't die. Then when I wrote Papa and asked him if I could stay in France, if I could study in Paris, he said yes. Yes, I could. I think he was a little proud that I wanted to. I was the first in the family to live in Europe since our forefathers had come to the Americas. He sent me letter after letter to look up the French branch of the family, and finally I did write to some distant cousins who lived not far from Paris. After several weeks I received a postcard from the curé saying that the couple I had written to had both died in the flu epidemic, but that there was a daughter, Telcide, singing somewhere in Paris. He gave me the name of the place—somewhere on the Left Bank—almost as though he were ashamed to do so; and out of curiosity I went to hear her sing. It was a long time before I made myself known to my cousin Telcide.

It seemed that I could never get away from my family. It was like one of the heavy mullet nets with the little iron weights around them. Even in my one futile splash for freedom I was caught in this net. Telcide was a Porcher. Neither Porcher, pronounced as it is spelled, nor *Puhshay*, but Porcher with a Parisian accent; a Porcher with short sleek black hair and a sardonic grin. "A Porcher is always a Porcher," Papa had said before I left for the North. "Never forget that, Henry."

How could I?

Even Ilsa.

Ilsa was inextricably mixed up with the family. Ilsa *was* family.

So now that at last I was returning to my home and to the people I had left with such reluctance, I wished to be able to blot out the past eight years, to make them nothing, make them not have happened.

But I couldn't blot them out; time that is passed is inexorably past, perhaps not for oneself, but for others. All that I could do was to take my part of the eight years, my part only; this I could fold and pack, like eight years' accumulation of goods and chattels into one trunk and valise and an empty violin case; sorting, discarding, throwing away as much as possible, so that when I got home there would be room for me to assimilate and hold what had happened while I was gone, so that somehow everything that had happened to Ilsa would become part of my experience, too.

You would think that I should have had enough pride to refuse to allow someone, into whose pattern I could never really break, to become so intrinsic a part of my own.

But I didn't.

I never did.

It was toward the end of June when I got back, and hot. I had forgotten our heat. When I climbed down from the train my sopping clothes clung to me; there wasn't a dry stitch on me; but I looked joyfully at the flushed, perspiring faces about me the men rubbing their foreheads and necks with their handkerchiefs, linen and seersucker coats dangling over their arms; the women corsetless, hair pulled high up off the napes of their flushed necks, stockingless feet pushed into loose sweat-smelling pumps.

I didn't expect a brass band. I didn't expect the whole family, but I had hoped there would be someone to welcome the prodigal home after eight years. I saw an occasional face I knew, but I wasn't recognized, and I felt too shy and strained to speak, with little inclination to do so, anyhow.

I got into one of the ten-cent taxis and started for home. It took a good half hour instead of the usual ten minutes because we kept picking people up and dropping them off here and there. In a way I was glad, because I was still frightened of Papa and welcomed the extra minutes to get used to being home. I sat on the sticky leather seat, peering out the taxi's windows, streaked from a recent rain storm, and looked at the dusty white houses on the burned-green lawns, at the gray tangled skeins of Spanish moss, the hot glare of flowers in the gardens, green shutters pulled to at the windows, rattan porch blinds lowered. The slurred nasal speech of the taxi driver and the people crowded moistly in beside me, sounded strange to my ears; I had forgotten the laziness of it, the carelessness, and the shrill uncontrolled whine that crept into the higher notes. It sounded untidy and slipshod to me; the hot perspiring faces were ugly; I was filled with a kind of despair because I knew I had made a mess of the life I had tried to make away from home, and to return and find that I was not only critical, but didn't even want to come back, was unnerving. I didn't want to come home, yet there was no place on earth to go.

I was so lost in misery that I didn't notice when the taxi turned into our wrought-iron gates. I gave the driver his dime and got my bag and violin case out of the back. Then I climbed up the white steps and pushed in through the screen door.

The house was filled with that peculiar summertime dusk we create to keep the hot light out. Shafts of yellow came through the bars of the shutters and caught on the motes of dust. Sunlight coming through the heavy foliage quivered with a yellow-green, under-water look. I could hear the ticking of the big clock in the parlor, but no other sound. The place seemed to be deserted.

"Hey! Silver!" I called, and then remembered with a shock that, of course, Silver wouldn't be there. She had married Eddie before he went to officers' training camp, and they were living with their three little boys across the river a few miles down from Violetta and Dolph.

I looked around the dining room. The picture of Aunt Elizabeth was gone from its place above the mantelpiece, and instead there hung one of the refined still lifes Aunt Violetta had painted—a dead bird, a green bowl with mangoes, and a silver candlestick. Somehow this added the last touch to my forlornness. I was filled with utter panic at actually finding myself home at last. I knew I couldn't face Papa yet, and I was afraid to go to Ilsa's, so I compromised by going to Cousin Anna's instead, on the off-chance that Ilsa might be there.

She wasn't, but Cousin Anna was sitting in her usual place under the magnolia tree. She surprised me by taking me in her arms and kissing me with real tenderness; I felt infinitely happier; the lostness that had enfolded me ever since I stepped unwelcomed off the train evaporated like the sultry early morning mists that the sun burned off on a hot day.

"You've changed," Cousin Anna said. "I don't mean that you're just eight years older. You've grown up inside, too. And how tall and thin you are, Henry boy, and look at the color of you, white as cotton. Barbara would say it was because you've been eating that northern rice, all gooey, with milk and sugar. She says if you eat it that way it makes you all white and pasty." She laughed up at me.

I was surprised and grateful for the effort she was making, though she talked leaning back against the tree, not moving, her voice coming low and slow. I think somehow she understood that I had come running to her for comfort, like a disappointed child.

"We didn't expect you till the evening train," she said after a while.

"But I wrote!" I cried indignantly.

"I guess your writing hasn't improved with age. Your father couldn't make head or tail of your letter and finally decided you were coming on the evening train."

"Oh," I said, relieved to know why I had arrived apparently so undesired. Then I remembered something I wanted to ask her. "Cousin Anna, the portrait of Aunt Elizabeth is gone from the dining room. Do you know where it is?"

As usual when Aunt Elizabeth was mentioned, a veil seemed to drop over her eyes, but she answered unemotionally, "Silver has her. Eddie asked if they couldn't have the portrait for a wedding present because of the resemblance between Silver and Elizabeth."

"Oh," I said.

"Well, Henry"—she turned her head slightly to look at me—"why did you stay away so long? What kept you in foreign parts all these years? There must have been something. Or someone."

I shook my head. I couldn't explain it to Cousin Anna, because I couldn't explain it to myself. I thought perhaps if I could talk to Ilsa about it I might understand. It was because I had to prove something to myself, but what it was I had to prove I didn't know, and I certainly hadn't proved it. I think I felt, perhaps, that I had failed because I had been too young; because Ilsa had married Monty; and I couldn't come home until I had proved that I wasn't a failure.

But how could I prove it? More than a year before I left Paris I had pawned my expensive violin. I had learned to love music, to understand it a little, and I had learned at the same time that making a toy violin when you are ten years old does not make you a musician when you are twenty. I looked well with a violin tucked under my chin; I would make a fine showing in the drawing room at home; but I was no musician. I wasn't an artist of any kind.

And now I was afraid to see Papa because I had pawned my expensive violin to buy presents for a French *diseuse* called Telcide, who was incidentally my cousin. I thought—only Ilsa would understand this, only Ilsa can I talk to. . . .

Cousin Anna was looking at me. She shook me gently.

Wake up,
Jacob,
Day's a-breaking.
Peas' in the pot
And hoe cake's a-baking—

she said laughing, using Nursie's old rhyme.

I blinked. "How's Silver?" I asked quickly.

"Silver's fine," she answered. "I think you'll be very happy when you see her. She loves Edwin and she worships her children, and I must say they're three of the finest little boys you've ever seen."

"And how," I asked, my voice hardening, "is my dear Cousin Monty?"

The corners of Cousin Anna's mouth twitched into a half-smile. "Your dear cousin Monty is as to be expected."

"How is that?"

"Well, just what did you expect?" She seemed suddenly to withdraw into herself, and we fell into a long silence.

After a while I asked, trying to subdue my eagerness, "How's Ilsa?"

"She's Ilsa," Cousin Anna said.

"But how is she?"

"I told you she was Ilsa. Isn't that enough?" Her welcoming flow of words seemed to have dried up. I was home now. I had been properly greeted. She evidently felt that she had exerted herself enough in my behalf.

"Well," I said. "I guess I'd better go see Papa."

"Haven't you?"

"No. You're the first person I've seen." My voice drooped.

She laid a hand gently on my knee. Her face softened. "Sorry you came home?"

"I don't know."

"It'll go in a few days," she said. "You'll slip back into the old groove." Then she added, as though to herself, "That's the trouble."

"Thank you for talking to me," I said.

She gave my knee another small pat. "I'm fond of you for some reason, Henry boy. You have a strange way of making people fond of you, though you're not worth it. I think you were born out of your time. You should have been a charming little page boy for a handsome Renaissance noblewoman, and when you grew up you should have been kept pleasantly and uselessly at court for the rest of your life, as a kind of background, a decoration."

"A delightful picture." I tried to laugh. I bent down and kissed her good-bye, then walked back up the cypress paving blocks of the garden path, through the gray coolness of the house, and slowly home through the heavy, still heat of the streets.

24

Papa seemed amazingly glad to see me. I stood with my hand in his and noticed how gray his hair had gone, how old he seemed for his age. We talked for a little while, shyly, each embarrassedly fond of the other; then he asked the question I knew inevitably must come.

"Well, Henry, when are we to hear you perform on your violin?"

"I'm afraid I haven't my violin with me, Papa," I said.

"Where is it?"

"In Paris," I said bluntly. I didn't add, as I was tempted to, "But I have the pawn ticket in my wallet."

"What do you mean?" Papa asked, in a rigid voice.

"I'm afraid I'm not a musician, Papa," I said, trying to keep my voice steady. "I worked hard and I enjoyed my work but I just don't have enough of a gift, and we both of us might as well face that fact, because fact it is."

"So you decided you didn't want to be a musician after all and left your violin in Paris, is that it?" Papa asked, still quietly.

"That's just about it."

"That was an extremely expensive violin. You will cable for it right away."

"I'm afraid I can't do that. I didn't exactly just leave it."

"What do you mean?"

"I sold it. At least—that is—I pawned it."

"Pawned it?" A dark mahogany flush began to rise in Papa's checks.

"Yes, Papa."

"A Porcher has never sunk to the depths of pawning his personal property."

"I pawned my violin," I said, taking out my wallet and putting the ticket on the desk in front of him.

"Why did you do this?" Papa asked.

"I needed the money."

"I thought I sent you sufficient every month."

"You did, Papa. You were more than generous."

I knew that I could get around him by telling him about Telcide. Not the truth, of course, but that she was one of our French relations, working hard, and desperately poor. But I couldn't use that way out; I knew Ilsa would think it cowardly.

Papa picked up the pawn ticket and held it with disgust between his thumb and forefinger. "And this is all the gratitude I get?" He was shouting now.

I stood perfectly still and tried to make my mind as blank and blind as a cloud. When I spoke my voice was devoid of life. "I don't mean to be ungrateful, Papa."

"Why—why—why the devil did you come home?"

"I thought it wasn't right to live in Paris any longer and take money from you under false pretenses."

"Oh, so you have a sense of right and wrong, have you, sirrah! And what do you intend to do now, if I may ask?"

"I don't know, Papa. I thought perhaps you might advise me."

"How old are you?" he said, in a loud voice.

"Twenty-four."

He seemed to gasp for breath. "Get out of this room!" he spluttered at last. "Keep out of my sight as much as possible! The family is going to the dogs and I don't want to see any more of it than necessary. Go on! Get out!"

I left hastily. He would calm down by the time I had to meet him across the table in the dining room.

I climbed the stairs and paused on the landing for a moment, kneeling on the hot brown-plush seat and looking across the garden. Then I went up to my room. It looked exactly the same. One of the servants was unpacking my bag.

"There're some soiled clothes in the violin case," I said, and went into Silver's room. The white candlewick spread on the four-poster bed was smooth and creaseless; it looked barren, a bed that had not been slept in for a long time, and filled me with an even greater sense of isolation than I had already.

I wandered downstairs, out the front door, down the white wooden steps, and walked slowly along the gravel path. The heat burned up through the soles of my feet. I thought of the chill damp grayness of Paris, and wondered if I would eventually forget that, as I had forgotten the heat at home.

25

I thought I would go around to the drugstore and have a soda or a sundae, something I hadn't had since I left home; something that might make me feel part of it again. Ahead of me on the street the heat lay coiled snakily. The red sign above the drugstore quivered like something seen under water. In one corner of the store a huge fan was whining, as were the ordinary ones hanging from the ceiling, stirring around a smell of cosmetics, medicines, stale dish water, ice cream. Flies stuck on the brown curls of paper hanging from the fans, and buzzed about the counter and the tables. At the counter sat three little girls wilted cotton dresses. They might have been Ilsa, Silver, and Violetta, years ago, if Ilsa, Silver, and Violetta had ever sat in a drugstore together.

The brownest little girl, whose bare black-soled feet twisted around the rungs of her stool, whose straight back and tanned, scratched arms might have been Ilsa's, said at once and with decision, "I'd like a chocolate sundae, please."

The second little girl, in white socks and sandals, in a corn-colored dress that somehow hadn't entirely wilted from the afternoon sun, the fair little girl who might have been Silver, said, after a moment of delicate deliberation, "I'd like a pineapple soda with chocolate ice cream."

The third little girl; with shiny corkscrew curls, exactly like Violetta's, clinging hotly to her face and neck, smiled sweetly at the soda clerk and said, "I think I'll have a douche. Mamma says they are *so* refreshing."

I looked up over their heads into the mirror and met a pair of amused blue eyes smiling into mine. Wheeling around violently, I practically knocked Ilsa over.

"Well, Henry," she said laughing.

"Ilsa!" I looked at her and relief flooded through my whole body; I felt all my doubts and suspicions and uncertainties being washed clean by the sea of her regard.

"Ilsa—"

"Silver said you might be coming home, but we didn't know when."

"I just got back this afternoon," I said.

"Glad?"

"I wasn't till now."

I noticed for the first time a child standing shyly close to Ilsa. She had a solemn sun-tanned face and great brown eyes that stared up at me under ruddy bangs.

Ilsa laughed again. "This is Brand. Johanna Brandes Woolf—after Father. Ladybird, this is your Cousin Henry."

The child put out an obedient brown hand. "How do you do, Cousin Henry. Are you the Henry who's been away playing the violin in Paris?"

"Yes."

"If you're Aunt Silver's brother, why aren't you Uncle Henry instead of Cousin Henry?"

"Because our family is far too complicated. But if you'd like to call me Uncle Henry, instead of Cousin Henry, I should be delighted."

"I think that would be easier," the child said. "Mamma says you've been in Paris almost ever since I was born and that's why I haven't seen you before."

"That's right," I said. "Ilsa, will you and Brand have some ice cream or something?" I looked at her happily. She looked just as she ought to look, in a faded blue-and-white-striped cotton dress and a pair of old sneakers, her brown arms and legs bare, her body as straight and firm as ever, her mobile face alight with amusement and pleasure.

"Oh, yes, some ice cream, please!" The child looked up at me eagerly.

"I'd love a dope," Ilsa said.

"A what?" I asked.

"Oh—a Coca-Cola, darling. I haven't started taking morphine yet. I forgot you wouldn't be having them in Paris." It was the first time she had called me "darling." I winced at the casualness of it.

We sat down at the counter next to the three little girls. The one who had asked for a douche was happily eating a banana split.

"How does it feel to be back in an American drugstore?" Ilsa asked.

"I expect in a week I'll feel as though I'd never been away," I answered slowly.

"Mamma said she'd love to go to Paris," Brand volunteered. "Mamma said she wondered at your coming back."

"All right, ladybird. That's enough."

"Papa said you thought you were too good to stay here, Uncle Henry," the child went on. "But he said he bet all along you'd come running home."

"Brand, what did I say to you?"

"I'm sorry, Mamma."

"When I say that's enough, I mean it."

"Yes, Mamma."

The clerk put our orders in front of us. Ilsa said, "Take your ice cream over to the empty table in the corner and cat it."

"Yes, Mamma." Brand drooped her way over to the small dark table and sat there, scraping little curls off the top of her ice cream with her spoon and staring at us with her huge brown eyes. When her gaze rested directly on Ilsa, her eyes were bewildered, but I knew that it was not because of her punishment.

"Really, Ilsa," I started.

"When I tell my child to do something I intend to be obeyed," she said.

"She's a pretty little thing."

"Yes. She looks like the Woolfs."

"How's Monty?"

"Oh, as ever. Have you seen Silver and Ed?"

"No. I've just been back a few hours. Papa and I had a fight and I didn't dare ask him for the car to go across the river and see them. I thought maybe I could get him in a better mood this evening."

"My car's outside. When Brand finishes her ice cream I'll drive you over if you like."

"I'd certainly appreciate it."

"Why *did* you come home, Henry?" she asked.

I stared at the melting pieces of stained ice in the bottom of my Coca-Cola glass. "I don't know exactly. Partly the reason I gave Papa—I didn't think it was right for me to play around Paris on his money while he thought I was seriously studying music and I wasn't."

"You weren't?"

"No."

"Why else?"

"Well, partly—partly—"

"Partly what?"

"I don't know. It was almost as if this place—not really this place, but something in it—was like a magnet. And I was a piece of iron and there was nothing in the world that could keep me from being drawn back to the magnet."

"Oh."

I didn't know whether or not she understood what I meant I didn't know whether or not I wanted her to. I looked over at Brand, who was still peeling tiny slivers off her ice cream and staring at us. "She must be about eight now."

Ilsa nodded. "She's a good child, on the whole."

"You and Monty are still in the old house?"

She nodded again. "It's getting run down. Paint's peeling off the pillars. Gloomier than ever. I suppose your father or Silver wrote you that Monty hasn't been doing too well with his father's law practice?"

I shook my head. Papa's letters contained only money and advice, and Silver would never say anything against Monty. "I don't know anything about what's gone on while I've been away. Silver wrote me that she and Eddie had a small orange grove, but it wasn't doing too well, and they had chickens, too, and that Eddie had a job as a salesman with some company and was always traveling about the State. She sounded very ashamed of it."

"She needn't be," Ilsa said sharply. "Eddie's working hard at something he doesn't like, to provide a living for her and the children, instead of taking your father's money and wasting himself with dissipation and getting into debt." She stopped suddenly. "I'm not sure I'm glad you've come back. For some reason I seem to talk to you."

She stood up and all at once I realized what made her look different, and yet more like herself than when I had seen her last. "You've cut your hair!"

She ran her fingers through her short wild locks. "Yes. Monty was furious. But it's so much more comfortable. I shouldn't be surprised if Silver bobbed hers one of these days. Violetta will go to the end of her years proclaiming hers to be a woman's crowning glory. When glory goes with discomfort I'll have none of it. Brand's finished her ice cream. Shall I drive you across the river?"

"If it's not too much trouble."

"I love to drive." She went over to the table where Brand sat obediently, watching the flies crawl around the edge of her empty ice-cream dish. "Come along, ladybird. You can rejoin society. I'm going to drive Uncle Henry across the river. Do you want to come with us or shall I drop you off at home?"

"Aunt Violetta's or Aunt Silver's?"

"Aunt Silver's," Ilsa said. They grinned conspiratorially.

"I guess I'd like to go, then," Brand said.

Ilsa drove a car the way she rode a horse, with great surety and considerable recklessness. It was a long Dodge touring car and we had the top down.

"I really ought to put the top up for you, Henry," Ilsa said after a while. "You're not used to this sun and I'm afraid you'll get terribly burned."

"I like it," I said. The wind seemed to be blowing my eyes back through their sockets, my breath down into my windpipe, but it was an exhilarating feeling, and it was good to have purely physical sensations drive out my unformulated miseries.

"Uncle Henry," Brand asked, "can you speak French?"

"Yes. I haven't spoken much English these past years."

"No," Ilsa said. "You've quite lost your southern accent."

"Was it hard to learn?" Brand went on.

"I don't think I really remember learning it. I didn't know a word of French and then the next thing I knew I was talking quite easily."

"Would you take Mamma and Papa and me to Paris sometime?"

"I wish I could."

"Will you play your violin for me sometime?"

"I'm afraid I can't do that, honey," I said. "I left it in Paris." I turned to Ilsa and glared at her. "I failed in that like in everything else."

She said quietly, "What else have you failed at, Henry?"

"Everything."

"Do you care passionately about your music? Does it mean your whole life to you?"

"No. Of course not."

"Then don't be so tragic about it."

"But what am I to do?" I asked. "What am I to *do*?"

"What do you want to do?"

"I don't know."

"Isn't there anything you want?"

"Nothing I can have."

"Your father'll give you work in the mill, won't he?"

"Oh, yes, I suppose so. That's not what I mean."

"No. I know," she said.

I had expected the gap between our years to be smaller now that I was twenty-four and she was twenty-seven, now that we were both grown up. But it seemed even greater. Because I had failed and I was lost. And though in a sense she had failed, too (I was certain her marriage with Monty was anything but a success), she was not lost; she might be disillusioned, but she was still clear and straight.

"Ilsa," I said. "I've lost my sense of humor."

She laughed. "I know you have, Henry. You'd better get it back."

"How does one go about getting back a sense of humor?"

"I don't know, exactly. People just strike me as funny and I laugh and then I'm all right. We're all really very funny."

"I just don't strike myself as being funny. Nobody does."

"Well, maybe you're in love. Love can often do very peculiar things to senses of humor."

"Can it?"

"Is that your trouble, Henny? Are you in love?"

"Maybe."

"Was it someone in Paris?"

"Good Lord, no!" I thought of Telcide and our happy animal relationship—the only simple and healthy contact I ever had with another human being in my life—and the way she had been so calm and matter-of-fact when I told her I felt I had to come back to America. "I mean, nothing that would make me unhappy. It was my own decision to come home and it didn't have anything to do with her. Besides, she had a marvellous sense of humor." I stopped suddenly, sheepishly, realizing what I had told her. "For heaven's sake, don't say anything to Papa!" I exclaimed.

"Of course not. Who was she?"

I looked down at Brand and then across at Ilsa questioningly. She laughed again.

"All right. Later."

We lapsed into silence. As we drove through the business section of town I noticed how much more crowded it was, how many new modern five- and six-story buildings there were. When we came to the bridge, it was no longer a rickety wooden affair with loose boards moving under carefully, slowly turning wheels, but a heavy modern drawbridge with traffic lights at either end. We didn't talk much until we got to Silver's.

A neat mulatto girl opened the door and told us that Eddie was downstate and that Silver was upstairs putting the children to bed, but would be down shortly.

We sat in the drawing room to wait. It was shady and quite cool. An electric fan was blowing from behind the asparagus plant in the fireplace. The portrait of Aunt Elizabeth was almost invisible in the shadows above the mantelpiece.

"I like that portrait of Elizabeth," Ilsa said.

I nodded.

"I've always felt rather close to her," Ilsa went on. "Not just because of Father and everything that happened, but almost as though somehow I did have a little bit of her in me. It's a funny thing. She had her revenge on your Uncle Montgomery, in a way, through me."

"What do you mean?"

"You knew he died of a stroke?"

"Yes. Papa wrote me."

"I found him lying on the floor with the port running like blood down his shirt. Monty and I carried him to his room and managed to get him to bed. I stayed with him while Monty went for the doctor. And all of a sudden he opened his eyes and stared at me in the most ghastly terror and half screamed, 'Elizabeth, don't! I beg of you, don't!' Then he made a dreadful sound and died. I hate to think of him, because that's all I see and hear. It's strange. I don't look in the least like Elizabeth. And anyone who didn't know would think that the portrait was of Silver, but I don't think it would have happened if Silver had been there instead of me."

"Cousin Anna said you were like Aunt Elizabeth."

"Yes, but why should I be? There's no reason. . . . Your Cousin Anna said she understood, though—about your Uncle Montgomery, I mean. She's been like a mother to me. Maybe even more, because we've never had the embarrassment of intimacy that inevitably comes when one woman has borne another. She's a wonderful woman, with a capacity for love that's been trampled on and trampled on, but that somehow stays alive. I love her very much. . . ."

"So do I," I said.

"Henry."

Silver stood in the doorway. I got up and hurried across the room to her. She kissed me in her usual cool undemonstrative way. Only her cold trembling hands told me that she was excited and glad to see me.

"Henry! Papa said you'd be over tonight! I didn't expect you till then!"

"Ilsa was good enough to bring me over."

She pushed me away from her and stood staring at me. "You're so tall and skinny, Brother! I can see you haven't been taking care of yourself or eating properly. And older—"

"Well, eight years is a long time."

I looked hard at her little face. The gray eyes had lost the look of fear that had lurked behind them in the old days; now they were serene and contented. Her expression was, as always, cool and unemotional, but her body had softened and filled out, though she was still slender. She wore a simple lemon-yellow dress that made her look very young—not at all the mother of three little boys.

"Ilsa—" she said. "Excuse me for not speaking to you. I'm every which way for Sunday. Thank you for bringing Henry over."

"I was glad of the drive."

"You never come to see us."

"I didn't think you particularly wanted me to."

"I'd always be glad to see you," Silver said. "After all, you're my sister-in-law."

"That needn't make any difference to your feelings."

"Perhaps not. But it does make a difference to my manners," Silver said coldly.

"It shouldn't."

Brand had been sitting quietly in the corner looking at an album of photographs. Now she called attention to her presence, saying, "Please, Aunt Silver, may I go see the chickens?"

"Darling, I didn't see you!" Silver said. "Of course, you may go see the chickens. Come with me and I'll get one of the men to take you around." They went off together.

"It's a funny thing with Silver and me," Ilsa said. "Sometimes we're the best of friends, and sometimes there's this cold thing like a sheet of ice between us. We can see each other, but we can't reach through to each other. I suppose it must still be Monty, though I thought she'd outgrown that long ago. God knows she ought to have."

Silver came back in, saying, "Henry, Violetta and Dolph and I had planned to go down to the beach tomorrow evening for a picnic supper. Could you come with us? Papa wouldn't mind, would he?"

"Papa said he wanted to see as little of me as possible. I'd like very much to come."

"Do you think you and Monty could come too, Ilsa?" Silver asked, a little tentatively.

"I'll have to ask Monty. I think it would be very pleasant. I'll call you tomorrow morning."

"Could you let me know tonight? I want to do the marketing first thing in the morning."

"I'm afraid Monty may not be home until too late. If I can't call you tonight I'll let you know by eight."

"Oh. All right," Silver said, and looked over at me. She sat curled up on a lime-green plush Victorian sofa. Although she had none of the spark that flashed at one from Aunt Elizabeth's picture, I was relieved to see that there was no longer anything of Mamma in her. The worry I had felt when she wrote me that she was marrying Eddie vanished.

"Come see the children," Silver said.

We followed her upstairs.

The house smelled of newness. It was quite a small house and the heavy mahogany furniture, the massive silver, the portraits in the huge gold frames, all seemed crowded and degraded. It was not so much that they belonged in another house as that they belonged in another time, an age that every new event pushed farther back into the impossible.

"Hush," Silver said, leading us into a small room off the landing, although neither Ilsa nor I had said a word.

I looked for a moment at the three hot sleeping babies, lingering at the middle one, the two-year-old, Henry Porcher Woolf, named after me. Then I looked at Silver as she went from crib to crib, looking down at the sleeping, heat-flushed little boys; and as I watched her face I knew why she no longer looked like Mamma. Mamma had never looked at either of her children like that.

26

We had a perfect evening for a picnic. I drove down to the beach with Ilsa, Monty, and Brand.

Monty was fatter; his face looked unhealthy under a superficial tan; there were deep puffy circles under his eyes. Much of his overheartiness was gone, and he had, instead, a kind of unsteady gentleman-of-the-old-South manner. He wore a spotless Palm Beach suit, and the handkerchief with which he mopped his brow was of the purest silk. He carried a portable gramophone and a batch of records. I climbed into the back with Brand. Ilsa got in and sat at the wheel.

Monty stood in the driveway. "I'll drive," he said.

Ilsa did not move and did not speak.

"I'm perfectly capable of driving my own car to the beach," he said.

Ilsa's mobile mouth twitched slightly. "You look tired, Monty. I'm afraid you worked too hard at the office again. Why don't you rest and let me drive? You know I enjoy it."

Docilely, he went around the car and sat down beside her. "Times hard," he said. "Buried in work, up to ears." I noticed that he was talking like Uncle Montgomery.

"Uncle Henry," Brand said, as we crossed the new bridge.

"What is it, Brand?"

"Isn't my Papa handsome?"

"Yes, he is," I answered with complete truthfulness. No matter what eight years had done to his face, Monty was still handsome.

"Don't you think I have the most wonderful Mamma and Papa in the world?"

"Yes," I said, answering only the first part of the question.

"Monty," I heard Ilsa say in a low voice from the front seat.

"What is it now?"

"Will you please be out of the house by ten tomorrow morning?"

"Why?"

"Beulah Jackson's coming over for a piano lesson."

"What did you say?" he said in a loud voice.

"Be quiet. I said Beulah Jackson was coming over for a piano lesson."

"And you propose to give her this lesson?"

"I do."

"Why, may I ask?"

"We need the money."

"We're getting along."

"The house needs painting. Brand and I need some new clothes."

"Oh, so it's your vanity."

Through the rear-view mirror I could see Ilsa's quick spontaneous smile, and felt like an eavesdropper.

"This is the first time I've been accused of being a vain woman. I'm rather flattered." She took one hand off the steering wheel and laid it on Monty's, not, I fancied, because of any impulse of affection, but because she knew instinctively the healing power of those hands and used them when necessary.

"No Woolf has ever stooped to giving piano lessons," Monty sputtered.

"This Woolf is going to start stooping," Ilsa said. "Come on, darling, stop glowering. It's a great deal better to teach than to lose one's self-respect. You might try to find me a few more pupils."

As she kept her hand strongly on his, he seemed like a bristling cat whose fur slowly lies down at the mistress's touch. I thought, as a matter of fact, it would probably have been a good deal better for them both if she had been his mistress instead of his wife. No doubt this was the decadent influence of Telcide and Paris.

Ilsa took her hand off Monty's and put it back on the steering wheel.

27

We met the others, Silver, Violetta, and Randolph, at the foot of the beach road.

"Shall we go toward July Harbour or down Myrtle Valley way?" Dolph asked. At thirty he was already quite bald and very cadaverous. His high forehead was the color of parchment, his nose long and wrinkled, not as though he were smelling something unpleasant, but as though he were puzzled and trying to find out what was wrong. He looked older than his few years more than the rest of us. I knew that he was helping Papa at the paper mill, since I was so unsatisfactory as a son and heir, and doing very well.

Violetta was the only one of the three women who was dressed in expensive, fashionable clothes. She wore a white-and-scarlet linen dress; her hair was waved, and her nails manicured. While Dolph had been getting thinner, she had been getting plumper, and with the added flesh her face, like Monty's, had become coarse instead of soft. She was still pretty and vivacious, though she looked more than twenty-nine, and I didn't think her continuous flow of conversation was going to amuse me. I thought how much nicer both Ilsa and Silver looked in their simple dresses and low shoes.

"When people ask me," Violetta started, "whether I want to go toward July Harbour or down Myrtle Valley way for a picnic, I never know which to say, do you, Henry? The beach looks just the same to me no matter which way you go—water and sand one way and sand and water the other—so, as far as I'm concerned, it doesn't make much difference. You don't care, do you, Randolph? Let's just go whichever way is quickest. Silver and I put up the prettiest picnic you ever laid eyes on. Silver's Willie May makes the best deviled eggs you ever bit into. Maybe it's because they're Silver's own eggs; I mean, her own hens lay them, not Silver, but I think the way Willie May devils them has something to do with it, don't you, Silver? Or are you going to give all the credit to the chickens?"

Monty ignored his twin sister. "Go down Myrtle Valley way," he said.

I had expected Ilsa to call loudly for July Harbour, so that she could go to her father's house, but she sat quietly, her hands loose on the steering wheel, and waited.

"Come on," Monty said. "What are we waiting for? Let's go. Does anybody object to going down the Myrtle Valley road?"

"Unhunh. It suits me fine, and Dolph, too," Violetta said. "How 'bout you, Silver?"

"I don't care. Let's just hurry. I don't want to leave the children too long."

"Well," Violetta said, "we better make our minds up one way or other. Randolph's been working hard all day and he's real hungry. Which way do you say, Ilsa?"

Ilsa's lips were pressed together impatiently. She started the car and turned around, heading down the Myrtle Valley road.

"You needn't be rude to my sister, Ilsa," Monty said.

"She wanted someone to make up her mind for her, didn't she?"

"Violetta's been very kind to you. When you married me she said she was going to treat you just like one of the family."

"That's more than you've done, isn't it?" she asked, in a voice so low I could barely catch the words.

We drove in silence, sprawling dunes to the left of us, scrub and swamp to the right. Every once in a while, poking tentatively, mockingly out of the dunes, you could see the tops of rickety picket fences. Once someone had stumbled across the magnificent idea of building these fences across the dunes to keep the sand away from the road, the way, I believe, it is done for snow in the North; but nothing can hold back the sifting restless sand. It goes where it will, as careless of poor little fences as revolution. Toward the road, and twisting in and out of the fences, were beach morning-glory vines; at the top of the dunes, waving triumphantly like ostrich plumes in a war horse's headdress, were the sea oats, their careless tarnished gold the color of Ilsa's windblown hair.

The road seemed to be a dividing line between life and death. Free sea and sand and sea oats on one side; on the other gnarled myrtle trees, twisted and tormented by the salt wind; stunted scrub oak; an occasional rusty palm sticking up tall and alone. Scorpions would be in that underbrush, and snakes, and strange wild birds' hidden nests. Where the inland waterways wound their serpentine coils, near the road, but hidden by the bowed secretive trees, alligators would raise treacherous heads in the, dark waters, flamingoes would arch their scarlet frightened necks, egrets would couch, hiding their secret, forbidden plumes, and sea gulls would hover for a moment, then fly screaming back to the ocean. Over this uninhabitable land, buzzards waited; wild razor-backed pigs grunted their way across the road in front of us, and disappeared into the swamp's dark recesses.

On one side of the road was all the clean life and beauty of home; on the other the rich decadent death.

Ilsa drove rapidly, angrily, until we reached one of the turn-offs at the edge of the road, with its small fountain of sulphur water. She pulled the car off here and stopped.

"I'd forgotten the sulphur water now that we don't have it in town any more," I said.

"They still have it across the river. That's one reason—only one—why I don't go over to see Silver or Violetta more often. Father and I always drank rain water. You'd better have a good drink, Henry. This is the real stuff. Take a mouthful of rotten eggs and you'll know you're home again."

I bent over the fountain and took a mouthful, spitting it out onto the sand immediately. "I'd forgotten how foul it was."

Ilsa and Brand laughed loudly. "I must remind Violetta to give you a lecture on its merits," Ilsa said.

Reaching into the back of the car, Monty got out his gramophone and records. "Come on and we'll have some music," he called to Brand.

Brand looked from Ilsa to him and back again.

"Go on with your father, ladybird," Ilsa said. "Uncle Henry and I'll wait here for the others. Your Uncle Randolph's a darling, but he drives like a cockroach."

"How does a cockroach drive, Mamma?"

"Get your father to tell you. Help him carry the records."

Stumbling in the soft sand, Brand and Monty disappeared over the crest of the dune. In a moment we heard the raucous rhythm of one of Monty's dance records.

"I should think he'd get enough of that tripe in town without having to buy records and drag them along everywhere. I loathe the hideous noise," Ilsa said.

I remembered the songs Telcide had sung in her deep, foggy voice, always a little wistful when they were most valiantly noisy, always crazily gay when they were most sad and despairing, and I suddenly realized that I had started going regularly to hear Telcide because her voice reminded me of Ilsa's. But I had never even heard Ilsa sing. This, I thought, is one of the times when I should laugh at myself; but I couldn't.

The others drove up just then, and Ilsa and I helped them carry the picnic things up the dunes. Dolph and I spread out the steamer rugs while Silver and Violetta unfolded the white linen tablecloth and began unpacking the picnic basket. Ilsa stood watching Monty and Brand for a moment; then she turned to help with the picnic basket.

28

After Violetta had gorged her fill—deviled eggs, fried chicken, sandwiches, corn dodgers, cake, watermelon, sweet coffee she had brought in a huge thermos jug—after the remains of the picnic had been cleared away and Brand lay sleeping on one of the dark steamer rugs, Ilsa said to me, "Come take a walk, Henny."

I stumbled eagerly to my feet and followed her. Dolph and Violetta sat close together on one of the steamer rugs. I thought that there must be at least a spark of passion left between them; Cousin Anna had known what she was talking about. That made up for a lot.

Silver sat near the gramophone, handing the records to Monty.

Ilsa stuck her finger in her mouth and held it up to the evening. "Let's go against the wind," she said. "I don't want to listen to *The Georgia Grind* or *Waiting for the Robert E. Lee*. And as for *When the Midnight Choo Choo Leaves for Alabam'*—" She Hung her arms wide. "This sea breeze is good. Henry, why didn't you say you wanted to go July Harbour way?"

"I—I don't know," I stammered. "I guess I sort of forgot I'd have any say in the matter. I've been so used to being here only mentally I still don't feel part of anything yet. You wanted to go back and see your father's house, didn't you?"

"Naturally."

"Why didn't you say so?"

"There wouldn't have been a chance of going, then. I thought maybe if someone else wanted to go that way Monty wouldn't say anything. The only way I got him to come tonight was pretending I didn't want to come because Violetta's such a bore. Heaven knows she is a bore, but I get so lonely for the ocean sometimes I feel as though I were going to burst. It's as though someone put the ocean into a box at low tide, and when the moon came along and said, hey, ocean, it's time for high tide, there wouldn't be any place for it to go. . . . It'll be night in a minute. Let's walk far away so they can't make us go home for a while."

She slipped off her shoes, pulled up her skirts and unfastened her stockings, then ran splashing into the water. "Come on, Henny, it's glorious!" she called. I took off my shoes and socks, rolled up my trousers, and followed her in.

"I wish we were kids again, so we could just take off our clothes and have a swim," she said. "If we were alone I would, damn it, but I'm afraid the others would find out and die of horror. You wouldn't be shocked, would you, Hen? After all, you're like my brother."

I turned and waded out of the water, sat down on the sand, and put my socks and shoes on over my wet, sandy feet. Ilsa followed me and stood looking down at me.

"What's the matter, Henny? You look so desolate, all of a sudden. I didn't shock you, did I? Oh, come now, after the life you've been leading in Paris!" She tried to make me laugh.

I forced a smile. "I guess I'm just not used to being home yet," I said; "I still feel strange and disoriented."

"On a night like this, at the beach! Look, there's the lightship." She pointed out over the water where the light flickered on and off. "When I look at that light coming over the ocean I can't be frightened or discontented. It's like magic for me. It makes everything clear and serene."

Ilsa had taught me her feeling about the lightship. At the time I could never quite get out of my mind Mamma's gruesome tale, or forget that, shining and secure though the light might be, the buzzards were always there, and the sharks.

I remembered how shortly after Mamma had chilled my blood with that horrible warning I had crept out of the house and ridden on Billy out to the woods. I left him tethered to a pine and was wandering along rather aimlessly. A number of buzzards were circling slowly overhead, and unconsciously I headed their way. Suddenly I was standing in the center of the circle—half a dozen buzzards were wheeling above me, their ugly naked heads half drawn into their shoulders, their wings absolutely motionless. Their shadows slid over the brush, around and around in the same track. They were almost hypnotic, sliding so regularly past, and I had a sudden strange feeling that they were weaving a web of some sort around me. If the sun hadn't been so bright I'd have been frightened out of my wits. It was like being in a dream that slowly, slowly, progresses to a dreadful end, in spite of your fighting to stop it midway.

"There's going to be a moonrise," Ilsa said. "Cheer up, creature. The stars are coming out. Let's go sit on a dune and watch it. It's been a long time since we've been on the beach together. If it weren't for Brand I'd walk down the beach to the house, and to hell with them."

"It's a long walk," I said.

"I know." She settled herself comfortably on the soft sand of the dune that seemed to accept her companionably, as part of itself. Me it rejected impassively; I had become a foreigner. I wriggled uncomfortably. Sand was in my shoes, in my hair, I ground it between my teeth.

"Henny, would it be proper for you to take me out dancing some night? It would be fun to stay out all night dancing again."

I didn't think the family would approve of this any more than my life in Paris. "Wouldn't Monty take you?"

"I don't know. I doubt it. Too many of the wrong people might recognize him."

"I—I'm sorry," I said, softly, miserably.

"For heaven's sake, don't be sorry for me, Henry! I have an awfully good time out of life. I can't think of anything in the world that would make me stop enjoying things. As long as I can have the beach once in a while I couldn't ever really be unhappy."

I couldn't very well tell her that I wasn't nearly as sorry for her as I was for myself.

After a while I said, "Ilsa, do you really need money?"

She nodded. "After the old Woolf died Monty pretty much let the practice go to pot. Edwin comes to the office every once in a while to try and straighten things out, but it's not much use. Monty resents having to work. He's firmly convinced he ought to be subsidized for life."

"I hate to think of you having to give piano lessons."

"Oh, I don't mind. It'll be good discipline for me, and I don't think I'll be a bad teacher."

"You play very well."

"Father used to make me work hard at it. He said it was one way to keep me out of mischief."

"You've never been serious about it?"

"Good Lord, no. I love music, but I want it to be for pleasure, not work. You take everything too seriously, Henry."

"I know . . . it'll be work for you if you have to give lessons."

"Well, that can't be helped. Let's not talk about it. Silver looks well, doesn't she?"

"Yes." I swallowed the bait and changed the subject. "I'm glad and relieved about her. I was afraid she was going to be like Mamma."

"Eddie's such a sweet little thing," Ilsa said, "and he'd do anything in the world for her. And then, there're the children. I think the children have been most important of all."

"Ilsa—"

"Yes?"

"Why haven't you had any more children?"

She looked at me quickly, then out over the dark ocean. "Nobody wrote you about it?"

"About what?"

"I wanted more children. I thought they'd help. Things were much better with Monty and me for a time after Brand was born. When she was two I had a miscarriage. I can't have any more."

"How did it happen?" I asked. "Would you mind telling me?"

"No. I don't mind. I told you I seem to talk to you. Well—Monty was going down to Miami on business. I wasn't feeling too well and he wanted me to come with him and see some doctor he'd heard of down there. He was just as crazy to have the baby as I was. He wanted a boy, of course. We planned to be in Miami about a month—that would have been till about three weeks before the baby was due. I had the trunks all packed. Monty always insists on traveling as though he were going to be gone for years. Then, the night before we were to leave, we had a quarrel. We'd planned to leave Brand with your Cousin Anna, and all of a sudden Monty decided she'd be a bad influence on the child and we'd have to take her with us. It was just a crazy whim. He'd been drinking. I was feeling miserable and hadn't learned yet how to cope with him when he was in that condition. When he hit me I wasn't prepared for it and I fell. I thought I was all right—but I guess that was what started it. It was really quite a fall, because I whacked my head against the marble-topped table and went out for a moment. When I came to, Monty had me in his arms and was weeping over me. He carried me upstairs and put me to bed. Sometimes he can be very sweet."

She spoke quietly, unemotionally. "I started the pains soon after. They tried to save the baby, but it was no use." She let the fine sand sift through her fingers. "The moon will be up in a minute. It's getting light at the edge of the ocean. Watch, Henny."

I looked out across the dark water to the horizon. Slowly, over the black edge of sea, the moon lifted itself, a great burnt-orange disc. It looked not prehistoric, but posthistoric. In its strange sulphurous light the ocean looked unbelievably old as it rolled in slowly, lecherously licking the sand. Close to the water's edge lay dark patches of tangled seaweed and clumps of water hyacinth that had come in by the river, had curled silkily around the jetties, and been washed ashore. They looked alive now, coiling and writhing like snakes, like the last living thing on earth. I wanted to reach over and take Ilsa's hand, but she sat there, her eyes absorbing the dark of night, and I knew that I must not break in on her isolation.

As the moon pulled itself dripping out of the ancient sea it became smaller and slowly turned from its appalling bloody color to gold, and finally, leaping triumphantly clear of the water, it swung white and pure up in the sky.

"There's a kind of fog around the moon tonight," Ilsa said. "I expect it will rain tomorrow—real rain, not just a thunder shower."

"Oh," I said. The moon seemed quite clear to me, but I have never been any good at seeing weather signs. I remembered once when Ilsa had tried to point out some of the constellations to me I had been unutterably stupid.

"I forgot to tell you before," she said. "Watch out for those clumps of hyacinth. Sometimes a water moccasin will drift in on one from the river. . . . It's a lovely night, isn't it, Henry?" She put her arm in mine, and I thought I would die from an agony of longing at her touch.

We walked back to the others. Brand was still sleeping on the steamer rug, the forlorn empty picnic basket beside her, her young sleep undisturbed by the raucous strains of *Waiting for the Robert E. Lee*.

29

On sunday I went to church with Papa. Violetta, Dolph and Silver had come from across the river; Eddie was still downstate, Ilsa, Monty, and Brand sat in the pew in front of us. Throughout the sermon there was the constant gentle sound of palm-leaf fans moving slowly back and forth, back and forth, creating a mild warm breeze throughout the church. The light was too warm as the sun pushed it through the stained-glass windows; the reds and yellows and greens of the small pieces of glass seemed alive with heat. I watched Ilsa fanning herself slowly, watched her amused look and Brand's proud one as Monty walked with elegant dignity up the aisle during the collection, reverently bearing the silver plate. Papa, Violetta, and Silver sang loudly and smugly:

Prone to wander, Lord, I feel it:
Prone to leave the God I love;
Here's my heart, O lake and seal it,
Seal it for Thy courts above!

Randolph cleared his throat and looked down his long nose at his hymnal. Ilsa looked around her with her clear eyes; it seemed to me that she was trying not to laugh at something.

Ignoring Papa's looks, I left before communion. Ilsa followed me out.

"Henny, walk over to your Cousin Anna's with me, and then come on back to dinner. I can't bear Sunday dinner."

"Well, Papa—" I started.

"You said he didn't want to see you. Come along."

"Oh—all right," I said.

Cousin Anna's house was not far from the church. We walked slowly, because of the midday sun beating down on our heads. Ilsa wore a coral-colored dress Cousin Anna had given her, and a wide-brimmed, natural-straw hat which her wild hair pushed onto the back of her head. Instead of being beaten down and killed by the merciless strength of the sun she seemed to take life from it, to diminish it by her own capacity for receiving its violent energy.

Cousin Anna was sitting out under the magnolia tree and, as we kissed her and sat down beside her, it felt as though only a few days instead of so many years had passed. I seemed to be back in that summer when I had spent so many evenings sitting silently under this tree with Cousin Anna, the heat and our thoughts weighing equally heavily upon us, while I waited, waited, hoping to see Ilsa's precise, graceful form come toward us down the path.

She seemed glad to see me, glad, as always, to see Ilsa, but she didn't want to talk, so after a few minutes we left and walked slowly back to the church. Monty and Brand were waiting in the car when we got there; Monty was hot and impatient.

"Where the hell have you been?" he asked.

"We went over to see Cousin Anna," Ilsa said.

"Oh, you did."

"Yes. Henry's coming back to dinner with us. Hop in, Hen."

I climbed in the back and Ilsa sat down beside Monty, pulling Brand onto her lap. Monty sat glowering, his hands clenched on the steering wheel. After a while Ilsa said, "If you're not going to drive, Monty, move over and let me do it. I want time to wash up before dinner."

Monty started the car roughly. As we careened around a corner on two wheels and almost ran down another car, I didn't think we had a chance in the world of getting home alive, and discovered abruptly how little I wanted to die. Ilsa sat motionless and unperturbed in the front seat, one arm firmly around Brand. Once, when Monty almost seemed to lose control of the car, she dropped the other arm lightly across his shoulders, and his hand seemed to steady at the wheel.

When we got to the house Ilsa went upstairs to wash. Monty wound up his phonograph, put on a record, then changed his mind, scraping the needle off the disc, and slammed out of the room after her. I went into the hall and phoned to say I wouldn't be home, then pushed through the rice portieres and sat down in the drawing room. After a few minutes Brand came in, her face shiny and new-scrubbed. She stared at me with sudden shy silence, then sat down in a corner with a picture book. I looked around this room which had gained importance, had, indeed, become a new room, since it now belonged to Ilsa, though actually it was little changed.

It was, at any rate, slightly less oppressive than the parlor which was hardly ever used. Two long French windows opened out onto a narrow stone terrace. Around the thin square pillars to this terrace a heavy wisteria vine was twisted, so thick and luxuriant that it formed a green screen that almost cut off the view of the ill-kept lawn going down in a mass of weeds and shaggy shrubbery to the river. Heavy brown-velvet curtains, lined with scarlet Chinese silk, always hung at these windows. In summer, muslin bags were pulled on over them so that they stood out, bulky and white, on either side. Between the windows was a black marble-topped table on which stood a large white marble statuette of Iago whispering in Othello's ear, which Monty had always admired greatly. And there was a Rogers group of two little boys standing by a horse at a watering trough. When we were very little Uncle Montgomery used to put it on the floor and let us ride the horse. A large picture of the Sibyl with her head in a turban hung over this.

I noticed that the dark brown carpet had been taken up for the summer and in its place were Japanese raffia mats. White linen covers were on all the furniture except the Japanese bamboo chaise longue and the sewing chair, giving the room a put-away, unused look. The walls were still papered with the same horrible brown paper. The only part of the room which seemed to have Ilsa's touch was the corner where the old square grand piano stood. It was piled with music now, instead of being covered, as in the old days, with a shawl on which had been placed a cut-glass vase holding dried grasses. Across the wall she had had bookshelves built, and the worn, well-read-looking volumes made one feel that perhaps someone alive came occasionally into this room. Above the shelves she had hung a water-color sketch of Aunt Elizabeth, evidently one of Aunt Violetta's pallid efforts—but even Aunt Violetta couldn't help letting some of Elizabeth's vehemence slip into the expression.

I went over to the piano and sat down. I had learned to play a little while I was in Paris; sometimes, when Telcide and I gave a party, I would accompany her while she sang. Now I began to play softly one of Nursie's old songs that I had taught Telcide, and which I hoped she was still singing successfully with that heavy accent of hers that somehow gave it an added charm. Brand came over and knelt on the piano bench beside me."

"You don't play as well as Mamma does," she said after a while.

I flushed and stopped. She put her hand gently against my cheek. "Please play some more. It's just *different* from Mamma. I like to hear you," she said softly, her face puckered with distress at having hurt my feelings. So I started again, with even more diffidence than before.

Ilsa came running down the stairs and in through the rice portieres. "Hen, wasn't that the rosy-bush song you were playing?"

"Yes, do you know it?"

"Father used to sing me to sleep with it when I was little. His mother used to sing it to him. It's the only thing he remembered about her—she died when he was just a little boy and his sister raised him. Play it again, will you?"

I played, and as she sang along with me I was relieved to hear that her voice *was* like Telcide's, though Telcide was a singer, and I had to admit that Ilsa wasn't.

I wish I was
A red red rosy bush
A-blooming by-ee
The banks of the sea,
For when my true
Love would come by-ee
He'd pluck an rose
From offen me.
A rosy rose,
A red red rosy bush,
He'd pluck an rose
From offen me.

Ilsa hugged Brand with excitement. "Ladybird, don't you remember that? I used to sing it to you when you were a baby."

Brand nodded. "I remember."

"Do play it again, Henny," Ilsa begged.

This time she listened while I played, and watched carefully. "I like your accompaniment," she said. "Will you teach it to me?"

"Of course. By the way, how did your piano lesson go?"

"Not bad. The child's a moron and I'll never be able to teach her anything, but I've got to the point now where money is money.

Violetta has promised to get me some more pupils. So at last a use in the world is being found for Violetta. Henny, play my darling rosy-bush song again."

She stood behind the piano bench, one arm around Brand, the other resting lightly on my shoulder. Monty came in. "A very pretty domestic picture," he said.

"Come and join us." Ilsa looked around and smiled at him.

He sat down on one of the white-shrouded chairs and pushed his fingers through his glossy hair. "Always been very fond of Ilsa, haven't you, Henry?" he asked.

"Of course," I answered, watching him closely. I was sure he had had something to drink while he was upstairs.

"Advise you not to get too fond of her."

"What do you mean?"

"Ladybird," Ilsa said to Brand, "will you go out to the kitchen and see if you can't hurry dinner up? I'm about to swoon with hunger."

Brand went slowly off. Monty waited until she had disappeared through the rice portieres. "Mean just what I say. Better not get too fond of my wife."

"Monty, don't be absurd," Ilsa said, going over to him. "Of course Henny and I are fond of each other. We've known each other most of our lives."

"Won't have my wife pleasuring herself with another man."

Ilsa laughed. "Monty, no one on earth but you would think of calling Henny, 'another man.' It makes me feel practically incestuous."

Monty grunted.

Ilsa laughed again, trying to make him catch her amusement. "Monty, you poor fool, Henny's like my kid brother. He's certainly not interfering with your rights as a husband." Monty was silent, looking with his dulled eyes into her clear ones. "I think you should apologize to Henny for your foolish ill-temper. This isn't a very hospitable way to behave toward your long-lost cousin."

"Will not have my wife behave like a loose woman," he said. "No matter what kind of woman your mother was, when you married me you were supposed to behave like a lady."

Ilsa became very pale. "How dare you," she said in a low voice.

"I'll say anything I like to my wife," Monty said.

"After the way you've behaved since the first week I married you, you'd have no right to say anything if I made you a cuckold with every man in town." Her voice was still very low very controlled. Standing a few feet away, by the piano, I had to guess at the words. When she had finished speaking there was a short silence like a suspension of time—not seconds passing, empty, with nothing in them, but a sudden complete stillness, time holding its breath, the hands of the clock not moving the heart not beating, the pulse empty in the wrist.

Then Monty struck Ilsa across the face. I sprang toward him, but quick as a flash she had caught him by both wrists. I stopped and stood waiting.

"You will apologize to Henry for your boorish behavior," she said. She held his flaccid wrists in so firm a grip that he couldn't struggle. "Apologize," she said again, through clenched teeth.

"Sorry, damn you," he said.

She continued to hold his wrists. "And you will behave like a rational human being at the dinner table. Not for my sake, or even for Henry's, though he is our guest, but for your daughter's. She still loves you and thinks you are the most wonderful father in the world. For some reason I'd like to have her go on thinking it."

She let go of his wrists, went over to the bamboo chaise longue, and threw herself down on it. Between her shoulders and under her arms dark wet stains from nervous exertion spread themselves on her bright Shantung dress; she looked white and exhausted. We sat in silence until Brand came in, saying, "Mattie Belle says we can come in to dinner now." Then Ilsa got up with her usual energy and led the way into the dining room.

30

During the meal she talked constantly, not paying much attention to what she was saying, watching Brand's face to make sure that nothing that had happened before dinner had reached her.

"I hope you appreciate these butter beans," she said. "I spent hours yesterday shelling them."

"Why didn't you let Mattie Belle shell them?" Monty scowled.

"Mattie Belle has plenty else to do. We wouldn't have had them if I hadn't shelled them."

"They're very good," I said.

She laughed. "I worked up such a grudge against them I didn't dare speak to myself or anyone else for hours. It's a good thing we had to go to church today. Skinny, flat, tight-shut nuisances. I don't mind English peas—though they are a little annoying when they get out of hand and begin to roll all over the floor. But butter beans! I can't think of an epithet to fit 'em. They have to be torn open by brute force and yanked from their hulls. Very hard on fingernails and not so good to eat anyway."

"Umph," Monty said, but Brand and I laughed obligingly.

There was a long silence. Mattie Belle passed the rice and gravy and butter beans around again. Monty helped himself and said, "Ilsa, does that man Ira build?"

"Yes. He built most of our house at the beach. Why?"

"Think you could get him to do some building around here?"

"He probably could be persuaded. But what do we need to have built?"

"Thought I'd have some kennels put in at the side of the house and get in some hounds, some pointers. Like to do some hunting with Eddie and Dolph next winter. Could Ira build the kennels?"

"Yes, I'm sure he could build them, Monty, but all you really need is a wire pen."

"Want kennels. If you're giving piano lessons we ought to have more money. Think I can get you a few pupils. When can you get hold of Ira?"

After a second she said, "We could drive down to the beach tonight if you like."

"Uh huh," he said, and pushed his chair back. "I don't feel like dessert. Going to see a man about the hounds."

"On Sunday?"

"Why not? Be back in time to go down to the beach tonight. About eight-thirty?"

"Very well."

Monty got up and left. He had to walk carefully to keep himself steady.

After we left the dining room Ilsa sent Brand up to the nursery. I knew she was trying to run the huge house with only Mattie Belle, her skinny little cook.

"Come on up to the bedroom if you don't mind, Hen. It's a little cooler."

I followed her upstairs. The bedroom seemed to have much more of her personality than the big room downstairs. The walls had been repainted a cool sea-green-gray. There were no curtains at the windows, only Japanese bamboo blinds which kept the sunlight out and allowed the breeze from the river in. The raffia rug on the floor was the same color as the walls. By the bed was a small bookcase; in a silver frame on this was an enlarged snapshot of Dr. Brandes on Calypso, a pair of field glasses in his hand, his eyes squinting against the sun.

Ilsa flung herself across the foot of the bed, kicking off her shoes in order not to soil the white seersucker bedspread. She rubbed her fingers over her forehead with a tired gesture that was unlike her. "Oh, Hen, I'm glad you're back. I haven't had anyone to talk to. These last few years your Cousin Anna's been even less communicative than usual. She keeps feeling that she ought to talk to me about Elizabeth and Father, but she can't do it without emotionally experiencing everything all over again, and she can't bear to do that."

I sat down on the bench in front of her dressing table, looking at her little bottles of perfume.

"I love good smells," she said. "Did you notice the wonderful scent Silver had on in church? I gave her that for Christmas."

"Um um. It was nice." I looked around the room, thinking how clean and cool it was. The bamboo blinds stirred slightly in the breeze. I sat there silently while she lay stretched across the foot of the bed, her eyes closed, her face relaxed, deliberately devoid of expression. I noticed with a kind of agony that there were little lines about the corners of her mouth and her eyes that she couldn't will away. After a while she sighed, opened her eyes, and rolled over.

"Oh, Hen, I'm tired. Not physically, not mentally, just tired. I don't know quite what I mean, so I know you don't."

"Maybe I do," I said.

"It's just," she went on, "that there's a funny deadness somewhere that I can't quite track down. A slightly out-of-love-with-life feeling. Sort of matter-of-fact and unenchanted. I need something—something to excite me—to do I don't know quite what. I want to go back to the ocean and find my roots again. . . . And then there's something else. If only I could be sure one way or other—"

"What?"

"Oh, nothing."

"Ilsa," I said.

"What?"

"May I ask you a very personal question?"

She smiled. "Why did I marry Monty?"

"Yes. It seems so—so out of character, somehow."

"What do you mean by 'out of character'?"

"It's—it's just not like you."

She laughed. I thought that as long as I could hear Ilsa laugh, with her beautiful, exquisite sanity, nothing could quite be entirely wrong. "Darling Henny, you haven't any idea what I'm like. You've made me up. I don't know why you've bothered."

"I think I'm the only person in the whole town who *has* any idea what you're like."

"Your Cousin Anna knows me," she said. "She knows every thing that's wrong with me: my stupid arrogance, my false pride, my uncontrollable passions. . . . To go back to your question, I was in love with Monty when I married him. Don't ask me why, because there's never an answer to that question—not an answer you can put into words, at any rate. But I was in love with him all right. Don't ever doubt that, just because you've always hated him."

"Well," I said, half to myself, "maybe it was because you didn't have any basis for comparison. Monty and Eddie and I were all you had to choose from, and God knows Monty was the likeliest then. And you were awfully young.

After a moment I realized that she hadn't heard me. She was sitting up, hugging her knees, and she said very softly, gently. "It was a lovely feeling, being in love that way."

"You're not in love with him now?" I knew she had every right to be angry with me for asking that.

But she answered, simply, "No." After a while she went on speaking in an unemotional voice that reminded me of Cousin Anna. "You don't understand Monty any better than you do me. I know you've never liked him, and I suppose because you're a man his charm is quite lost on you. But I can assure you that he has charm. I can still feel very fond of him. I can also feel quite *in love* with him—although he's made it impossible for me to *love* him. . . . Do you see what I mean?"

"I think so."

"I'm terribly sorry we were both so awful before dinner."

"It wasn't your fault."

"Oh, yes, a lot of it was. . . . It's funny, you know—he's really very dependent on me in a strange sort of way. Sometimes, when I find myself quieting him down, calming him, I feel as old as the moon, and just as burnt out. Twenty-seven's really not so ancient. . . . Sometimes I feel as alive and violent as the sun. . . . I can't stop him from drinking or carrying on the way he does, you know. I've honestly tried. But me being me, and Monty being Monty, the chemical reaction's just wrong. When I try to stop him I make him worse. For his sake it would probably have been better if he'd married Silver. She might have been able to manage him, with her little sphinx face. For her sake I'm glad she married Eddie, even if she is ashamed of him for earning a good living. Henry, you seem to act on me like 'shine liquor. I haven't talked like this since you went away. How long is that?"

"Eight years."

"That's quite a time. . . . I'd like to ask you to drive down to the beach with us tonight, but I guess with Monty in this mood I'd better not."

"I've got to get back home anyhow," I said. "Papa wants me to start work in the mill office tomorrow and I guess he'll want to talk to me about it tonight. I'm not looking forward to it."

"No, I guess you're not," she said.

I suddenly thought of something. "You know what might be fun?"

"What?"

"There's a stock company going to be in town week after next. I'd like to go."

She sat up, that quick interested excitement flashing into her eyes. "Let's! I've never seen a play."

"I don't suppose it'll be any good."

"I don't care how awful it is. It'll be fun and a change. You haven't been home long enough to remember how much the same every day is in this town. At the beach every day's different. Henny, let's go to the play the very first night. Will you get the tickets?"

"How many?"

"I don't know—let's see. I know what would be best. We'll get Silver to phone and ask Monty to take her. He's more apt to go that way. I don't think Eddie'll be back. She said he'd be gone till the end of the month. Four tickets, then. Henny, you're an angel to have thought of it. . . . I suppose you saw lots of plays in Paris."

"Quite a few."

"Henry," she said, "do you realize that here I am twenty-seven years old and the farthest I've ever traveled is from here to the beach and back again? I didn't even get to Miami that time. You don't know how lucky you are."

"I don't think I'm lucky," I said, hearing the echo in my ear of her voice saying that I was like her kid brother, that she felt practically incestuous when Monty talked of me as "another man."

"I suppose you've seen snow," she said.

"Yes, of course."

"Is it very wonderful?"

"No. It's horrid and wet."

"You're crazy. I know I'd love it. And mountains—have you seen mountains?"

I nodded. "Telcide and I went to Switzerland once for two weeks."

"Telcide?"

"My—friend."

"Tell me about your—friend," she said, grinning.

I tried to tell her a little about Telcide. She listened lazily, still lying stretched across the foot of her bed.

"My darling immoral Henny," she said. "I'm sure you felt terribly guilty about her."

"I guess I did, with part of me."

"Did you offer to marry her?"

"Of course."

"And she'd have none of you?"

"She didn't want a husband."

"And a very wise girl she is." Her voice was mocking in a way I didn't like. But after a moment she went on, in her usual candid tones. "I think I'd like your Telcide. Do you miss her very much?"

"Very little."

"That's not nice of you."

"I'm sure she doesn't miss me at all."

"Of course she does. You're very attractive." She looked at me again, mocking, teasing, and I wanted to cry out, "Stop! Don't you know what you're doing to me!" But I just sat there for a long time, trying to miss Telcide, looking at Ilsa's three bottles of perfume and the silver comb and brush on the clean top of her dressing table. A pair of spectacles lay carelessly by her comb and brush.

"Are these yours?" I asked.

As I looked toward the bed for her answer I realized that she had fallen asleep. Her bright hair and the coral dress made splashes of color on the white spread. From the distance came the restless calling of a train. She didn't hear me as I tiptoed out.

31

We went on Monday to the opening night of the stock company—Monty, Ilsa, Silver, and I. The old Lyceum Theatre is gone now, a modern movie house in its place, but in the old days it used to get the best actors in the country: Mrs. Drew and John Drew, Joseph Jefferson, William Gillette, and all the others. Everybody used to buy tickets by the season. Papa always took a pair, but he seldom used them, because Mamma didn't approve of the theater. The ushers used to stand around and chatter; they seldom had anything to do, since people had the same seats year after year.

I knew that the stock company that was going to introduce Ilsa to the theater must be a Second-rate one, or it wouldn't have been there. None of the good companies played this far south any more. But Ilsa was so pleased with everything that it didn't seem to matter. As she looked around with her blue delighted eyes at the tarnished gold of the boxes, the faded, moth-eaten velvet of the curtain after the asbestos went up, the restless perspiring audience, fanning itself with programs or palm-leaf fans as it waited impatiently for the tawdry curtain to rise, I thought that, in spite of everything, Ilsa was still very like the little girl at the beach who had talked with such vivid interest to the chain gang.

I was so hot in my white linen suit that I thought the curtain would never rise. I looked over at Monty and his face was blanched and wet. When the rest of us got crimson from the heat Monty grew paler and paler, and if you touched him accidentally, his flesh felt cold and clammy. Neither Silver nor Ilsa, in their short-sleeved dresses, seemed as unbearably hot as Monty and I and the mass of heat-flushed humanity surrounding us, but I could see that Silver was becoming as sleepy as I from the oppressive atmosphere. I had spent the afternoon at her house across the river admiring the little boys and the chickens; between them they had run us ragged. And Silver had picked that afternoon to visit the grove, which was not doing too well. She allowed her head to droop down to my shoulder now, and was half asleep when the curtain rose—on *Hamlet*. Well, I thought, it couldn't be a better play, or a worse, for Ilsa's first. Silver sat up with a jerk, furious with herself for having made what she would have termed a spectacle of herself in public by leaning so openly against me, and glued her eyes to the stage. I looked across at Ilsa, who was leaning forward, her eyes brilliant, her lips eagerly parted. Then I slouched down in my seat to watch, trying to diminish my awkward narrow height, bored and disgusted from the first with this production, which I compared most unfavorably in my mind with the plays I had seen in Paris.

Queen Gertrude was not a day under sixty and wore a horrible red wig and a fuchsia-velvet dress that clashed with it; she struggled indifferently through her lines, obviously about to pass out with heat prostration. The king was what I had learned to call an old ham, who should never have been allowed in a pair of tights; nevertheless, he rolled out his lines with a kind of authority, though not until he had walked to the footlights and deliberately looked the house over. Ophelia was a desiccated girl with huge feverish eyes. Her blond hair was unhealthily stringy, and even her make-up couldn't hide the fact that she was ill.

But Hamlet—Hamlet infuriated me just because he was so damn good and I knew he shouldn't have been. He spoke with a distinctly foreign accent; peering down at my program I saw that his name was Franz Josef Werner. Physically, he made a beautiful Hamlet, dressed in inky-black tights, with masses of soft black hair waving back from a high moon-white forehead. His nose was a thin, handsome beak, his lips full and sensuous, his eyes dark and romantic enough to cause at least a minor flutter in every feminine heart in the audience. His fingers were long and had a kind of flexible strength that he evidently knew was a great asset, because he used them as much as possible, or rather more, I thought, than possible. I realized that he was overacting abominably, and yet one couldn't help believing in his performance. In spite of everything I knew to be wrong with him he had the power to make an audience care about him.

When the curtain went down at the intermission I was surprised when Ilsa turned to me and said, "I want to come every night!"

"You really like it?" I asked.

"It's probably nothing compared with the plays you saw in Paris," she said, "though I wouldn't know. But I've never seen words brought to life like this before and it's a wonderful thing."

"Go as often, as you like," Monty said, in a surprisingly tolerant voice. I think he was ashamed of his last Sunday's outburst. "Stock companies don't come down to this hell hole much any more. God knows when we'll get another. Just don't expect me to come with you. Got better things to do with my evenings. If you can persuade Henry, all right with me."

"Would you, Hen?" Ilsa asked eagerly.

"Of course," I answered, equally eagerly, delighted at the prospect of spending so many evenings with her.

The curtain went up again. Hamlet leaped about the stage like a hunted animal, agonizing his way to a most graceful and lingering death in, Horatio's arms. Ilsa clapped until her palms were scarlet, and almost every nose in the audience was blown with emotional violence.

32

The second night's show was a western thriller during which Hamlet played a noble and sharpshooting cowboy. Even Ilsa couldn't help laughing at the ludicrous foreign accent, though after the first moment we somehow forgot it and all shrieked and cheered when he finally flung the villain over an embankment.

"You really don't mind coming with me, Henny, do you?" she asked.

"Of course not. What a silly question," I said.

"It isn't just—just being frivolous. Although I'm much more frivolous than you think I am. But I do have a particular reason for wanting to see things and have fun right now. I don't mean to sound mysterious. I'll probably have to tell you about it soon."

The third night was *Hamlet* again. I had managed to get seats in the center of the front row, and before the first speech I realized that Franz Josef Werner had spotted Ilsa. I was miserable with mortification because he so obviously directed his entire performance at her; people were staring at us. But Ilsa seemed completely unembarrassed. I wondered if she realized what he was doing; heaven knows I should have given her credit for that much perspicacity.

After the performance we stopped in the drugstore next door to the theater for sodas. As I was paying the check I paused to buy some cigarettes, and bumped headlong into Franz Josef Werner, who was buying cold cream.

We both apologized profusely, and, gauche as a schoolboy in spite of my backstage experience with Telcide and her friends. I stared at him standing there in his beautifully tailored linen suit, and stammered. "We—we enjoyed your performance very much, Mr. Werner."

Ilsa had come up and was standing beside me. "Especially Hamlet. Thank you very much for Hamlet, Mr. Werner. It was beautiful."

His mobile actor's face flushed with pleasure. In a spontaneous gesture he reached out and clasped Ilsa's hand. "I am so happy. You do not know how happy that makes me. You—you have come every night, have you not?"

"Yes," she said, withdrawing her hand thoughtfully and putting it in her pocket.

"You don't mind that I noticed you?"

"Why should I mind?"

"You are coming again tomorrow?"

"Yes."

"Ah. Would you and the gentleman perhaps care to come backstage for a moment after the performance and see me in my dressing room?"

"We'd be delighted."

"Splendid! I will see you tomorrow night, then!" He bowed and left us, forgetting his cold cream.

33

The play the next night was a violent and rococo tragedy about Cardinal Wolsey. Mr. Werner met us at the dressing-room door after the performance, still in his costume and make-up. He was perspiring under his grease paint and the heavy filthy costume that reeked of cleaning fluid, but he bowed to me with old-fashioned courtesy and kissed Ilsa's hand in the grand manner. Her eyebrows went up, and she grinned.

He waved his long fingers at a dilapidated chaise longue covered with tattered brown-and-green chintz, and we sat down.

"Couldn't you take off some of that crimson velvet, Mr. Werner?" Ilsa asked.

"Dear lady," he said, bowing again, "with your permission I should be most grateful." He retired behind a screen, and emerged pulling a Chinese-silk bathrobe about him. It was wiled with make-up and quite threadbare, but it must once have been very beautiful, and I was reminded somehow of Dr. Brandes in his riding habit.

"Perhaps you would forgive me if I take off some of this grease paint?" he asked.

"Please do," Ilsa said, and laughed. "It makes me hot to look at you."

His long fingers plunged into a tin of paint-stained cold cream which he spread with slow delicate strokes over his face. As he rubbed it off with a torn scrap of soft linen his own pale complexion began to show under the ruddy coloring.

"This is quite fascinating, Mr. Werner," Ilsa said. "I'd never even seen a play until I saw you do *Hamlet* last Monday, and to get behind the scenes like this is an added and unexpected bit of excitement."

"I hope"—he smoothed more cold cream onto his face and neck—"that you did not consider it an impertinence of me to ask you to come back to my dressing room."

"Not at all," Ilsa said. "We were delighted and grateful."

"You see," Mr. Werner went on, "I could not help noticing you several times in the audience. Perhaps you realized last night that I was playing for you, especially for you?" His dark eyes smouldered as he wiped off the cold cream.

Ilsa laughed again. "Yes, I realized."

—So she did see, I thought. I should have known she would.

"It is so rare in these insufferable times"—Mr. Werner went over to the cracked and rust-stained washbasin and sloshed water over his face—"to find even one person in an audience who appreciates the art of acting, and I could tell from the light in your eyes, most gracious lady, that you were the one person in a million who understands what the theater, what playing can and should mean. You say you had never been to a play before?"

Ilsa nodded.

"It is all the more to be wondered at and applauded, then. Perhaps may I have your comments?"

"I'd never seen words brought to life like that," Ilsa said. "It was very exciting to me. It gave me a feeling of the power of words, their potentialities, that I'd only guessed at before, never realized. I'm most grateful to you for that."

"Perhaps you should have been an actress," he said. I don't think he realized that she hadn't mentioned his performance. "You have an interesting dark quality to your voice. It might be arresting on the stage. And your speech is so much less—lazy—than most of the speech one hears around here. Would you like to be an actress, perhaps? Has this experience awakened the desire in you?"

"No," Ilsa said, and laughed again. She always laughed a great deal, a free open laugh that expressed for me the objectivity with which she seemed, at any rate, to look on life. But I thought I detected a new note in her laughter tonight, a kind of secret question and-answer quality between the actor and herself. Perhaps it was only imagination on my part. I know I've always had a tendency to read more into her least gesture than she ever intended.

"I'm much too lazy to want to be an actress," she went on. "I don't want to be anything. My father was a naturalist, and though he never once urged me, it would have made him very happy if I'd followed in his footsteps. But I don't want to study nature; I just want to enjoy it. When you've pulled the petals off a flower in order to learn about it, you've destroyed the flower. . . . Henny here"—she nodded over at me—"would like me to take music seriously, to practise scales and finger exercises and become boring and intense about it. I don't want to take anything seriously, and, of course, there's no point in doing anything if you don't. . . . No, the height of my ambition at the moment is to see mountains and snow."

"Ah!" Mr. Werner exclaimed. "You should see my birth place, then! I was born in a chalet in the Bavarian Alps. My father was a famous Viennese opera star; my mother a Bavarian peasant girl. I was," he said, "what you call a child of love. My mother kept me until I was fourteen; then I was sent to Vienna where my father introduced me to life and the theater. Only you, dear lady, perhaps can imagine what it must mean to me to have to play in a theater like this, and before such audiences! What it must mean to one who has played in all the great cities of Europe to be forced to use a dressing room like this. Would you," he said, taking two silver brushes and smoothing his masses of curly dark hair, "would you and your husband do me the honor of coming back to the hotel with me and perhaps having a little supper?"

"I'm afraid we forgot to introduce ourselves," Ilsa said. "This is Henry Porcher, a kind of brother-in-law of mine by marriage. I am Ilsa Brandes." Then she added, as though as an afterthought, "Mrs. Woolf."

"But how unpardonably discourteous of me!" the actor exclaimed, rising and pacing about the room in what seemed to be real distress. "I simply assumed—"

I don't know exactly what he *did* assume at that point, but I knew from the way he looked at us that it was quite far from the truth. I flushed painfully. Ilsa saw my embarrassment, and put her hand lightly over mine.

"My husband doesn't care much for the theater," she said, "so Mr. Porcher has been kind enough to indulge my whim by coming with me. We're like brother and sister—"

I wished she wouldn't keep harping on that; how I wished she'd stop!

"—we've known each other forever—but Henry has traveled—he lived in Paris for several years—while I've never been farther from this town than to the beach, where I was born."

"Ah, Paris!" Mr. Werner murmured. "Paris! You loved Paris, of course?"

"Yes," I said, conscious only of the excitement, the in-love-with-life-ness that seemed to have awakened in Ilsa.

"Perhaps you would consider having supper with me anyhow?" he asked.

Ilsa looked over at me. I didn't shake my head, as I wanted to, because I knew that if I did she would accept promptly. So I simply looked blank and watched a stain on the wall as though I hadn't seen her looking toward me.

"Why don't you and Henry both come back to my husband's house!" she said suddenly. "I'm sure he'd enjoy it."

"That seems like a great imposition, Mrs. Woolf."

"Not at all—if you'd like to come."

"I can think of nothing that would give me greater pleasure. I have always had a burning desire to enter a real Southern home."

"I'm not sure that's what you'll be entering," Ilsa said, "but you're welcome to enter. In the drawing room there's a marble group of Iago and Othello that I'm sure will give you great pleasure."

She and Franz Werner laughed heartily. Then she turned to me. "Hen, would you go across the street and phone Monty—just to make sure everything's all right? You know what I mean."

I knew what she meant. But Monty was at home and his voice as he answered the phone was quite steady and agreeable.

"Oh, hey, Henry. How was the show?"

"Fine," I said. "You know what happened, Monty?"

"Unh unh, what?"

"The actor who played Hamlet—you remember—"

"Uh huh."

"We bumped into him in the drugstore—"

"You don't say—"

"—and he asked us to come backstage and see him—"

"I wondered what all you'd been doing."

"—and he wanted us to go to the hotel and have supper with him, but Ilsa suggested that he come back to your house, if it was all right with you, because she thought you might like to meet him, and he's never been inside a southern home, so she asked me to ask you if it was all right." I sounded like a nervous fool and I knew it.

But Monty's voice was still agreeable. "Sure, it's all right with me, Henry. You come right on out and I'll dig up a bottle of something. Ilsa'll have to root in the kitchen. Mattie Belle's been in bed and asleep for hours. I been seeing a man about my hounds. Ira'll have kennels finished end of the week and I can have my hounds Monday. I'm right pleased about it."

"Oh, good," I said vaguely. "Well, we'll be right on out. Good-bye, Mont."

"Good-bye, Henry." We hung up.

34

Rather to my surprise, Monty and Franz Josef Werner got on very well. They drank up a couple of pints of corn liquor while Ilsa and I had ginger ale, and we all ate quantities of ham sandwiches. Werner talked incessantly, obviously delighted with his audience. Ilsa lay sprawled on the bamboo chaise longue, but her eyes were flaming with excitement. From time to time Monty looked at her, the old admiration reawakening in his gaze.

Franz Werner said to Monty, waving his newly filled glass and splashing corn liquor down his shirt, "My dear sir, with your appearance and your manner you are wasted here. You belong in the great capitals of Europe—Vienna, Berlin, Copenhagen, Budapest, Paris—"

Monty sighed heavily into his drink. "Paris. Mm. Always wanted to travel. Henry here knows Paris."

"Ah, Paris," Mr. Werner breathed. "I was born in Paris. My father was one of the principal actors at the Comédie Française, my mother the daughter of a noble English family. Of course, they would not countenance the marriage—"

Ilsa and I looked at each other. For a moment a vague shadow went over the actor's face; then he went on, with a commendably brave flourish, "and so I remained a child of love. I am told," he added with a smile which to me was amusingly naïve, "that children of love have an advantage that so-called normal children can never enjoy."

Monty refilled their glasses. Ilsa went out to the kitchen to make more sandwiches. As soon as she had slipped through the rice portieres

Monty took her glass, emptied it into the brass bucket of sea oats in the fireplace, and filled it up with corn liquor, grinning to himself like a pleased child.

"I have heard that this is a noble climate for consumptives," Franz Werner said, swallowing the burning corn as though it were water.

Monty nodded, a gleam suddenly coming into his dull eyes. "Have a friend who makes his living out of the consumptives who come here. Come by boat or train?"

"Boat."

"Notice a funny old fellow standing at the foot of the gangplank, with a long fishing rod?"

"Now that I think back I believe I do recollect such a man."

Ilsa came in with a plate of sandwiches. She smiled at the sound of Werner's labored, elaborate speech.

Monty went on. "Well, this fellow, he measures the passengers on his pole by guesswork as they come down the gangplank, and when he sees one who looks especially ill he makes a coffin to fit."

"Holy Mother," said Franz Werner, "I hope he hasn't made one for me. I am so sensitive to the power of suggestion that I am sure if anyone made me a coffin I would immediately oblige by dying."

"I didn't know you knew that old ghoul, Monty," Ilsa said. "Father used to tell me about him."

"See him at Togni's bar," Monty mumbled unwillingly.

"Oh." Ilsa put the plate of sandwiches down between the actor and Monty, and reached for her glass. She didn't smell it or even raise it to her lips, but went over to one of the long windows and threw it out. "You know I don't trust that stuff of Togni's, Mont," she said, and poured herself a glass of ice water. She filled it too full and some of it spilled onto the table, but she didn't notice, so I pulled out my handkerchief and wiped it up. She gave me a peculiar look, then turned to Franz Werner. "Father told me about one forehanded invalid who brought his own coffin with him, and after a year or so sent it back North, filled with oranges. Most of them aren't so lucky, poor creatures. . . . I should think it would be rather damp down here for people with lung trouble. How did you get going on the subject, anyhow?"

"One of the young ladies in our company, our Ophelia, you remember," Franz Werner said, "is suffering from a bad cough, and though she is the queen of *kvetch* we are unquiet about her health."

"What's *kve—kvetch*?" Monty asked.

"I suppose it is what you would call ham acting. Literally translated, it means 'push.' About our Ophelia, we were wondering whether, after our tour closes, she ought to come back here."

"I'm sure a drier climate would be better," Ilsa said. "Father always thought so. It's so flat here—have you noticed the way mold gets on things?"

The actor nodded.

"I should think Arizona—or Switzerland—some place with less humidity. The air here often seems heavy and oppressive to people unless they were born here and love it, as I do."

"You are very kind to advise me," Franz Werner said. "I wonder, Mrs. Woolf, if I could beg a tremendously large favor of you and your husband—"

"What is it?"

"Tomorrow is Friday—there is no matinée. I understand you have a famous beach here—so wide and hard that many cars can drive on it at once, side by side. It would give me the most extraordinary pleasure if we could take a little excursion together—all four of us—and at my expense—of course. Perhaps we could hire a car."

Ilsa tensed and said nothing. She was waiting for Monty to speak, and I noticed how she relaxed with relieved pleasure when he said, waving his glass, and bowing waveringly with what he considered old southern courtesy, "Splendid! Take our car, of course. Wife has a house at the beach—belonged to her father, distinguished naturalist, John Brandes, native of our own State—" His voice rumbled pompously. Ilsa stifled a grin.

"Ah, yes, Brandes," Franz Werner murmured politely.

"Could have an early meal there. Time do you have to back to the theater, Werner?"

"Seven-thirty at the very outside I like to be in my dressing room."

"Can be arranged," Monty said, with what was a great deal of enthusiasm for him. I knew he was pleased to have found a drinking companion of whom Ilsa seemed to approve. "You free, Henry?" he asked. "You not needed at the mill?"

"No," I said. "I'm not. I'm no earthly use there. I just sit around and do nothing all day, and Papa gets mad if he comes in and finds me reading. I'll get away."

We arranged to meet in the morning. I set off for home on foot. Ilsa was to drive Franz Werner back downtown to his hotel. As she stood under the street lamp, the light flickering with soft gold and amber shadows as the wind shook the green palm branches in front of it, rattling them like paper in the night air, her face lit more from an inner radiance than from the moving light, I thought that she had never looked so beautiful.

Out of the night a train wailed.

"Listen!" Ilsa said, holding up her hand.

"What?" Werner asked.

"The train. It's the most restless, searching noise in the world, a train calling like that. The way I feel."

"The way I feel, too," Werner said.

35

The day at the beach was a tremendous success. Werner was as pleased as a child with the house and the water. Ilsa drove the car onto the beach from the main road and he made her drive him up and down the beach, up and down, and then spent hours running in and out of the waves, and collecting shells which he insisted on tying up in his handkerchief to carry back with him. He had obviously never been much out of the city, which made the story of the childhood spent in the mountains of Bavaria questionable, to say the least. As for Paris—I didn't think he had a French father and an English mother. But that he was a child of love I didn't doubt for a moment.

It was a freak sort of day, hot and oppressive, but beautiful in that sultry sullen way I have never seen anywhere else—a few hours of dead calm and brilliant sun, then a few hours of tearing wind and solid rain. As the first drops of rain hit the beach they made round dents in the sand, tiny, where the beach was hard, large as a silver dollar on the loose grains of the dunes.

The changes in the day were so complete and so rapid that after we went into the house, when it began to rain, we kept turning toward the windows to watch. One minute the horizon would be curving out to infinity, the way it can do only on the ocean; then everything would close in quickly, with just a brief moment in between when you seemed to be looking from inside a closed dark globe out into the sun. Horizons disappeared completely; nothing was left but grayness, which seemed so close you could touch it, but which still stretched out without end.

As I watched out of a window, then, the idea of space seemed very confusing; there was no space in sight; the gray couldn't be placed as near or far. Suddenly in a spot I could almost have touched with my hand a moment before, a shrimping boat appeared. There was no ocean beneath it or beyond it—just a boat floating in grayness. Then it melted away, and I wasn't really sure I had seen it at all. A few minutes later the sun was pouring over the water as if it hadn't been washed almost out of existence.

Monty had brought his records and phonograph. We were all so full of sea air and broiled mullet, grits, and greens, and a kind of excitement because Werner was something so out of, so alien to, our way of life, and we to his, that we were seized with a kind of childish gaiety and danced by turns with Ilsa until she was breathless. Werner was a magnificent dancer, smooth and intimate as only a Continental can be; when she was dancing with him she seemed as light as the spindrift that flew off the waves and scudded along the sand.

At six-thirty we climbed into the car, laughing like children, and set off for home, singing all the way. Monty invited Werner to come and have dinner with them the next day between the matinée and the evening performance, and we all planned to go down to the beach after the performance at night and have a midnight swim, and perhaps dance a little. Ira would be through with the kennels and could go down ahead of us and boil us some crawfish for supper. The company was staying for a second week, so Werner didn't have to catch a train in the morning, and we could sleep all the next day.

I could tell that Monty was terribly pleased with himself at his lavishness in dispensing hospitality. He was showing off and talking big, as he always had done when he was little. But somehow I could no longer hate him; I was only sorry for him, though I was angry at myself for being weak enough to feel pity.

I couldn't tell what Ilsa was thinking, as she sat next to Monty, relaxed, her head thrown back against the seat, singing in her smoky dissonant voice. But somehow I was more jealous at the way she looked back over the seat and smiled at Franz Werner than I had ever been at any way she had looked at Monty.

After a while she began to sing the rosy-bush song. I didn't join in with her, but let her sing it through to the end, alone.

I wish I was
A red red rosy bush,
A-blooming by-ee
The banks of the sea,
For when my true
Love would come by-ee
He'd pluck an rose
From offen me.
A rosy rose,
A red red rosy bush,
He'd pluck an rose
From offen me.

"What's that?" Franz Werner asked.

"An old song of my grandmother's."

"Would you be gracious enough to sing it once more?"

She sang it through again. When she had finished, Werner said, "Why, it is almost like an old Elizabethan love song. It is one of the most endearing little melodies I have ever heard."

Monty said, "I don't remember it, Ilsa. Why haven't you sung it before?"

"I used to sing it to Brand," she said quietly. "You just didn't listen."

36

It was almost one o'clock Saturday night when we got to the beach. Silver had driven over from across the river for dinner with Papa and me and was coming with us, having sent the children over to Violetta's for the night. Monty had wanted to ask Violetta, but I managed to dissuade him, saying Silver couldn't come then, and anyhow, with Dolph, the car would be too crowded.

None of us was accustomed to staying up that late; Silver got to bed most of the time by nine or nine-thirty, I always went upstairs at ten, though I read in bed, and I don't think even Ilsa or Monty stayed up much after midnight. We were filled again with a sense of excited adventure.

Ira met us with his usual grumpiness. He had prepared a marvelous supper, which we ate ravenously. Then we went upstairs to change to bathing suits. It was a hot sultry night, the kind of damp weather in which nothing ever dries. Our bathing suits were still sticky and wet from the day before, although they had been rinsed out in rain water and had been hanging out all day. The sand, still holding on its surface the penetrating rays of the sun, felt damp and warm under our feet. Great clumps of water hyacinth had come in with the tide and lay sprawled, brown and dead from salt water, on the beach. There was no moon; great jagged knives of lightning ripped the sky down the beach where sand and water joined together at the curl of the horizon, but there was no thunder. The stars were tremendously thick and low; where they hung over the ocean they seemed to be dripping wet and salt-crusted from the water.

The ocean was very quiet. After we had waded out to our waists we were beyond the breakers. The water was warm. Werner ducked himself up and down with naïve pleasure. "In the Bering Sea," he said, "the water is so cold that it collapses your lungs in less than five minutes. No one can live in the Bering Sea." He lay on his back and kicked his long graceful legs that had looked so handsome in Hamlet's tights.

Ilsa was swimming with fast precise strokes out toward the flickering arm of the lightship. After a while she turned and swam back to us, much more slowly. She stood up panting. "There's a terrific undertow tonight. I was afraid there might be."

"You were foolish to swim out that way," Silver said, her little face pale and sphinxlike above the dark moonless water.

"I wanted to test the pull."

"You shouldn't have risked your life to do it."

"I know how to swim, Silver."

"Many strong swimmers have been dragged out and drowned by the undertow."

"I didn't go out that far."

"There's always the danger of a barracuda."

"Really, Silver, I'm here safe and sound. Let's stop caviling about it."

Silver turned away, her face cold and expressionless as always when she was angry. She never raised her voice when she was aroused—perhaps that was one reason why she could be so infuriating. After a few moments she waded in to shore and went back to the house. I could see her shoulders drooping a little forlornly as she went up the long white ramp, her limbs gleaming wetly in the starlight. I wondered if she were missing Eddie. Then I sighed and, with a brotherly sense of duty, followed her to the house. Monty came in while I was dressing. I was sitting on Dr. Brandes' narrow ascetic bed and pulling on my socks.

"Funny kind of room," Monty said. "Like a few more gewgaws myself. Like this when the old boy was alive?"

"Yes," I answered. "Exactly. Where's Werner?"

"He and Ilsa still in the water." Monty pulled off his suit and dropped it on the floor at his feet, where it lay in a salty damp puddle. He took a towel from the one chair, which he had cavalierly appropriated for himself, humming *The Georgia Grind* through his nose. I noticed how white and flabby his body was, and remembered how I had envied his strength and suppleness when I was a kid, having been always ashamed of my own long skinniness.

"That Ira built me the best little old kennels you ever did see," Monty said. "Come along over Monday and see the hounds if you can get away from the mill, Henry."

"How many are you getting?"

"Five. Three grown, two puppies—nine weeks. Funniest little old bastards." He pulled on his shirt and drawers. They were both clumsily patched. I knew that Ilsa would hate to sew. Monty stretched, then reached up and scratched the thick black hair on his chest and under his arms. "Oh, Lord, getting old, getting old," he said. And it was true; he no longer looked young. "Glad to be home, Henry?"

I nodded.

"Have a gay old time in Paris?"

"Pretty gay."

"Hoped I'd get to go there during the war, but neither Eddie or I got to go overseas. Think you'd have gone there if it hadn't of been for the war? Think you'd ever have stayed there?

"I don't know."

"Lot of girls, huh? Wine, women, and song? Kind of a serious feller, aren't you, Henry; student? Well, how's about

A book of verses underneath the bough,
A loaf of bread, a jug of wine, and thou
—something—beside me in the wilderness,
Ah, wilderness were Paradise enow.

How's that, hey? Guess where I learned that? From a Minorcan feller down at Togni's. That surprises you, hey? Pretty good, i'n't it?"

"Yes," I said.

"Nice girls in Paris? Nice little armfuls? Or don't you like that sort of thing?"

"Oh, I don't know," I said.

"Was that why you stayed over there so long, hey?"

I didn't say anything. I went over to the damp-spotted mirror. My face peered out at me, wavering and distorted, as though I were looking at myself from endless leagues under the sea. I started to comb my salt wet hair. My body felt sticky and good from the salt water, and cool.

"Not so bad here, you know," Monty said. "I could show you a good time. Want to come out with Werner and me tomorrow night? Come to Togni's?"

"I'm going over to Silver's for supper," I said.

"Okay, Henry, some other time. You just let me know when you want me to show you some fun."

I was disgusted with him.—You poor fool—I thought—how can you have so little taste? I knew that this was his way of apologizing for having created a scene about me that Sunday but he couldn't have picked a worse way. And I was angrier still that he was was taking Werner down to Togni's with him Monday night after the show; it seemed as if they were both betraying Ilsa. I was angriest of all because Werner was still in the ocean with Ilsa. I forgot that I had come back to the house because of Silver, that I had intended to go in to her as soon as I was dressed. Without saying anything to Monty, I slammed out of the room and down the stairs.

Ira was bending over the piano, reaching in and doing something to the hammers.

"Hey, Henry Porcher," he said, scowling at the piano.

"Hey, Ira."

"Half these keys stuck. Don't know why Ilsa keeps it here when she never uses it. Thought if I shifted the lamp down toward those lower notes might help. You been gone a right long time, Henry Porcher, away from your good home and kin."

"Yes, it was a long time."

"Back for good now?"

"I guess so."

"You don't look much different."

"I feel different."

"Don't think you'll ever change much. You'll go on being about the same Henry Porcher till the day you die. Glad to be home?"

"Very," I said, thinking that Ira, too, never changed.

"I used to think you might be kind of like Johnny Brandes when you growed up, but you turned out in another direction. I don't know is it too bad or is it just as well. That actor feller looks kind of to be like him in a black sort of way. . . . You have a good time all these years?"

"Oh, yes, I guess so, thank you, Ira," I said. "Did you?"

"I've had my ups and downs like everybody else." He bit off a plug of tobacco. "Sure have missed Johnny Brandes and Ilsa. Most fun I've had since I've been alone's a couple of years I spent rum running."

"You were a rum runner!" I exclaimed.

"Sure. Over at the island off from July Harbour. Good place for it. Took them government chaps a long time to get wise to us. Then there was a fight, a regular sea battle, fire everywhere you could see, on the island, and boiling, oil and kerosene on the water. A lot of men got killed that night."

"Did you kill any?"

"I don't know, Henry. I used my gun like the rest, but whether I got anybody or not I don't know, there was so much scurrying about. I remember being thrown out of a motorboat and swimming out in the open water with the tide pulling me out to sea, and suddenly a whole sheet of flame come at me over the ocean, so I ducked and swam under water until I thought my ears would burst or my heart split me open, it was pounding so. But I didn't dare come up as long as I could see that glare above me. When finally I saw a dark patch I come up and breathed and then went down again. I had to do that about half a dozen times before I got out of the fire. Then I was so far out to sea I could hardly see land. I swam down the coast and then I managed to get to shore. When I pulled myself onto dry sand I just dropped and lay there until the sun came around twice before I could get strength and breath enough to crawl back."

"Golly," I said.

"See them kennels I built for Ilsa's husband?" he asked.

"I'm going over to see them Monday when the dogs come."

"You think Ilsa's happy?" he asked suddenly.

"I—I don't know," I answered.

"Seems to me something's been troubling her these past months," he said, opening the smallest blade to his knife and scratching inside his ear.

"What?" I asked.

"That's what I been asking you. Other day she came out to talk to me while I was building them kennels, and she tripped and fell flat smack. Said she felt kind of dizzy. Not like Ilsa to trip over things. You think maybe could be she's going to have another baby?"

"No," I said. "It wouldn't be that."

"Didn't think it would be. Didn't think she could, after she was so sick that time. I purely hate to have her peely wolly."

"Yes," I said, immediately beginning to be anxious.

37

I turned as Silver came downstairs. In the warm muted light of lamp and candle her pale little face glowed gently; only the sudden dark eyebrows sharpened the soft blur of it.

"I thought you were still in the water," she said.

"No. Everybody's out now except Ilsa and Franz Werner."

"Oh."

"Let's go sit on a sand dune," I said, "and wait for the others."

We climbed to the top of one of the highest dunes, white in the starlight like the snow-covered hills that Ilsa wanted to see. The tiny grains of sand were cold under us. The stars were so quiet and serene that it was difficult to feel troubled about anything.

"Look at the stars," I said to Silver. "They never seem so dense and so close except over the ocean."

"I don't like them." She wrapped her arms about her knees and shivered.

"What?"

"I don't like stars."

"But why?"

"Oh, I don't know, Brother. They seem to give me such a sense of—of futility—I mean, when you really think about them, they're so immense out there and so far away and so long ago—they make us so small and so pointless—and kind of deserted by God. . . . I don't like them. . . . They're impersonal and cruel . . . and then they seem sort of like little points of knives pricking through that black old sky and you never know when one of the knives is going to go piercing right through the night and right into your heart."

"Good heavens, what a thing to say!"

"That's the way I feel." She rubbed her little face, pale and luminous, against her knees; in the starlight she looked very childlike, all the soft womanly lines washed from her face.

"I never think of them like that," I said. "I just see them as being small and beautiful and exciting—stars are very exciting to me—but not dangerous—not any more dangerous than the Easter lilies when they come out like stars all over the fields."

The sand of the dune felt comfortable beneath me tonight; I began to feel that I was home again, accepted once more by my land. The surf came in to the shore with a low rumble; even though the breakers were small, swelling and curling over when they were near the shore, lapping against the sand in gentle, whispering crisscrossings, there was an almost subterranean roar to the ocean, steady and loud. I looked beyond the long white lines of the breakers to the quiet swells beyond searching for Ilsa and Franz Werner, but I couldn't see them; if Ilsa had worn a bathing cap it might have caught the light and helped me to find them; but she always went in the ocean bareheaded.

"Are you sleepy?" I asked Silver, waving away a mosquito that had begun to buzz about my head in spite of the lavender oil I was covered with.

She shook her head. "I was at first. I thought while we were eating the crawfish I'd just put my head down in my plate like little Henry Porcher and go to sleep. But I'm wide-awake now."

We sat together for a long time, quietly, more at peace in each other's company than we had ever been when we were children. I had always been fond of Silver because she was my sister; now I found myself at ease with her because she was herself. I realized all at once that it was the repose that Silver gave people that was so wonderful. She would sit silently, her little hands dropped like two small shells in her lap, and if you wanted to talk, she would listen. Sometimes she wouldn't even look at you, but you would know that she was listening, and caring. With Ilsa it was different. She could sit just as quietly, and listen for just as long, but she would be concentrating on you so intently with all the fire of her being that you were filled with a sense of the excitement, the infinite, unlimited potentialities of life. She gave you anything but repose.

I wondered—I wondered what she and Franz Werner were saying to each other all that time in the dark ocean.

❖ ❖ ❖

Then I saw them come out of the waves, and walk, side by side, across the beach and up the long white cement ramp to the house. The actor moved with the panther-like grace that was his greatest asset on the stage.

"That actor," Silver said, and I knew she had seen them and had been watching them, too.

"What about him?"

"I don't mean to be nasty, Brother, but—"

"But what?"

"Maybe I oughtn't to say it."

"Go on. If you've started you may as well finish."

"I know. . . . I don't want to sound like Violetta."

"You couldn't. Go on."

"I don't like the way he's been looking at Ilsa. I don't like the way she's been looking at him."

"You're just imagining things," I said uncomfortably.

"Henry, be honest. Haven't you noticed?"

"I've noticed that they like each other. And that Monty and Werner get on. And that's a good thing. It keeps Monty away from that dreadful Togni's." I thought I could change the subject by getting her angry over Monty, but she wouldn't fall into the trap.

"I don't know anything about what Monty does. Whatever it is—*if* it is anything—it doesn't give Ilsa an excuse to—"

"To what?"

"To—to do anything that might cause gossip."

"After all, Silver, it was Monty's idea, coming here tonight."

"Oh, you'd stick up for her through thick and thin, wouldn't you, goosey?"

"I don't think she needs sticking up for."

"Henry, tell me something."

"What?"

"What do you see in her? What do you see in that Ilsa?"

I didn't say anything, but sat staring out across the ocean to where the night bent down at the horizon and became one with the wayward, irresistible water. From the house the sound of the piano and voices singing crashed suddenly across the darkness.

"Brother, I don't understand," Silver said. "You've always been crazy about her. Why? What for? She doesn't give a hoot about you. I don't believe she really thought of you once the whole time you were away, and that's all your letters were full of, asking about Ilsa. Whenever I saw her and told her you'd sent your love she'd always just smile, only you'd never know what it meant or what she was smiling at, because I'm sure I don't see anything particularly funny about your sending her your love from across the ocean, and then she'd say to thank you and send you hers."

"You never sent it to me."

"I had other things to write about. When we cabled you about little Henry Porcher being born we didn't get a letter from you for over a month. That wasn't nice of you, Brother."

"I know it wasn't."

"But, Brother, it's not good for you to go on being crazy about someone this way when there isn't any point to it. It just makes you turn into a kind of nothing—a nobody! You never think of anything just yourself. You're always wondering what she'd think. Everything you do is in relation to her. And she isn't worth it. She simply isn't good enough for you just in general, and for you to waste yourself on—"

This was a long and impassioned speech for Silver, and proved, if I needed any proof, how deeply she cared for me. But all I could feel then was anger. I cut in furiously, "You're wasting your breath."

"It's not that I don't like Ilsa, goosey," she said. "After all, she's my sister-in-law, and I'm fond of her. And if it'll make you any happier I'll admit she's got a funny kind of thing that makes you enjoy being with her—she kind of seems more alive than other people, and she makes you seem more alive, too. But it's nothing she does or says. You can't put your finger on it. Sometimes I think it's black magic. After all, Brother, I know her better than you do. *I* haven't been away for the past eight years. I've seen her. I've seen the kind of wife she's been to Monty."

"Have you seen the kind of husband he's been to her?"

"Oh, I might have known you'd say something like that!" she cried.

"What about the time she lost the baby? You were there."

"I never should have talked to you about that. I don't know what got into me. And *she* certainly shouldn't have said anything about it—*ever.*"

"Oh, for mercy's sake, Sister, I told you it was because I asked her. She never accused Monty, but the fact remains that it was his fault. What if she'd died?"

"Maybe it would be better if she had."

"Silver!"

"You always stick up for her," she said defensively. "You're sticking up for her now about this actor. I think you're crazy. I should think it would make you furious."

—But it does, you fool, it does—furious and jealous. I lay there on the cold white sand of the dune, and jealousy oozed out of me, hot and sticky, like blood from a wound.

"There's no use arguing with you," Silver said. "There's no use saying it's her fault about Monty because you wouldn't believe it, you're so infatuated with her."

"No, I wouldn't believe it. And if you want to talk about infatuations, what about you and Monty? What about the way you've always gone on about him?"

She sat up straight. "At least I *know* Monty, Brother. And you forget. I'm married to Eddie and I love him—when he's here for me to love." Her mouth twisted and she put her head down on her knees again.

I reached over and touched the nape of her neck where her sun-blanched hair was knotted. "I'm sorry, Sister. Let's not quarrel."

"No. Let's not quarrel," she said. She reached over and took my hand, and we sat there together until the phonograph music, that had been an unlistened-to background to our words, stopped, calling attention to itself by its cessation. I turned and looked back at the house.

38

After a moment the door opened and yellow light poured out onto the stone ramp and the dark night-green of palmettos and scrub. The Spanish bayonettes were in bloom, wonderful chimes of flowers, like carillons sounding on the sweet dark air.

Ilsa stood in the doorway, Werner and Monty behind her. She raised her hands to her mouth and called, "Hoo—oo! Henny! Silver!"

"Hoo—oo!" I called back. "We're here!"

They left the house, shut the door behind them, came down the ramp, and clambered over the dunes toward us.

"What all you been doing?" Monty asked.

"Oh, talking," Silver answered.

"What about?"

"Oh, you."

"You come walk down the beach and tell me what you were saying about me." He reached out a hand and pulled her up. She slipped her hand out of his and stood for a moment, stamping to get the stiffness out of her legs and the sand out of her skirts, before she followed him down to the water's edge.

Ilsa flung herself onto the dune. She never sat down carefully, like Silver and Violetta and I suppose most other women, but threw herself with abandon into its impersonal (but somehow for her, personal) embrace. This was her home, and it was as like her as she was like it. Franz Werner stretched his agile and graceful body beside her, while I sat up stiffly because I no longer felt welcome or accepted. We didn't say anything, and it seemed to me that a hundred words hung above us like a cloud, waiting to be spoken. And I thought that I was the thing that was keeping them from being spoken, so I got up and stood on the top of the dune, awkwardly. It was nearly morning. The stars were still bright, but the night and the ocean were no longer lost together in a dark embrace; they were separate, mutable, divided.

"What's the matter, Henry?" Ilsa asked.

"I—I think I'll go back to the house. I'm awfully sleepy." I waited a moment for her to tell me not to go, to sit down again; but she didn't say a word. Under the low breathing of the ocean I seemed to hear hers, a little too quick. I turned away, but before I had gone more than a few steps there came a shout from Monty, and then a scream from Silver. Ilsa sat up.

"Henry!" Silver called. "Ira!" Then, "Ilsa! Ilsa! Come quick!"

Swift as a gull Ilsa flung herself over the dune and across the sand to them. Werner and I followed as quickly as we could. Monty was sitting on the wet sand near a clump of salt-blackened water hyacinth, holding his ankle. Silver stood by him, her hands clasped in terror.

"Give me your handkerchief and a pencil, Franz," Ilsa said sharply as we came up. He handed them to her; she tore a strip from the handkerchief and made a tourniquet below Monty's knee, fastening it with the pencil. "Now your knife," she said.

Werner reached into his pocket and handed her a penknife. As she unclasped the blade she turned to Silver and said, "For heaven's sake, don't agonize so, Silver. It isn't a tragedy. He'll be all right." She knelt down beside Monty and pulled off his shoe and his sock. "Strike me a match, someone," she said.

Before I could reach for mine Werner was kneeling beside her, holding a cigarette lighter. Just over Monty's ankle I saw two tiny red dots, and knew what had happened. A moccasin had come in on the hyacinth; Monty had probably kicked the clump, and the snake had struck at him defensively. I looked at the hyacinth clusters, which looked like masses of snakes twined together, anyhow, but could see no sleek dark body moving.

"Did you see the snake, Silver? Where did it go?" Ilsa asked.

"I don't know—it glided away so quickly—"

"It didn't touch you?"

"No—" Silver's voice was pale and wavery like a reflection in moving water.

Ilsa said, the blade of the knife poised just over Monty's ankle, "Silver, go back to the house and get Father's bed ready for him.

Then put on a kettle of hot water." As Silver hesitated, she said, "At once, please."

As soon as Silver turned she bent very close over Monty's ankle and cut two deep crosses, one over each red dot. For a moment she squeezed with her fingers; then, as the blood didn't come freely enough to suit her, she bent down and put her lips to the cuts to suck the venom out. Werner and I stood watching her, useless, not offering to help. At the edge of the ocean a streak of light began to show.

What Ilsa sucked from the cuts she had made she spat out onto the sand. After a while, not looking at us, but still bending close over the cuts, she said, "Henny, have you a handkerchief? A clean one?"

"Yes," I said, "it's clean," and gave it to her. She bound the place and said, "Now if the two of you can make a chair we can get him back to the house."

"I can walk," Monty said. It was the first time he had spoken. He had sat there on the wet sand, watching Ilsa through the long fringes of his eyelashes, looking frightened and pitiable.

"Don't be absurd," Ilsa said. "Franz and Henry will carry you."

We Stood together stupidly; she had to show us how to clasp our hands so that they made a chair for Monty to sit on; she half lifted him onto it, then stalked on ahead of us to the house. Monty was very heavy; it seemed an unhealthy weight. We carried him in silence, except for Werner's saying quietly, "You have a wonderful woman for a wife, Woolf."

In the bedroom Silver was walking nervously about. "Is he all right, is it all right?" she asked as we came in.

"Sure. Fine," Monty said.

Ilsa came upstairs with a kettle of steaming water. Silver turned to her. "Where's Ira? I couldn't find him anywhere."

"He's gone off on his own business," Ilsa answered sharply "After all, he's not a servant." Although she tried to hide it, the hand holding the kettle trembled a little from nervous reaction. "Go on out and I'll undress him," she said.

"Christ!" Monty yelled. "Beg your pardon, Silver, Ilsa. But what the hell do you think I am? Undress myself."

"Do you mind going?" Ilsa said to us again.

We left.

39

After a while she came downstairs and ran up the flag for Ira, saying that Monty was asleep in her father's bed. She took one look at Silver's white tired face and sent her upstairs, then took out a book and sat down in her father's big chair at the table. I could tell that she wasn't reading, although from time to time she turned the pages. Franz Werner excused himself and went to walk on the beach. Standing at the window, I watched day come, the light over the horizon widen, the ocean turn from black to the gray on a gull's wing to its own mordant shade of blue, as the stars dimmed and went out, and the sun rose in a sea of flame, spreading a deep flush over sand and sea and sky. Down by the ocean Werner was a small, dark silhouette, bending at the edge of the water and turning over the shells.

"Henny," Ilsa said abruptly, "are Franz's eyes brown? They are aren't they? Very dark brown, almost black?"

"No," I said. "They're blue. Deep blue."

"Oh. I forgot for a moment. Stupid."

I thought that it was a strange thing for her to forget, and stranger for her to have asked, if she had forgotten.

"Is anything the matter?" I asked.

"What do you mean?" Her voice and scowl were ferocious.

"Nothing—only I thought maybe you hadn't been feeling well lately. Ira was wondering—"

"Ira had better mind his own business. And so had you."

"I'm sorry. But is anything the matter?"

"No. Certainly not. . . . I wish Ira'd come back and look at Monty's ankle. I want to go home to Brand—she'll worry. She's almost as bad a worry wart as you are. . . . I'm sure Monty's all right. There's no discoloring and it's not swelling, but I want Ira to look at it and make sure, now that it's daylight. I couldn't see very well in the dark."

As she could perfectly well go and look herself, now that day had come, I knew there was something not exactly right with that argument, but I was too tired to be able to put my finger on what was wrong and I wouldn't have dared dispute her anyhow. She rose and stood listening. A moment later Ira came in.

"I seen the flag," he said. "What you want? Something wrong?"

"Yes," she said. "A moccasin bit my husband. I think I got all the venom out but I want you to look at it."

"All right. Come on upstairs," he said, and went up ahead of her. I waited by the window until they came down.

"He's fine," she said. "Ira said I did all right. We'll stay over till tomorrow, I think, though. Franz says it's all right with him. If you need to get back I can drive you to the bus."

"I don't need to get back."

"Good. I'm going over to the nearest filling station to phone so Brand won't be worried. I won't tell her about her father—just say we're staying over." She went out to the car.

I noticed on the way back to town the next morning that she seemed to be driving more carefully than usual. It was, of course, necessary to drive very slowly and cautiously on the rut road that led up to the house, avoiding the soft shoulders of sand in which automobile wheels turned futilely as on a treadmill; but even when she got to the hard oyster-shell Beach Road she didn't relax and drive with her usual swift abandon but held the steering wheel in a tense grip and sat leaning forward, staring through the windshield.

We dropped Silver off, crossed the river, took the actor downtown to his hotel, and then went back to the Woolfs'. I could walk home from there. But after she had taken Monty up to bed to sleep until his hounds came, after she had scolded and comforted Brand, who burst into frightened tears when she heard what had happened, Ilsa turned to me.

"Henry, will you do something for me?"

"Of course. What?"

"I have to go downtown again. Stay here with Brand, will you? The poor baby worried herself sick in spite of my phoning—had us all drowned or murdered or lying dead in a ditch with the car on top of us. I hate to leave her again, and I'll probably be a couple of hours. I usually give her lessons in the morning. Would you mind having her read to you? Or whatever you like."

"I should be delighted," I said.

"Bless you, Henny. I shall feel much easier if I have to take longer than I expect. Mattie Belle is sweet and kind, but I'd feel happier if you were here—in case Monty should want anything, too."

"Of course," I said. "I'll just go phone Papa and tell him I can't be at the mill."

While I was phoning Papa—who fumed and sputtered, but didn't mean a thing by it, as I had learned to know, because in his own way Papa was almost as weak as I was—Ilsa ran upstairs to change. As she came down I saw her stuffing into her pocket the spectacles I had seen on her dressing table.

40

Papa was still pretty mad with me when I got home just before dinner that night, and I had to stick to the mill for the next few days. I heard from one of the men there that Werner had got into trouble by socking a barber downtown because he had cut his hair too short, and Monty had had to rescue him by taking them both to Togni's. Luckily, the barber went there a lot and knew Monty well, and I guess for once Ilsa was grateful for Togni. I knew it must have made Monty pleased as punch to play the noble host and rescuer.

Some of the girls who worked in the mill office had gone to see *Hamlet* and they were all agog when they discovered that I knew Werner. During lunch hour they crowded around me, begging me to get his autograph and pictures for them. I couldn't see what there was about him to get them so excited.

"He makes me think of a black panther," one of the girls said. "You know, terribly frightening, and terribly exciting." I didn't see it. But, then, not everybody felt about Ilsa as I did.

It was Friday before I saw her again. On Wednesday I met Beulah Jackson's mother in the drugstore. She lived next door to Monty and Ilsa and sometimes Beulah played with Brand. I hated the whole family. As usual, Mrs. Jackson cornered me and talked for an hour. The only important thing she said was that she had seen Ilsa at the theater.

"Oh, my, Henry," she said, "she seemed to be enjoying the play so much! I just wish I'd liked it half as well. Didn't understand a word of it, though that man with the foreign accent who took the part of

Cardinal Wolsey was surely gorgeous. You ought to go see it, Henry; it's the kind of thing you'd like, what with your having lived in Paris and everything. Isn't Ilsa a striking-looking woman, though, Henry? With those big eyes and that bright dress, so pretty, and I hear Mrs. Silverton gave it to her, too. Mrs. Silverton sure has been good to her, treating her like her own child, and her no kin at all."

—So—I thought.

She was still going to the theater every night. I wanted to rush over; I was filled with insane jealousy. But what right had I, of all people, to be jealous of anything Ilsa did?

By Friday I couldn't stand it any more. I left the mill after lunch and took the trolley over to Ilsa's. She and Monty weren't in the house; but Mattie Belle told me they were in the yard with the dogs. I went on out.

As I approached I saw Monty pull an envelope out of his pocket and hand it to Ilsa.

"What's this?" I heard him say.

She snatched it out of his hand. "That's mine!" she exclaimed furiously. "How dare you open my mail?"

"Opened it by mistake. Thought it was for me. What does it mean?"

"It's my own business," she said. "The old fool! The fat old fool!"

"Who's a fool?" I asked.

She turned and saw me. "Oh. It's you," she said.

"Yes. . . . I've come to see the hounds." I was momentarily crushed by the ungraciousness of her greeting, although I knew it was only the overflow of her anger at Monty's opening her letter. "Hey, Monty," I said.

"Hey, Henry." He opened the door to the wire enclosure behind which the dogs had been jumping and barking. They came tumbling out now, leaping up at us and almost knocking us down. The two puppies bowled themselves over immediately, all long ears and great clumsy feet that were continually getting in their way. One minute they were chasing their tails around in circles, digging frantically on the way to China, bumping against our legs like battering rams; the next they were flinging themselves down on the ground, tongues lolling, ears dragging in the soft gray sand; a split second of rest, and then up and off again, the limpest, clumsiest, sweetest things I'd ever seen. The littlest one had long silky black ears and a tongue so long that it hung way out on one side of its mouth. I couldn't help laughing as it galumphed about chasing little yellow butterflies and the shadows of birds, falling over those huge feet and rolling limply over and over, then scrambling up and bouncing around again. A cuckoo puppy never looks as though it would grow up into a serious hunter.

After a few minutes of proprietary grinning, Monty put the three full-grown dogs back in the enclosure, but left the puppies out.

"I want to know what that was about," he said to Ilsa.

"What what was about?"

"You know what I mean."

"You saw it." For a brief second I thought that it must have been a letter from Werner. Wild conjectures as to what it might have said raced through my mind. But she went on, "It was just a bill."

"What do you mean by going to the doctor?" His voice was angry and suspicious.

"For heaven's sake, Monty, don't sound so ferocious. My eyes have been bothering me. I don't seem to see so well. I went to him last month and he gave me a pair of glasses. That's what the bill's for."

"Then why didn't you wear the glasses?"

"They didn't do me an atom of good. I could see better without them."

"You'd better go back and tell him so, then."

"I did."

"When?"

"Last Monday."

"Couldn't have gone last Monday. Home all day because of my snake bite."

"I went while you were asleep. Henny stayed in the house with Brand, and so he could go to you if you needed anything."

"Why'd you pick that time to go?"

"I had an appointment," she said wearily.

"What'd he say?"

"Not a damn thing. He doesn't know what's the matter. He tried some more glasses on me, but none of them did any good. He says I'm probably just tired and it'll get better. I don't think he knew what he was talking about. To tell you the truth, I'm worried. I don't like not being able to see. I'd like to go up to Baltimore and talk to the doctor up there who used to write to Father—an eye specialist."

"Do you think he'll see you for free?" Monty asked.

"I certainly wouldn't ask him to."

"Why not?"

"Don't be absurd, Monty." She turned to me. "I'm rather relieved this has come out. Do you think Silver would keep Brand for me while I'm gone? It wouldn't be more than a couple of days."

"She'd be glad to."

"She can stay right here with her father, where she belongs," Monty said angrily. "Can take care of her myself. Anyway, how can you go if he won't see you for free? Train takes money; haven't any extra this month."

"I have the money from my piano lessons."

"Need that." Monty took his rifle, which was leaning against the fence and examined it closely, avoiding Ilsa's eyes.

"What for?"

"Said I needed it, Ilsa. Wife supposed to honor and obey without asking questions."

"You took some vows, too, Monty," she said.

The little bitch, the smallest of the puppies, stopped chasing butterflies and began to batter joyfully against Monty. He pushed it away savagely.

"I'll lend you the money, Ilsa," I said. "You can pay me back from your piano lessons any time you like." Then I realized I had done a very stupid thing, interfering like that. But Ilsa simply nodded, running her hand along the white, freshly painted rail to the dog's pen. The puppy rushed at her and she caressed it absently. I had no idea what she was thinking.

Monty glared at me. "When are you planning to go to Baltimore?" he asked her.

"I thought I'd leave Sunday. The early morning train. Then I could go see the doctor late Monday after I got there," she answered; she seemed to be concentrating on the three dogs in the pen.

"Sunday, hey?"

"Yes."

Monty turned to me. "That's the day the actors leave town isn't it?"

I nodded.

The puppy flung itself at Monty again. He struck at it wildly with the butt of his gun. It fell to the ground and lay there whimpering. Ilsa snatched it up and held it in her arms, cradling it, soothing it with little tender noises. I have never seen such anger on any human being's face as on hers when she turned on her husband.

He looked sheepishly down at the ground, his long lashes shading his eyes.

"Put that gun down before you do any more damage," she said in a low voice.

He leaned the gun against the fence again and approached her slowly. "I hurt it?" he asked.

"Naturally."

"Bad?"

"Yes."

"What you going to do?"

"Take her to the vet's. Henry, will you drive me, please?"

"Of course," I said, surprised, knowing how she loved to drive.

"I'll drive you," Monty said.

"Henry will drive me."

"Didn't mean to hurt it," he said, still looking down at the ground, his ashamed eyes hidden by the curtains of lashes. She didn't answer, but stood there silently, stroking and comforting the whimpering dog.

I got the car out of the garage and she climbed in beside me, still holding the puppy against her breast.

"I don't dare drive alone in town any more," she said, as we turned into the street. "I can't see the traffic lights. I was almost given a ticket the other day, driving Franz to the theater."

She was in the veterinary's office quite a long time. When she came out the puppy was still in her arms, a little groggy, but apparently all right otherwise. "Is she O.K.?" I asked.

"She'll live. The vet says she'll probably be deficient mentally, but she'll be perfectly healthy. I'm going to keep her for mine. Monty can have the others for hunting. . . . Look here, Hen, don't say anything to anyone about this business about my eyes, will you?"

"No, but what about when you go to Baltimore on Sunday? You'll have to say why then, won't you?"

"No. Why should I?" She climbed into the car and sat down beside me. The puppy leaned against her like a sick child, but it was quiet now, the thin shrill whimpering had stopped.

"Well, if you don't, people might think—might think—"

"People might think what?"

"Well, you know how people are—"

She was mercilessly determined to make me say what people might think, and what even I could not quite dismiss from my mind.

"No, I don't know how people are. How are they?"

"Well, they might think you weren't going to a doctor; they might think you were going off to pleasure yourself."

"With whom?"

"Oh, I didn't mean exactly that, but they just mightn't be—be charitable about it. People hardly ever are."

"No. God knows I know that," she said. "All right. If it will make you feel better I'll announce the fact that I'm going to the doctor, but if people take it into their heads to gossip about me, my giving a reason for my departure won't stop them. Heaven knows why they bother. I'm not worth it."

"People resent anyone who doesn't conform to their ways," I said.

"You mean me, I suppose?"

"Yes."

"Good God, Henry, it seems to me I've conformed for nine years now, and I'll probably go on conforming for another nine, if not longer. Let's drop it. They bore me, those people. Why talk about them? . . . I don't feel like going home," she said, as we turned down her street. "Let's drive on out a bit, toward the Fort. Do you mind? Have you anything else to do?"

"No, of course not. I came over to see you all this afternoon. Shall we stop for Brand?"

"No. She's down the street, playing with Beulah Jackson."

I drove on out of town, past the cemetery. Old Cousin Belle, in her flowered muslin dress, was puttering about her lot as usual with her watering pot and shears. It would certainly be familiar ground when she came there for her final rest. She was kneeling by her sister's grave, our Cousin Josie, whom everybody except Mamma and Aunt Violetta had hated for her biggetiness. Cousin Josie had had a drawer in her bureau in which she had kept all her mourning clothes, including a long elegant black veil. By the side of these had been her shroud. She had slept in clean sheets and a clean nightdress every night in case she should die in her sleep. When she did die it was in a dingy hotel room on her way to her summer home in North Carolina. All her props were far away. "Man proposes, God disposes," Mamma used to say with a contented sigh when telling this tale. Cousin Belle had a very thorny rose bush growing at either end of Cousin Josie's grave, and a prickly pear at one side, which always made us laugh.

"I suppose your mother's in there?" Ilsa asked, peering at the cemetery.

"Yes. Silver goes out every first Sunday. I've never been. Papa thinks I'm awful because I won't go with him."

"You are. That's why I love you," she said.

—Don't say it like that, not meaning it—I begged her silently.

Almost seeming to understand, she went on, "I do love you very much, you know, Henny. You seem to be part of me, to belong to me. I hope you don't mind."

"You know I don't."

"Brand's very fond of you, too. She's always asking when Uncle Henry's coming over."

"I'm glad," I said. "She's a sweet little thing."

We were silent again until we got to the heavy gray walls of the Fort, leaning out toward the river. I turned off the road and stopped the car under a tree by the river bank.

"All right?" I asked.

"Yes. Let's just sit awhile before we go back. Not long, because I've got to help Mattie Belle with dinner and it's warm in the car, but just a few minutes."

"All right."

"What have you been doing with yourself this week?" she asked. "We haven't seen you since the fatal night when Monty got his snake bite."

"Oh, I haven't been doing much. Just working at the mill during the day and going to bed early and reading at night." I didn't want to talk about myself. "What about you?"

"I've had a good week. . . . Oh, Henny!" she said excitedly, "Franz and I went out to the lightship yesterday afternoon."

"How was it?"

"Thrilling. You know, it was the first time I'd been! Father and I kept talking about going, but we never did. There always seemed to be so much time ahead of us. Sometimes I think it's good to know there isn't much time, because then you don't miss out on the chance to crowd a lot into a short space. . . . Yes, the lightship was lovely. The men were beautiful, and they liked Franz and me and wanted us to stay and have supper with them. It would have been fun if we could have, but of course Franz had to get back to the theater."

"Were there sharks swimming around the lightship, and a buzzard on the topmost tip?"

"Yes."

"Didn't that spoil it a little?"

"No. It just made it more exciting." She was stroking the puppy with her strong gentle touch as it lay contentedly on her lap. "I wish you could have come. You'd have loved it."

"I wish I could have come, too," I said. "Have you been going to the theater a lot this week?"

"Yes."

"Do you still love it as much as ever?"

"Yes. . . . We'd better go on back now," she said. "Thank you for being so patient and bringing me out here."

"Oh—I enjoyed it," I said awkwardly. I turned the car around and started back for town.

41

When we got back to the house Monty was gone. He had left a note with Mattie Belle saying that he wouldn't be back for dinner. Ilsa set her lips and fed the dogs. As they flung themselves at the pans of food, she started to laugh, and said, "I bet when Monty was little and had pets he made Violetta and Eddie do all the dirty work. I can just see him being given rabbits and standing over the others with a stick while they cleaned out the hutch for him."

By the big iron stove in the kitchen, which was never used in summer, she placed a pan for her puppy. The poor little creature ate as though famished, then rubbed affectionately against Ilsa's ankles as she sat stringing the French beans. It seemed quite recovered.

"What are you going to call it?" I asked.

"Would you like to name her?" She smiled at me with sudden affection. "I'd like it if you would."

I grew warm with pleasure. "Would you call her Médor?" I aid suddenly. "Telcide had a dog called Médor, a little old mongrel she picked up off the street. It's a very common name for dogs in France." I didn't know why all at once I wanted to be reminded of that time when I lived with Telcide in Paris, a time that had become more like a dream than a remembrance of actuality.

"Médor would be lovely," she said. "A lovely name for a beautiful pup. Come here, Médor."

The puppy stopped chasing itself around the kitchen table and ran over to her posthaste, but because it didn't want to be clumsy and stumble over the bar of sunlight on the linoleum it made a ludicrous miniature hurdle, landed in a heap on the other side, and looked tremendously pleased with itself because it had outwitted the silly sunbeam.

Ilsa laughed. "You see, you couldn't have thought of a better name for her, Hen! She answers to it already. . . . Will you stay to supper? There's plenty of food, since Monty isn't here."

"I'd like to. I'll go phone Papa. He's beginning to think I live at your house."

Dinner was early because Ilsa wanted time to help Mattie Belle clean up, and time to bathe before she left for the theater. As we were finishing our coffee the doorbell rang, and Mattie Belle let Franz Werner in. He shook hands with me with as much enthusiasm as though I had been his long-lost brother. Then he chucked Mattie Belle under the chin and asked for some coffee. She beamed all over and brought him a cup.

"Don't you worry about the dishes, Miz Woolf, honey," she said. "Won't take me a minute to do 'em." She turned back to the actor. "You like some ice cream, Mr. Werner? I got some awful good peach ice cream for dessert. Homemade. With a freezer."

He bowed deeply. "But of course some peach ice cream for my parched and dried palate. My performance will be immeasurably better this evening because of you, Mattie Belle."

She hurried out into the kitchen and came back with a heaping dish. He took one good look. "No, no! Take it out and warm it up, Mattie Belle!"

She bent doable and broke into shrill shrieks of laughter. It was evidently not a new joke with them. As he attacked the ice cream he turned to Ilsa.

"Liebling, I've got to go in three minutes. Come sit in my dressing room with me while I make up. You don't mind, do you, Porcher? There's so little time left. This is Friday evening already. Only tonight's performance and the two tomorrow."

"I don't mind," I said.

"Ilsa, I think I should not come here for dinner tomorrow between performances."

"No," she said, watching him eat his ice cream.

"Mamma."

We looked around and Brand was standing in the doorway in her thin summer nightgown.

"Where's Papa?"

"He had to go out, ladybird," Ilsa answered.

Now, by my maidenhead, an eight-year-old—
I bade her come. What, lamb! What, ladybird!
God forbid! Where's this girl? What, Brandy!

Brand stood shyly in the doorway as the actor declaimed.

"Well, come here, little one," he said. She didn't move.

"Speak to Franz, Brand," Ilsa said.

"Good evening," the child murmured, still standing motionless on the threshold. "Mamma, when will Papa be back? He said he'd come say good night to me tonight and tell me a story about when he was little."

"I don't know when he'll be back, darling," Ilsa said. "I'm afraid it may not be till long after you're asleep. Uncle Henry will tell you a story about when he and your father were little, won't you, Hen?"

"Thank you very much, Uncle Henry," the child said politely, but with no enthusiasm. "Will you come up when you finish? Mattie Belle wants to wash my ears. She says I never remember I have ears. Will you come up and say good night, Mamma, and prayers and everything?"

"Of course, ladybird. I'll be up in just a moment. Run along."

Brand watched her mother for a moment, then her eyes flickered toward the actor. Her little shoulders drooped and she went slowly out.

"Where did you get hold of 'ladybird,' Ilsa?" Werner asked "Shakespeare?"

"It was Father's name for me. I'll go up and get Brand to bed while you finish your ice cream. It's late so we'd better take a taxi. I'll phone for one." At the door she paused. "Hen dear, do you think you could possibly let me have that money tomorrow morning? I'll have to see about my ticket right away if I'm to leave on the early train Sunday."

"Of course," I said. "I'll send it over tomorrow morning if I don't come myself."

"That would be wonderful. Are you sure it's convenient? You can spare it?"

"Yes. I'll take it out of the money Mamma left me. Papa won't have to know."

"You're an angel, Hen."

I was watching Werner out of the corner of my eye when Ilsa mentioned her ticket and the money. He looked at me just for a moment, then went on eating his ice cream without a change of expression.

After a moment he said to Ilsa, "You remind me of a fairy story my mother used to tell me. A story of Hans Christian Andersen's. My mother was a Danish singer, you know."

Ilsa leaned against the door frame. "Oh?"

"It's about a woman who lost her child. So she went to try and find her. She came to a huge lake and there was no way for her to cross it, so she lay down to drink the lake dry, although it was an impossible task. So the lake said, 'You can't drink me dry no matter how hard you try, but I admire your courage, so I am willing to help you. I adore jewels and you have the most beautiful eyes I have ever seen. If you will give me your eyes I will set you down on the other side of me.' So the woman gave up her eyes, which sank to the bottom of the lake and became two perfect pearls, and she herself was carried across the water and put down in a huge forest. She set out to reach the other side of the forest, but as she could not see where she was going she soon lost her way. Then a thorn bush said, 'I'll help you if you'll do something for me.' And the woman agreed. 'I am freezing to death,' the thorn bush said, 'and turning to ice. If you will warm me at your heart I will show you the way.' So the woman held the thorn bush close against her breast in order to warm it, until it was stained crimson with her heart's blood." He paused.

"Well?" Ilsa asked.

"I forget," he said, smiling. "The woman learned that she was wrong, though. She should have let the child go."

"And married the prince and lived happily forever after?"

"Yes."

"But she didn't?"

"No."

Ilsa smiled what seemed to me a very strange smile. "And that story reminds you of me?"

"Yes."

"I'm afraid I don't get the connection." She smiled again and went out.

Werner went on eating his ice cream in silence, frowning at it fiercely. Suddenly he ran his fingers through his black hair in a despairing gesture, but when he spoke his voice was light. "Mattie Belle is the queen of ice-cream makers. I could eat this all night instead of *kvetching* myself to pieces over the egregious Cardinal Wolsey. You should try those red-hot robes. They are not things to wear in the jungle."

"The jungle?"

"This God-forsaken town. Tell me, how did a woman like Ilsa come out of a place like this?"

"I don't think it's God-forsaken," I answered coldly.

"Oh, come now, Henry, you who've lived in Paris. . . ." Then suddenly he seemed abashed. "I am sorry. It was unpardonable of me to speak like that. There is a very small village in the mountains about which I feel the same way—but only because I don't ever have to go there again, I am afraid."

"Where do you play next week?" I asked.

"Some repellent town in South Carolina." He leaned back in his chair and lit a cigarette.

"So you and Ilsa will be on the same train?"

"Yes, for part of the way. It will be very pleasant for me. One gets understandably tired of constantly seeing the same people. Besides, there is no one in the company with whom I am particularly compatible. And your sister-in-law is an extraordinary and wonderful woman."

"She's not my sister-in-law," I said irritably. I felt guilty for being frightened by his words, but I was.

I was sure that if Ilsa left for Baltimore she would never come back. I did not, in fact, believe she was going to Baltimore at all. I did not believe she was really troubled about her eyes. I began to search wildly in my head for ways to keep her from leaving on Sunday morning.

She came running down the stairs, hat and bag in hand, the puppy, Médor, at her heels.

"All right, Franz, let's hurry. Good-bye, Hen darling. Brand's waiting for you. I'll see you tomorrow morning, then?"

"Yes."

"If Monty should come back before you leave, tell him I may be late. I think I'll stop off at the station on the way home and see about the ticket, and then I can just pick it up tomorrow. Good-bye."

"Good-bye," I answered, watching them leave. Through the open window I saw them get into the waiting taxi and drive off. Mattie Belle came in to clear the dining room.

"That Mr. Werner sure a pretty man." She paused at the kitchen door with her tray full of dishes. "He slip me a dollar bill every time he come. You want anything you just let me know, Mr. Henry."

"I will."

She went out to the kitchen and I lit a cigarette. After a moment I heard her singing in her piping little voice:

I'se so glad I'se been baptized,
I'se so glad I'se been baptized—

over and over to a tune of her own devising.

I was grateful that Ilsa had a good and faithful servant. Mattie Belle was tiny and wizened, with a face like a little eager monkey. When I saw her I was never in doubt as to the origin of the species. When I listened to Violetta I was even less in doubt. Mattie Belle had never weighed over ninety pounds in her life, but she was strong as a man and had never known a day's illness, and I knew that she worshiped Ilsa. Now she came back and stuck her head in the doorway.

"You want anything, Mr. Henry, I'm out by the insinuator. I got a lot of trash to burn."

"All right, Mattie Belle. Thank you. But I don't think I'll need anything."

"Mr. Henry," she said, "Kin I ask you for something?"

"Of course."

"Could you maybe loan me a car token to get home? Miz Woolf, she forgot to pay me tonight. She always pay me Friday night."

I reached into my pocket. "Here're two tokens, so you can come to work tomorrow."

"Thank you, Mr. Henry." She took the tokens in her little brown monkey's claw and put them in her apron pocket. "I worried about Miz Woolf. It not like her to forget to pay me. She ain't been feeling so good. I sure do hope she's not fixing to get sick. You think she's all right?"

"Oh, yes, I think she's all right. I don't think she's sick," I said.

"I sure do hope not." Mattie Belle waggled her little head and went back out to the kitchen.

I finished my cigarette and started upstairs, Médor tripping over her feet and mine. Médor was the strangest dog I'd ever seen, with wild blank eyes, rather yellowish and sloping, Chinese fashion. Most dogs, hound dogs at least, have heartrendingly melting eyes, but Médor's always looked as though she were going to jump up like a bucking bronco and make a wild dash across the yard.

Brand was sitting up in bed when I came in, her top sheet kicked down to the foot. Her bamboo blinds were down to keep out the light and the clean white room was stifling. Her mahogany-colored hair, which Ilsa kept cut short, curled in soft moist ringlets around her face and neck. I raised one of the blinds and sat down beside her. Médor managed to clamber up onto the foot of the bed, tangling herself inextricably in the sheet, and lay there panting.

"Hello, Uncle Henry," the child said shyly.

"Hello, Brand."

"Have Mamma and that man gone?"

"Yes."

"Papa isn't back?"

"No. Not yet."

"Uncle Henry, Mama never used to go out all the time like this. I wish she'd stop. Is it because of that man she goes to see at the theater every night?"

"Well," I said, "your mother doesn't get a chance to see plays very often."

"Beulah Jackson said that her mother said that actors weren't nice people. She said people you knew never got to be on the stage or they weren't quality."

"Well, that's a pretty broad statement," I said. "Perhaps a good many theater people aren't persons you'd like to know very well off the stage, but that's certainly not true of all of them. I used to know someone very well who was an actress—a sort of actress."

"Who was she? Was she any kin to us?"

"Yes. She belonged to the part of our family that never came to this country. I knew her when I was living in Paris. She sang songs in a very special way that was all her own. That was how she made her living. But she was one of the nicest people I've ever known, kind and gentle and honorable. She had real quality."

"What was her name?"

"It was a French name that I expect will sound a little strange to you."

"What?"

"Telcide de Publier Porcher."

"That is a funny name."

"Yes. So you see, Mrs. Jackson isn't always right, and I expect Beulah isn't either." I was afraid she might hear something distressing about Ilsa.

"Beulah's so biggety," Brand said. "I don't much like her. And her brother, Lee, he thinks he's so smart. Uncle Henry, do you think when the actor goes on Sunday everything'll be the way it was before?"

"I don't know," I said. "I guess so."

"Tell me a story now?"

"What kind of a story?"

"About when you were little." She lay down and clutched my hand, staring up at me with beseeching eyes.

The conscious part of my mind was thinking unhappily and nervously. The unconscious part was making words come out of my mouth. I told her about the gentle thudding sound of mallet against wooden ball in the evening when I was very small and Mamma and Papa and their guests would play croquet on the soft green stretch of lawn Papa had tended so carefully. Silver and I, in our thin white night clothes, would lean out of our window and watch them, our eyes gazing drowsily at the graceful pastel sweep of the ladies, and the gallant adagio elegance of the gentlemen, until dark suddenly faded them out like Mamma's old daguerreotypes.

And I told her about the birthday parties given for Monty and Violetta, the gay lights, red and yellow and green, of the Japanese lanterns strung about the boathouse and hanging from the trees; and how every once in a while there would be a sudden flame as one of the lanterns would ignite, and the grinning yard boy, his dark watchful face suddenly visible in the flare, would quickly put it out.

And I told her about the first time I saw Ilsa, sitting on the burnt-out fence talking to the men on the chain gang, and about going down to the beach and swimming in our birthday suits, and Ilsa flashing, brown and glistening, out of the water, and the sandpipers and gulls and foam from the waves seen through new eyes, and at night the bar of light from Ilsa's lightship flashing across sea and sand, strong, secure. . . .

Long before I had finished, the child was asleep. I pulled my fingers gently from her clasp, untangled Médor from the sheet, and tiptoed out.

42

I stayed at home all day Saturday reading Beaumont and Fletcher and getting extremely irritated at the two of them because I couldn't keep my mind on them. I got so mad at *Philaster* that I could have chewed nails. I kept looking in the direction of the Woolf house, willing myself not to go over; I had sent Nursie with the money for Ilsa in an envelope.

Every time the phone rang I jumped up, thinking that it would be Ilsa to thank me for the money and to say good-bye. But it rang for the stupidest reasons—wrong numbers, and people who should have called the mill office, and Cousin Belle to say that it was the anniversary of Cousin Josie's death, and Violetta to say she'd called Ilsa and couldn't get any answer and was she at my house and Monty wasn't in the office and where was he? I couldn't choke her off for about half an hour, and then Silver called to tell me that Eddie was back from downstate and he'd brought some wonderful new chickens, and I had to talk to Eddie, and I grew more and more distracted.

Shortly after midnight I gave up and went to bed; I was so depressed and miserable that I couldn't sleep. I didn't think that Ilsa would just accept my money and walk out of my life, and, incidentally, out of Monty's and Brand's, forever, without even bothering to say good-bye.

A little after two I turned on the light and started to read. Shortly after, I heard the telephone. I tore downstairs.

"Hello," I gasped, breathless.

"Henny?"

"Yes—"

"It's Ilsa."

"Yes, I know. What is it? Is something wrong?"

"No, not really. Did I wake you?"

"No, I was reading."

"Hen, I'm sorry to have called you at this ungodly hour. I didn't realize it was so late. I hope I didn't rouse the house."

"No."

"Listen, Henny, Monty seems to be off on a toot. He hasn't been back since Friday. Undoubtedly he'll turn up tomorrow or the next day in a vile humor, but I suppose I can't go to Baltimore till he does. Franz has gone down to the station to return my ticket."

"Oh," I said. "I'm sorry."

"What I called you about was to ask you if you'd mind awfully driving me to the station tomorrow morning? I want to see Franz off and I don't want to crash into anything on the way—I'm afraid I might if I try to drive in that stupid gray light before the sun comes up. I'm awfully sorry to be such a helpless bore, Hen. I'll go to Baltimore as soon as Monty condescends to return and then I'll be all right and won't bother you any more."

"It's not a bother," I said. "Don't be like that. I'll be over for you at six."

"Maybe you'd better make it a quarter to. Is that too horribly early for you? I'm awfully sorry."

"No, of course not. I'll be there."

"Bless you, Henny. Good night."

There didn't seem much point in going back to bed. It was so late, and I was afraid that if I went to sleep I wouldn't wake up, so I dressed and sat down with a book. At five-thirty I slipped downstairs.

When I got to Ilsa's she was sitting on the porch steps waiting for me, though I was ahead of time. She was silent as we drove to the station. The early morning was gray and misty; the street was blotted out a few yards ahead of us, and I had to drive slowly. I could feel her pushing the car along as she leaned forward, straining to see through the windshield.

"This'll burn off by noon," I said. She nodded.

As the station came into view, she said, "We're nearly there, aren't we?"

"Yes," I told her, and she fumbled for the handle of the door.

The company was assembled on the platform. The little Ophelia was huddled into a heavy coat, in spite of the heat, and was smoking a cigarette in a long yellow holder. Queen Gertrude sat on her suitcases and dozed. Werner was not among them. Then I caught sight of him at the far end of the platform, almost hidden by the fog. Ilsa had gone close to the company and was looking strainedly for him. Queen Gertrude looked up from her nap.

"He's down there, honey," she said, pointing.

"Thank you very much," Ilsa said, and hurried off into the gray distance. I stood in the station doorway and watched the two of them walk up and down, up and down, just out of range of the others; two dim, mist-blurred shadows. I was grateful that there were very few people at the station besides the theatrical troupe. As far as I could see there was no one who might recognize me, or, what was more important, Ilsa, and she was out of view of the station master's desk.

I turned and went back to the car to wait for her. I had a sudden feeling that she was going to get on the train with Werner and go off with him just as she was, but I knew that I must not watch. I sat in the car and closed my eyes.

—If I can count to a hundred before the train comes, she won't go, she'll come back—I said to myself, reverting to an old superstition of my childhood. But when I had reached sixty I heard the train roar in and scream to a stop. For a moment there was the excited sound of voices raised in farewell and greeting, the tapping of hammers against wheels, the thud of mailbags, the sound of water, all the sudden busy noises, then the long roar as the train pulled out, and silence under the fog.

One by one the other cars filled and pulled off. Mine was the only one parked on the dirty gray sand. I watched the station door and thought that in a moment I would have to go.

Then Ilsa came out and walked slowly toward the car. I was filled with shame and self-reproach as I saw her fumble for the handle of the door. She slouched down in the seat and lit a cigarette.

"Franz said to say good-bye to you," she said.

"Thank you."

I turned the car around and drove her home.

"You'd better come in with me and have some coffee," she said in a flat voice.

I followed her in. Brand was just coming down the stairs dressed in a fresh cotton frock, and she rushed headlong at her mother. Ilsa clasped the child to her, suddenly trembling violently. "Oh, darling," she whispered, "darling, darling, darling. . . ."

43

Two weeks had gone and Monty had not returned. It was the longest he had ever stayed away, and Ilsa had a hard time quieting Brand and convincing her that all was well. She herself began to imagine that something must have happened to Monty, but she told everybody in her definite voice that he had gone downstate to look up an old mortgage for a client. Nobody but I knew that Monty had just disappeared, though I think that Mattie Belle guessed, because she was much more solicitous than usual, and hovered over Ilsa like an anxious little marmoset.

Ilsa was more depressed and irritable than I had ever seen her. She gave piano lessons nearly every morning, and the housework kept her busy, but in the afternoons she would sit for hours staring at the marble Othello and Iago; or at the piano, not playing; or she would hold a book in her lap and not read. Sometimes I would push through the rice portieres and find her sitting there, and she would not even turn around or acknowledge my presence. Médor would climb onto her lap and sleep there and she would smile down at the ancient puppy face; sometimes she would walk down by the river with Brand; and sometimes, when the wind blew the train whistle, searching and clear, a strange expression would come to her face. But her vitality, the tremendous aliveness that seemed to be the essence of her—for the moment this was gone.

We had day after day of overcast skies and rain, and I remembered how the furious sun, that seemed to wilt everyone else, seemed, in Ilsa, to light answering fires. And I thought that if only the sun would come out she would be all right again. This heavy humidity was infinitely more exhausting than the febrile sunlight.

I almost made myself sick with impotent worry.

We were sitting out on the porch one afternoon, watching Médor stumble over her own shadow. Brand and Beulah Jackson were playing behind the house down by the river; their voices drifted back to us, changed and blurred by the wind. Ilsa lay in the hammock and fanned herself slowly with a Chinese fan I had found in the attic. I sat on the rail in my shirt sleeves, too lazy and worried to move, though the sun struggling through the clouds was sending perspiration down my back.

"If Monty doesn't come home soon I'll have to do something about it," Ilsa said.

"I suppose you will."

"I'm going to give him till the end of the week."

"Then what will you do?"

"I haven't decided yet."

We lapsed once more into silence. Médor was chasing a chipmunk. Brand and Beulah came running around the house, then disappeared again. After a while Brand came back, her face scarlet with heat, her hair as wet as though she'd plunged it into a bucket of water.

"Mamma?"

"Yes, ladybird?"

"May Beulah and I go make some lemonade?"

"If it's all right with Mattie Belle. You ask her."

Brand ran off. "I'd like to forbid her to play with that Jackson child," Ilsa said.

"Why?"

"She told me last night that Beulah had said we were decadent. Neither of them knew what it meant. I suppose Beulah nicked it up from that frightful mother of hers. I'd just make things worse if I didn't let Brand see Beulah. She hasn't anyone else to play with, anyhow. Poor little thing, she can't seem to get on with other children. She hasn't enough guts. I don't know what's the matter with her. I'd have been ashamed to let another child boss me the way she lets Beulah. But that's something she's got to fight out for herself. I just wish I could stop her from being hurt by things that *aren't* her fault."

Ilsa dropped her hands loosely into her lap, like Cousin Anna—a gesture most uncommon to her. I watched her for a moment, as she lay in the hammock, then looked back out at Médor who had caught her chipmunk, but, with her poor battered little brain, couldn't think what to do with it. Some kind of instinct told her that she ought to kill it, but she couldn't figure out how. She would hold it in her mouth and look over at Ilsa with a puzzled expression, then she would drop it and pick it up again, hold it, and look beseechingly at Ilsa. But Ilsa was staring straight ahead of her, engrossed in her thoughts. Finally Médor dropped the chipmunk, and before it could run away, she had rolled over on it, and was lying very still, looking over at us for approbation. When she finally wobbled unsteadily to her feet and twirled around to look at her prey, she saw that she had succeeded, for the chipmunk was dead, smothered. With a joyful yelp Médor picked it up and came tearing toward us, falling all over her huge puppy feet, stumbling up the steps and dropping the chipmunk, picking it up and dropping it, picking it up, and finally laying it in triumph at Ilsa's feet. Ilsa didn't move. Médor looked up at her uncomprehendingly and barked, loud and sharp. Ilsa rose and went into the house, not noticing the dog or her trophy. Médor's tail went down and she backed, bewildered, into a corner of the porch and sat there, hurt and betrayed.

I picked up the dead chipmunk and put it in the incinerator; then I went into the house after Ilsa. She was in the drawing room, standing by the piano, picking out the rosy-bush song.

"Ilsa," I said. "You've hurt Médor's feelings awfully."

"Why? What did I do?"

"She caught a chipmunk for you and brought it to you and put it down in front of you, and all you did was to get up and stalk into the house." I don't know why I was so upset about that crazy hound's being hurt.

Her face went blank for a second. "Oh," she said. "I didn't see it. Where is she?"

"Nursing her wounded feelings on the porch."

She went out and I sat down at the piano, staring up at the watercolor sketch of Aunt Elizabeth.

After a moment the phone began to ring, so I got up to answer it. I was surprised to hear Cousin Anna's voice, because she never talked on the phone.

"Hello," Cousin Anna said, shouting into the phone as though she were trying to make her voice carry over the rooftops from her house to the Woolfs'. "Hello, Ilsa?"

"No," I said. "It's me, Henry."

"Who?" She almost deafened me. I had to hold the receiver away from my ear.

"Henry Porcher. Your cousin."

She couldn't seem to understand. "Oh. . . . I must have the wrong number. Can you tell me what to do? I want to talk to Ilsa Woolf."

"Cousin Anna, this is Henry Porcher. I'm over at Ilsa's," I said. I found myself shouting into the phone almost as loudly as she was. "Ilsa's out on the porch. I'll get her in just a minute. Are you all right?" I yelled.

"For heaven's sake, Henry, what's the matter?" Ilsa's low voice came behind me. "You're bellowing like the bull of Bashan. Who is it?"

"It's Cousin Anna. She wants you."

"Oh." She took the receiver from me. "Hello, darling," she said. "Are you all right? What are you doing on the telephone?"

I heard Cousin Anna's voice, blurred and raucous, from the other end of the wire, but no words were distinguishable. The gull-like squawking was so different from her usual well-modulated speech that I almost burst out laughing.

"Good heavens," Ilsa said. "When? . . . Didn't they write you or anything? . . . But why didn't you tell us before? . . . Of course we'll come over. . . . Right away. . . . Are you happy, my dear? . . . I'm glad, then. . . . All right. . . . Good-bye." She turned back to me, looking baffled. "Anna's brother William is home."

"What!"

"Yes. I was bowled over, too."

"But why? He hasn't lost his New Jersey church or anything, has he?"

"No. His wife died last year, and he's retiring. . . . It'll be good for your Cousin Anna to have someone in that huge house with her besides Barbara. Barbara's an angel but Anna needs someone to talk to. . . . She was always very fond of William. . . . Go round up Brand and send the Jackson child home, will you, Hen? I want to put Médor in the pen so she won't run off and get lost while we're gone."

"Hunting dogs don't get lost."

"Médor does. Hurry, please, Henny. I told her we'd be right on over."

"Do you think I should come? I mean—"

"You'll have to drive me."

"Oh. All right." Ilsa was so careful with her gestures and movements that only occasionally was I reminded of the trouble she was having with her vision, although I still felt hot with shame when I thought how I had disbelieved her motive in wanting to go to Baltimore.

When we got in the car she said to Brand, "Your Cousin William has brought a boy with him, bird; Lorenzo Moore, I think your

Cousin Anna said his name was. A little orphan from the parish he and his wife adopted a few years ago. He's about ten now. Maybe he'll be someone good for you to play with, Brand."

"I don't think I like boys," Brand said.

"Perhaps Lorenzo won't be like most of the boys in town. Don't decide not to like him before you meet him."

"All right. Mamma, why is Uncle Henry driving instead of you?"

"Well, it's more polite to let the gentleman drive, you know, ladybird."

"But you always used to drive."

"I'm just learning manners in my old age."

As we drew up to the house Barbara came hurrying down the white steps. "Miss Ilsa, Miss Ilsa," she called as she ran panting up to the car.

"What is it, Barbara?"

"Mr. Woolf he just called and he say you come home right away. He sounded real mad. I told Miss Anna and she say you better go on back home. She say why don't you leave Brand to meet Lorenzo and they all bring her back after supper and pay you a call."

"That's a fine idea," Ilsa said. "Hop out, ladybird."

"But Papa's back! I want to go home and see Papa!"

"I expect your father's tired," Ilsa said. "He's been off on this business trip for a long time, you know, and he probably wants to wash and have dinner and get a little rested the very first thing."

"I wouldn't bother him."

"Darling," Ilsa said. "I want you to do as I say without any fuss. Cousin Anna'll bring you home right after supper. In the meantime you are to be nice to Lorenzo. He's a stranger here, and he probably feels lonely and shy. He'll be very grateful to you if you make him feel at home, and so will I."

Brand got out of the car slowly. "I've never talked to anyone who was adopted before," she said.

"He won't be any different from anyone else," Ilsa assured her. "Except if your Cousin William wanted him, he's very likely nicer. Run along, now."

"Well, good-bye—"

"Good-bye, bird."

We waited as Barbara took her by the hand and drew her up the steps and into the house. Then I turned the car around. Ilsa leaned back on the seat and closed her eyes.

Monty came out on the porch as we drove up. His face, white and puffy, was bruised and swollen under his eyes. "Where the hell you been?"

"We went over to your Cousin Anna's," Ilsa said quietly, going ahead of him into the house. "You know that. You phoned there."

"Oh, yes, uh huh. Thought I might find you there. Well, aren't you going to give me a kiss? Fine welcome you're giving your husband."

Ilsa stood still in the dim ancient-smelling hall and raised her face. Monty grabbed her roughly into his arms, kissing her hard against the mouth.

"Well, what are you staring at, Henry? Never seen a man and woman kiss before? Never kiss a woman yourself?"

"Monty, be quiet," Ilsa said, pulling away from his embrace. "Henry was good enough to drive me back from your Cousin Anna's."

"Why'n't you drive yourself?"

"It's been difficult for me to drive lately." She went into the drawing room, and Monty and I followed.

"Why? Very good driver." He picked the marble group of the little boys and the horse up in his arms and put it on the floor, almost unbalancing himself with its weight and falling on top of it.

"I told you my eyes were bothering me, Monty."

He straddled the horse. "Used to ride this when I was little. Remember, Henry? Pa used to put it on the floor and let us ride it. Must give it to Brand to ride." He turned suddenly and shouted at Ilsa. "So you didn't go to Baltimore?"

"No."

"Why not?"

"The obvious reason. I was waiting for you to come back."

"Why?"

"I was worried about you."

"Hah!"

"And I didn't want Brand frightened."

"Could have sent her to Silver, or Cousin Anna. Thought you had it all arranged." He slid down the tail of the white marble horse onto the floor.

"That wouldn't have kept her from worrying, and I didn't know when you'd come back or in what condition you'd be. She picked up the marble horse with much more ease than Monty and put it back on the shelf. "I'm going in the kitchen to get you some food and coffee."

"Not hungry."

"Just the coffee, then."

He flung himself down on one of the shrouded chairs. Ilsa went out to the kitchen. It seemed to me that she flinched as she went through the rice portieres, as if she had come to them before she expected to.

"God," Monty said. "What a time. What a time. Been down to Miami. What a time." He turned around in the chair so that he was lying down, his head dangling over the seat, his legs up over the back. "What a time," he kept saying over and over. I knew I ought to leave, but I just sat there at the piano bench and watched him.

"Over at the Silverton house?" he asked suddenly.

"Yes."

"What for? What all you go over there for?"

"Cousin William has come back from New Jersey."

"Cousin William? Who the hell Cousin William? We got enough kin already without having a Cousin William sprung on us."

"He's Cousin Anna's brother, the one who had a church in Charleston and then in New Jersey," I said.

—The one who was engaged to Aunt Elizabeth, the one who never forgave your father and who kept Mamma from taking communion in Charleston and lost his church because of it; the one who sent us into retirement in a hotel with a yellow veranda and doves sobbing on the summerhouse roof; the one who kept us away from home till Mamma died. That one—I thought.

"What he want to come back here for?" Monty asked. "Done enough damage already. Let him keep away."

"He's retired," I said. "I guess he just wanted to come home."

"Home," Monty said. "That's right. Can't stay away too long. Start to feel lonely. Had to come home." He twisted himself around suddenly, knocking the chair over. He then looked about the room, and walked toward Ilsa's straight desk chair. With a great effort, as though it were very heavy he moved it in front of the door so that anybody entering would have to walk around it.

"You'd better move that chair away," I said.

He shook his head craftily. "No. Leave it be. Want to see something."

Ilsa had evidently gone out to the kennels and let Médor out for the puppy came galloping into the room, skidding on the floor and rolling up one of the raffia mats. I got up and started to straighten it as Ilsa came in with a pot of coffee. Before I knew what was happening or had time to shout a word of warning she had walked into the chair. The coffeepot fell from her hand and crashed to the floor, spattering the scalding liquid over her feet and ankles. She didn't say anything or stoop to pick up the pot, but turned and walked out of the room. Monty stared after her, his mouth open.

"You better clean that mess up," he said to me, and followed her out.

I got some rags from the closet under the stairs and mopped the spilled coffee up. The glass top to the percolator was broken and I put the pieces in the wastepaper basket by Ilsa's desk. Then I took the pot and went out to the kitchen.

Ilsa was standing very tense, very still, in front of the stove. Monty had his arms about her, bending over her and rubbing his cheek against hers. She stood stiff in his arms, her face white, her lips set.

"Honey, does it hurt much, did I hurt you much?" he was pleading.

"It's all right."

"Sure enough you didn't see the chair? You didn't see it at all?"

"No."

"You better go to that doctor in Baltimore."

"That's what I told you."

"We'll go tomorrow. Come with you. Made some money on the horses in Miami."

"Thank you. I want to go alone."

"You be all right on the train alone?"

"Naturally. I'm perfectly capable of taking care of myself."

"Bumped into that chair."

"Chairs don't usually stand in front of doors."

"Honey," Monty said, "Ah, honey, honey. . . ."

I put the coffeepot down on the kitchen table and went back to the drawing room.

44

Cousin Anna, Cousin William, and Lorenzo Moore came over with Brand shortly after nine. It was the first time Cousin Anna had left her own house and grounds in years. She looked around the drawing room.

"Couldn't change it much, could you, Ilsa?" she asked. "I remember Violetta and Cecilia thought this a most elegant and beautiful room. William and Elizabeth and I always hated it. William, this is Ilsa Brandes Woolf, John Brandes' daughter."

"How do you do, my dear," Cousin William said. He was a kind, tired-looking man, with thick ash-blond hair and a well-groomed Vandyke beard, the color of Cousin Anna's hair and Silver's, the color that does not turn with age. He wore thick spectacles; through them his eyes were a vague brown blurr. He took Ilsa in his arms and kissed her. "I saw you the day you were born," he said, "so I'm afraid I'll have to remark on the way you've grown."

"This is Ilsa's husband, Montgomery Woolf," Cousin Anna said.

Cousin William held out his hand. "Yes. You look like your father. How do you do."

"How do you do, sir." Monty took his hand and bowed. "We are delighted to welcome you home."

Cousin Anna snorted and turned to me. "And Henry Randolph Porcher, son of our sainted Cecilia and Henry Randolph Porcher, the elder."

Cousin William shook hands with me, as Cousin Anna beckoned to Lorenzo, who was standing shyly in the corner with Brand. "And this is Lorenzo Moore."

"How do you do," Lorenzo whispered to us. He was a skinny little boy with beautiful big gray eyes and a fine beak of a nose. He stood with his pale legs wide apart and his small bony hands clasped behind his back as though bracing himself against our regard.

Cousin Anna and Cousin William both looked at the water color of Aunt Elizabeth.

"That's new since I was here last," Cousin Anna said.

"What?" Ilsa asked.

"The picture of Elizabeth."

"Yes. I found it in the attic."

"One of Violetta's attempts, I see." Cousin William went over to the picture and peered at it through his glasses. "Funny how Elizabeth's personality managed to come through even Violetta's artificiality."

"Tell me," Ilsa said in a low voice, going over to him. "How did you happen to see me the day I was born?"

"I baptized your mother shortly before she died."

"Did you know Mother at all?"

"No, my dear. I'd never seen her before." He looked at her intently. "I see what Anna meant when she said you were like Elizabeth. I pray that none of the unhappiness and horror that came about before your birth will visit itself upon you."

"The sins of the fathers," Ilsa said. "Isn't it seven generations?"

"Yes. But you weren't related to most of the people involved until you married young Montgomery."

"I was related to Father, though, and he seems to have caused—or at any rate started—most of the trouble. I wish you'd known my mother. Father never seemed to want to talk to me about her, and of course I never asked him. I'd like to know what she was like, what kind of a person she was."

There was a loud thump as Monty put the marble horse on the floor and offered it to the children. They were both too big for it, but both, fortunately, too tactful to refuse. Monty would probably have forced them to climb onto the patient white horse that Mattie Belle scrubbed once a week with soap and water, if they hadn't obediently straddled it without being told.

After a while Lorenzo left Brand sitting on the horse, and went over to the piano, stroking the smooth rosewood box with loving fingers. He looked at Ilsa on the bamboo chaise longue with Médor on her lap, then went over to Cousin Anna and stood shyly by her chair. She put an arm about him. She was making a tremendous effort to rouse herself from her customary apathy for Cousin William's sake, but her face looked strained and exhausted, deeply shadowed about the eyes and white about the mouth.

"Miss Anna—"

"What is it, Lorenzo?"

"You don't have a piano, do you?"

"No."

"Do you have any musical instruments at all?"

"There's a harp in the small upstairs sitting room. I haven't played it in a long time, though."

"Might I try it, sometime?"

"Whenever you like."

His face lightened. He went back to Brand, who was still sitting on the marble horse.

"That's Othello and Iago over there," Brand said, pointing.

"Yes, I know." Lorenzo ran his small bony hand down the horse's slanting neck as it bent toward the water trough.

"How do you know?"

"Because once Mr. William took me in to New York to see *Othello* on the stage, and we read and studied the play for a long time beforehand. It was very exciting. Mr. William took me to see quite a few plays."

Brand folded her lips to a thin line. "I don't like the theater," she said. "I don't like plays or actors." She slid off the horse and went over to Monty, climbing onto his lap. He held her close to him, burrowing his nose in her thick ruddy hair.

Ilsa watched them for a moment—at least her eyes were focused in their direction. I was no longer certain how much she could see. Then she got up and went over to Lorenzo, who was sitting forlornly by himself on the sofa.

"Oh, please," he said seriously as she sat down. "Would you mind standing up just for a second? You're sitting on my tail.

Ilsa rose instantly. "Oh, I'm very sorry."

"That's quite all right," he said. "People don't expect to find tails lying around on sofas."

"Tell me about your tail." She smiled at him. "I've always wanted to know someone who had a tail."

"It's just an ordinary tail," he said. "Rather long. When I have to go to school it drags on the ground, but when I'm happy it sticks way up and wags."

"Lorenzo," Cousin William said.

"Sir?"

"I thought we had a talk about your tail a few days ago."

"Yes, sir, I remember. And I think it is a little shorter. But it's still there." He turned back to Ilsa. "Mr. William thinks I'm too old to have a tail now that I'm ten, because older people just don't have tails, but I shall feel awfully lost without mine. It's such an expressive part of me."

"Of course it is," Ilsa said.

"If you have a tail to express things with," Lorenzo went on, "you don't have to do it with your face, and that's a great help."

"I'm sure it is." Ilsa leaned back against the sofa, relaxing a moment. I saw Cousin Anna looking at her with worried eyes.

"If I had a tail," Ilsa said, "I'd never want to lose it, but I expect that's one of the penalties one pays for the privilege of growing up."

"Is it a privilege to grow up?" Lorenzo asked.

She nodded. "When I was little I thought it wouldn't be because it seemed to me that grownups didn't play and have fun and they had to pay taxes. But unless you're very foolish—and of course a great many people are—there's really much more for you to enjoy when you're grown. Go on about your tail. How about when you're mad?"

"Oh, when you're mad it's lovely!" he said. "You've no idea! You turn around and stalk out of a room with your tail bristling and you look much madder backwards than you ever could forwards."

She laughed. "Oh, wonderful!"

"And when Mr. William spanks me for something, as long as I have my tail to put between my legs I don't have to cry."

"Lorenzo," Cousin William said. "You have talked quite enough. See how quiet Brand is being."

"Well, I haven't a tail, so there isn't anything to talk about," Brand said.

Monty put her down off his lap. "How about something to drink? Got some good stuff from a man I know."

Cousin Anna rose. I knew she didn't trust Monty's bootleg liquor any more than Ilsa did. "Thank you, no, Montgomery. William and Lorenzo are tired after their long trip."

I watched Ilsa while the good-byes were being said. She stood with her hand resting lightly on the back of the bamboo chaise longue, a strained look about her eyes. I noticed that Monty was watching her, too.

When they were gone he said, "Ilsa." His voice was rough.

"What is it, Monty?"

"How soon could you leave for Baltimore?"

"Any time."

"Could you be ready to go by the early train tomorrow?"

"I haven't a ticket."

"Do you still have the money Henry lent you?"

"Of course."

"I'll go down to the station and see about your ticket while you pack then."

Brand had been sitting in the corner. We had completely forgotten about her. Now she said in a frightened little voice, "Why must Mamma go to Baltimore?"

"Ladybird," Ilsa said. "I—I didn't see you. You should be in bed."

"You told Mattie Belle she could go home."

"I'm a neglectful parent. Come on upstairs with me now."

"Mamma, why must you go to Baltimore?"

"Don't sound so frightened, my bird. It's nothing very terrible. I think I just need a pair of horrible horn-rimmed glasses like your arithmetic teacher, and the best place to get them is Baltimore."

"Will you be gone long?"

"I don't expect so. Just a couple of days."

Monty picked the child up with a sudden return of his old strength. "How about a piggy back?"

"All right, Papa. Thank you."

"Would you like to stay here with me while your mother's away, or go over to Aunt Silver's and help her take care of the chickens and the babies, or over to your Cousin Anna's and play with Lorenzo."

"With you, please."

"Will you do everything your father and Mattie Belle tell you to do?" Ilsa asked.

"Yes, Mamma."

"All right, then. It's settled. You'll stay and take care of your father for me. Take her upstairs, will you please, Monty?"

She stood by her chair, listening to Monty go upstairs with Brand on his shoulders. "Henny," she said. "I don't know what William looks like, or that funny little boy, Lorenzo Moore. I couldn't see them—only shadows. I didn't realize. . . . I haven't tried to see anyone I didn't know before. But I couldn't see them—I couldn't see them at all."

Médor was circling about her, sniffing at her and whimpering nervously. Ilsa pulled one of the dog's ears, then sat down in the chair. Médor continued her worried circling. We heard Monty coming downstairs.

45

At the first ring of the telephone I was wide-awake. Daylight was coming in the windows but the sun was not yet up. I tore downstairs, not stopping to put on slippers or robe. "Hello," I shouted into the phone.

"Henry?"

"Yes."

"It's Ilsa."

"Yes—are you back?"

"Yes. I promised I'd phone."

"What—what did the doctor say?"

"It was too late," she said in that very careful voice. "If I'd gone to him months ago, when I first went to that fat old fool here in town, it might have been all right. But now there's not a thing in the world to do."

"You mean—you—you—"

"Oh, say it, Henry. Don't be afraid. I'm going blind."

"Ilsa—" I could only stammer inarticulately.

"I can't see much now," she said. "There won't be long to wait."

"Oh, my God—but what—but why—"

"Decay of the optic nerve. Atrophy, he called it."

"Oh, my God," I groaned again.

"Now listen, Henry." Her voice was brittle, as though it might be snapped off as easily as the telephone connection. "Will you do something to help me?"

"Of course—anything—"

"I want to go down to the beach and stay until I learn—well, the fundamental things I'm going to have to learn. Eating and so forth." Dimly through the wires I heard Médor yowling and Ilsa's voice commanding, with a momentary return of resonance, "Médor, be quiet!" Then she went on. "I don't want Brand to have to watch me while I'm still struggling clumsily to get—to get adjusted. She's a sad enough little creature as it is. And it would do bad things to Monty. It would just make everything worse. I don't think it'll take me long. I've always been quick at learning things. Now, will you be an angel and drive me down to the beach this afternoon?" She was speaking in an even rapid voice, hypnotizing herself by it, hypnotizing me. . . .

"Of course," I said in the same flat way. I knew now that I had known all along that this would be the outcome, that the trip to Baltimore would be useless except as a confirmation of what we already knew. "But do you think that's the right thing?" I asked. "Do you think you ought to go down there—I mean—how can you, all alone—" my voice began to break again.

"Ira'll be there. Another thing, Henry. Will you tell the others—Cousin Anna and Silver and all of them?"

"Yes, of course. Have you told Monty and Brand?"

"Yes." She stopped. There was a long silence. I couldn't say anything. I stood there agonizedly clutching the telephone receiver and listened to the bleak silence at the other end of the wire. Then I heard Médor's voice raised again in an anguished howl and Ilsa quieting her, soothing her. At last she said, "One other thing, Henry. Would you just drop over to the house once in a while and see that everything's all right? I think it will be—this has sobered Monty up—he's being his very sweetest. And he adores the child so that I think if I'm away he'll behave for her sake. At least he won't let her see anything. . . . Well, I guess that's all. Will you come by for me at about two?"

"Yes, of course."

"Hen, darling, don't sound so shaky," she said. Her own voice was suddenly quite unsteady. "It's going to be all right."

46

I was over at my sister Silver's one afternoon several weeks later. We had heard nothing from Ilsa since I had driven her down to the beach, raised the flag, and waited silently with her until Ira arrived. I spent my days vainly trying to gather enough courage to drive down and see her, knowing that I mustn't. During this period I didn't go once to the mill office. In any case my working there was pretty tacitly acknowledged by everyone to be a farce. Papa fumed and fretted but he didn't do anything about it except make a big noise.

If Papa had only made me work at the mill, or really sent me off to earn my own living as he so often threatened to do, I might have turned out to be more of a person. But I always had enough money, and enough time in which to be sorry for myself, to keep me from ever doing a useful day's work. It is indicative of my intense selfishness at this period that I was far more sorry for myself than I was for Ilsa.

It was lovely at Silver's; after our early supper, after the little boys had been put to bed and were asleep, Silver and Eddie and I went out in the woods and picked armfuls of daisies to decorate the porch; not the prim white kind Milton was thinking of when he wrote: "Meadows trim with daisies pied" (I had recently looked up Milton's *Sonnet on His Blindness* and gone on to read more and more of his work), but bright yellow ones with red-brown centers, long slender petals, and stems a yard long, the kind that go with pine scrub and wire grass instead of neat meadows. Fireflies came out on our way home and whippoorwills began calling all around us. The combination of those two, or even the whippoorwills alone, is the very essence of summer to me. Their calling goes on all night long, sometimes slow and soft from across the fields, sometimes so rushed and fast that they seem to feel that time is flying past and they must crowd in as much as possible as it flies. Eddie's favorite hound, Bone, came along with us, having a wonderful time pointing lizards and grasshoppers, looking ridiculous padding around with his big feet after the blue-tailed lizards and the big red-and-yellow hoppers.

When we got back to the house, our arms cradling huge masses of daisies, we saw the Woolf car. For a moment my heart leaped within me like a sea gull rising to the sun, but I knew that it could not be Ilsa.

Monty was sitting in the living room with Brand and Lorenzo Moore. When we came in he sent them out to play. The sun was setting over the river; the water was like a red snake curling between the cypress and the oaks. The children went down to the dock and lay watching the water; we sat on the front steps in order to keep an eye on them.

"You all right, Mont?" Eddie asked his brother.

"Sure. Why not?"

"Thought I'd come down to the office tomorrow and look things over," Eddie said.

"Might be a good idea."

"Think I may have to go down to Fernandina for a couple of weeks, and then over to Augusta."

"Uh huh," Monty said, not listening. I got up and wandered down to the river and out onto the dock. The children had taken off their shoes and socks and were dabbling their toes in the dappled water.

". . . and my mother tells me stories or sings to me before I go to sleep and sometimes in the night when I've had a bad dream or something I get in bed with her and Papa, and my mother and I have jokes we laugh at together and she's so strong she could pick me up and throw me over her head with one hand if she wanted to," I heard Brand say.

"I never knew my mother, and my father didn't like me very much," Lorenzo said. "I wish I had your mother for mine."

They looked around and saw me. "Hello, Uncle Henry," Brand said.

Lorenzo stood up and bowed politely. "Good evening, Mr. Porcher."

"Oh, you'd better call me Uncle Henry, too, don't you think?"

"May I?"

"Of course. How do you like it here?"

"Oh, I like it very much," Lorenzo said, sitting down again and dipping his toes delicately into the water. "It's different, but I like it."

"Uncle Henry"—Brand looked at me earnestly—"Papa said he thought Mamma would be back from the beach soon. Do you think she will?"

"I don't know, Brand," I said. "Has your father heard anything from her?"

"No. But he said he'd try to find a way to make her come home and then he said we'd take care of her. We're awfully lonely without her. The house is a different color."

"Yes," I said. "I know."

"Do you think maybe you could get Mamma to come home? It would make Papa and me so happy."

"I'm afraid she'd resent it very much if I tried, Brand," I said. "You know how she likes to make up her own mind for herself, and not have other people try to think for her."

"Yes, I know, but she likes you very much, and I thought maybe if you told her how lonely Papa and I were—I guess I was wrong, though. It wouldn't do any good. She'll come home when she's ready."

"And she's the only one who'll know when she's ready," I said.

Lorenzo nodded his little bird head wisely.

The long last shadows were spreading themselves across the wrinkled skin of the river. In a moment dark would be upon us like a clap of thunder. "We'd better go back to Aunt Silver," I said.

The children scrambled to their feet and followed me up the path.

Monty was standing on the steps, his arm about Silver. Eddie sat on the rail, chewing a long piece of grass.

"Run on out to the kitchen and ask Willie May for a cookie, children," Silver said. When they had vanished inside the house she turned to me. "I'm going down to the beach tomorrow to try to get Ilsa to come back, Henry."

"Do you think that's wise?" I asked.

"I don't know. Monty thinks she might come if I persuaded her."

"Oh," said. "Well, it's on your own head."

"I know it is, Brother," Silver said in her maddeningly cool and collected way. "I just thought you'd be interested."

47

Early the next afternoon I went across the river to wait until Silver came back from the beach, though I didn't have much hope that she'd bring Ilsa with her.

Eddie was out in the grove, so I sat on the porch while the children played around and over me like puppy dogs. Violetta came by to return some sugar she had borrowed. I didn't tell her where Silver was and I hoped she would go away when she saw that Silver had gone off in the car and that Eddie was busy in the grove. But she plunked herself down in the big black wicker rocking chair.

"Henry," she said. "I just can't get over Ilsa. It's just awful and I thought I'd die when Silver came over and told Dolph and me. She's always been such an independent girl, and now I suppose she'll have to resign herself to being waited on hand and foot for the rest of her life. Though who's going to do it I'm sure I don't know. I bet she regrets ever having gone down to that theater."

"What's that got to do with it?" I asked.

"If you ask me, this looks to be a judgment on her for the she carried on with that actor. I was surely humiliated the way Mrs. Jackson talked about it, and right to my face, too."

"Honestly, Violetta!" I cried. "If you believed all the malicious gossip that goes on in this town no woman would trust her own husband out of her sight."

She bridled like a wet hen. "Henry Randolph Porcher, I will not have you talking about Dolph like that."

I shrugged my shoulders in despair.

"But I am perfectly sorry for Ilsa," she went on, "though I don't see why she wanted to run off to the beach like that and leave her own good home and family. I never did trust that Ira person. People are going to begin talking if she doesn't come home soon."

I scowled down at the floor and didn't answer.

After a while Violetta heaved herself, in her expensive pink chambray dress, out of the black wicker chair. "I can see you're determined not to be sociable today, Henry. I'll get along home. I gave Willie May the sugar and told her to tell Silver, so you don't have to remember about it. I know you'd forget, anyhow. And mark my words, you better get Ilsa back from that beach."

I was so mad I wouldn't walk with her to the car but stayed sitting on the porch and watched her drive off. When Silver came back she came alone.

She came up to the porch where I was waiting and sat down wearily, kicking off her sandals. Grains of sand from the beach dropped onto the pine boards of the porch floor.

"You couldn't get her to come?" I said.

She shook her head. "Go out in the kitchen and get me a dope or something, Brother. I'm parched to death."

When I came back out with her drink her stockings were off too, and she was fanning herself with the paper.

"What happened?" I asked.

She took the glass from me and gulped half of the iced liquid down. "Well," she said, "I stopped the car at the edge of the road because there hasn't been a shower for a week, and I thought it would be better if Ilsa didn't hear me drive up to the house anyway. It's a good thing I didn't try to make it because the road was filled with soft shoulders and I'd have gotten stuck for sure. The sand got into my sandals and it was hotter than Tophet. But you should have seen the flowers, Brother. Sunflowers all over the place, and prickly pear, Gaillardias, lavender Bee Bane, and those lovely purple sea morning-glories. They were all over the road. You'd think it was months since a car'd driven over it instead of a few weeks. Goatsfoot-Gillia, you know their lovely scarlet stalks, and scuppernong vines in bloom all over the sand—I'm going to ask Ilsa if I can pick some of the grapes later on and put up some jelly."

"Go on," I said. "What about Ilsa?"

"Well, I picked my way to the house, pushed open the screen door, and went in. It was very quiet, very bare, clean as a pin. A broom was leaning against the big table Dr. Brandes used to use, so I knew someone must be about. The shutters were almost closed to keep out the sun, and the light filtered through and lay on the floor in sandy yellow stripes. It was so hot I most couldn't breathe. I couldn't hear a sound except the ocean and a little old mockingbird out in the chinaberry tree singing and singing. And I felt so peculiar, Brother, sort of the way you feel going into a deserted house when you're not sure who you may see coming through the sagging door and suddenly you find you believe in ghosts. When I heard the screen door slam behind me I didn't dare turn around because I had the strangest feeling that Dr. Brandes was standing behind me, holding a rare plant in his cupped hands."

"Ilsa?" I asked.

"No. Ira, and not a bit pleased to see me. He just said what was I doing there and did Ilsa know I was coming. I told him no, that I'd come to take her back with me, and he got real mad, said she was much better off where she was and why couldn't we leave her alone when that's what she wanted. I didn't know what to do. I asked him where she was, but he wouldn't tell me. He just stood there glowering at me and looking at that big old hunting knife of his. I bet he cuts his hair with it. It certainly looks it."

"Well, what did you do?"

"I just sat down and said I'd wait. He said I'd be a long time waiting, but I said I'd wait anyhow. He stood chewing tobacco and staring at me like I was a snake or something. Finally he said, 'You never much liked her, did you?'—'Who?' I asked—'Ilsa.' That made me kind of mad. It's not that I don't like Ilsa. I just don't understand her. And now—oh, I guess I do kind of like her after all. So I told him that and then I asked him how she was. He just said, 'All right. How else would she be, being her?' Then he told me if I wanted to look for her she was walking down on the beach. So I went out. And when I knew that I'd have to go up to her on the beach—Brother, I don't know when I've been so scared."

"Why?"

"I don't know. I suppose because I thought her being blind would make her different. I didn't know how I ought to behave. I just stood on that cement ramp and looked around as if I'd never seen the place before. That Ira surely is a good worker. Keeps the ramp clean of sand and it's so white as it goes down through the scrub it hurts your eyes. I'd kind of forgotten how wild it was, what a heavy dark green, the bushes and weeds, palmettos and myrtles—they grow so close together there doesn't seem any room for anything to breathe, and I felt stifled. And you know how hot it's been today. The sun was banging down and even right by the water there wasn't much breeze. I guess it's seemed worse today because yesterday was so cool."

I felt nervous and impatient, but I knew there was no use hurrying my sister. She always told a story her own way and that was usually the longest way.

"I stared up and down the beach," she said, finishing her Coca-Cola and putting the glass down on the floor beside her black wicker chair. "At first I couldn't see anything in either direction; then, far in the distance, I saw a small black speck. It was so far away I couldn't tell whether it was coming or going, but I knew it must be Ilsa because there isn't another house around there for miles. So I went in that direction. I surely was relieved when I saw she was coming toward me. She had on a pair of old blue jeans, rolled up, and a red shirt. That moron hound of hers was beside her, walking close to her feet in the funniest way, as though she thought she was protecting Ilsa. I started to call, and then I just couldn't. I couldn't even go on walking. I stood still, right where I was, and let Ilsa come up to me. And I still couldn't say anything, Brother. I just stared at her and then I went on walking beside her. She didn't look any different, Brother, she looked just the same, only I knew she couldn't see me because when she looked as if she was looking at me, it went right on through me, it didn't stop anywhere at all, it just went on and on. So I just went on and walked with her. That dog didn't pay me any mind at all. And Ilsa was walking so fast—I almost had to run to keep up. Sometimes she started to walk crooked—she'd get into the water, or the loose sand, but then she'd straighten out again. And then, Brother, all of a sudden she said, 'Well, Silver?' I was so startled I almost dropped dead in my tracks. And then she began to laugh, and when she laughed like that, just the way she always did, I wasn't scared of her any more. She said, 'If you don't want me to know when you're around you shouldn't wear that perfume I gave you Christmas. What are you doing here?'—'I just came,' I said.—'Monty send you to spy on me?'—'No,' I said, 'he just wanted to know how you were. He's lonely.'—'How is he otherwise?'—'All right, I guess,' I said.—'And Brand?'—You know that funny sort of tenderness her voice always gets when she talks about Brand, Brother? 'She misses you awfully,' I told her. We walked along without saying anything for a minute; then she said, 'How are you, little Silver Woolf?' And Brother, when she said that I had the funniest feeling that if anything went wrong she would fix it—and there I was, supposed to be helping her! She asked about Eddie and the children and you. Then I asked her to come home with me. She just laughed and said Ira wouldn't like it. And I told her how much Monty and Brand missed her and needed her. We'd come to the house by then. The dog ran on up the steps to the ramp and started barking and Ilsa turned up the beach after it. I wanted to take her arm when we got to the soft sand but I was afraid she wouldn't like it. When we got near the steps she started walking very slowly, and frowning, as though she were trying to hear something. But she found the steps all right and started up. I could see she was counting the steps till we got on the ramp; then she kept her hand on the rail. The screen door was closed but the big door was ajar and she banged right into it. She must have given her head an awful wallop, but she didn't turn a hair. She went in and yelled for Ira and then she blessed him out for leaving the door ajar. You should have heard her. It was real frightening, she was so mad. And he just stood scowling at her till she was finished and then he said she'd have to learn to be careful about doors because people weren't going to remember about them for her. I thought it was awful of him to speak to her like that, but she didn't seem to mind. She kept striding about the room as though nothing was wrong and mostly she managed pretty well, but every once in a while she'd knock into something, and oh, Henry, it was right pitiful. I wanted to take her into my arms and tell her to stop fighting, but I guess she just has to fight. I guess there isn't anything else for her to do. She said once after she'd knocked into something, 'You see, I wouldn't be any good to Monty or Brand yet. Go away and leave me alone. I'm in a vile mood. I've got a temper like a madwoman. I'm much better off down here.' I just couldn't bear to think of her there alone with no one but Ira, and him not much comfort, it didn't seem to me, so I begged her again to come back, but she just kind of laughed and said, 'I'm not like you. You know I don't give a damn about the comforts of life when I can have the ocean, and Ira takes wonderful care of me. I've told you I'm in a hellish mood. It wouldn't be good for Brand to have me around. It wouldn't be good for Monty. If he's behaving well because I'm away, maybe I'd better not come back for a year. But don't you see—I want to be down here where my roots are, where it's wild and lonely and I can learn things and make my mistakes in private. I want to stay until I'm—sufficient unto myself again, and the ocean has breathed peace back into my heart. Come back later.' 'When?' I asked her. She laughed again, but this time it wasn't a good laugh. 'Oh, in a few years.' I didn't know what to say. I didn't know what to do. She just sat there, her elbows on her knees, her chin in her hands, looking as though she were seeing right through me. Then she said, 'Listen, Silver. I'm not ready to come back. Give me two weeks more. Go home and give my husband and my child my love. Tell them that when I come back I'll be all right—that everything will be all right.'—'And you promise to come home in two weeks?' I asked. Well, I got her to promise. That was the best I could do."

Eddie had come up while we were talking and now he sat down on the steps. "How is she for money?" he asked. "Does she need anything?"

"I don't know," Silver answered. "Oh, she asked me to tell the mothers of her piano students that she'd start teaching again the first of October."

Eddie looked skeptical. "How can she?"

"That's what I wondered," Silver said. "But she played for me. I don't know much about music but it sounded all right to me. She said she'd spent about five or six hours a day at it."

"I wish there were something we could do for her." Eddie frowned unhappily. "I've always liked Ilsa and I think she's had a rotten deal. Wish there was some way to help."

"There isn't. Not till she gets back, at any rate," Silver said. "You staying for supper, Henry? There's plenty."

48

But Ilsa came back from the beach in less than two weeks.

Three mornings later I went over to the house to see how things were, on my way to the mill. Brand was sitting alone at the breakfast table. I sat down near her.

"Where's your father?" I asked.

Brand took a swallow of milk. "I don't know, Uncle Henry. At supper last night he said he had to go to town on business and not to worry if he didn't get back till today, but he'd surely be back in time for dinner. I wish he'd come soon. It's awful lonely here with both of them gone."

Mattie Belle came in with a plate of porridge for her. "You here, Mr. Porcher? Good morning."

"Good morning, Mattie Belle," I said. "How are you?"

"I can't complain, though a hoot owl kept me awake awhile. It was so close it sounded as though it was on my window sill, hooting and hooting so scary, it never does mean no good. I choked it, though, and it quit hollering."

My eyes opened. "How on earth did you catch it?"

"Oh, Lord, Mr. Henry, I didn't catch it. If you hear a hoot owl hollering and catch hold of the wrist of your left arm with your right and squeeze hard, you choke the owl and it stops. Some people tie a knot in the sheet but the fust way's the best. It's purely sure to work. I didn't hear it hollering no more after that. You hear it, Baby?"

"No," Brand said.

"I don't like them hoot owls. They come so close, they always mean no good. You eat all your breakfast now."

She went back out to the kitchen and I to the mill.

Shortly after lunch I had a frantic phone call from Violetta and I went tearing down to the beach in the car, faster than anyone ought to drive, recklessly turning off the oyster-shell road and bouncing along the sandy ruts to the house.

No one was there. I called and heard no answer. I flung out of the screen door and ran down the ramp, shouting. To my left I heard Médor barking wildly and saw Ilsa rise from the shelter of a dune and stand listening. I ran, stumbling and slipping, toward her.

"Ilsa! Ilsa!" I called. She didn't move, but stood very still, waiting in her damp bathing suit until I had come up to her. Médor barked and pranced around me in greeting, nipping at my trouser legs.

"What is it, Henry?" Ilsa asked. "What's the matter? What brings you here in such confusion?"

"Ilsa, come quickly," I gasped. "Monty's terribly sick."

She started back toward the house with rapid steady steps, her bare toes feeling the sand beneath them. I took her arm but she shook me off. "What's the matter with him?" she asked.

"I don't know, but he's dreadfully sick. Violetta and Dolph were over. Dolph went for the doctor. Violetta's with Monty. He kept calling for you. We thought I'd better come."

"Of course. Write a note for Ira, will you? You'll find pencil and paper in the drawer of Father's table. And we'd better leave Médor."

I scrawled a note to Ira.

"The car's outside," I said.

She was halfway upstairs. "I'll just get into some clothes."

In a few moments she hurried down, and we went out to the car. This time she let me take her arm, walking carefully over the rough ground, balancing herself delicately like a tightrope walker. "What do you think it is? Do you think it could be that rotten gin he gets from Togni's?" she asked.

"I don't know," I said. "I don't know what bootleg gin does if it's bad."

"Has he been drinking much?" she asked. "I thought silver said he hadn't."

"I didn't think he had," I answered. "I've been going over about every other day for some reason or other, the way you asked me to. He wasn't always there, but when he was he seemed pretty all right. But he wasn't in last night."

"And Brand?"

"She just keeps asking for you."

"Poor baby," Ilsa said. "All this has been hellish for her."

We drove for a good while in silence, then. I dislike driving very rapidly because I never feel that I'm really in control of the car, and I have to concentrate so desperately on the driving that it is difficult for me to talk. I kept wishing that I could ask Ilsa to take the wheel for me, knowing how she adored to speed.

"It smells like autumn," she said once. "It's been a long summer."

We got into traffic as we crossed the bridge and had to slow down. I could sense Ilsa's nervousness as she sat beside me. "I bet it's the gin," she said.

When we got into the house she took my arm and we hurried upstairs. We could hear Violetta talking in a terrified voice that I guess was meant to be soothing.

"It's all right, Mont, just you don't worry and everything's going to be all right. Here comes somebody and it's either Henry with Ilsa, or Dolph with the doctor. Oh, Lord! I don't know what's taking Dolph so long. I guess the doctor's out on his calls this time of day. Here, Monty, let Violetta wipe your mouth. Could you hold a piece of ice in your mouth to take the taste out? Could you do that for Violetta, Monty?"

Monty groaned.

"Get Violetta out," Ilsa said as we went into the room. Monty began to retch violently into a basin Violetta was holding for him. Brand was sitting on a chair by the window, her eyes wide and frightened, her body tense.

"Mamma!" she cried as Ilsa came in, and ran to her. Ilsa held her closely for a brief moment, then said, "Henny, take Brand downstairs. Send her into the kitchen with Mattie Belle. Tell Mattie Belle to bring me up a big pitcher of milk and a glass. Violetta, please go downstairs and wait for Dolph and the doctor."

"Ilsa, what are you talking about!" Violetta cried. "I'm certainly not going to leave my own twin brother when he's sick and needs me."

"Henry!" Ilsa stormed at me. "Get Violetta out of this room. Brand, go ask Mattie Belle for the milk, quickly! Obey me, both of you!"

She fumbled for the bed, sat down, and took the basin from Violetta.

"Ilsa," Monty groaned. "Ilsa, please—"

"It's all right, Monty, I'm here, I've come home," she said, putting the basin on the floor at her feet.

Brand ran from the room, and I pushed Violetta, protesting, ahead of me. "Stay at the door and don't you dare come up those stairs," I said.

She was so astonished at being ordered about in this rude fashion by me, of all people, that she obeyed. I ran out to the kitchen, grabbed the pitcher of milk from the weeping Mattie Belle, and ran back up, slopping milk on the stairs.

Monty was shivering so violently it seemed as though he were having convulsions. Ilsa had her arms about him and was holding him tightly against her to try to control the jerking of his muscles.

"Pain, pain," Monty kept saying.

"Henny?" Ilsa said as I came in.

"Yes. Here's the milk."

"Put it right down at my feet. Right here where I can feel it. That's right. Now go to the hall closet and get me one of the big double blankets."

I hurried out again. When I came back she was speaking to him sharply. "Monty. Try to tell me. Did you have anything to drink? Did you? Monty! Answer me. It's all right. I just want to know. Did you have anything to drink?"

"Yes," he managed to gasp out.

"Here's the blanket," I said.

"Wrap it around him."

While I was doing this she leaned down, felt for the milk, and poured a glass, hardly spilling a drop.

"Can't drink milk," Monty groaned. "Makes me sick."

"Exactly," she said. "That's why you'll drink it."

He jerked wildly away, spilling most of the glass.

"You'll have to help me hold him," Ilsa said to me.

I sat down on the other side of the bed and tried to pinion his arms. Ilsa refilled the glass and forced it to his lips. As soon as he had swallowed the milk he began to retch, and she reached for the basin. He vomited into it, moaning. "It hurts," he moaned. "Pain. Oh, God, pain."

"Where?" she asked.

"My stomach. Oh, God, my stomach."

"Empty the basin and come back as quickly as you can," she said to me.

When I came back she had her fingers on his pulse. "How is it?" I asked.

"Very weak. Very rapid."

"Could it be appendix?" I asked.

"No. He had that out while you were in Paris. I'm sure it was the gin. He's cold and wet. The vomiting. Everything. He's got all the earmarks."

"How do you know?"

"Franz told me about a woman in his company who almost died from bad liquor a couple of weeks before they came here. Hold him again. I want to give him some more milk. If I can just clean his stomach out—"

The telephone rang. "Get it, Henry," Ilsa said sharply. "I don't want Violetta up here again. I'll manage the milk."

I ran downstairs. It was Dolph to say that he couldn't get hold of the doctor. He'd been following him from house to house, missing him everywhere, and now he was miles across the river on a case.

"My God, aren't there any other doctors in town?" Ilsa said. "Come on. We'd better take him to the County Hospital. Get Mattie Belle to help you carry him to the car."

She kept him held tightly in her arms until I came up with Mattie Belle, pressing the glass of milk against his teeth, and holding the basin for him to throw up into. He was delirious now, talking wildly about things that had happened at Togni's, about the part of his life that was the most shameful. As Mattie Belle and I got him off the bed, Ilsa went downstairs ahead of us, holding on to the banister, her feet feeling for the steps.

"Violetta," she said. "Have you got your car here?"

Violetta came into the hall from the drawing room. "Yes, of course." All her string of words seemed to have been frightened out of her. She looked like a pouter pigeon stuck with a hat pin.

"Then please take Brand over to your Cousin Anna's. Tell them to keep her until I come for her. Henry and I are taking Monty to the County Hospital. You can follow us there."

"The County Hospital!" Violetta shrieked.

"Be quiet! It's the nearest and what Monty needs is help as soon as possible."

"We're going out to the car now," I said to Ilsa, pushing out the screen door.

"Violetta, help me out to the car," she commanded.

She sat in the back, holding him. He was quieter now, moaning only occasionally. I drove recklessly through the lights, dodging cars and pedestrians, and we were at the hospital in ten minutes.

But it was no use.

Monty died that evening.

PART FIVE

49

I sat on a dune at the beach and watched the surf. The waves came inexorably, rolling into dark pregnant swells, then rearing themselves up in a luminous green concave wall capped with white, and finally spilling over in a million little crossings and crisscrossings, white-veined and lace-edged. Close to the water were lucent bubbles of foam, rainbow-colored as they caught the sun, instead of the sallow yellow they were when you came up close.

I watched the waves roll in for a long time, until their constant repetition left me almost hypnotized, each wave so similar to the one preceding it, and to the one following, yet each with its own infinite variations. As no leaf on a tree is ever precisely like another, so each wave of the ocean is in some way different, has its own individuality. And it came to me that if we could look at our own lives a thousand years from now, our years would be like that, too, each with its individual wars and passions, its cities rising and falling, its people dying and being born, each so closely related to the others, yet each rounding itself out, full cycle, individual, isolated, alone in itself, like each leaf torn from the branch, each wave rejected by the sea.

As I looked back on the past eleven years, the eleven years since Monty's death, I could see only the similarities, the rise and fall of the days, the hours and minutes swelling and receding, one after the other, one after the other, crepuscular in their sameness.

Morning after morning uselessly spent at the mill, getting in Papa's way, getting in Dolph's way, knowing and despairing of my own uselessness, yet doing nothing about it. Papa had quite given me up. We lived together, but saw each other only occasionally at the mill office, or across the long mahogany dining table at home, where we ate in antagonistic silence, seldom speaking except to comment on the weather, or to ask for the corn bread. Then evening after evening, like the tide following the involuntary command of the moon, I would go to Ilsa's, to find Lorenzo Moore there before me, evening there before me, darkness there before me, knowing what a weak fool was Henry Porcher, Henry Randolph Porcher, and yet not caring enough to remedy it, not caring enough to be unhappy about it.

Lorenzo would sit playing on the mandolin I had given Ilsa; Brand would hunch over the desk doing the accounts, Ilsa standing beside her, dealing with complaints, giving orders to Mattie Belle. Soon after Monty's death she had started taking in boarders to help pay off the debts which were all that Monty had left her, and to support herself and Brand. It was one of the few things a southern lady could do to earn her living, this turning of her home into a boarding house, and about the only thing *she* could do in her blindness. At first I was horribly against it. Then one night something happened that, in a way, reconciled me, because then, at any rate, she would not be alone at night in that huge house with only the child for protection.

50

It was quite late. Mattie Belle had gone home and Brand was upstairs asleep. Ilsa was alone downstairs. It started to rain and she groped her way around to the windows, holding out her hand to see if the rain were coming in, when suddenly she sensed that someone had come in by one of the French windows and was standing in the drawing room.

She was in the hall. She stood very still and listened. She could hear breathing, and a faint creaking of the boards when whoever it was shifted his weight. She knew the floors of the old house like the back of her hand. Stealthily, avoiding the most creaking places, she tiptoed to the big closet under the stairs, where the coats were kept, and in the back of which Monty had hidden his liquor and his gun. She knew the gun was loaded. Very quietly she fumbled for it, tiptoed out again, stood still, just out of sight of the drawing-room door, listening. She could still hear the breathing. Quickly and with determination she walked into the drawing room, holding the gun. She knew from Ira and her father how to hold a gun and how to shoot.

She said that she stared where she heard the breathing so that the intruder would think she could see him, and said, "Get out of this house and stay out."

There was no sound of anyone moving. She could still hear the breathing, fast, a little frightened now.

"Get out," she said, "or I'll shoot, and you can see by the way I handle this gun that I know how."

She heard him turn and leave the room. She heard him on the stone flags of the terrace and she heard him brush through the grass on the way to the river. He walked silently and stealthily as a cat. A few weeks ago, she said, she would not have been able to hear him like that.

When she knew that he had gone she went around and bolted the windows, and spent the rest of the night sitting up straight in a chair, the gun across her knees. She was grateful that Médor was asleep up in Brand's room. There was no telling what the poor half-witted dog might have done otherwise.

I nearly died when she told me.

"Now, for heaven's sake, Hen, don't breathe a word about it to a soul. I won't have Brand frightened, and if Mattie Belle ever got wind of it she'd never cross the threshold again, fond of me as she is. The only reason I told you was because I want you to see if there are any footprints. Maybe I dreamed it. I don't know. I didn't dream sitting up with the gun, at any rate. Go have a look, will you?"

There were footprints.

"You're not to sleep in this house alone another night!" I shouted at her.

"Henry, don't get hysterical," she said crossly. "Where would I sleep?"

"At Cousin Anna's."

"I am no longer of an age to be anybody's ward. And I proved to myself last night that I can take care of myself. I'm glad I didn't imagine it. That really would be something to worry about. If you're nervous about my being here alone, see what you can do about digging me up some boarders."

I gave up and left for the mill. There was no use arguing with her. She came out onto the porch as I left and stood there, her hand on one of the weather-grayed pillars. The rain of the night before had stopped, and the air was fresh and clean-smelling. She stood on the porch, the wind blowing her wild hair on end and whipping the skirt of her cotton dress about her legs. I thought, as she stood there, her head thrown back, breathing the free fragrant air, that she looked like one of the golden figureheads on the huge sailing vessels that first came bravely across the ocean, breasting the wild unknown.

Ilsa had once shown me an old explorer's map that had been her father's. According to this map the sea was peopled with all sorts of strange monsters. Nothing that Ulysses encountered in his voyages was more terrifying or more unknown than the fancied dangers of the early explorers—dangers perhaps more frightening to them than the actual ones.

But on the prow of the boat was a golden figurehead, with bits of cold blue glass for eyes, breasting the dark waves with courage and excitement in her face.

51

"Well, Henry, when you and Ilsa Woolf going to get married? We're all waiting," Mrs. Jackson cooed in the drugstore, Mrs. Jackson sniggered on the corner, Mrs. Jackson giggled as she poked me in the ribs at the parking lot by the butcher's.

"I hear Ilsa Woolf is going to marry you, and we'll all have to find somewhere else to stay," Myra Turnbull said acidly, passing me on the stairs. "I thought she had better taste than that."

Well, perhaps not better taste, Myra Turnbull, but certainly different.

I wanted to write, to pour everything out of my soul in a wild impassioned torrent of poetry, in the ecstatic ravings of novel. Paper and pen before me, my mind seethed, my brain seemed to quiver like sunlight on a hot day, and all that would come out was *Oh God, oh God, oh God*—nothing but that agonized repetition—nothing, nothing else.

Now as I sat on the warm cradling sand of the beach, I knew that I was not strong enough to absorb strength from nature, that I must as usual go running to the only human being who could put courage into my precarious soul and who dispensed this intransigent stability with the lavishness of ignorance. Or did she know? That is something, I suppose, that I shall never know.

I looked again at the ocean and begged for help, but received none. It rejected me as unimpassionedly as it accepted Ilsa. She saw only the impersonal vastness and strength of the sea, while I could not help personalizing it. Its very indifference troubled me. I would watch the waves carelessly caressing the shore and caring nothing for it, and remember that three years ago, not far from where I sat, Lorenzo had been attacked and badly bitten on the leg by a barracuda, that further down the beach Silver's little Henry Porcher had been caught in the undertow and nearly drowned trying, uselessly, to save the life of a companion. And while we waited, trying to hold and fan the flame of his faint breath, the moon had come up radiantly over the dark water's edge, proclaiming her light-hearted self-satisfaction. I watched the ancient skin of the sea and remembered the storms that tossed the wreckage of fishing vessels on the shore and the storms that came down the coast to destroy homes and lay waste the land.

I walked back up the beach to the car. I was quite near July Harbour; the houses of the village caught the gleaming sun. We were no longer able to use Dr. Brandes' house when we went the beach except in the winter, because in the summer, when many of the boarders were away and there was not so much money, Ilsa rented it.

How she had hated to do that.

"But I have to, Henny," she said. "There's so much to do to this horrible old house in town. By the way, the boathouse went in the last storm, and the dock's a mass of debris. I'll have to have it cleared."

"But do you think you'll be able to rent it?" I asked.

"Why not?"

"It's so far away from everything and everybody."

She shrugged. "There are probably a few people," she said, "who still feel about privacy as I do."

I got into the car and started back to town. I was in a bad mood, had been for several days, and I wasn't sure why. The past eleven years had been very peaceful and happy on the whole, and I couldn't put my finger on the reason for this gloom that had suddenly descended on me. I felt like a sulky child in need of comforting instead of the rational, if not dynamic, adult I presumed I was.

I tried to clutch at memories that were pleasant in order to throw off my mood. This coming down to the beach instead of running pellmell to Ilsa had been in itself an unusual (and futile) declaration of independence.

How does the Declaration of Independence begin? All men are created equal. . . . Beautiful utter nonsense. As long as some men are born with more intelligence, more will power than others, how can there be anything but inequality?

—Enough of that—I thought—That will get you nowhere. The happiest time I could remember was one Christmas when Ilsa had left the house and the boarders in Mattie Belle's charge and gone down to the beach with Brand for a week. I went too, in spite of Papa's protests. He was sure that people would talk, but he calmed down a bit when I told him that Ilsa had asked Cousin Anna, with Barbara to take care of her, to come too, and Cousin William and Lorenzo Moore.

I remember all of us standing around the piano after the lamps were lit and singing Christmas carols—Ilsa, Brand, Ira. Cousin Anna, Barbara, Cousin William, Lorenzo, and myself. I remember trimming the Christmas tree Ira brought in from the woods, and Ilsa flinging tinsel at the branches and laughing. And I remember Ilsa walking for miles on the beach wearing a pair of Eddie's old gray flannel trousers—he was so slight they were the right size for her—and a sweat shirt of Ira's, and Médor continually getting under her feet and tripping her. And then the day before we went back to town it was suddenly, unseasonably, hot.

"I know I'm foolish," Ilsa shouted at us, "but I'm going swimming!" And she found her old blue-serge bathing suit and ran recklessly down the beach, stumbling over a washed-up log and rolling over and over, picking herself up and tearing into the ocean, flinging herself at the breakers that tossed her about like a bit of driftwood, while that moron hound Médor rushed at the surf and barked hysterically, furious with it for daring to buffet Ilsa, running in screaming terror whenever a wave lapped at her toes, and finally dashing into the churning water to rescue Ilsa and, of course, having to be rescued herself; and then Ilsa, blue with cold, coming back to the house and standing in front of the fire in her bathrobe, warming her hands around a bowl of donax soup. . . .

52

I remembered these things all the way in to town, but I was still depressed. The porch was deserted as I drove up to the Woolf house; the sun was still beating down on it, and it was too hot. On my way in I bumped into Joshua Tisbury, one of the boarders, an ugly young man with a weak chest who spent most of the day hunched over a typewriter in one of the small back rooms. He greeted me cheerfully as I went through the rice portieres and into the drawing room. Brand and Lorenzo were there, Lorenzo sitting on the piano bench, Brand on the bamboo chaise longue, eating a persimmon.

At nineteen Brand was pretty in a quiet way; her brown eyes had Monty's long lashes, her thick curly hair the ruddy sheen of his. But she always looked lost, to me, as though she were outside a house on a dark night, forced to look through the windows at the warmth and life inside, in which she would never be allowed to participate.

"Hello, Uncle Henry," she said as I came in.

"Hello, honey. Where's your mother?"

"Down by the river."

"Alone?"

"Yes."

"She shouldn't be," Lorenzo said. At twenty-one he still looked like a skinny little bird, his eyes as huge, his nose as beaked as ever, but he had a kind of serene determination that continually astonished me.

"Of course she should," Brand said angrily. "I wouldn't have let her go, otherwise."

"You do anything your mother says, whether it's right or not." Lorenzo rested his arms on the keys of the piano.

"I don't."

"Of course you do," Lorenzo said. "Everybody does. . . . I ought to go home and work on my harpsichord, but I'm too hot."

"Still making the harpsichord, Lorenzo?" I asked, seating myself on one of the white summer-shrouded chairs.

"Yes."

Mattie Belle stuck her little marmoset head in the doorway "Where Miz Woolf?"

"She went down by the river," Brand said.

"Did she take a parasol?" Mattie Belle asked.

Lorenzo laughed, leaned away from the piano, and put his elbows on his knees. "You know she didn't."

"She oughtn't to be out walking in this brilin' heat," Mattie Belle said. "Enough to scorch the fur off a tarantula. Ain't nothing I can do to manage her. Baby, can't you—"

"Don't you talk to me." Brand shook her head. "You know I can't manage Mamma." She took her spoon and scraped the last shred of persimmon from the skin.

"I guess you got to raise a person like Miz Woolf to be able to do anything with her," Mattie Belle said. "Old Miz Anna Silverton's the only person I ever saw who could boss her and even she can't keep her from being purely pigheaded. Well, I s'pose I better go down to the river and look for her. There's something I don't get about the ice bill this week, and I ain't aiming to pay it till I is satisfied we not being overcharged. If you smell anything in the kitchen, go have a look, Brand.

"Uh huh." Brand pushed her damp hair off her forehead with a tired gesture. "What we having for dinner?"

"Bacon and grits and baked eggplant."

"Oh, grits again, Mat!"

"Miz Woolf went whipping off this morning and forgot to give me the orders. I had to figure out the best I could. And I couldn't ask you because you was nowhere to be found, and the linen to be sorted."

"Oh, Mat, I forgot! I'll go do it now."

"You perfectly well know I did it for you," Mattie Belle said, but with no ill-humor, and stomped out, almost colliding with Myra Turnbull.

I'll never forget the day I walked into the drawing room and saw Myra Turnbull sitting there, talking to Ilsa. I felt as though I were a very little boy once more, in one of Miss Myra's classes. My mouth fell open and I let out a startled noise that sounded more like a razorback pig grunting than anything else.

Myra Turnbull turned around and eyed me with distaste.

I looked at her, at Miss Myra, wearing the same heavy steel-rimmed spectacles, the short, straight nondescript-colored hair pushed behind her ears, the thin shapeless body in the thin shapeless dress. Now that I was older I saw, too, the fine eyes, the flawless complexion, the beautiful pointed ears pressed like little shells against her head. Still feeling like a child in the schoolroom, I managed to gasp out, "He—hello, Miss Turnbull."

"Yes," she said, and I stared open-mouthed as she pulled a package of cigarettes out of the pocket of her shapeless silk jacket. "I thought you looked familiar. Who are you?"

"Henry Porcher," Ilsa said. "Do you know each other?"

"She—she taught me English in school," I stammered.

"And you probably don't remember a particle of it."

"Oh, but I do—I'll never forget your classes."

"That," said Myra Turnbull, "could be either a compliment or its diametric opposite."

"Is she—are you—" I couldn't seem to stop stammering.

"Yes, I'm staying here," Myra Turnbull said. "For a month or so, at any rate."

That was five years ago.

Now she came into the room, looking around for Ilsa. Brand and Lorenzo, who had been in her English classes not so long ago, rose awkwardly. I had long since thrown off my shyness and become extremely fond of Myra Turnbull, so, although I rose too, I greeted her with a "hey" I wouldn't have thought possible or permissible five years before.

"For an omnivorous reader you have primitive modes of greeting, Henry. Good evening, Brand. Good evening, Lorenzo."

Lorenzo bobbed his head.

"Good evening, Miss Turnbull," Brand said. "Just getting back from school?"

"Yes," Myra said. "I had to keep most of the class in. It is insufferable that the schools have to open in this September heat. Well, Lorenzo, why aren't you at the theological seminary this year?"

Lorenzo looked at the floor to hide a grin. "I don't feel I've been called yet," he said.

"Lorenzo, hold up your head and speak like a man and not like a gangling schoolboy. You are twenty-one years old and you would do well to remember it."

"Yes, Miss Turnbull."

"And you, Brand. Why your mother didn't send you to college this year I will never understand. You may not be brilliant, but you have a reasonably adequate brain and it would have been good for you."

"You know we can't afford it," Brand said. "And Mamma needs me here, anyhow."

"In that case you will speak to Miss Wells. She spends an hour in the bathroom every evening just when I want my bath and she sprays that cheap perfume of hers all over the place."

"I'll speak to her, Miss Turnbull," Brand said, again pushing her hair back with that weary gesture.

"And if I have grits one more night for dinner I shall pack my bags and leave." Myra started out.

"She'd better begin packing then," Lorenzo whispered.

"What's that?" Myra wheeled on him.

"Nothing, Miss Turnbull." He looked down at his feet until Myra had gone out through the big folding doors. Then he sat down again, this time on the floor.

"I heard they weren't going to ask her back to school this year," Brand said. "I'm glad they did."

"Who told you that?" Lorenzo asked.

"I don't remember."

"Why wouldn't they ask her back? She's the best teacher they've ever had in the school."

"Because of—oh, you know why, Lorenzo."

"Because they say she drinks? Well, I've been around here plenty and I've never seen any signs of it."

"You wouldn't know anybody was drunk unless they passed out cold, and then you'd just think they were dead."

Brand got up and put her plate with the remains of the persimmon on the table by the folding doors.

53

I looked up quickly as Ilsa and Mattie Belle came in the French windows. Ilsa went over to the piano, her feet in their soft sandals touching the floor with the peculiar intimacy of a ballet dancer; Mattie Belle went back to the kitchen.

Outwardly Ilsa had changed very little in the past eleven years. She was thinner, but her body was as firm and strong as ever. The lines of determination about her mouth and eyes no longer disappeared when she laughed, but she still laughed a great deal. Her hair had kept its old tawny color of the sea oats, her skin its burnished sunny gold. But it was her hands you noticed now as you never had before.

Although she did not move them a great deal, they seemed to stand out from the rest of her, startling in their sensitive touching beauty. Her most casual gesture was fraught for me with an indescribable importance.

Her sightless eyes still mirrored her moods, flaming with amusement, freezing cold and sharp with anger, smouldering with determination. Now that she could not see, she took less pains to control her facial expressions. Sometimes, when I wondered that blind eyes could have the life and intensity of flame, I would remember that flame cannot see.

"Hello, Ilsa," I said. "I went to the beach today."

"Did you, Hen?" Her fingers were moving gently over the piano keys, soundlessly, not striking the notes. "How was it?"

"Wonderful. I wish you could have come."

"I wish I could, too."

"Hello, I'm here," Lorenzo said shyly, scrambling up from the floor, and, as usual, bowing awkwardly as though she could see. Ilsa was the one person before whom Lorenzo lost his serenity.

"Oh, hello, Lorenzo, dear. How are you today?"

As soon as she spoke to him he sat down again. "Oh, I'm fine, thank you. How are you?"

"I'm fine, too."

"Does anyone want a coke?" Brand asked. No one said anything. "Must you always sit on the floor, Lorenzo?" Her voice had a thin edge of irritation to it.

"It's cooler on the floor."

"It's not that hot."

"Does it bother you to have me sit on the floor?"

"Do whatever you please. I don't care. How's the harpsichord coming along, Lorenzo?" Brand's voice was unpleasant. I thought it was because this fag end of summer had worn us all out.

"It's nearly finished," Lorenzo said quietly, looking over at Ilsa, who sat silently, her cold blue eyes seeming to stare sternly down at the piano.

"Miss Darlington is complaining because we have grits so often," Brand went on. "Everyone's sick of them, but Miss Darlington's the worst. I wish we could put her out, but she pays more for that room than anyone we've had so far. Not that it does any good. Joshua Tisbury hasn't paid his rent again this week. Why do you let him stay, Mamma?"

Ilsa began to strum softly. She appeared not to have heard.

"And Miss Turnbull said if we had grits again she'd leave, and we're having them tonight. What should we do?"

"Nothing," Ilsa said.

"I don't think you'd care if we lost all the boarders." Brand's voice was not pretty when she complained.

"I wish to hell we would. And Myra won't leave." Ilsa got up, took her mandolin off the piano—I had given it to her the year after she became blind—and began stroking the chords.

"It was so nice when we were here alone," Brand sighed. "You and Papa and me. It doesn't seem to me it used to get so hot then. Doesn't anybody want a Coca-Cola? What I'd really like is lemonade."

"Why don't you go make some?" Ilsa suggested in her low voice, dark as the sea. When I read the other blind poet, Homer, I was always reminded of Ilsa's voice when he talked of the wine-dark sea.

"Mattie Belle's getting dinner," Brand said.

"You wouldn't be in her way if you stayed in the pantry."

Brand sighed again, heavily. I noticed that each time she sighed, a worried shadow crossed Ilsa's face. "You'd think we could rent the back room," Brand said, "when the house is so close to the river and everything. It's just that it looks so hot. Oh. . . . I'm too lazy to go make lemonade."

"I'll do it for you," Lorenzo said, scrambling off the floor and shaking himself to settle his feathers.

Ilsa called after him, "Tell Mattie Belle to make a soufflé instead of the grits for tonight, will you, Lorenzo? It'll make Brand much happier."

After she heard his footsteps diminish as he went through the dining room, she turned toward Brand. I think she had forgotten, as she often did, that I was in the room.

"Do you love Lorenzo?" she asked.

Brand made that trapped rabbit-like movement of the head. "I've told you I don't know."

"If you did, would you marry him?"

"I've told you I don't know."

"I like Lorenzo."

"He'll never have a cent."

"Is that so important?"

"I don't know. I—I'm tired of being poor."

"You simply don't understand him, do you?"

"I guess not."

"Does he know that?"

"Yes."

"But does he really know it?"

"You can't make someone really know something by just telling them it's so."

"Brand—"

"What, Mamma?"

"Why don't you go spend a week with your Aunt Silver and the children—just for a change?"

"She hasn't asked me."

"Of course she has. She told you just to let her know any time you could come and she'd love to have you."

"That's not a real invitation."

"You don't need a real invitation from Silver."

"I can't help it."

"You mean you won't go?"

"I can't trust you."

"I'm perfectly capable of taking care of myself."

Brand pulled a small box out of the pocket of her yellow cotton dress and took it over to Ilsa, putting it in her hand. "What's this?"

Ilsa took the box, feeling it with a quick light stroke of her fingers. "My sleeping tablets."

"How many have you got in the box?"

"I don't know, dear. Quite a few."

"Mr. Bell told me you only get two on each prescription. What do you want all these for?"

"It saves me extra trips to the store in this hot weather to have them on hand."

"You didn't have this many two weeks ago and these have been the hottest two weeks this summer. You must have made a good many trips to get all these."

"Well?" Ilsa said.

"I'm going to keep them."

"You are not."

"Please let me keep them, Mamma. I can't sleep if you don't let me keep them."

Ilsa slipped the pills into her pocket as Lorenzo came in with the lemonade.

"Here we are," he said, putting the tray carefully down on the table.

Ilsa put her mandolin back on the piano. "Lorenzo, you're an angel. There's nothing I love more than lemonade in hot weather."

Lorenzo poured her a glass and took it over to her. "There's plenty more."

"Did you use up all the lemons?" Brand asked.

Lorenzo grinned. "I wanted to, but Mattie Belle wouldn't let me."

Ilsa drank down half of her lemonade. "Brand, my darling, I love you dearly, but Lorenzo makes much better lemonade than you do."

"I've watched him," Brand said, sipping hers gingerly. "He isn't very sanitary about it."

Ilsa laughed. "There's a very comforting saying that what you can't see won't hurt you. I'll take Lorenzo's unsterile lemonade."

Lorenzo refilled her glass and said, "I think I can finish my harpsichord tonight."

"Lorenzo!" Ilsa exclaimed. "How exciting!"

"I feel quite queer about it," Lorenzo said.

“How long has it been?” I asked.

“It’s three years, Uncle Henry. Lorenzo’s spent three years making a harpsichord.” Brand’s voice was metallic with antagonism.

“Oh.” I looked over at Lorenzo, who plunged his hands into his pockets and shrugged his thin shoulders.

“It must be very beautiful,” Ilsa said.

Lorenzo looked at her gratefully. “It is. Very.”

“May I play it?” she asked.

“It’s over the garage. The stairs are quite bad.”

“Darling, I’m not an invalid.”

“I’d love to have you play it,” Lorenzo said.

Ilsa went over to the mantelpiece and took down a picture she’d had taken of Brand on her eighth birthday. “Lorenzo.”

“Ma’am?”

“You know this picture of Brand?” She took it to him.

“Of course.”

“I’ve always meant to ask someone who could really *see*. You’re one of the few people I know here who can. Brand was eight when this picture was taken, just before I lost my sight. Does she still look anything like it? I mean, the expression?”

“The eyes are different,” Lorenzo said slowly.

“I was afraid of that,” Ilsa said.

“What do you mean?” Brand asked in a hard little voice.

Ilsa returned the picture to the mantelpiece, went back to the piano and sat down. “I’ll ask Joshua, too.”

“Why do you let Joshua stay!” Brand cried.

“Because.”

“You’ve always listened to me before, Mamma.”

Ilsa laughed.

I thought that she was indeed in a strange and cruel mood that afternoon.

“More lemonade, Brand?” Lorenzo asked.

“Yes. I’ll get it. I think it just makes me hotter, though.”

As Brand went and poured what was left in the pitcher into her glass, Ilsa straightened up and seemed to be listening suddenly.

“Where’s Médor? Is she in here?”

“No, I don’t think so,” Lorenzo said, getting down on his knees and looking under the sofa and the chairs. “No, she isn’t here.”

“She was down by the river with me,” Ilsa said, “and she was so hot I sent her in. I suppose she got lost on the way to the house.”

“Shall I go look for her?” Lorenzo asked.

"Would you mind awfully, Lorenzo?"

"No, of course not." He got up and went out the window. We heard him whistling as he went toward the river.

"Poor Médor," Ilsa said, laughing. "Remember how she used to sit in the yard and cry when we first got her? In such an undoglike way, as though she were frightened of something. The way children do when they're frightened and lonely and need someone to tell them they're loved and wanted. She just used to cry off in a corner, not at the door or under a window, but just off by herself, until I heard her and came out so she could crawl up in my lap and be soothed. She wasn't in pain, she was simply unhappy and frightened. You remember sometimes how she used to keep on her funny shivering sort of crying five minutes after I came out and began rubbing her and telling her that everything was all right, we were all here, nobody was going to take her away or hurt her. She hasn't done it for a couple of years now."

"I don't know why on earth you've kept her all these years, Mamma. She isn't any help to you," Brand said, stupidly; she ought to have known it would infuriate her mother.

"You might as well ask why I've kept you all these years," Ilsa flashed back.

"You remember," I said quickly, "how proud you were when Dolph and Eddie took her hunting?"

The anger ebbed from Ilsa's face and she grinned. "Yes. I felt just like a gratified parent when she turned out to be their best hunter. The fashionable hunters may have laughed because she squatted instead of pointing properly, but that was just her way."

I had gone hunting with Eddie and Dolph a few times, though it was not a sport that I enjoyed. When Médor was hunting with them they had to do their best not to hunt in fence country, because Médor had to be helped over. She never learned to jump; she just went up vertically and stiff-legged and came down on the same spot, or just *on* the barbed wire. And as though that were not enough, another of Monty's dogs (Eddie and Dolph had bought them) and Bone, Eddie's favorite dog, had to be helped over because they were too old and grandfatherly to jump, and Médor had to see that I got over, having some idea that she must bring me safely back to Ilsa. Even when she was on a scent and someone else had lifted her over a fence she'd circle right back, leaving the birds completely, and worry at the fence till I was safely over. Eddie and Dolph would be swearing at the damned dog acting as though I were her brood of chicks, and I would do my best to send her on, but Médor hovered helpfully till the fence had been safely navigated. Several times I got hooked up and Médor was distraught, and twice I fell into creeks when the log I was on rolled or twisted. Médor was a nervous wreck by the end of those days, so we had to try to avoid creeks as well as fences. It was like having a critical onlooker peering over your shoulder. Before I'd done it with no trouble and no thinking, but the worried watching made me muff it.

Then there was the time, about two years after Monty's death when there was the accident. Ilsa remembered it now, too, because she said, "You've never gone hunting since, have you?"

"No," I answered.

54

There has been a hunting accident. There has been an accident at hunting. That was what they said. That was how they told you. In Mamma's books. In Silver's books. *Madam, I regret to inform you. There has been a hunting accident.* She grows very pale. Her fingers fall from the piano keys. Not—she gasps. He nods. His face is very solemn, the color of parchment, a face like a skull, Dolph Silverton's face, but it is not Dolph, it is from Mamma's books, from Silver's books, the paragon in tails bearing a silver salver with a white card, chastely engraved: *Henry, Lord Randolph, ninth earl of Porcher.* But now there is no salver, now he stands looking with impersonal sorrow at the blanched figure at the piano. *Not*—she gasps. *Yes, Madam. Lord Henry.*

> *O, where have you been wandering, King Henry, my son?*
> *O, where have you been wandering, my pretty one?*

Oh, Mamma, my head pains me. Mamma, hold my head

But she turns away in distaste, "You will get blood on my dress," she says.

One minute I was standing there, Dolph, with his gun leveled, near me, Eddie somewhere not far away; the dogs silent, pointing; Médor squatting, ecstatic; the smell of salt in the air; the sky the color of cotton, and the birds rising, beating their wings against it.

Then there is a flash of lightning and a clap of thunder.

But we do not have thunder in December.

And after it the birds hang suspended against the white, the dogs are petrified in the act of leaping forward, a black pine tree with a crooked branch is nailed like a cross against the sky.

There has been an accident at hunting, Madam. I regret to inform you. The silver salver falls from his hands and clatters on the piano keys. *King Henry, Madam, yes, Madam, I regret to inform you. O, where have you been wandering King Henry, my son.*

Something hot and sticky, that is what they always say about blood; yes, something hot and sticky drips into my eyes and blinds them. The cotton-colored sky darkens with blood, the dogs drown in a pool of blood, the birds fall, their wings weighted by it, unable to move in the dense crimson heaviness.

Now I must lie down, I say to myself, because I am shot and I am dead. When you are dead you do not remain standing, your gun in your hands, fingers cold against metal, cheek cold against sky. When you are dead you lie down.

So I lie down.

I can feel the sharp grasses against my face as I press into the earth, but there is nothing else, no pain. I feel the sharp grasses, cold and wet; then I feel nothing. I see nothing. Blackness.

Now I know what it is like, I tell her as she rises from the piano and holds her fingers tightly together. *Henry! I must go to him!* she cries. Now I know what it is like, I tell her—darkness—now I know what it is like for you.

Then the blood is cleaned from my eyes, someone is wiping it away, and the immaculate figure in tails is bending over me the impeccable parchment face.

"Tell her there has been an accident," I said.

"Henry," the voice said. "It's Dolph."

"Henry," a voice echoed. "It's Eddie."

"Henry," another voice said. "We'll get you right home."

"But I'm not going home."

"What?"

"I'm not going home."

"Never?"

"Never."

"I'm afraid your father will have something to say about that."

"Please let me stay to supper."

"I really do not see how Ilsa or I could contaminate you but the Porchers are such rare creatures that they are very afraid of contagion."

Something was being tied around my head. A handkerchief. I reached up and felt it about my forehead, a tight band like a crown.

O, where have you been wandering, King Henry; my son?
O, where have you been wandering, my pretty one?
I've been to my sweetheart, mother, make my bed soon,
For I'm sick to the heart and would fain lay me down.

Someone held me. Someone held my head against the jouncings of those roads, those tracks through the swamp, through the fields; someone held my head against the joltings of Eddie's sharp-angled hunting Ford. Someone pressed tight fingers against the place on my forehead that was beginning to spread out like flame and consume me, to burn my brain, my mind, my soul, in an intense dry fire.

"I don't want to go home. I won't go home," I said.

"Henry, it's me, it's Eddie. I'm taking you home with me. I'm taking you home to Silver."

"Oh, Henry," she cried. "Oh, Henry," Silver cried, and there had been nobody to tell her, nobody to warn her, no one said: *There has been an accident at hunting.*

Out of the blackness her face flashed above me, pale and anxious, her white face flittered above me. "Oh, Henry," she cried.

I am like the moon, I thought, as I felt the bed hard under me and my head being held up from eternity by the cool cup of Silver's hand. I am like the moon on a cloudy night. Sometimes I am alive; I shine clear and bright. Like now. Everything is quite sharp and clarified. There has been an accident. Hunting. There is a bullet in my head. In all probability I am dying. Someone will tell her there has been an accident and she will come to me.

This is when the moon is clear of the clouds. And sometimes it is partly obscured by them. It shines dimly, unable to penetrate the mist.

O, where have you been wandering, King Henry, my son?

Hold my head, Mamma, hold my head. Save me from the buzzards, Mamma, with their naked necks; save me from the white-bellied sharks.

She pulls away her skirts. She holds her hands in the white-kid gloves tight to her body; she will not touch me. "You will get blood on my dress," she says.

And then there is blackness. There are only the clouds. Dark as mountains, thick as hills, untransparent as high earth and rock. There is no moon. The moon is dead.

Man, that is born of a woman, hath but a short time to live, and is full of misery. He cometh up, and is cut down like a flower; he fleeth as it were a shadow, and never continueth in one stay.

Man, that is born of a woman. . . .

But I was not born of a woman. I was born of Mamma.

If you are a wicked naughty boy, Henry, the overseer will come for you. He wears boots laced up to the knee and he has a gun in a leather holster on his hip. The chains will clank behind you as you walk, and you will never be allowed to be alone. You will become dirty and you will smell like the others.

I will be good, Mamma, I will be good!

If you are a wicked naughty boy, Henry, you will be sent out to the lightship. They are waiting for you there. The buzzard sits on the topmost mast, and the sharks circle round and around the ship. They are waiting for you.

"Ilsa!" I cried. "Ilsa! Ilsa!"

"Hush, Henry. Hush, Brother." Silver's voice. "Ilsa's coming."

The lightship is a strong arm of light, the lightship is the clear eye of courage, the lightship is comfort in darkness.

It has been a long time since Ilsa has seen the lightship. It has been a long time that Ilsa has been in darkness.

"Ilsa!" I cried. "Ilsa, look at me!"

"Hush, Brother. Ilsa is coming. You mustn't talk. The doctor says you are to be perfectly quiet."

In the midst of life we are in death. . . . Thou knowest, Lord, the secrets of our hearts; shut not thy merciful ears to our prayer; but spare us, Lord most holy, O God most mighty, O holy and merciful saviour, thou most worthy Judge eternal. . . .

Monty lies very quiet, very pale, his eyes closed and more blind than Ilsa's, his mouth shut to the sun, his ears to those words, his body numb to the clods of earth, thrown on the coffin. I stand next to Ilsa. Silver stands on the other side of her. She cannot see the curious eyes on her, the eager staring people, the white and black clothes, Mrs. Jackson in white, handkerchief to mouth, all the Mrs. Jacksons, Violetta in black, sweating, weeping, all the Violettas in black voile, in white silk, and the sun beating down on us all, see, you were fooled, summer is not over—

Ilsa cannot see the prying, probing eyes but she can feel them, more cruel than the sun, beating her, flaying her; she knows they are there—she knows. Her face is very set, her blue eyes seem to stare fiercely at the words pushing open the humid air, at the grave pushing open the heavy earth. *Forasmuch as it hath pleased Almighty God, in his wise providence, to take out of this world the soul of our deceased brother, we therefore commit his body to the ground; earth to earth, ashes to ashes, dust to dust. . . .*

But the handkerchief, the large silk handkerchief, rolled into a ball and moist Only from the sweat of her palms, moist not at all from tears, that handkerchief belongs to the graceful-limbed Hamlet, the dark-eyed actor, Franz Josef, Franz Josef Werner. Her grief is not for the dead man, the desolation in the blind eyes is not for her widowhood—If thou didst ever hold me in thy heart, Absent thee from felicity awhile, And in this harsh world draw thy breath in pain. . . . No, Henry, no, you are imagining, you are making it up; he was not important, he didn't matter. . . .

And we beseech thee, that we, with all those who are departed in the true faith of thy holy Name, may have our perfect consummation and bliss, both in body and soul. . . .

Mamma's limbs are stiff in the coffin, in the narrow black box; Mamma's face is still angry at death, death for having dared to touch her, for having presumed to violate her. Silver stands beside me, her eyes as dry as Ilsa's. Papa clutches the silver top of his cane.

O, where have you been wandering, King Henry, my son?

And Mamma is bending over me, her hair fragrant against my cheek, her gloved hands gentle against my body.

"I know I was wicked not to love you, but I couldn't help it," she says. "I couldn't help it."

"That's all right, Mamma," I say, awkwardly.

"I know it was wicked to frighten you with the chain gang and the buzzards, but I had to frighten you. I had to frighten you so you would never frighten me."

"It's all right, Mamma. I understand," I say.

"Henry, it's Silver. Are you in pain?"

"No, go away!" I cry.

Mamma draws back. "You're sending me away. There is blood on my dress."

"No, not you!" I cry. "Mamma, come back! Come back!"

But she shakes her head. She puts one hand up to her mouth. Under the gloves the rings bulge. She stands away from the bed and with the other hand she holds her skirts close about her so that they will touch nothing in the room.

O, where have you been wandering, King Henry, my son?
O, where have you been wandering, my pretty one?

I've been to my sweetheart, mother, make my bed soon,
For I'm sick to the heart, and would fain lay me down.

And what will you leave your sweetheart, King Henry, my son?
O, what will you leave your sweetheart, my pretty one?
A rope for to hang her, mother! Make my bed soon,
For I'm sick to the heart, and would fain lay me down.

She stands with her eyes blindfolded. You don't need to do that, I cry, you don't need to blindfold her eyes; she is blind; she will not be able to see the noose when you slip it over her head.

But we always blindfold them. It is the custom.

Yes—but here we do not hang people.

She speaks. Her words come dark as the ocean at night, calm under a moonless sky. "You said I was to be hanged. Don't argue. Let's get it over with as quickly as possible."

"No, no!" I cry. "I didn't mean it! Stop! Ilsa! Ilsa!"

Hands were strong against my shoulders. Someone was pushing me. I was falling. In panic I opened my eyes and the four mahogany posts of Silver's bed struck wildly at the ceiling.

"I am here," the wine-dark voice said. "Henry, be quiet."

She pushed me back against the pillows.

"There has been an accident," I said, "an accident at hunting. Madam, I regret to inform you—"

"Be quiet," she said.

The moon came out of the clouds.

Her hand rested on the bed but it didn't touch me. I wanted to reach out for it but I was afraid that if I moved she would disappear. Her hand stayed very still, very steady. The gold band of the wedding ring was strong in the light which pierced the blinds.

"Are we alone?" I asked.

"Yes."

"Where is Silver?"

"Downstairs."

"There is no one in the room?"

"No one."

"We are alone?"

"Yes."

"Will you marry me?"

"No."

"Monty is dead."

"Yes."

"Then you are free."

"No. I am not free."

"Your fingernails are not clean," I said.

She withdrew her hand, with the broad band of the wedding ring, from the bed.

"Don't feel badly," I said. "I know you can't see them." Then I went on, almost shouting. "Do you love him, then? Do you love him so much?"

"Yes!" she shrieks. "I will defy you all," she cries, jumping up. "You, Montgomery; you, Cecilia-Jane; and you, Violetta, so pure, so refined! I love him and I will marry him! You are all cold and frigid and dead. But I am alive, and even if you try to kill my love you cannot because it is stronger than you are!"

"Elizabeth, you are out of your mind," Mamma says, pulling on white-kid gloves. "You are *out*"—the snap at one wrist is fastened—"of your *mind*," and the snap at the other.

"I love, I hate! I love, I hate!" Elizabeth cries. She shakes the four posts of the bed. She beats her head against the walls, and Mamma ties her up so that she cannot move, and she lies there, bound and screaming, groaning, shrieking—animal noises like Mamma fighting death. It is worse when there is a moon. When there is a moon she is not human.

"I am dying," she whispers. "Anna, hold my hand, don't let go."

Man that is born of woman . . . full of misery . . . cut down, like a flower . . . in the midst of life we are in death . . . who for our sins art justly displeased . . . Yet, O Lord God most holy, O Lord most mighty, O holy and most merciful Saviour, deliver us not into the bitter pains of eternal death.

"Anna, hold my hand, don't let go."

But not once did she say she was afraid.

"I am dying in childbirth. That is a good way to die, Henry. No. That's not right. I didn't die in childbirth. It's her. The other one. The dancer. Her mother. But I should have been the one. I should have been the one, Henry."

"O, where have you been wandering, King Henry, my son?"

"Hold my hand, don't let go."

Again the moon was out of the clouds.

"Please hold my hand. Please don't let go."

She took my hand in both of hers. "Go to sleep, Henry," she said. "I won't leave. Go to sleep."

"Hold my hand, Ilsa. Don't let go. Don't let go."

"I won't," she said. "Go to sleep."

"Will you kiss me good night, then?"

She nodded. She rose from the chair Silver had placed by the bed. She felt for my face with her hands. They moved very lightly, very gently, so that she would not find me with an abrupt movement. For a moment her fingers traveled over me. Then my face was caught between her hands and she bent down and her lips touched mine, warm, and full of life.

"So I am not going to die after all," I said.

55

Brand collected the empty lemonade glasses and took the tray back to the kitchen.

"Hen?" Ilsa said.

For a moment it was difficult to jerk myself back from my memories. It seemed that I still felt her hands gentle on either side of my face, her mouth strong against mine.

"Yes, I'm here," I said.

"I've only got ten piano pupils for this winter." She walked restlessly over to one of the windows and leaned against it, trying to catch the breeze. "And only three this summer. The more this town grows the more it's convinced I can't teach because I'm blind. This town is the worst size a town can be. I don't know why we don't just not pay the mortgage on the house and let the bank take it."

"Where would we go, and with what?" Brand asked, coming back in and flinging herself down on the sofa.

"To the smallest village or the biggest city. To the ocean. To mountains and snow. Everywhere. Did you hear Miss Corinne Waley's piano recital at the Woman's Club last winter, Henry?"

"No."

"I've lost most of my pupils to her. Isn't that funny? She's the queen of *kvetch*—" She broke off and started to laugh.

Brand said, "What's the matter, Mamma?"

"It's too funny. I haven't thought of that word for years."

"Why did you think of it now?" Brand asked.

"I knew someone once who used it a lot."

"Who?" Brand didn't sound really interested, but she couldn't seem to stop talking.

"Oh—someone," Ilsa said.

I remembered who it was but I didn't say anything.

Ilsa went on. "It's perfect. Miss Corinne Waley. I hate people who play with buttery fingers and backs. I could hear her fingers and back being buttery."

Making her own fingers and back very buttery she went to the piano and started to play a pseudo-oriental dance, breaking off in disgust.

"I thought you hated teaching," Brand said.

"I do. But I have a conscience. Not a sense of duty, though, thank God. You have a sense of duty, don't you, Brand?"

"Yes."

"I wonder where you get it from? Certainly not your father."

"Why do you always call him my father?"

"He was, wasn't he?"

"He was your husband, too."

Ilsa played the Wedding March with one finger. "You'd like to marry, wouldn't you, Brand?"

"Of course."

"Just legally or really?"

"I think you're acting very strangely in front of Uncle Henry," Brand said.

"Nonsense. Henny's family."

"Are you angry with Brand?" I asked.

"Yes," Ilsa said. "Because I love her."

"I don't understand you, Mamma," Brand said.

"Children aren't supposed to understand their mothers. Mothers are supposed to understand their children. And that's just as silly."

"Why are you being so funny today, Mamma?" Brand asked.

"Am I being funny?"

"You know you are."

"Maybe," Ilsa said slowly, "it's because someone—funny—has been on my mind all day. Isn't it strange how you can suddenly begin to think of someone you haven't seen in years—and he just won't go out of your mind? . . . Usually when I feel people like this it means they're near. But he couldn't be."

Lorenzo came in with Médor, who flung herself frantically at Ilsa, whimpering and sobbing. She never acted like the old dog she was. Ilsa said it was because she didn't have enough brains to realize she was old, so she'd always be a puppy.

"I guess she thought she was lost," Lorenzo said. "She was down at the corner sitting on the curb and shrieking to high heaven. She was awful glad to see me."

"Thank you, Lorenzo. You're a darling." Ilsa was still stroking and soothing the quivering old dog who slowly quieted down.

"I'd like to have enough money to air-condition the house," Brand said inconsequentially.

"If we had that much money we wouldn't be here." Ilsa pulled out the threadbare silk handkerchief that had belonged to Werner, and wiped her face.

"Why not?"

"Maybe you would, my child. I wouldn't."

"This would be a good night to go to the movies," Brand said, sighing again.

"Why don't you go?" Ilsa asked.

"I don't want to go by myself."

Lorenzo said quietly, "I'll go with you."

"You were going to finish your harpsichord," Brand said.

"But if you want to go to the movies . . ."

"No, Lorenzo. I don't really want to go. I'll go to bed and read."

Valdosta, Mattie Belle's inadequate helper, shuffled in without knocking. "Mr. and Mrs. Randolph Silverton is here, Miz Woolf," she whined, and shuffled out, wiping her nose on a corner of her apron. I was thankful Ilsa couldn't see this.

"*Why* must Violetta come to call!" Ilsa cried. "Really, it's too much, in weather like this!"

"Sh," Brand warned, as they came in.

"I won't 'sh,'" Ilsa muttered.

"It's so hot I knew you'd be home," Violetta cried, trotting over to Ilsa and kissing her, then embracing Brand. I had to be kissed, too. Dolph cleared his throat and patted Ilsa on the shoulder.

"How nice to see you," Brand said politely. "You haven't been over in ages."

"Little Brand!" Violetta let out a fulsome sigh and smoothed the skirt of her white linen suit. It was a very good and a very expensive suit, but it made her look like a not too amiable sea cow who had suddenly taken it into its head to have too many permanent waves. "Little Brand! You're really a woman now, aren't you? I said to your Uncle

Randolph as we were coming up the path, 'Brand's really a woman, now, really a woman,' didn't I, Dolph?"

Dolph cleared his throat. He looked more like a cadaver than ever in his wrinkled seersucker suit that seemed to hang like loose flesh on his bones and his yellowed parchment-like skin.

"I've got to go home now," Lorenzo said. "Good-bye."

When Lorenzo didn't like anything he had a way of quietly walking out on it.

"Good-bye, Lorenzo." Ilsa smiled at him.

"I'll be over tomorrow, Brand," he said.

"All right." Brand nodded indifferently.

As soon as he was gone, Violetta cried, raising her hands with their blood-colored nails heavenward, "Now, why does that boy always run off like that when anyone comes around? He's over here a lot, isn't he, Brand? He must be interested in you. Uncle Randolph thinks so, too. I was telling Mrs. Jackson just this morning, not Beulah Jackson's mother, but Mamie Jackson who lives across the river, 'Lorenzo Moore must be interested in my little Brand.' And then coming up the path I realized you aren't a little girl any more. I guess I was sort of a long time realizing it because you've never been interested in boys like most girls are. I guess you take after your mother, though she married real young." She moved her chair closer to the table and picked up a paper to fan herself with. "Though Mrs. Jackson did say to me the other day it's because you're with your mother so much. I think it's right wonderful the way you give up so much to your mother. Poor Lorenzo Moore, I do declare. Fancy his being interested in my little Brand. And how is your mother feeling today?"

"I am neither deaf nor dumb nor a half-wit," Ilsa said in her resonant voice.

Dolph cleared his throat.

"Oh, dear!" Violetta cried. "Now I've gone and hurt her feelings."

"Would it be possible for you to address yourself directly to me?" Ilsa asked.

"Ilsa dear," Violetta said, "please don't misunderstand me! I wouldn't hurt your feelings for anything in the world! I wouldn't hurt a mouse! Have you been having trouble with ants? I've had to put my stockings in glass jars with the tops screwed on tight or the ants eat them, and I mean perfectly eat them! I've put ant poison all over the house, but they just seem to thrive on it. Have you been bothered with them? But maybe it's just across the river they're so bad. I love living across the river—you really feel so much more in the country. But you know, I do think there are more insects. Don't you, Dolph?"

"Possibly," Dolph said.

Violetta ran on like a brook running over stones and completely unaware of them. "And how are you feeling the heat, Ilsa?"

"I imagine I'm feeling it in about the same way that everyone else is, thank you, Violetta."

"Well, it *is* real hot," Violetta said. "I've just been over at the hospital visiting old Cousin Belle. She fell down the stairs the other day and broke her hip. Poor old Cousin Belle, I do declare. Why don't you go see her, Brand? She'd adore to see you. But don't take any flowers. You've never seen as many flowers as she's had. I hope for her sake she doesn't die with this hip. People won't feel like sending flowers so soon again. Mrs. Jackson took her some Pyrus japonica out of her hothouse, though how she gets it to grow even there this time of year is beyond me. Mrs. Jackson wanted someone to get her little boy from camp in North Carolina—you know, she'd pay the way and everything; she hates traveling. She thought maybe you might like to go, Brand, but I told her you never leave your mother. 'Oh, no,' I told her, 'Brand wouldn't leave her mother.' How're your piano lessons going, Ilsa?" When Violetta talked directly to Ilsa, which was rarely, she always raised her voice a little as though she expected her to have difficulty in hearing. It infuriated Ilsa. "Mrs. Bennet was going to send little Dorothy to you but then she decided to send her to Miss Corinne Waley. She wants little Dorothy to have the best. Not that you aren't *good*, Ilsa, and I always advise anyone who asks me to send their children to you. But teaching must be so tiring for you and—"

Valdosta stuck her little head in the door and droned, "Miss Brand, Miss Beulah Jackson say she want to see you. Do I say come in?"

"Of course, Valdosta," Brand said.

"Mattie Belle say I was to tell you Mr. Joshua Tisbury didn't get clean linen this morning."

"Oh—well, I forgot."

"You never forget anyone else," Ilsa said sharply.

"I'll put it in his room later."

"Mattie Belle, she done it. She say just don't forget again." Valdosta's voice was like a little mosquito. "Come in, Miss Beulah," she droned as she went out.

Beulah Jackson paused effectively in the doorway, then came in. I never cottoned to Beulah and I knew that Ilsa didn't like her any more now than she did in the days when she wanted to forbid Brand to play with her.

"Hey, everybody," Beulah said. "I'm not interrupting a family conference or anything, am I?"

"Of course not." Brand got up, offered Beulah the bamboo chaise-longue, and sat down by Ilsa on the piano bench.

"Hey, Mr. and Mrs. Silverton," Beulah said. "Haven't seen you on our side of the river in a long time. Hey, Mr. Porcher."

"We don't come over often in the summer." Violetta fanned herself briskly with the paper. "It's really hotter over here. I was talking to your aunt about it just this morning."

"Oh, Aunt Mamie! How she?"

"Well, I think she looks real pale from the heat, but she says she's feeling all right."

"How you feeling, Mrs. Woolf?" Beulah asked politely in her sweet honeyed little voice. I had to hand it to Beulah; she was a pretty girl with her yellow curls and frilly dresses, and she had a nice manner.

"Very well, thank you, Beulah," Ilsa said.

"Brand"—Beulah smoothed down the skirts of her pale green percale dress—"I just ran over to see if you wanted to go to the movies tonight. I'm going with Bennet and I wondered if you'd like to go with Lee."

"You've got a real handsome brother there, Beulah," Violetta said.

After a moment's hesitation Brand answered, "I'd love to, Beulah, but I can't, I'm afraid. I've promised to go with Lorenzo."

"Ah!" Violetta purred.

"Oh, I'm sorry," Beulah said. One of the things I disliked about Beulah was that she always sounded so sincere and half the time I was sure she wasn't. "Lee'll be real disappointed. Maybe we'll get to see you there, though. What you going to see?"

"We hadn't thought. Where are you going?"

"To see Gary Cooper's new picture. I hope you come see it, too. I've got to run along home now and tell Lee—he'll be real sorry. Good-bye, everybody. I'll just run across the lawn, if you don't mind. Oh—how do you like my new dress? I made it."

"Well, if you aren't the clever one!" Violetta exclaimed, "I didn't know you could sew like that. Girls don't sew any more the way they used to. I'll tell your aunt about it the next time I see her."

"It's awfully pretty," Brand said wistfully. I knew she was comparing her own plain shirtwaist dress unfavorably with it.

"How do you like it, Mr. Silverton?" Beulah was dancing around, avid for praise.

"Very fine," Dolph said.

"Mrs. Woolf?" Beulah asked, still twirling.

"Come let me feel it," Ilsa said. "I'll find out if you're as good a seamstress as everybody thinks."

"Oh—" Beulah stopped in confusion. "I forgot—I'm so sorry—gee, I'm sorry—"

"My dear, it doesn't matter in the least."

"I've got to run—" I must say for Beulah that she was crimson with embarrassment. "I'm so sorry you can't come, Brand. Please forgive me, Mrs. Woolf. Good-bye Mr. Porcher. Good-bye, Mr. and Mrs. Silverton. I wish I could stay and chat, but Lee made me promise I'd hurry and he'll be mad if I don't. See you soon, Brand." She ran out one of the long windows.

"Why wouldn't you go with her, Brand?" Ilsa asked.

"She's going out with Lorenzo Moore!" Violetta cried. "Didn't I tell you our Brand was a woman, Dolph!"

"Would anyone like anything to drink?" Brand was obviously trying to change the subject. "I'm afraid we've finished the lemonade, but there's lots of Coca-Cola and Dr. Pepper and ginger ale in the icebox."

"Oh, no, thank you, sugar," Violetta said. "We've got to be getting back for supper. I said to your Uncle Randolph in the hospital when we left poor old Cousin Belle, 'Why don't we go see Ilsa, too?' So we came right on over. You'd be surprised now many people I know in the hospital. I always enjoy visiting a hospital." She stood up, pushing her chair still further away from its original position. "Dolph, come on, honey. We've sot to be getting home. Brand, if your mother feels equal to it, you must come over and have supper with us soon and *see* how much cooler it is across the river. I'll ask little Beulah Jackson and Mamie, too. There's a sweet child if there ever was one. How're your boarders doing? I expect they bring you in quite a lot, don't they? But then your mother mustn't want for anything. Are you ready yet, Dolph?" She went over to Ilsa and kissed her. Ilsa immediately wiped her mouth. "Good-bye, Ilsa, honey, and we'll come see you again real soon. Every time we see you I say to Dolph, we must see Ilsa again real soon, but I don't know how the time slips by."

"Come along, Violetta," Dolph said. "Good-bye, Ilsa, Brand, Henry."

"I'll go out to the car with you," Brand said.

Violetta tucked Brand's arm under hers. "I wish you could see your little Brand, Ilsa. It would do your heart good. She looks more like her father every day. Come along out to the car, too, Henry. We never get to see you any more."

I started to follow Violetta and Brand out, but paused as I saw Dolph walk over to Ilsa and bend close to her. "She may not be leaf or dumb, but she's certainly a half-wit," he whispered.

Ilsa squeezed his arm. "Oh, darling—" she said.

56

As I followed Dolph into the hall I saw Joshua Tisbury going up the stairs. He hailed me, and I went to him, glad to have an excuse to stay in the house instead of going out to the car for one of Violetta's prolonged farewells.

"Are they going?" he asked. He was one of the nicest men I'd ever known, and one of the ugliest, even taller than I, with a huge bony nose that seemed to walk all over his face, and extraordinarily bushy eyebrows springing from his forehead.

I nodded.

"Thank God. I wanted to go talk to Ilsa for a bit. Coming?"

"Well, if you want to talk to her—"

"Oh, it's nothing private. I just want to relax for a few minutes before I go back to my typewriter."

"How's the book coming?"

"Which one?" His smile was crooked and rather bitter.

"Oh, either."

"Well, opus number one is still making the rounds of the publishing houses. I forget which one has it at the moment. It will probably come winging its way home in a month or so. God knows why they keep them so long. It's been gone two months now. Opus number two is about halfway through. I read the new chapter to Ilsa last night."

"What did she think of it?"

"I think she was too kind."

"You know Ilsa well enough to know that she is never too kind. Especially about something like that," I said.

In the drawing room we heard a crash as though Ilsa had walked into something, and I remembered that Violetta had moved her chair. We heard Ilsa swear, softly, but with horrible intensity. I don't think she ever realized how that low voice of hers carried.

"God damn it to hell."

Then, as we hurried downstairs, "Brand! Brand! The furniture has been moved."

She was standing stock-still and tense as we came in.

"Ilsa, it's Joshua and Henry," the young man said. "What is it?"

"Somebody's moved the furniture," Ilsa answered, and I noticed that Beulah, too, had pulled a chair out of place so that it was directly in front of her. "It gives me the most frightened feeling to be lost in my own room—even though I hate it."

"Where did you want to go?" Joshua asked as I set about putting the chairs back in their places.

"Upstairs to change."

Joshua put his arm around her. "Don't go up just yet. You've plenty of time." His northern tones always sounded harsh and strange beside our gentler ones. "Sit down and talk to me."

"All right. I think I'll have a cigarette."

"You and Myra Turnbull are going to burn the house down with all your smoking," he said.

"Might be a good idea."

Joshua went with her to the sofa and sat down by her, holding her hand—something, despite all the years, I would never have dared to do. I stretched out on the bamboo chaise longue.

"Brand thinks you should make me leave because I can't pay the rent," Joshua said. He spoke with no bitterness or resentment; it was simply a question that perhaps ought to come out in the open for discussion.

"She didn't say that, did she?" Ilsa asked sharply.

"No. But it's true."

"You'll pay sometime." As far as Ilsa was concerned, it was something that needed no discussion.

"Sometime may be a long way off."

Ilsa shrugged. "I wish you'd fall in love with Brand," she said, half laughing.

"Sorry."

"I know you couldn't. I—I just wish she was someone you could. . . . You left a girl up North you loved?"

"Yes."

"Is she nice?"

"As nice as you," Joshua said.

"Does she love you?"

"Yes."

"Poor Joshua. Poor girl."

"Why do you let me stay?"

She laughed again. "I like to be read aloud to. . . . You'll be strong again soon and then you'll be able to go back to her."

"That's right," Joshua said.

"I know how an illness can turn things around." Ilsa leaned back against the sofa. "Mine helped out my moral sense, but that's all. I don't like moral senses. Oh, God, Joshua, I feel so strange today. I don't know what's the matter with me. Maybe it's Brand. I'm worried about her."

"I know."

"Are you still here, Henry?" she asked.

"Yes. Do you want anything?"

"No. I just wondered. . . . Is anything in the way of the piano?"

"No," I said. "I put everything back in its place."

"Thank you, darling." She rose and went over to the piano. Joshua made a motion to help her, thought better of it, and sat down again. After a moment Brand came in.

"Good evening, Miss Woolf," Joshua said.

"Good evening."

Ilsa stopped playing. "Brand, someone moved the furniture. Probably your Aunt Violetta. Your Aunt Violetta would have just loved it if I'd fallen over a chair and broken a hip. Then she'd have had someone else to visit in the hospital."

"I'll see you at supper," Joshua said, laughing, and went out.

"Brand." Ilsa swung around on the piano bench and faced her daughter. She always seemed to be looking at people when she talked to them, but I noticed that her eyes were always directed too low when she spoke to Brand, as though she were still seeing, in her mind's eye, the child she had last looked on. She often laughed and said that when she met new people she visualized them at approximately the right age, but those of us she had known when she could see had eternal youth as far as she was concerned.

"What is it, Mamma?"

"Why wouldn't you go to the movies with Beulah and her brother tonight?"

Brand was silent.

"Why wouldn't you?"

After a moment Brand burst out, "Mamma, you know perfectly well that Mrs. Jackson made Lee say he'd take me and he wouldn't even ask me himself. Beulah had to. And you know why she had to run back so quickly. So Lee'd have time to ask a girl he wanted."

"Dearest," Ilsa said, "if you'd even go out with Lorenzo more, you'd meet more people."

"I don't want to leave you." Brand continued to look stubbornly at her feet.

Ilsa stubbed out her cigarette and lit another. "You don't need to have such an excessive sense of duty. It doesn't make me happy to have you sticking around missing fun you'd have normally. I know you *want* the kind of fun Beulah has. Don't you?"

"Of course."

"Brand, it irritates me to have you around all the time," Ilsa said sharply.

"I don't dare leave you any more," Brand said in a low voice.

Ilsa took the pills out of her pocket and held them out to her. "Oh, take the damn pills if it will make you any happier."

"Why did you want to do it?" Brand implored.

"What do you mean by prying into my private affairs?"

"To have your mother attempt suicide isn't very pretty."

"I promise you I won't, Brand. I wasn't very serious about it."

Brand began to cry softly.

"Ladybird," Ilsa said. It was the first time she had called her that in a long time.

"What?" Brand said in a hard choked voice.

"What are you thinking?"

"I get—I get so frightened." Brand tried desperately to control her voice so that Ilsa wouldn't know she was crying. But Ilsa knew.

"Dearest—don't—" she said.

"I can't help it," Brand wailed.

"Come here, my bird," Ilsa said, and put her arms around her. "You're getting wrinkles in your forehead from frowning. You're too young to have wrinkles. Smooth them out. There. That's better."

Brand clutched at her as though she were, indeed, a child. "Mamma, what's happened? Why does everything have to be like this?"

"Don't frown so, darling. You'll never get rid of those wrinkles. . . . You're all muddled up, aren't you?"

"I wish I weren't! Are other people ever muddled up?"

"Often."

"They don't seem so to me."

"Don't frown, ladybird."

"Mamma—"

"Yes, dear?"

"When I was little do you remember what good friends we used to be?"

"Yes."

"It isn't because of your eyes . . . it's only the past three or four years . . . since I've been grown up, I guess."

"Yes."

"Why?"

"I don't know."

"Sometimes I think you don't love me."

"Brand."

"I've tried to be a good daughter, to see that you don't want for anything—"

"I used to be able to tell what was going on in that little head of yours by looking at you," Ilsa said. "If only you wouldn't hide yourself so."

"I can't seem to help it. I don't think I mean to."

"Brand—"

"Yes, Mamma?"

"Tomorrow—just to please me—be selfish all day. Make Lorenzo take you to the beach, swimming. Go to the movies in the evening. Stay away from this house all day."

"I'm needed here."

"Mattie Belle and I can manage very well without you."

"Why do you want to get rid of me?"

"Because I know you want to get away."

"Then why don't you marry Uncle Henry?" Brand cried.

"Brand." Ilsa's voice was frightening in its anger. "Henry is in the room."

"I know that!" Brand's voice was hysterical. "I wasn't sure you remembered. He's always here, just sitting around. You might just as well be married to him and then we wouldn't have to run this dreadful boarding house."

"Brand, you will apologize to your Uncle Henry at once."

"Why?"

"If you can't see for yourself, you will do it because I tell you to."

"I'm sorry," she mumbled. She sounded very like Monty.

“It doesn’t matter,” I said.

“It does matter.” Ilsa’s voice was still angry. “There is no reason why you should be humiliated and hurt.” Then her voice softened. “Hen,” she said, “you know how fond I am of you, don’t you? I love having you over here as often as you care to come.” She got up from the piano bench, came over to me, and cupped her hand gently around the back of my neck, stroking it. “But you know why I couldn’t marry you, don’t you?” she asked.

“I guess so.” As usual when she touched me my body seemed to dissolve, to burn into a hot vapor. I didn’t know how much of the feeling that her touch gave me was the enormously healing power of her hands, which I had always noticed, and how much the added sensitivity her blindness gave them. Myra Turnbull had once told me that in the tips of our fingers we all have a tiny bit of the gray matter that forms our brains. I think that Ilsa must have had more than the usual share of this, and during the past years had cultivated it with double intensity. It seemed that I could feel her fingers quiver and vibrate with life as they traveled softly over my neck and ran up into my hair.

“It wouldn’t be fair to you, you know that,” she went on. “And Brand knows it, too. She can be very selfish. She will have to learn to break free and stand on her own feet without having her sense of duty taken care of. God knows why she has a sense of duty about me. She’s not in the least necessary to me. I can manage better by myself.”

I know that she was being cruel deliberately because she felt she had to be, but she couldn’t see Brand’s face quickly drain of blood and her mouth open breathlessly, as though she had been struck.

Ilso continued, leaving me and going back to the girl: “Brand, you keep talking about the time before your father died. You weren’t so twisted up, then. Ever since his death, or really more since you’ve grown up, you’ve become like a stranger. There’s nothing of me in you, God knows. There’s not even anything of your father.”

“You don’t want me to be like Papa, do you?”

“No.”

“You’re trying to tell me you didn’t love Papa.”

“You’ve always known that.”

“I didn’t want to know it.”

“You’ve got to face the truth.”

“Do you love me?”

“Brand, do you want me to love you?”

“Oh, God, Mamma, of course I do.”

"Brand," Ilsa said. "I—I'm most hateful when I'm loving you most."

"Sometimes I'm that way, too." Brand leaned against Ilsa like a child again. "How is it," she said, "you can't know how you feel about people and things—how you can *feel*, can feel completely and definitely—and yet you don't know *how* you feel? Do you know what I mean?"

"Yes, dear."

"I'm like that so often. I feel something so it wants to burst out of me—and yet I don't know what it is I'm feeling."

Valdosta peered around the door. "Supper ready. Miss Brand—"

"Yes, Valdosta, what is it?"

"The soufflé done fell so Mattie Belle had to hot up the grits." She disappeared.

"Hurrah!" Ilsa shouted.

"Mamma, please be nice to the guests tonight. There've been so many complaints lately and we can't afford to offend them."

"I hate their guts," Ilsa said.

"Mamma!"

"You're such fun to shock."

"*Please* be nice to everyone at supper," Brand begged. "You ought to realize how important it is. You're being very unfair when you *try* to antagonize them."

"I don't want any supper," Ilsa said.

"Why not?"

"I'm too hot to eat."

"You must eat."

"Want me to be rude?" Ilsa leaned back lazily against the piano.

"No."

"Then don't try to make me go into the dining room."

"I'll get Mattie Belle to fix you a tray."

"If you do, I'll throw everything on the floor."

"All right," Brand said. "If you're going to be childish, there's nothing I can do." She started out.

"Darling—"

"Yes, Mamma."

"Take me for a walk after supper and let's have a talk."

"All right." Brand's voice was cold and antagonistic.

"Every day we add another stone to the wall between us. You don't like to talk, do you?"

"It depends."

“Say a nice long grace,” Ilsa said. “It will please them all.”

As Brand went out, Ilsa stretched, long and wide. “Oh, God, what an afternoon! That’s enough soul-baring to last another ten years.”

“Yes,” I said. “Well, I’ll be getting along now.”

“Will you be back after supper?”

“Maybe I shouldn’t come so often.”

“Henry, don’t be an idiot. You’re not going to let what Brand said bother you, are you?”

“It’s been bothering me for a good many years.”

“If it gives you pleasure, there’s no reason why you shouldn’t come as often as you like.” She seemed to have forgotten momentarily some talkings she’d given me.

“Maybe I will, then.” I watched as Médor crawled out from under the piano and put her head on Ilsa’s knee, half closing the yellow slanting eyes so that she looked like a sinister Chinese.

“But why haven’t you ever married, Henny? You’d make some woman such a lovely husband.”

“There’s been no one I wanted to marry.”

“Why don’t you go to Paris and find your French girl?”

“I told you she wouldn’t marry me.”

“Why don’t you go back and look her up, anyhow?”

“I don’t want to.”

“Well, that’s reason enough,” she said dispassionately. “God knows I don’t want to interfere with anybody else’s life, Hen; it’s just that I’m so fond of you.” She gave Médor’s ear a final pull and pat and the dog returned to her place under the piano.

“I know,” I said awkwardly, and started out. “I’m going now.”

57

I went out of one of the long French windows and stood a moment on the stone terrace, looking into the room through the lush evening green of the wisteria vine. It was quite dark in the room; it seemed that night had already come, though it was still light outside. Ilsa sat at the piano, her hands in her lap, leaning forward, thinking. I walked on down toward the river and sat where the roots of a water oak stretched out over the bank and formed a seat. Faintly on the wind I could hear voices from the dining room, and in the drawing room Ilsa began to play something on the piano. And I felt suddenly that I must speak to her, that I couldn't go home without going back to her and telling her once and for all how desperately I loved her.

As I approached. I saw a man emerge from the shadows of the bamboo grove and go toward the house. I thought for a moment that he might be a thief, and followed him, quickly and silently, trying to avoid the dry twigs under my feet. A long strand of Spanish moss brushed duskily against my face.

The man stepped through the French windows and stood inside, very still, watching Ilsa at the piano. I knew then what I had felt at once, that he was no burglar, but someone I knew. For a moment I couldn't place him. There was something of Monty about his shadowed form, something of Dr. Brandes. I knew it could be neither and I didn't believe in ghosts. Then he spoke and I knew who he was. I stayed very still, hidden by the wisteria that clutched and smothered the narrow square pillars of the terrace, because I could not move. My legs were as paralyzed and lifeless as those of the poor prince in the fairy tale whose legs were turned to black marble.

"Play the thing with the tune—the little tune—you remember—" the man said.

Ilsa stopped playing. Her hands fell onto the keys and struck a discord. "Who is it?"

"Turn around and have a look at me, my love," he said. "I haven't changed so terribly in eleven years."

Slowly she turned toward him.

"What's the matter?" he said. "You're not seeing me—" Frightened, he cried out, "Ilsa!"

"I've been thinking of you all day," she said in a voice so low I could scarcely hear. "Isn't that strange?"

"It was true, then," he said.

"I never lied to you, Franz."

"I thought it was just another of your excuses for not coming with me. I didn't believe it could be true. I didn't believe it could happen to you—"

"But I never lied to you, Franz."

For a moment he stretched his arms out toward her, a gesture full of infinite tenderness, infinite protection, as she sat with her face upturned toward him. Then, very slowly, he dropped his hands.

"Play me the little thing with the tune," he whispered.

Ilsa started, very softly, to play the rosy-bush song. Franz stood behind her, and she stopped playing and leaned against him, weakly. He sat down by her on the piano bench and took her in his arms. After a moment she began to feel his face gently.

"You need a shave," she said.

"I know."

"You aren't much changed?"

"Not much."

"That lovely mop is still there. Is it gray?"

"No."

"Are you sure?"

"Um hm."

"Positive?"

"Um hm."

"You wouldn't lie to me?"

"No."

"I can't believe you. You always lied to me. Franz—"

"What?"

"Have I changed? What do I look like? You're the first person I've been able to ask. Isn't that funny?"

"You're more beautiful," he said.

"You're lying."

"No."

"Your hair isn't gray at all?"

"I've found three white hairs," he said.

"Mine isn't gray?"

"No."

"You've still got those thick sharp eyelashes. Do my eyes look strange?"

"No, darling. Just lost."

"My face has lines. I can feel them." She took his hand and pressed it against her face. "See? So has yours."

"How is Whisky or Gin or whatever she's called?" he asked.

"She's growing up."

"Was she worth it?"

"You won't recognize her," Ilsa said. "She's not a little girl any more."

"How's your husband?"

"He's dead"

"When?"

"Not long after you left."

"That's ironic, isn't it?"

"Is it?"

"What did he die of?"

After a moment Ilsa answered, "Heart."

"He never had a heart," Franz said.

"Yes. Yes, he did. That was another reason I couldn't."

Brand came in, carrying a tray which she put down on the table by the door. Then she turned on the lights. As Werner and Ilsa suddenly became clearly visible human beings again, no longer dim shadows in a dream, I realized that I had been listening to something I had no business hearing. I knew now that I ought to go away, that I ought to go quickly, that what I was doing was unpardonable. But still I couldn't move. Agonized and ashamed, I crouched by the wisteria vine and peered through its leaves into the drawing room and listened. Time seemed to be a new thing. Many days and nights were compressed into the moments I stood there. It seemed to me that I remained motionless, my breath coming quickly, as long as it would take summer to end and winter to come, and spring, the wisteria to billow purple on the vine, the Judas tree to blossom like flame, the magnolia to hold up white waxen cups, the petals to fall on the ground, brown-stained, betrayed, and summer to scorch and dry the land again. But still I could not move.

"Mamma, please try—" Brand said, and then she saw Werner. She stood stock-still.

"Brand, you remember Franz Werner," Ilsa said.

"Yes. I remember." Brand's voice went rigid.

"Brandy! That's it." Werner exclaimed triumphantly.

Now that the lights were on, I could see how shabby and down-at-heel the actor looked. His Palm Beach suit was wrinkled and thread-bare and hung loosely on his thin frame. His hair, though plentiful as ever, was shot through with white; his cheeks were hollow, his eyes sunken, though they still had the same passionate fire and he moved with the old beautiful conscious grace.

Brand picked up the tray and carried it over to Ilsa. "Mamma can you eat this?"

"I'm not hungry. Have you eaten, Franz?"

"No."

"Give it to Franz, Brand." As Brand, with compressed lips, put the tray in front of the actor, Ilsa said, "How's everyone? Did they all scream at the sight of grits?"

"They think you're ill because you didn't come to supper, and that's cheered them up," Brand answered.

"Your Aunt Violetta ought to come and live here," Ilsa said. "She'd feel right at home, and maybe Dolph could have a rest." She laughed. Although she still laughed a great deal, it was the first time I had heard that particular laugh in a long time, and I had almost forgotten it.

"Will you murder me if I tell you you've grown, Brandy?" Werner asked. "Ilsa, you didn't *want* to give such an inebriated name to a poor defenseless baby, did you?"

"Brand is a family name," the girl said tightly.

Ilsa laughed. "It's my maiden name. She's called Johanna Brandes, after my father."

"I like my name," Brand said.

Werner smiled at her. As I remembered, he had a singularly sweet smile. "No frills. It suits you."

"Are you going to be in town long?" Brand asked.

"No. I just stopped off on my way North."

I tried to see Ilsa's expression then, but I was too far away and the wisteria leaves were blocking my view.

"Where are you staying tonight?" she asked.

"You have a sign up."

"All the rooms are full," she said quickly.

"What about the back room?" Brand asked.

"No."

"I'll go to a hotel then," Werner said.

Ilsa nodded, then asked suddenly, "Have you enough money?"

"I've plenty of money."

"Does he look prosperous, Brand?"

"Quite," Brand answered, after a second during which the actor gesticulated to her violently.

"I've been successful since you last saw me," he said. He was eating hungrily.

Brand turned away. "I've got to get back to the dining room. They'll be wondering what's kept me. I'll see you after supper?"

"You will, Brandy, my girl." He crammed food into his mouth as though he hadn't had a decent meal in weeks.

Brand went out toward the dining room, her shoulders drooping in an utterly defeated manner.

After a moment of sitting very still, Ilsa said to Werner, "When must you go?"

"Day after tomorrow."

"Where are you going?"

"Back to New York. Helstone thinks he's got something for me in town again."

"Helstone's your agent?"

"That's what he calls himself."

"You haven't done anything in New York for a long time?"

"Not for five years."

"Why?"

"No luck." He seemed to have forgotten his big talk of a minute ago.

"Where have you been?"

"All over the goddam place from the Borstch circuit to South America. I even did a couple of lousy pictures in Hollywood. Playing sinister gangsters. You know the kind of stuff. You ever go to the movies?"

"No."

"Blind guy I know, divides his life between the movies and—well, never mind. . . . I was down in Panama when Helstone called me. When I knew I'd be coming through here I wanted to wire you—and then—well, I didn't know how things would be—I thought I'd better just stop and see for myself."

"Yes. . . . I—I hope it'll be good, whatever Helstone's got for you."

"I'll take it, whatever it is. I can't afford to be choosy any more." He had finished his supper and was slumped exhaustedly over the table. "Mind if I use your phone later on?"

"Of course not darling."

"Can you afford it or should I make it collect?"

"One of your telephone conversations to New York? You'd better make it collect. . . . But can't you do anything besides act?"

"Not a thing. I tried."

She smiled. "What did you do?"

"I started a religion. I grew a long beard and looked wise and kind and rented a hall on Fifty-seventh Street. I was the apostle of *kvetch*."

Ilsa threw back her head and laughed.

"All the middle-aged ladies came," he went on. "I felt so sorry for them. It was so unfair."

"Yes," Ilsa said.

"They all loved me so."

"Yes."

"I had music in the background always, and beautiful dim lights."

"Cruel Franz."

"It kept me comfortably alive for a year."

"Franz, come here."

He went and sat down beside her. She raised her hands and caressed his face.

"You do need a shave," she said.

He nodded. "Yes."

"Your hair's too long. But that's like you."

"Is it?"

"Your coat feels worn."

"Does it?"

"It feels quite threadbare."

"Your cheeks feel hot," he said.

She held him tightly. "You'd better stay here tonight."

"Yes," he said.

"Where would you have stayed?"

"Down by the river."

"Do you still have a hard time getting to sleep?"

"Yes."

"It's too hot to sleep now, anyhow," she said.

"Play me that little thing again," he said. "That little thing with the tune."

She turned around at the piano and began playing softly the rosy-bush song. She sang in her smoky voice:

I wish I was
A red red rosy bush,
A-blooming by-ee
The banks of the sea.
For when my true
Love would come by-ee,
He'd pluck an rose
From offen me.
A rosy rose,
A red red rosy bush,
He'd pluck an rose
From offen me.

58

It was as though that song was the magic key to my paralysis. Slowly, as though I were a somnambulist, I moved away. I walked down the driveway and out onto the street. I walked as though I were a stranger, as though I had never been in this town before and the tangled streets were new and confusing to me.

At the corner of Ilsa's street I saw some children playing in the last light before they were sent off to bed. Two of them belonged to a family that had just moved into the big house across the way. As I went by I heard the little boy say, "I saw the blind lady today."

One of the little girls said, "Oh, that's nothing. We see her all the time. She even came to our house for tea once."

I walked on quickly. The words were as much of a shock to me as the first plunge into the ocean in the spring when the water is still icy.

Ilsa was so integral a part of my life that I never thought of her as being someone whom you would mention seeing, as those children had. *I* never thought of her as being blind; *they* had talked as though she were some sort of freak.—But they're the freaks—I thought.—Cruel little beasts. But after all, what had been so cruel? They had simply mentioned seeing a blind lady.

My anger and shock at hearing her referred to in this way momentarily blotted out my turmoil at the scene I had just unpardonably witnessed. But before I had gone another block it rolled over me again like mist over the ocean.

I stared down, in my shame, at the sidewalk, at the octagonal pieces of cement, laid together like bathroom tiles magnified many times, the bright spears of grass and weed pushing up between them; and I wanted to run, to run forever through time as well as space, until the past hour dwindled and diminished in the distance. For a long time the persistent honking of a car didn't penetrate my fog of misery and reach me, though, when all at once I realized what it was, I knew that I had been hearing it for several yards. I turned slowly toward the street, moving my body with difficulty, as though an illness had suddenly come upon it.

The car was Silver's. She sat at the wheel with the three boys crowded in around her.

"Hey! Henry! Hey! Brother!" she was calling. When she saw my face she sprang out of the car and ran around to me. She grabbed me by the shoulders. "Brother, what is it? Are you sick?"

I shook my head.

"You come right with me," she commanded. "Boys, get in the back. Come on, Henry, get in."

I didn't speak while she drove rapidly across the river and home. The three boys went off to their evening chores and I followed Silver upstairs to the bedroom. I lay down on the huge four-poster bed, watching her as she stood beside me in her pongee dress, looking down at me with her quiet little face, her eyebrows so strong, her eyes so gray and steady, her hair the color of her dress, still unfaded, her pale little face almost unlined. And around and around in my head went the rosy-bush song, beating and beating against my brain like the little hammers against the wheels of a train when it is pausing at a station. I wished I were a red red rosy bush or magnolia vine smothering the oaks or a twisted little fig tree—anything, anything but Henry Randolph Porcher.

"Now, Brother," Silver said. "Suppose you tell me what's the matter."

"I'm sorry. I'm sorry, Sister," I said.

"Never mind about being sorry. Tell me what's troubling you."

"I've done something—something terrible," I said.

"What have you done?" She didn't look away from me. But I could tell by the way her dark brows drew slightly closer together that my words frightened her.

But I couldn't bring myself to say it. "Something terrible," I repeated.

"All right, Henry. You needn't be afraid to tell me. You know whatever it is, Eddie and I'll help you."

"If I'd killed someone," I asked, "would you and Eddie still help me? Would you hide me away from the police?"

"Have you killed anyone?" Her voice was very steady and I knew that she was ready for anything I might have to tell her.

"No."

"What is it, then?"

"It's—oh, Silver, that man is back!"

"What man?"

"That actor."

"What actor?" Her voice was beginning to show a faint tinge of impatience, like the stain coming to the edge of a white magnolia petal.

"Werner. Franz Josef Werner."

"You mean the actor who was here with that stock company just before Monty's death?"

"Yes."

"How do you know?"

"I saw him."

"Where?"

"At Ilsa's."

"And what have you done that was so dreadful?"

"Oh, Sister," I said, "I started to go home and then I felt that I must go back and talk to Ilsa and he came out of the bamboo grove and went in through the French windows and I stood by the wisteria vine on the terrace and listened. I listened and watched. I saw them together. I heard them. For a long time. It was something I wasn't meant to see or hear."

She was silent. At last she said, "You mean you spied on them?"

"I guess if you want to put it down in black and white, that's what it was. But it didn't seem like that at the time. I—I wasn't aware of what I was doing until after I'd left. I couldn't move. I just stood there and I couldn't move."

"Well, it's done now and there's no undoing it," Silver said "It's hurt no one but you, except you shouldn't have told me.'

"I know."

She wandered over to her chiffonier, picked up her silver comb and brush and mirror, and set them down again. Then she came back to the bed and sat down beside me, running her fingers gently over the polished mahogany post. "Henry I wish you'd go away," she said.

"Where?"

"Anywhere. It doesn't much matter, so long as it isn't here. Go back to Paris. Or go up North. Just anywhere to get away from here."

"Why?"

"Oh, Brother, you know why. I hate to see you like this, and every year it just gets worse. You're still young. You're only thirty-three. It's not too late to go off somewhere and begin over again."

"Begin what over again?"

"Your life."

"Does it matter that much?" I asked. "Is it worth beginning over again? I don't think my life's that important. I don't think it much matters what happens to it."

"That's no way to talk."

"Why not? I think the importance of the individual is horribly overestimated."

"Then why do you overestimate the importance of one individual?"

"What do you mean?"

"You know perfectly well what I mean."

I rolled over and buried my face in her lap. "Yes," I said, "I suppose I know."

"You know, Henry; it's a funny thing," she said. "I guess we've both changed. I know I take for granted now things that would have shocked me horribly ten years ago. It's probably having a contented marriage and a bunch of uninhibited children. But you always used to be so worried about my turning out to be like Mamma. And now I think you're much more like her than I am."

"No!" I shouted.

"I know you always hated Mamma, and I suppose that was because it was certainly unnatural of her the way she never loved you. But the way Mamma never could get close to people even when she did love them. You've got a lot of that in you."

"I don't know what you're talking about," I said.

"Yes, you do. I'm talking about you. And Ilsa. The way you've always put her up on a pedestal and kind of bowed down to her and worshiped her as though she were some sort of Greek goddess. When everybody talked about maybe you and she would get married after Monty died, I knew you wouldn't. I knew there wasn't a chance of it."

"Well?"

"Did you ever even ask her, Henry?"

"I don't think so." Had I asked her that time or was it just part of the delirium?

"You don't know? Why not? You had plenty to offer her. Love and a home. It can't have been much fun for her running that awful old place all these years with all those awful people complaining about this, asking for that, being disagreeable about the other. I had to lend her some money a couple of years ago. Oh, she paid me back—she'd rather die than be in debt—but it hasn't been easy for her, and she's made of flesh and bone like the rest of us. She's no marble statue. Even if she is blind. I'm glad Franz Werner's back. The Lord knows there's been no one here who's understood her since he left."

"He's only on his way through," I said.

"Then I hope he takes her with him. Maybe if she gets out of here you'll be able to stand on your own feet and behave like a man. Oh, I know why you never had the nerve to ask her to marry you, Brother. You like her up on that pedestal. You've got her in a niche like your own personal patron saint. If you ever discovered that she was just another human being in relation to you, you'd be terrified. You'd run like mad. As long as she's a distant goddess for you to worship like a child it's fine. You've been giving her all these years the kind of love you'd like to have given Mamma. That's no kind of love to offer a woman like her. I know it's not a nice thing to say, Brother, but I believe you'd die of horror if she offered to sleep with you. I know you're upset because you saw her with a man she loves. I mean that way. You're really more upset about that than you are about having spied on her. Oh, Brother, wake up!"

She took me by the shoulders and shook me.

"It's not true! Not a word of what you've been saying!" I cried. My teeth were chattering as she shook me back and forth.

She released me. "All right. It's not true. What difference does it make? I guess you're right, Henry. You're not worth much. It doesn't make any difference about you." Her eyes filled with tears. "But it does. You're my brother and I love you and I mind what happens to you. And if God cares about the smallest sparrow I guess it makes a difference to him, too."

I put my arms around her. "Ah, Silver, I'm sorry. . . ." It was always unnerving to me when my sister cried. She so seldom showed it when she was moved.

She turned away from my embrace. "If you wanted a job out of town I think Eddie could arrange one for you."

"Thanks," I said. "I'll let you know."

She smiled a very little smile. "All right, Brother."

We sat for a time in silence. Then she said, "I know Ilsa hasn't meant to just keep you hanging around, but I do think she should have tried harder to—to—"

"She has," I said.

"Has what?"

"Tried to get me to go away. She was quite awful about it once. Cold and cruel. The way she is to Brand sometimes. But this summer it's been so hot and she's seemed so tired. I guess she just gave up trying."

"I see," Silver said. Then, after a moment, "I expect you want to go back to town now?"

"Yes."

"I'll drive you to the bridge. You can take the bus from there."

"All right. Thank you."

She waited until she saw me step aboard the bus. It was the one which went past Ilsa's house. I had resolved to go straight home and spend the rest of the evening reading, but then I remembered that I had promised to come back after supper, and since the bus went right past the house . . .

I looked at my watch. A few minutes past ten. I would just drop by to say good night and the next day I would talk to Silver about getting out of town.

59

As I walked between the Ligustrum hedges up to the house I heard voices and laughter. Ilsa and Werner were sitting on the veranda steps; Werner had Ilsa's mandolin on his lap and was picking out the rosy-bush song. Lorenzo sat on the railing, chin in hand, his little hummingbird face flickering out white and peaked in the heat lightning that was brooding over the horizon.

I went up the steps. "It's Henry," I said.

Ilsa sprang to her feet. "Hen! Bless you, darling! Hen, look who's here!" Without giving me time to look, for which I was very grateful (and in any case it was too dark on the steps to see), she went on. "It's Franz! Franz Werner! You remember him, of course!"

"Of course." I held out my hand to the actor in his wrinkled Palm Beach suit.

"Porcher! I'm delighted to see you again after all these years," he murmured, not taking his eyes away from Ilsa. The long fingers of the hand with which he still held the mandolin were nervously moving over the strings.

"Please don't stand," I said.

"Franz made a very special punch." Ilsa sat down close to Werner, leaning slightly against him. "It's in the big silver bowl on the table. Give yourself some."

"Thanks. I will." Filling myself a glass of punch, I wandered about the veranda. Myra Turnbull lay in the hammock, smoking, her eyes closed. Joshua Tisbury sat on the floor near her, his legs stretched out in front of him, leaning back against the house, waving the mosquitoes away with a fly swatter. He nodded to me as I passed. Brand I saw nowhere. I went up to Lorenzo.

"Where's Brand?" I asked.

"I don't know. In the house, I guess," he answered.

From her hammock Myra Turnbull sighed heavily. Werner rose, went to the punch bowl, refilled his glass, and looked over at Myra on the hammock, where the hall light glimmered on her lean face.

"Maybe there'll be a thunderstorm to cool things off," Lorenzo said. "We haven't had one for a couple of days."

"Not with this heat lightning," I answered, pulling myself up onto the railing beside him.

"Have some more, Miss Turnbull?" Werner asked.

"Yes, I will," Myra said. "The only other person I ever knew who could make a punch like this was my grandfather."

"Mrs. Woolf taught me," Werner said.

"You've known her before?"

"Yes. For years. Here you are." He handed her a glass which she drained at one gulp.

"Much obliged," she said, handing it back to him to be refilled. When he gave it back to her she turned away, looking into the blank wall of the house, and lit another cigarette. The conch shell on the floor beside her was already full of butts.

"Give me some more, Franz," Ilsa said.

"You haven't finished that glass."

"I want some more anyhow. I'm glad I had one bottle of really good whisky hidden away." She turned and listened as he went over to the table and filled her glass. "Thank you, my darling," she said as he put it into her waiting hand.

It was a dark night. The moon was old and would not rise for another hour. It was always dark on the porch anyhow, because the trees and bushes pressed close against it, veiling it in the daytime in a moving green light and in the nighttime in a lush velvet blackness. The darkness on the porch, with faces visible only in the flashes of lightning, gave one a false sense of privacy. You felt that because you could see only the dim shadow of whoever sat closest to you, you could voice your thoughts aloud and they would be as unheard as they were unseen. Ilsa and Franz Werner on the steps were almost invisible, lost in darkness for minutes together and then appearing faintly as they were touched by the heat lightning which barely penetrated the shrubbery.

"You haven't changed, Ilsa," Werner said.

"Neither have you."

"I look very different." His voice was bitter.

"I must look even more different."

"No," he said quickly.

"Not even my eyes?"

"No. . . . Darling—"

"What?"

"Could we go to the beach tomorrow? Please?"

She nodded. "Yes. I let it only till the first of September this year. It's all closed up, but we can open it."

Lorenzo said, "Why don't Brand and I drive down early tomorrow and run up the flag for Ira and get it ready?"

"That would be wonderful, dear," Ilsa said. "If I know Franz he won't be ready till noon." She turned to the actor. "I don't suppose you've got round to learning how to drive?"

He shook his head. "No, but I can ride an elephant."

"I'm afraid you'll have to be satisfied with a Ford. Hen, could you drive us down? You'd like to come, wouldn't you? Are you busy tomorrow?"

"No, I'd love to," I answered.

"Good, it's all settled, then!" She clapped her hands together with pleasure.

"Liebling," Werner said, "I don't suppose you've a razor I could use?"

"I'll get Joshua to lend you his."

"I don't think I like that Joshua," Werner muttered. I looked toward Joshua, still leaning against the house, illuminated by a shaft of light from the hall, but he seemed lost in his brooding.

"Don't be absurd." Ilsa laughed. "He's wonderful. And don't raise your voice."

"He can't hear me. Do you like him?"

"Very much."

"Do you think he's attractive?"

"Yes."

"Do you think he's handsome?"

"I've never seen him."

"Do you love him?"

"No."

"Don't lie."

"I don't love him, Franz. And stop shouting."

"You're lying."

"I've never lied to you."

"You love him."

"He's much younger than I am."

"That wouldn't matter."

"Darling, why does it bother you? Because I don't love him."

"He loves you."

"No."

"Yes."

"He has a girl in the North. Now shut up."

"How do you know?"

"He told me."

"I love you."

"I know."

"What are we going to do?"

"Nothing."

"Why?"

"I have no money. You have no money. I am blind. Brand."

I got down from the rail, realizing suddenly that Lorenzo had gone before me, and went over toward Myra. Inside the house the telephone began to ring and Lorenzo went in to answer it.

Ilsa's voice came from behind me.

"Joshua—"

The young man scrambled to his feet and stood facing her. "Hello, here I am."

She turned in the direction of his voice. "Joshua, have you a razor?"

"Of course."

"Will you let Franz use it?" She put out her hand and felt for his.

"Certainly. Right now?"

"I might as well." The actor put his arm possessively about Ilsa.

"Make him shave well, Joshua," Ilsa said.

"I promise." He smiled, then reached out and touched her hand gently, remembering that she couldn't see the smile.

"And don't let him stare at himself in the mirror too long."

Joshua started out. Werner held back, his gaze seeming to cling to Ilsa. "If someone," he said, "who had never seen were suddenly given sight and saw for the first time a square and a sphere which he knew by touch, would he know without touching them which was which?"

"I don't know." With one finger Ilsa traced the line of his lapel, then plunged her hands back into the pockets of her linen dress. "I shouldn't think so. And you can't put off shaving that way. Run along."

"Will you come this way?" Joshua asked.

"Thanks." Werner followed him out.

Myra Turnbull rolled over in the hammock and faced Ilsa. Abruptly she asked, "Do you want to live?"

"Yes, very much." Ilsa smiled, a smile that was entirely to herself, as her facial expressions often were. "Why?"

"That's what I want to know." Myra's voice was flat. "Why?"

"Perhaps because we're all afraid of death," Ilsa said. "It's perfectly natural." But that wasn't her reason. That was not the way she had reasoned earlier in the day.

"But why live?" Myra asked desperately. "Life isn't attractive. We have to struggle to eat, struggle against the weather, we ride in crowded buses, teach stupid children things they don't want to know, we drink and smoke and walk down the street to the drugstore, go to church and sing hymns in shrill nasal voices, go to recitals at the Woman's Club—and why? For what? Just because we want to live? I don't think so. I used to think it was because of an unquenchable belief in the potentialities of the future. I used to have an unquenchable belief in the power of man to rise beyond himself to something greater than himself, an unquenchable belief in what man will ultimately become, and a feeling that my own life was part of that becoming. . . . But now . . ."

Brand pushed open the screen door and came out onto the porch. She stood for a moment looking around, speaking to no one, acknowledging no one. At last she murmured, "I guess I'll have some punch."

"Help yourself, bird," Ilsa said, turning toward her.

". . . but now," Myra went on, "every year I find myself further off from what I might be. My students seem to me more and more crass. The world is turning away from Christ and toward Jehovah, and Jehovah is destroying us. God made the world," Myra said, "and made a mistake, and now he is finishing it off. God is a vengeful creator, annihilating his own creation."

Lorenzo heard her as he came out. "If God were to destroy the world, Miss Turnbull," he said, "since God is the world and the world is God, it would be suicide. Somehow I don't believe in a Divine suicide."

"I don't want to believe in God," Myra said fiercely, sitting up in the hammock and lighting another cigarette with trembling fingers. "But I've got to because I'm afraid. Even a cruel, despotic, Old Testament God is better than none. To be lost in a Godless world is the most terrible of all punishments."

Lorenzo said shyly to Ilsa, "Would you mind if I had some punch?"

"Of course not, dear." She had gone back to the shadows of the steps and her disembodied voice came out of the incomprehensible darkness in which she always lived. "Help yourself. Who was the telephone for?"

"Joshua Tisbury."

"Did you find him? He went in to lend Franz a razor."

"Yes," Lorenzo said. "It was long distance."

Myra could not seem to stop talking. She lay back in the hammock, her cigarette hanging loosely from her fingers, and talked, almost as though to herself. "Most of us feel," she said, "that the only point in our living at all is because of the few great individuals who inspire us to rise out of our mediocrity. But my God, my God in heaven, it is these individuals who have caused our downfall, who have made the world the confused and agonizing place that it is. Because they are greater than we are, they have betrayed us. They've made great discoveries, especially in science, and they've been able to teach us the mechanical side of these discoveries. But the more important, the spiritual aspect hardly anybody can understand. We haven't progressed far enough along in civilization to be *able* to understand. It's all wrong, the way we've grown intellectually, scientifically, much too quickly. In understanding we haven't begun to catch up, we're still back in the dark ages. I am forced, therefore," she said, the slight slur suddenly sloughing off the edge of her words, so that she sounded like a schoolteacher once more, "to realize that the great individuals who are our only hope of salvation, instead of saving us, are destroying us."

"What made you think of that just now, Miss Turnbull?" Lorenzo asked.

"Because I'm not at all sure that Mrs. Woolf isn't one of the people I've been talking about."

Sitting over there on the steps Ilsa, with her quick listening ears, had heard. "Don't talk rubbish," she said angrily.

Myra pulled herself out of the hammock. "I'm going in. I've got to correct two batches of papers before tomorrow, and it's late. Good night."

"Good night, Myra."

"This has been such an awful month," Brand said, watching after her. "I saw the new moon through glass, so it's to be expected. And a mockingbird flew into the kitchen tonight. It took me five minutes with the broom to get it out. Thank goodness I managed before Mattie Belle came back."

"Come sit over here, Brand," Lorenzo called, climbing up onto the railing again. Languidly, Brand crossed the porch and pulled herself up beside him.

The screen door burst open and Werner came out, Mephistophelean in a sudden flash of lightning. "Feel me!" he crowed. "Soft as a baby!"

"Franz, you were quick," Ilsa said, laughing like a child. "What happened?"

"I always do everything you tell me to, my love. Feel me Brandy."

"Lorenzo's going to finish his harpsichord tonight," Ilsa said as Werner flung himself down on the shadowed steps beside her.

"He's making a harpsichord?" Werner asked.

"Yes."

"That's quite a feat, isn't it?"

"It took him three years," Ilsa said.

"May I see it?" Werner asked.

Lorenzo's voice was unenthusiastic. "If you'd really like to."

"We'll go over tomorrow when it's finished," Ilsa said, "and I'll play the rosy-bush song on it. I'd like the rosy-bush song on a harpsichord."

"My mother used to play the harpsichord, my boy," Werner told Lorenzo. "She was a Greek actress. I was born, though, as a matter of fact, in Norway, in Grieg's town, Bergen."

In the lightning I could see Ilsa's lips twitch with amusement.

We fell into silence. The hammock was still swinging gently. Brand slipped down from the rail, went over to it, and stopped its motion, then climbed up beside Lorenzo again.

Every once in a while, out of the darkness we were staring into, a branch of palm like a draggled bird's wing, or an oak branch burdened with Spanish moss, would stand out in sharp silhouette against the sheet lightning. Down by the river crickets were shrilling, katydids calling, frogs complaining. There was something hypnotic about their songs and the continuous flickering of the lightning. My thoughts stopped turning in my mind and I began to listen to the katydids, my mind beginning to imitate the rhythm and the pattern of their notes until everything else dropped back. I felt that I didn't want to think of anything else for two weeks, I could no longer say to myself, "Here I am, and this is where I must be." Suddenly there were no more heres and theres to put my finger on. But katydids don't need heres and theres and concrete facts. They never did, so they don't change. One shrills from this tree, one from the grass, another from the shrubbery—each has his own note and his own tune. They're like Ilsa's ocean, infinitely soothing and relaxing. They slip in and everything else slips out.

The screen door burst open again and Joshua came tumbling onto the porch. "Ilsa! Brand! Everybody!"

Brand jumped down from the rail nervously. "What is it?"

"The most amazing thing—I can't speak—I can't believe it!"

"Is it good?" Lorenzo asked.

"Yes, it's very good. It's so good I'm completely staggered."

Ilsa got up and went over to him, resting her hand on his shoulder. "What is it, Joshua?"

"It was my publisher on the phone. Do you hear that? My publisher!" He whirled around toward Werner. "Did you find the shaving things all right? Did you have everything you needed?"

"Yes, thank you," Werner said.

Joshua grabbed Ilsa about the waist. "It's so silly—but it's so enormous, it means so much to me that I seem to have lost all my words—all I can do is laugh. Now I can go back, now I can go home, don't you see? I've been well enough to go back to the paper for a long time, but I couldn't. I couldn't get away from the Illness of my failure, strangling me like the water hyacinth choking up the river."

"When are you going?" Brand asked.

"The day after tomorrow, as soon as I can get packed and on a train, as soon as I can get myself together—I'm going to New York, bless New York, I love it so—away from the South and the filthy Spanish moss hanging off the trees like dead men's beards; away from scorpions and bats and hoot owls—I'm going to New York!"

"But what's happened?" Lorenzo asked.

"My novel has been accepted," Joshua cried. "My novel that I wrote with my life's blood and that drove me down here to die, I thought—" He caught Ilsa about the waist and began waltzing around the porch with her. "Play something, Lorenzo; play something gay and triumphant and mad! Oh, my darling, what a glorious, glorious night, what stars, what a river coiled like a dark snake between the trees—" He flung her off, then caught her to him again. "Oh, you must let me dance with you, so beautiful, so wonderful, so mysterious—" They whirled around the porch again, then he let her go and caught hold of Brand. "And you, too, little solemn one, little disturbed confused creature, just wait and something wonderful will happen to you, too.

Weeping may endure for a night
But joy cometh in the morning—

Do you remember that?"

"You'll leave Saturday?" Brand asked as he stopped dancing and released her, panting, laughing, gasping for his breath.

"Yes—I can't believe it—I've been concentrating on it for so long; somewhere in the darkness of my mind was a flicker of light that said it would all work out eventually—but oh, to be free again—to be free!"

"I've played so hard my fingers are numb," Lorenzo said, putting down Ilsa's mandolin.

Joshua caught hold of my hand and laughed childishly. "I must sit down and get my breath. I'm behaving like a madman."

"Have another drink," Werner said, handing him a glass.

"Yes—thanks." He clutched the drink and stood there grinning.

"What train do you plan to take Saturday?" Werner asked.

"I don't know. Whatever train I can get. I suppose the new noon train would be best."

"Maybe we could travel together," Werner suggested.

"*Must* you go so soon?" Ilsa said in a low voice.

"I'll probably have to. I'll be surprised if Helstone doesn't give me hell for stopping off here this long." He took one of her hands and held it tightly in both of his.

"When are you going to call him?" she asked.

"There's no point in trying before one or two. He wouldn't be in."

"I'll go down to the station later on," Joshua said, "and find out about trains. It would be very pleasant if we could go up together. I'll have to go by day coach, though."

Werner laughed, rather bitterly. "So will I."

"Well, see you later," Joshua said, and hurried into the house.

Werner pulled Ilsa to him. He didn't seem to care who saw him, and her discretion, too, seemed to have fled into the heat of the late summer night.

"Let's go down by the river and walk until it's time for me to phone," he said.

She leaned close to him. "All right."

"Remember the last time we walked down by the river?" he asked.

She nodded. "Um hm."

"It's almost time for the moon to rise. Another moon for me to look at you by tonight. Most considerate of it."

"You know, it's a funny thing," Ilsa said.

"Hm?" Werner asked.

As they stood there on the steps, the shadows of the Ligustrum bushes closing them in, the darkness seemed to me almost unendurable.

"The subconscious mind is so much cleverer than the conscious," I heard Ilsa's voice say. "I could see you so beautifully and clearly in my dreams—so really you—but when I tried to remember you when I was awake I could never really do it, could never visualize you completely. And the most irritating, the most infuriating, the most damnable part of it is that I still have to count on dreams. . . . It doesn't matter. . . . It was never your face I fell in love with, but your foolish, gaudy, blatant soul."

"Come along," Werner said.

As they walked down the path they became visible again in the flittering lightning. Then they turned around by the side of the house and disappeared into the darkness.

60

"Who is that man?" Lorenzo asked.

"Why ask me?" Brand's voice was hard. "Mamma told you. Ask Uncle Henry if you want to know more."

Lorenzo turned to me. "How did he happen to come here?"

"To see Ilsa," I said.

"But why?" Brand asked angrily. "What right has he got?"

"He seems to think he has a lot of right," Lorenzo said quietly. He got down from the porch rail and flung himself into the hammock. "I don't think I'll show him my harpsichord," he said.

I wandered over to the steps and sat down. They were still warm where Ilsa and Werner had been sitting on them. Lorenzo heaved himself out of the hammock and went over to Brand again.

"It might interest you to know, Brand," he said, "that I'm going west in October."

"West? Where?"

"Wisconsin."

"What on earth are you going to do in Wisconsin?"

"Study ancient instruments."

"Why?"

"Because it's what I want to do."

"But why Wisconsin, Lorenzo!" Brand cried.

"Because the best man happens to be teaching there. I have a scholarship at the University. I just got the letter in the evening mail."

"Why didn't you say anything about it before?"

"I wanted to be sure I'd be accepted. I did tell your mother."

"But I thought you were going to be a minister!"

"Everybody thought that, it seems."

"You aren't?"

"No."

"But why not?"

"I don't like dogma, I don't like sects, I don't believe half the things I'd have to believe if I had any sense of honesty about it, and I want a private life, not a public one."

"I see," Brand said, kicking her feet against the horizontal bars of the porch rail.

"Do you?" Lorenzo asked.

"I don't know. I'll try to. But what are you going to do when you finish studying?"

"Teach."

"Oh," Brand said, in a small voice.

"What do you think of it, Uncle Henry?" Lorenzo asked politely, drawing me into the conversation.

I looked at his small bird face glimmering on and off in the lightning, the determined beak of a nose, the small firm chin. Lorenzo knew what he wanted and he usually got it. He wanted to study ancient instruments instead of going into the ministry, and that was what he was going to do. He had made up his mind to marry Brand and I had no doubt that he would do that, too. She would make a good teacher's wife and he would know how to manage her. His fragile, almost weak-looking appearance was entirely deceptive.

"If you have the courage of your own convictions, more power to you," I said, sounding almost jealous.

Lorenzo was going to Wisconsin. Joshua was going to New York. Myra thought she was going to pieces. Franz Josef Werner had returned as I had known one day he must, and now I must leave, too; I saw that. But where? To hell, like Mvra Turnbull, or to some definite destination like the others?

I got up and wandered down the path. The odors of the summer night were so hot and heavy that I felt stifled. We were due the northeaster that would mark the end of summer, and, for me, the end of everything. I remembered that when I was little and had suddenly been brought face to face with infinity as I contemplated the dark night ocean fading into the horizon, as I watched the stars burning forever above me, I had felt almost the same way I did now. All space and all time had seemed to confront me, as I stood, a tiny particle on all the tiny particles of sand that made the beach. To a sand crab, I thought, it must seem that this world of shifting sand is the only thing there is. To a starfish it must seem that there is nothing but the cool luminous water. And yet suddenly the starfish will find itself tossed carelessly up onto the beach, spewed out and ignored by the ocean it adores, left impartially to dry on the burning breathless sand. So is it not, I thought, consistent to wonder if there is not somewhere an end to our space, to our infinity? Beyond that purple sea of sky and stars what arid sands may not lie? Beyond our own clumsy conception of time—seconds, hours, days, weeks, years, centuries—what may there not be? And my child's heart was afraid.

Well, I thought now—coming back to the particular with the usual human inability to forget the self for long—I have come to the end of one small space, one small infinity. I knew that I no longer had the courage to go on being a coward. I did not have Lorenzo's serene indifference to what people thought of me. I valued my sister's opinion, Cousin Anna's, Joshua's, Myra Turnbull's, most of all Ilsa's. If I left home now and took whatever job Eddie could get for me, I would lose my life of being a dead, burnt-out satelite forever revolving around a living sun that had no use for me, no need of my inadequate convolutions—an existence certainly not noble, and desirable to no one but me. If I flung myself out of my accustomed course, they might at least say, "Look, there goes a shooting star," as I flashed briefly across the sky.

When I turned and went back to the house Lorenzo and Brand were still perched on the rail, talking.

"It'll be all right when he goes," Brand was saying. "I was afraid he was going to stay, but I don't think he will."

I climbed the steps. "It's late," I said. "You should both be in bed. Won't they be worried about you at home, Lorenzo?"

He slid down from the rail. "Yes. I'd better go," he said. "I'll be over tomorrow at nine, Brand."

She answered with more respect than I had heard her use. "All right, Lorenzo. I'll be ready."

Most of the lights in the house were out now; only the dim hall light was burning. Fireflies flittered in the bushes. Lightning still hovered over the heavy air. I saw a shadow at the door, and Myra Turnbull drifted onto the porch, her toothbrush mug in her hand. Brand nudged Lorenzo.

"Where's Ilsa Woolf?" Myra asked.

"She's down by the river, Miss Turnbull," Brand said.

"I want to talk to her." Myra leaned against the railing, and some of the liquor in her mug spilled over onto the bushes. She jerked back. "I want to talk to her. Out of the morass of my memory I've pulled something that I want to say to her. Where is she?"

"She went down by the river, Miss Turnbull," Lorenzo said.

"Come on in with me," I suggested, taking her arm. She pulled away, ignoring me.

"But I wanted to talk to her," she said again. "There was something I wanted to say to her—pulled out of the morass of my memory. It's not fair. . . . Brand, Lorenzo. It's very late. You should be in bed."

"So should we all, Myra," I said.

"You leave me alone, Henry Porcher." Urgently she caught hold of Brand's arm. "When your mother comes back, tell her I want to talk to her. Tell her it's very important. Before it goes back into the marshes of the mind a little poem out of the morass of my memory. . . ."

She turned abruptly and went in as we heard voices coming around the corner of the house. Ilsa and Werner came up the Steps.

"I guess I'll go in and phone Helstone," Werner said.

"Collect," she reminded him.

"Yes, liebling." He slammed the screen door behind him. Ilsa flung herself down in the hammock.

"Who's here?" she asked.

"I am," I answered. "Henry. And Brand and Lorenzo."

"Children, you should have been in bed hours ago."

"I'm just going home. It was my fault." Lorenzo went over to the hammock and shyly touched her sleeve.

"It doesn't matter this once. All the punch we drank—I guess we all got a little tight. I know I did. Poor Myra—" she laughed sleepily.

"Good night," Lorenzo said.

She pulled him to her for a moment. "Good night, dear."

She listened as he went running down the steps and his footsteps sounded and diminished along the path.

"Brand," she said.

"Yes, Mamma?"

"Go to bed."

"I'm just going, Mamma." The girl, moved toward the door.

Hearing the footsteps, Ilsa called, "Come kiss me good night."

"No," Brand said. "I—can't. Not tonight. . . . Good night, Mamma." She ran into the house.

Ilsa sighed deeply. "I feel so guilty, Henry," she said.

"What about?"

"Brand."

"Why should you?"

"It's my fault, because I let her get dependent on me and now she wants to break away and she can't. She's afraid of freedom. I'm glad Lorenzo's going to Wisconsin. He's got too skeptically searching a mind to make a good preacher. I hope she'll marry him. I think they belong together. Thank God he hasn't any ties of blood to the family at any rate." She started to laugh and kept on until I wasn't sure whether she was laughing or crying. "Forgive me, Hen," she said at last. "It's this fag end of summer—I'm tired."

"Ilsa Woolf." It was Myra's voice. She had come out on the porch again.

"What?" Ilsa said.

"You're back!"

"Yes. I'm back. What is it?"

"Something I want to say to you—I pulled it up—up by the roots from the muddy meadows of the mind, the meandering morasses of the memory—"

"What is it?" Ilsa asked.

"It's a poem. A little poem. I want you to hear it. He should hear it, too. In the marvelous mazes of the mind I found and plucked it up with its bleeding roots. May I say it?"

"Of course."

Myra almost whispered the words:

I hear a sudden cry of pain!
There is a rabbit in a snare:
Now I hear the cry again,
But I cannot tell from where.

But I cannot tell from where
He is calling out for aid;
Crying on the frightened air,
Making everything afraid.

Making everything afraid,
Wrinkling up his little face,
As he cries again for aid;
And I cannot find the place!

And I cannot find the place
Where his paw is in the snare:
Little one! Oh, little one!
I am searching everywhere. *

"Are you?" Myra demanded.

Ilsa didn't answer She had turned away in the hammock. I couldn't see her face.

Myra went on. "You must, you know. The blood runs fast and in the snare we die. You must find us and set us free. Are you searching or will you leave us, will you turn from our cry?"

Ilsa got up from the hammock and stood beside her. "Come inside."

Myra shook her head, fumbling for her handkerchief. "It's so dark, it's so dark," she wept.

"When I was little," Ilsa said gently, "I used to go along the dunes with one of Father's specimen jars and catch fireflies to make a lantern for myself." Her voice sounded muffled by the night which seemed suddenly to press inexorably about them both. She put her arm about Myra and took her indoors, soothing her like a very little child. Her shoulders, too, were shaking with sobs. It was the first time I had ever heard her cry. From the distance a train wailed.

---

* "The Snare." From *Songs from the Clay*, by James Stephens. By permission of The Macmillan Company, publishers.

61

The first thing in the morning I called Silver.

"If you still think Eddie can get me a job somewhere out of town, I want it," I said.

There was a short pause at the other end of the wire. "All right, Brother. Eddie has to go to New Orleans next week. Wait just a minute till I talk to him." Afer a few moments she came back. "He says he thinks he can arrange to have you go down with him Monday. Can you be ready by then?"

"Yes," I said. We both knew that if I didn't leave immediately I would never leave.

"Come on out for dinner tomorrow night, then," she said, "and talk things over with him."

"All right. Thank you, Sister."

"Don't thank me, Henry," she answered. "Thank yourself."

62

I went over to Ilsa's shortly after breakfast, though I was sure she and Werner would not be ready. As I heard music I paused at the rice portieres, my hands pushing them slightly apart. In the drawing room Ilsa was giving a piano lesson.

"Bring out the tune in your left hand, child. Don't you hear it? The little tune you start with. Listen to it in your left hand." I heard the stumbling notes of the music and Ilsa saying "That's better."

I wandered upstairs and knocked at the door of Myra Turnbull's room. I knew that on Friday she had no classes till afternoon so she wouldn't be at school.

"Come in," she called crossly.

Setting my shoulder against the door, which always stuck in summer, I pushed into the room, went over to her bed, and sat down. I ran my fingers over the slender coolness of one of the brass bars. She was sitting at her desk correcting papers.

"Don't sit on the bed," she said. "You'll make it sink down on that side."

I moved to a chair. "What's the matter?"

"I should think it would be quite obvious that I've got what you would call a hangover." Her voice was acid. "Did you want anything?"

"Just to talk."

"Why talk?"

"Well, I did want to tell you I was going away."

"Away? Where?"

"New Orleans. Eddie's going to get me work there. I'm going with him on Monday."

"It's about time. It seems that everybody's going away, doesn't it? Joshua Tisbury, you, Franz Werner . . ."

"Ilsa," I said.

"No." Myra closed her notebook and screwed on the top to her pen. It took several attempts before she could fit it together. "I don't think Ilsa will leave."

"Why not?" I asked. "What's to prevent her?"

"Use your head, Henry," Myra said. "Everything. Her intelligence, primarily."

"What do you mean?"

"Oh, be quiet!" she said irritably, not to me, but to a vine that was tapping against her window. "Her room's next to mine."

"I know that," I said. "Well?"

"The walls aren't too thick and I've got sharp ears."

"And?"

"They were talking together last night after I'd gone to bed."

"You mean you listened?" My heart began pounding against my ribs the way imprisoned cargo must pound against the ribs of a wrecked ship.

"Oh, let's be honest, Henry," Myra said. "You sit around and listen to a lot of conversations that aren't meant for your ears and you know it. So do I. Why shouldn't we? We're both shadows."

"I—I never mean to listen. I don't do it intentionally. I—I just forget to go away," I stammered.

"Oh, of course!" She laughed her little dry laugh. "You're here all the time. You're quiet, unobtrusive. People forget Henry Porcher's in the room. They forget you exist. And you don't. You're not as real as Ilsa's piano or that old bamboo chaise longue or the marble horse eternally trying to drink out of the marble fountain. Why should people feel strained about talking in front of you? . . . It's not quite the same with me. I have an unfortunately aggressive personality. It's better to be nothing, like you. Far less torturing."

"You don't know what you're saying!" I cried.

"No," she said. "I don't think Ilsa'll go."

"Why?" I asked slowly.

She laughed again. "You see! You're not above listening to someone, else's eavesdropping. Personally, I think it's better to do it deliberately, knowing what you're doing. . . . God knows it's not with malicious intent. I love Ilsa more than anyone in the world. All I want is for her to be happy. It's funny. Most people have either a capacity for loving or a capacity to inspire love. She has both. And she's right. She'll be happier staying here than she would if she went with him."

"But she loves him!" I cried, then added tentatively, "Doesn't she?"

"Of course. Dear God in heaven, yes!"

"What did they say? I mean—I mean—just about her leaving?"

Myra went over to her wardrobe, took out a bottle from among her shoes, and poured a drink into her toothbrush glass. "Do you mind if I have a drink, Henry?" she asked. She didn't offer me one. "I've discovered the only way to get over one hangover is to prepare yourself for another. I don't have school till afternoon, so what difference does it make?"

"Go ahead," I said, I knew there was no use trying to stop her though it was obviously not her first drink that morning.

"I suppose I ought to apologize to Ilsa for last night."

"Why? We all had too much of that punch."

"Yes. . . . Do you know, Henry, in all my life nobody's ever loved me. And there's been no one I could go to and say 'I love you.' One more penalty of being a woman. There's even a theory now that if a man milks a cow he'll get more milk out of it than a woman. Rot. Just let Ilsa try milking a cow. She's got a will of iron. If anyone argued with me the way he argued with her last night, I wouldn't need asking twice. I wouldn't even stop to pack my bags. Did you know he was born in Budapest? His father was in a circus there."

"Oh," I said. "Did he tell you that?"

"Yes. He's very charming."

"You can have him."

She drained her glass. "No, my dear, I can't." Her voice was suddenly sad. "He loves Ilsa. He said that it was only because he had a puny conscience that he let her go before. He said he'd ached for her, his whole body, until sometimes he cried with the pain of it. I know what he meant. Oh, God, I know!"

I turned away and stared out at the river. Soon it would storm.

"In his strange way," she said after a while, going to the window and pushing aside the vines, "he's the only one among us who is big enough for her."

"What do you mean?" My voice was scornful.

"He's the only one of us who's had the courage to accept her blindness as she has accepted it. He didn't insult her by pity, or by pretending to ignore it. That's what she said. It's a companion in the house just as much as that half-witted dog of hers. And with him only could she forget it because he was the only one who was willing to accept it, to realize it, and yet not make a barrier of it. Dear God knows there was no barrier between them. . . ." She tore at the vines for a moment, then turned abruptly from the window and took the bottle out of her wardrobe again. "Well," she said, filling her glass, her hand trembling so that the bottle clattered against the rim, almost breaking it, "I turned to the Bible. . . . Do you remember, Henry," Myra asked, "in Mark, I think it is, Jesus is hungry and He goes up to a fig tree and there aren't any figs on it, because it isn't time for the figs to be ripe yet. And He is angry and says that nobody should ever eat any fruit from that tree forever. And the tree is blighted and withered. That's not fair. It wasn't the fig tree's fault that its fruit wasn't ripe. And it seems to me that's typical. God goes around blighting and withering all the time for no known reason."

"Don't, Myra," I said gently.

"Why not?" she asked, her voice rising shrilly. "Why isn't this as good a time to be hysterical as any? I went to the Bible for comfort. I needed comfort. I remember once walking on the beach, when Ilsa asked me down. And there was the imprint of a woman's body stretched out like a crucifix in the sand; desolate, betrayed. That's how I felt. That's how I feel. But there's no comfort anywhere. And my God, to what lengths we go to deny woman any power or positive goodness. If Ilsa were a man she could leave; it would be all right. . . . The Adam and Eve story is the most typically masculine one I know. Men can't bear the knowledge, the indisputable fact, that woman gives birth to man—so the original woman had to come from man!" She laughed uncontrollably.

"Why won't Ilsa go?" I asked.

"Oh, haven't you enough intelligence to think of the reasons, Henry? Because of the girl. Because she's blind. She knows she'd be a burden to him. He's not a man who can support a burden. He'd hate her eventually. She knows it even if he doesn't. And she won't betray the girl."

"Why would it hurt Brand?" I persisted.

"Are you a complete fool? Blind woman elopes with former lover. It would just rake up the old scandal. Her blindness and Monty's death smothered it before but the embers are still alive. They could be married a hundred times over and it wouldn't stop the tongues. The girl wants to make her life here. Why, God knows. If Ilsa went away, it would make it even more impossible for her here than it is already. . . ." She turned violently and took a book from one of her shelves. "Here.

Give this to Joshua Tisbury for me, will you? Something for him to remember me by."

"Why don't you give it to him yourself?" I asked her.

"I'm not very good at giving things."

"He'd be awfully pleased."

"Are you going to give it to him or must I ask Ilsa?"

"I'll give it to him." I took the book.

"Do you remember Sidney Carton's last words?" she asked. "'It is a far, far better thing that I do than I have ever done. . . .'"

"Why do you think of that now?"

"Because I choose to." She went over and looked at a small snapshot of Ilsa she had stuck in her mirror. Then she looked at the threatening sky reflected behind her.

"It's going to storm in a minute," she said. "For heaven's sake, go down to the dock and see that that damn rowboat is well tied."

"All right," I said.

I went downstairs, pausing a moment at the drawing-room door. Ilsa sat at the piano playing, cleanly and precisely, the music her student had been struggling with. Werner stood behind her, gently caressing her head and neck.

"That the last lesson for today?" he asked.

"Yes," Ilsa answered, leaning back against him. "You know, when they're gone I feel I have to wash the piano of them, play it clean and unfuzzy."

I turned away from the drawing room and went out the front door instead of taking the short cut through the French windows.

63

I walked slowly down to the river. It was quite pointless to tie the boat. If the storm was bad, the boat would just float off and carry the flimsy old dock with it. But it gave me an excuse to go down to the river, and Myra had upset me. I stood on the dock, the sudden northeast wind blowing about me. The river seemed strange, so high from the summer rains that I felt as if it were choking and I should pull a plug out somewhere and relieve it. Everything was a dull dead black. Then a bar of sunlight came from behind the masses of clouds, and the black took on a glittering purple tinge. The trees shivering in the wind seemed to have a black veneer. Even the light seemed black, coming so eerily from behind the purple-black clouds. I expected such awesome weather to make the very squirrels peer timidly from behind their moss curtains, but everything was in a frenzy of activity. All the dogs in the neighborhood were racing around; jays and gulls were squawking and screaming, water bugs were scooting about. I tied the boat more firmly, and went back to the house, heading for the French windows to the drawing room. As I reached the terrace the wind began to blow violently, sounding almost like rain as it swished through the dry leaves and dusty Spanish moss.

Ilsa and Werner were standing close together. As I stepped into the room she moved away from him and stood by the piano.

"It's Henry, Ilsa," I said. "I just went down to the dock to see that the boat was tied tightly."

"Oh." Ilsa nodded, frowning slightly. "Thank you, dear. I didn't know you were here yet."

"I was up in Myra's room."

"How is she this morning?"

"She doesn't feel so well. Good morning, Werner."

"Good morning," he said. "Ready?"

I nodded. He put his arm around Ilsa and we went out to the car. I noticed that he was allowed to lead her when the rest of us would have been angrily pushed away because he did it with an utter lack of self-consciousness.

In spite of the heat we all crowded into the front seat. "Brand and Lorenzo got off at nine," Ilsa said. "I don't know what I'll do without Lorenzo this winter but I'm glad he's going." Then after a moment, she added, "It feels like a northeaster."

"It looks like one," Werner answered.

"The ocean will be rough, then. Good," she said.

I stopped my car at the edge of the dirt road near where Lorenzo had left Ilsa's. If the northeaster did strike, the road would be washed out for about a week and we would be marooned. Werner held Ilsa firmly, almost carrying her when she stumbled in the loose shifting sand. I noticed that in spite of his shabbiness he seemed physically much stronger and firmer than he had eleven years before. There was no longer any softness about him; time and whatever his experiences had been had whittled his body thin and hard.

As we came up to the house the wind seemed to swoop down on us like an eagle. There was a great clamoring of mockingbirds quarreling, sea gulls screeching, palm branches rattling, and a piece of wood banging somewhere in the old empty stable. A branch snapped off the chinaberry tree and fell at our feet as we approached.

That musty sandy odor that belongs to houses at the sea when they have been shut up even for a few hours greeted us as we pushed in the screen door. Lorenzo, Brand, and Ira had evidently been hard at work. The floor had been swept; the windows and the front door were wide open; a fire had been laid in case the storm should turn the weather cold. As we came in, Brand and Lorenzo hurried down the stairs and Ira came out of the kitchen.

"Hello," Lorenzo said. "We've got all the windows open."

"Hello, Mamma; I think there's going to be an awful storm. Ira says the warnings are out all along the coast. I've cleaned and filled all the lamps. Hello, Uncle Henry." Brand nodded at me, kissed Ilsa, then threw an ungracious "hello" over her shoulder to Werner.

"Storm isn't going to be bad. Just a plain old northeaster," Ira said. "I've got a rabbit stew in the pot." He nodded to us, looked searchingly at Ilsa, then went back out to the kitchen.

"Let's go swimming now before the storm breaks," Ilsa said, and we went upstairs to change to bathing clothes.

The waves were rough and wild. The shallow water was dirty, unpleasant, filled with sand and ground-up shells. The waves rolled over and pounced on us, trying to fling us down and grind us into fine dry particles like the sand and shells. Ilsa and Werner, Brand and Lorenzo, holding hands, stood up against the noisy buffetings of the waves, managing to push forward till they were beyond the sandy water. The only thing to do, then, when you saw a wave, was to dive under it in order to avoid being tossed onto the shore like a piece of driftwood. As each concave gray mountain approached, Werner would call out, "Wave!" and Ilsa would dive down, and as she came up on the other side of the churning water Werner would be there to take her hand.

Laughing and shouting, a few yards away, Brand and Lorenzo were diving and jumping, their skins pink and bright from the sharp impersonal slaps of the water. After a few minutes they came out and started walking up the beach, still hand in hand, but Ilsa and Werner continued to battle the waves, seeming to exult in their supremacy over the blind forces of nature, forces that could not cow Ilsa, supposedly as blind as they.

I stood at the edge of the water, shells and sand swirling about my ankles. There didn't seem much point in going in when there was no one for me to protect and no one to protect me. I went back up to the house and dressed; when I got downstairs it was so dark with the approaching storm that I lit the lamps, though they would make the room warmer; and as I turned them up, their golden light brought color and life to the day. I picked up a magazine that the summer tenants had left and sat down to wait for the others. Ira looked in at me once, but he didn't say anything. Except that his hair was shot with white, he seemed unchanged; he was part of the house, part of the beach, remaining, immutable; though the rest of us might grow old and die, Ira would stay as long as the coquina and cypress house, much of which he had built with his own hands, stood erect.

After about an hour Ilsa and Werner came up the ramp. They were laughing and singing; their voices were wild and excited almost as though they had absorbed some of the stormy abandon of the ocean. As they came in the door, Ilsa sniffed.

"The mantle on one of the lamps is burning," she said.

I looked over at the big Aladdin standing lamp. The mantle was half blackened over with carbon and I turned it way down to give it a chance to clear up. I wouldn't have noticed it till it was burned beyond repair.

Ilsa and Werner ran up the stairs. At the landing she paused. "Where're Brand and Lorenzo?"

"Still walking on the beach, I guess," I said, and turned back to my magazine though there wasn't a word of interest in it. One of the shutters at the windows came loose and began to bang in the wind. I got up and went over to the window, pushed up the screen, and fastened the long rust-covered hook again. As I pulled the screen down I heard Ilsa on the stairs. I turned to watch her come down, hurrying, her fingers lightly touching the banister. She wore her usual beach garb of jeans and a bright shirt. Her strong slender feet were bare; they seemed to caress the boards beneath them as she crossed the room to her father's chair.

"Have a good swim?" I asked.

"Wonderful. Children back yet?"

"They're coming up the ramp now," I said, looking out the window.

As Werner came down the stairs, Lorenzo and Brand burst in the screen door, shouting for food.

"All right, now, hold your horses," Ira said, coming in from the kitchen. "Ilsa, you'll have to move. I want to use the big table." He thrust a handful of silver at Brand. "Here. Lay this. You, Lorenzo, get some napkins and put them out if you're that hungry." He went back to the kitchen and returned a moment later with a steaming fragrant earthenware pot of stew.

After eating three large bowlfuls, Werner suddenly said, "Ilsa—"

"What, darling?"

"The awful thing is that I have learned how to act."

She leaned back in her chair. "Why is it awful and what do you mean?"

Werner fixed himself a piece of bread and sugar. "When I was here before, I played Hamlet, Cardinal Wolsey, all the leading roles. I was the star of the company, such as it was. Now, if I were ever in another production of *Hamlet*, the best I could hope for would be Rosencrantz or Guildenstern."

"My two schoolfellows whom I trust trust as I will adders fanged," Lorenzo said with relish.

Werner nodded, taking a large bite of bread and sugar. "Yes. And the unhappy part of it is that while I was playing Hamlet I didn't have the faintest idea how."

"And now you do?" Ilsa asked.

"Yes. I think I can come somewhere near playing it now. In the first place I have far less accent than I had. In the second place I've learned to act in the past eleven years. I've played all over the world, with all kinds of companies, to all kinds of audiences. That has helped. And I've lived and suffered during these years. There is more in me to come out. The best performances—and probably the last—of Hamlet that I ever gave were last year in Australia."

"Tell me about them," Ilsa said gently.

He put his bread and sugar down, pushed his chair back, and stood up. His eyes flashed; a light seemed suddenly to have been illuminated behind his face. "Do you remember in the very beginning of *Hamlet*," he said, "in Hamlet's very first scene on stage—Claudius, his father's murderer, his mother's lover, tells Hamlet that he does not want him to go back to the University. Hamlet pays only scant and scornful attention. Then Queen Gertrude says, 'Let not thy mother lose her prayers, Hamlet.' When I did it here before, I had my queen simply lean forward and say the words lightly. And I answered just as lightly. I quite lost a very important moment."

"How should it have been?" Lorenzo asked.

Werner turned to him for a moment, but it was not long before his eyes were back on Ilsa's listening face. "You see," he said, "I used to think of Hamlet as a role that could do something for me, rather than of myself as an actor who might be able to do something for Hamlet. It wasn't so very long ago that I suddenly realized that Hamlet was more important than Franz Josef Werner."

Ilsa leaned toward him. "Go on," she said.

He was walking restlessly up and down. "The scene I mentioned may not be very important, but I think it is indicative of Hamlet's main problem right at the outset of the play. He was hurt, I think, far more by his disillusionment in his mother than he was by the death of his father."

Brand sat up erect in her chair. "What?" she asked sharply.

"It is Hamlet's disappointment in his mother that overwhelms him," Werner said. "He is lost in a horrible welter of inactivity and procrastination not because he is insane or because he is not brave enough to kill Claudius, but because there is no action he can possibly take that is large enough to express his horrible disillusionment. Killing Claudius would do to avenge his father, but it would do nothing toward clearing his mother."

"When we studied *Hamlet* in school I didn't see any of that," Brand said. "It makes me understand—a lot of things. Please go on."

She spoke almost breathlessly. It was the first time I had seen her speak directly to Werner, interest in what he had to say outweighing her antagonism.

Werner rested his hands on the back of the girl's chair but looked over her ruddy hair at Ilsa. I felt that he believed it was desperately important that he convince Ilsa that he *had* become a better actor even while his star had been sinking; and I, for one, believed that he had.

"When I did Hamlet last year," he said, "I tried to show my audience this relationship immediately, and that no matter how he felt about Gertrude he was still powerless before her will. So I directed my queen—fortunately the director was a good friend of mine and let me do what I liked with my scenes—to get off her throne and come down to me, and look right into my face, her hand on my shoulder. So even before she said a word to me I was weakening. And then when she spoke, in a deep moving tone, 'Let not *thy mother* lose her prayers, Hamlet'—tears came to my eyes and I could do nothing but give in."

Ilsa sat back in her chair once more.

"You see, Ilsa?" he said. "Isn't that better? Isn't that more right?"

"Yes," she said, "much more right."

The shutter broke loose again and began banging violently against the wall. Out back we could hear a great clattering as the wind worried the stable.

"Hamlet so adored both his mother and father," Werner went on, "that he could not see anything better than either one. And when Gertrude married Claudius, he could not see how she could possibly prefer anyone to his father. He had idealized her so that he could not realize that she could have passion, and be weak enough to yield to it."

With a violent motion Brand flung out of her chair and ran out of the room, slamming the screen door behind her. Through the back window I saw her beating against the wind toward the refuge of the stable.

"Brand!" Ilsa called. She sat tense, waiting, for a moment, then sprang from her chair and ran after her daughter. She still moved with electrifying rapidity when she wanted to. She was halfway across the yard before we were out of the door. We all saw the wind tear a board off the stable and fling it at her, and there was no way to warn her. From the stable door Brand screamed. Werner called her name hoarsely, then rushed toward her as the board struck her and she fell to the ground. He reached her first. Brand was kneeling beside her a moment later.

"Is she dead? Is she dead?" she kept asking him hysterically.

Lorenzo put a slender hand firmly over her mouth.

"Be quiet, Brand," he said.

The sky was completely covered with sullen lowering clouds. The light was yellow and angry, and in a moment great drops of rain began to fall, splashing with cold impartiality on Ilsa and the rest of us. Werner picked her up and carried her back to the house.

—She is dead—I thought—She is dead, so now the storm can break. I felt quite numb, quite feelingless. Nothing could feel in this lurid electric weather.

But before Werner had reached the house Ilsa began to stir in his arms. Lorenzo opened the screen door and the actor carried her in. As he laid her down on the old red sofa she raised her hand to her head and spoke in quite a clear voice.

"I think someone tried to finish me off. I got an awful wallop on the head."

Brand broke away from Lorenzo and ran to her mother, pushing Werner away. "Are you all right, Mamma? Mamma, are you all right?"

"Certainly I'm not all right," Ilsa said crossly. "I've got a perfectly frightful headache and all I want to know at this moment is who hit me and why."

"Nobody hit you, liebling," Werner said. "It was the wind blowing a board off the stable."

She relaxed. "Oh. I was a little confused. I think I thought I was Queen Gertrude and Ophelia was after me with a baseball bat." She laughed. "I'd love a cup of coffee. I feel as though I had a hangover, so maybe it'll help. Brand, would you beg Ira to make me some coffee? I've a lump on my head the size of an ostrich egg. Feel, Franz. But gently."

Werner rubbed his fingers softly through her hair as Brand went out to the kitchen. In a moment Ira came in, scowling. "What's this I hear about you rushing into the yard and nearly getting yourself killed?"

"Oh, Ira darling, don't scold," Ilsa pleaded, using the child's voice in which she had begged him to sing the Napoleon song and which I had never heard her use with anyone else. "Just make me some coffee."

"Brand's making it," he said. "Let me see where it hit you." She raised her fingers to her hair and he felt the spot with strong, harsh fingers.

"Ow!" she cried. "Have pity, Ira!"

"You're all right," he said crossly. "Just a little old bump. Always did have a skull hard as a rock." He went, muttering, back to the kitchen.

"Why was I out in the yard?" Ilsa asked. "Brand was upset about something and I went after her. What was it?"

"Never mind," Lorenzo said. "Here she comes with your coffee."

Brand came in with a cup and put it into Ilsa's waiting fingers. "Are you really all right, Mamma, please?"

"Of course I'm all right, ladybird," Ilsa said.

And I thought that no matter what happened she always *would* be all right. That had always been the most *Ilsa* thing about her.

64

We went back to town after midnight. Although the storm made me nervous and neither Brand nor Lorenzo cared for it, Ilsa and Werner could scarcely bear to leave the house.

The rain came in great drenching waves, splashing against the windows, then receding, then rushing at the house again. Palm branches cracked from the trees and flailed against the walls of the house. At high tide the waves thundered against the bulkhead and splashed over it, drenching the ramp halfway to the house with water and salt spray.

Werner insisted on carrying Ilsa to the car. "I know quite well that you are capable of walking," he said, "but I don't want a branch of a tree to snap off and crack you on the head."

Lorenzo and Brand drove ahead. We followed close behind. We had to go very slowly. The wind and the rain were so heavy that the automobile lights did not penetrate more than a few inches ahead of us. The windshield wipers were practically useless. Sand had washed over the road and it was difficult not to skid. Just a few yards ahead of us Brand and Lorenzo were nothing but a rain-drenched shadow.

It should have been the most difficult driving I had ever known, but somehow I felt quite calm as we pushed slowly through the night. Beside me Werner began to hum the rosy-bush song and somehow I no longer felt jealous. Ilsa reached up and ran her fingers through his thick gray-shot hair.

"You know," he said dreamily, "once I read in a book about a scientist who grew from a cocoon a very rare and beautiful moth. It was the only moth of its species in that country. And yet at mating time there was another moth of the same species beating against the window to get in. Extraordinary, isn't it? But scientific fact."

"Um," Ilsa mumbled. She was asleep, her head down on his shoulder.

65

In spite of the late hour at which I had gone to bed and the even later hour at which I had gone to sleep, I woke up early the next morning, remembering that I had forgotten to give Joshua Myra's book. After I had dressed and had some coffee I put on my raincoat, a shabby but sentimentally loved reminder of the days of my manhood in Paris, and set off with the book, wrapped in newspaper, under my arm.

I decided to stop for a few minutes at Cousin Anna's. It would probably be my last chance to say good-bye to her if I was to spend the evening at Silver's talking things over with Eddie. The next day would be spent packing, getting ready to go, and early Monday morning the train left for New Orleans.

The wind was still strong as I splashed through the wet streets, although not so angrily violent as it had been at the beach. Cousin Anna would be unable to sit in her usual place under the magnolia tree, I knew; and she was not in the pearl-gray living room where Cousin William sat cradling his pipe in his curved hand and reading the newspaper. I greeted him, and we talked for a few minutes; then he told me that Cousin Anna was in the small upstairs sitting room and to go on up if I had anything I wanted to talk to her about, which he could tell by my manner that I had. He stroked his trim little Vandyke beard, faded, but still ungrayed, and his eyes smiled at me through the thick lenses of his glasses.

I smiled back, rather sheepishly, and climbed the stairs. Cousin Anna was lying on the delicate rose chaise longue in the little sitting room, her silver shawl about her shoulders. Her eyes were closed and I didn't know whether she was asleep or just thinking. I entered the room very quietly and stood by the huge gold harp that I had so seldom heard her touch, tracing with my forefinger the fine carvings of the wood. She looked old and fragile as she lay there, her lips puckered and almost colorless, the blue veins raised under the scarred tissue of her hands.

After a moment she opened her eyes, looked at me as I stood uncertainly by the harp, and said, "Come in, Henry."

"Good morning, Cousin Anna." I pulled a straight chair near her and sat down.

"Did you see William?" she asked.

"Yes. He told me that you were here and I might come up."

"Naturally. How does Ilsa like the storm?"

"She loves it."

"You look very wet. Take off your coat."

"I can only stay a moment."

"I hear by the grapevine," Cousin Anna said, spreading her fingers apart slowly and looking at them as they lay on the arm of the chaise longue, "that Ilsa's actor has returned."

"Yes," I said.

"Have you seen him?"

"Yes."

"Is that all you have to say?"

After a moment I said, "We went to the beach yesterday."

"We?"

"Ilsa and Werner, Brand and Lorenzo."

"And you."

"Yes."

"Is she happy?"

"I don't know," I said. "Yes. But I don't think being happy with Ilsa is the same as it is with the rest of us."

"Did it upset Brand to have him come back?"

"I think it did."

"And you?"

"Yes. But—"

"But what?"

"I couldn't hate him this time."

"I didn't hate him before. I liked him," Cousin Anna said. "Though Ilsa only brought him over once. How long is he going to be here?"

"He's leaving today. He has to get back to New York."

"I see." Cousin Anna closed her eyes. I felt that I had been dismissed, but I still had not said what I had come to say; I had not said good-bye; so I sat looking down at her, waiting for her to open her eyes again.

When she didn't, I finally said, "Cousin Anna, I came to say good-bye."

Without raising her finely wrinkled eyelids she spoke. "So at last you're leaving."

"Yes. Eddie says he can get me work in New Orleans."

"That's fine." She opened her eyes suddenly and looked at me with that old penetrating regard—that look that has nothing to do with the actual structure of the eye itself, but that comes from the essence of the person. "What decided you?"

"I don't know," I said. "Just everything seemed to be coming to an end all at once."

"You remind me of something Elizabeth once said to me." Cousin Anna let her hand fall from the arm of the chaise longue to join the other one in her lap. "We were watching the stars one night at the beach, and she picked out one star that was especially beautiful, almost blue, almost with a living pulse in its light. It was shortly after she had met Ilsa's father. And she said to me, 'That's my favorite star. It always has been. If one could fall in love with a star, I'd be in love with it. But John Brandes told me that that star is dead now. Burned out, utterly lifeless. The light that we see and that I love, that is so ecstatically, frighteningly passionate and beautiful, has been extinguished for thousands of years. And we're only seeing it now.' We stood there and watched the star for a long time and that cold scientific fact was difficult to understand."

"But why do I remind you of that, Cousin Anna?"

She smiled, her faint almost imperceptible turning-up of the corners of her mouth, the slight lightening behind the eyes. "It wasn't like Elizabeth to fall in love with a star thousands of years too late. But it's exactly like you. I hope you're going to New Orleans in time, Henry."

"I hope so, too," I said. "I have to go now. I have to give a book to Joshua Tisbury. Good-bye, Cousin Anna." I stood stiffly by the chaise longue.

"Come here," she said. I bent down to her and she put her arms around me with tenderness; her lips were gentle as she brushed them against my cheek. "Good-bye, Henry boy. Bless you," she said. And then, as I reached the door, "Give my love to Ilsa."

66

I heard voices in the living room when I got to Ilsa's. When I looked through the rice portieres I was grateful and pleased to see both Joshua and Ilsa there, and no one else. Joshua saw me, smiled, and beckoned, so I went in, stripping of my dripping raincoat. I heard Ilsa saying:

"—if I were like most of the good people down here, I'd believe that I didn't deserve happiness for what I've done."

"For what you've done? You haven't done anything," Joshua said.

"I've deliberately killed life for years. If it were just me, it would be bad enough, but I've pulled Brand into this pool of nonexistence with me. And you, too, Henry."

I had entered very quietly, but her sharp ears had caught my step.

"No," I said.

"And that's what I have to pay for. That's why there's no answer now. Except the wrong one."

"It'll be all right," Joshua said, his voice very tender. "It'll be all right somehow, Ilsa."

"Yes," she said. "I know. Thank you, Joshua."

"It sounds so strange to have you thank me—when it's you I want to thank."

"Me? Whatever for?"

"For just being, I guess. I think you knew when I first came here that I wasn't just physically ill. I was beginning to go to pieces inside. I couldn't write any more. . . . I don't know. Just watching you up against so much more than I was—coming out so strong and fine—"

"I was bitter and sarcastic," she said.

"Some day I'll show you what you're like. I'll put you in a novel—not your story, but you as a person."

"You'd better write a play for Franz first." Her laugh rang out again.

"I'll do that, too," he promised.

"I'd like to meet your girl—the one you're going back to."

"You will," he said. "You will."

"Will I?"

"Yes. . . . Now, good-bye."

"Good-bye, Joshua. God bless you."

He bent down and kissed her mouth, then walked quickly out. I followed him to the door and gave him the book. Then I came back in.

"Well, Henny?" Ilsa said. The rain that was still pouring down outside the long windows plunged the room into an unreal submarine light.

"Here I am."

She felt for my hand. "I know how strange it seemed to me," she said, "when Father used to apologize for keeping me at the beach. And Anna for taking me away. I know a little now how they felt and what they meant. I shouldn't have let you get so dependent on me. You see, I truly didn't realize that I—I could be really important to anyone—even Franz."

"Ilsa," I started, then knew I couldn't tell her yet, though I knew, too, that now there was no getting out of my leaving. Just as there was no escape from autumn once the northeaster broke, so there was no longer any escape from my departure.

Werner came in. "My bag is all ready, Ilsa. Hello, Porcher. Ilsa, where's Brandy?"

"She went over to see Lorenzo's harpsichord. It's finished."

"Ah."

For once Valdosta knocked before sticking her head in the door. "Miz Woolf?"

"Yes," Ilsa said impatiently.

"I got to give my notice." The shrill little voice was insolent.

"Very well."

"I don't like living on premises and I is got to be careful where I works. Miz Jackson she asked me to come work for her."

"Splendid!" Ilsa said.

The little mosquito voice cracked. "You ain't angry with me?"

"Why should I be?"

"You don't mind my going?"

"Not at all."

"I could stay if you really want me."

"I don't want you."

"Well . . . all right. . . ."

"When do you want to go?" Ilsa's voice was matter-of-fact and businesslike. "Tonight? I'll ask Brand to make out a check for you."

"Well . . . all right, Miz Woolf. I'se real sorry to leave you. . . ."

"You'd better get along out to the kitchen now." Ilsa's voice remained cold and unmoved.

"Well—" Valdosta's shrill mosquito drone wavered in bewilderment as she trailed out.

"Little she-cat," Werner said. "She must have eyes and ears all over her body. It's incredible that you should have to put up with this sort of thing. Ilsa, you're coming with me and no more foolishness."

He didn't seem to care whether or not I heard.

Ilsa's voice was trembling. "You say it's incredible that I should have to put up with this sort of thing. Have you thought what this sort of thing means to Brand? *I* don't give a damn. You know that. But it's the most important thing in the world to the child. For some reason she's chosen the people of this town as the people she wants to live with, to belong to. They're not all as warped as Mrs. Jackson, nor as malicious as Beulah, but they lap up the same dirt with as much greed."

"That's still no reason for you to stay among them."

"If Brand marries Lorenzo, she has a chance of happiness, as long as I don't ruin it. God! It's amazing what a difference a wedding ring makes down here! . . . I love my child, and I want her to have her chance. And you. Franz Josef, my darling. The most important reason of all. The real reason. I'm not going to be a stone hanging around your neck. That would be a new part for me, and one I'm not going to play. I'm independent here and I've got to keep my independence. And I want to keep your love, too."

Werner started to speak, but Mattie Belle hurried in excitedly. "Miz Woolf, we purely don't need that no-good girl. She'd do you for a fare-thee-well any day. The way she been carrying on is something scandulous. How she think *she* can talk! We get along fine without her. She'll get her come-uppance, don't you worry. I'll shut anybody's face who think they got anything to say."

"Thank you, Mattie Belle. Bless you," Ilsa said.

From somewhere down the block we heard Médor raise her voice in a long-drawn-out wail. Ilsa sighed. "She thinks she's lost again."

"I'll get her, Miz Woolf," Mattie Belle said. She curtsied to Werner, grinned at him, and bobbed out.

"Who'll be next to leave, I wonder?" Ilsa lightly struck a discord on the piano.

"Does it matter very much, when you lose roomers?" Werner asked.

She shrugged. "The rooms fill again eventually. . . . I wonder if Joshua ordered a taxi."

"I'll go see," I said, reminding her of my presence.

But just then Joshua knocked and came in. "The taxi's here," he said. "We'd better take the suitcases out and go."

"So soon!" Ilsa cried.

"If we want to get seats," Werner said gently.

"I've taken my bag out. I'll get yours, Werner," Joshua said. "If you want to say good-bye—or are you going to the station, Ilsa?"

She shook her head, without speaking.

"I'll wait in the taxi for you then," Joshua said.

"I'll give you a hand with the bags." I followed him out.

67

It was less than five minutes later that I burst back in.

"Ilsa—oh, Ilsa—" I cried.

"What is it?"

"It's Violetta—she's coming up the path—"

"Get rid of her, for heaven's sake."

Brand pushed in behind me, her face strained and white; she must just have come back from Lorenzo's, for she was still wearing her raincoat, dripping with rain, and her hair lay in sopping wet rings about her face. "Mamma, Aunt Violetta—" she cried. "I'm sorry."

"I know," Ilsa said brusquely. "Tell her I died and was taken away in the night."

But there was no stopping Violetta, who broke upon us with the inexorability of a full-breasted wave. "Well, I bet this is a surprise!"

Ilsa made no effort to hide her anger. "It certainly is."

Her rage was lost on Violetta. "I had to come over to this part of town this morning so I thought I'd just surprise Ilsa and drop in. Bet you didn't expect to see me so soon. Well, Henry Randolph Porcher, what do you mean by turning tail and running like that when I wave at you? My land, am I busting into a meeting or something?"

"Mr. Tisbury and Mr. Werner are going North," Ilsa said between clenched teeth.

"Oh!" Violetta exclaimed. "Brand, I don't believe I know this gentleman."

"Violetta, Mr. Franz Werner. Franz, my sister-in-law, Mrs. Silverton," Ilsa said harshly. Her clenched fingers were trembling.

"Pleased to meet you, I'm sure." Violetta said. "Are you one of my brother's old friends? Monty had so many friends."

"My friend," Ilsa said.

"Why, Ilsa, you sly thing!" Violetta's face beamed with joy and sudden recollection of the name. "I do believe you've been hiding something from us! Just wait till I tell Mrs. Jackson. Just you wait!"

"I can't," Ilsa said.

Joshua returned. "The suitcases are all in the taxi. We'd better go."

"Yes—" Ilsa breathed.

"Going to be mighty hot on that train," Violetta laughed gaily.

"Good-bye, Ilsa." Joshua pressed her hand and left quickly, nodding to Werner to follow him.

I stood stock-still, trying desperately to think of some way to get Violetta out so they'd have a chance to say good-bye; but of course my mind completely failed me. I waited for Ilsa to turn on Violetta with her usual violence and throw her out, but she did nothing, standing quite still in the middle of the room, breathing rapidly, her wide-open eyes seeming to stare above our heads.

Werner walked restlessly over to the marble Othello and Iago and back again.

And then, as I stood there helplessly, listening to the rain pour down upon us from a full heart, I seemed to hear again Myra's voice saying scornfully, "Are you a complete fool?" And I knew why Ilsa couldn't drive Violetta from the room, why she must stay and deal with her. She would hurt Brand as much by giving Violetta more food for gossip as she would by leaving.

Myra came in, looking grimly determined. I guessed that Joshua had told her about Violetta's arrival.

"Good morning, Mrs. Silverton," she said.

"Why, Miss Turnbull, how you?" Violetta held out a fleshy, manicured hand which Myra ignored. "Not at school?"

"It's Saturday," I said, pushing Violetta out of the room with my mind. Get out, get out, get out, I whispered, but she didn't move. She seemed to fill the entire room with her corpulent presence.

Médor catapulted into the room and threw herself in an agonized frenzy at Ilsa, who bent down and pulled her ear gently, then straightened and stood tense again. Médor crawled rheumatically under the table with the Othello and the Iago, almost upsetting it.

"Why, so it is Saturday!" Violetta cried. "I forgot! The days go by so fast I can't tell one from another. Now, if you'd asked me I'd have said it was Thursday."

"Won't you come out on the veranda with me, Mrs. Silverton?" Myra urged tensely.

"Out on the veranda? In this rain? What a peculiar thing, Miss Turnbull. Whatever for?"

"Well—I—I though you might be interested in hearing some—some rather interesting things about the school. As one of the trustees—"

"You can tell me right in here, can't you; Miss Turnbull? I'm sure it would interest Ilsa, too. She's so interested in *everything*!"

"I've got to go now," Werner said in a low voice.

"I'll go out with you," Ilsa answered.

"We'll all go out!" Violetta exclaimed. "I love to see people off for things. Don't you, Miss Turnbull?"

"I loathe it," Myra said.

"But why? I think trains are so exciting. And good-byes always make me cry."

Myra's hands were shaking with nervousness. "I don't like people," she jerked out.

"You don't like what?" Violetta tried to sound puzzled, though there was no mistaking Myra's meaning.

"People."

"Then *you* wouldn't be here, Miss Turnbull." Violetta was arch.

"Nobody'd miss me," Myra said angrily. "Look at the mess people have got things into. Much better to be a wisteria vine climbing up the white pillars of the veranda, or one of the sea oats waving golden tassels at the beach, right out with the wind and sun and rain and stars. Take away people and the world would be a happier place . . . much happier without people who think they're so good and who breathe out evil as naturally as flowers breathe out oxygen. There shouldn't be any people. Just trees and flowers and animals. Evolution's a mistake." She stalked to the door, then paused and said to the room in general. "I did my best. I'm sorry. I can't help it."

We heard her hurrying upstairs.

"My, she *is* peculiar, isn't she?" Violetta's little eyes were eager. "Certainly makes me have a mind to believe the stories they tell about her drinking and everything. Well, shall we go out to the taxi? I'm so wet I don't mind getting a little wetter for a few farewells."

"Yes, let's go, Violetta," I said quickly, trying to pull her out.

"Come along, Ilsa," she called.

"You go, Violetta." With a great effort Ilsa made her voice calm. "I'll stay here."

"Now, I'm not going to leave you alone, Ilsa Woolf," Violetta cried. "It's not good for you to be by yourself so much. Either you go or I stay."

Werner raised his arms in despair. Then he went over to Ilsa and took her hand. "Good-bye."

"Good-bye," she answered.

He kissed her quick and hard on the mouth. Then he ran out. The rain came down in fresh torrents. It was difficult to hear above it.

"I thought we'd settle down and have a nice chat this morning, Ilsa," Violetta said, ignoring the fact that Ilsa was standing rigid as a statue, listening. "We haven't chatted in a long time. Yesterday I was in such a hurry I didn't have time to say a word."

The doorbell rang harshly. Ilsa moved slowly away from Violetta.

"I'll go, Mamma," Brand said, and hurried out.

Ilsa stood still, listening. Violetta's words poured over her like rain, drenching her.

"You seem real strained about something this morning, Ilsa." Violetta's face was eagerly prying. "What is it? I guess the heat's getting you down. But this northeaster ought to break it, though I must say it feels mighty close. I had to keep the windows of the car closed on my way over, it was raining so hard, and I was like to stifle, it got so hot. It sure is going to be hot for those two men on the train. Summer's over at any rate, though. It won't be bad from now on, and about time. Now, Ilsa, I want you to tell me all about you and that fascinating Mr. Werner."

Brand came back in. "Mamma—"

"Yes?"

"It's someone to see about a room, Mamma."

"Have they gone?" Ilsa stood clutching the back of a chair for support.

"Yes. The taxi just drove off. Shall I see him, Mamma? Or will you tend to it?"

"To what?"

"The man who came about a room."

Ilsa straightened up. "I'll tend to it. I'm afraid you'll have to wait, Violetta."

"That's quite all right, Ilsa, honey." Violetta settled down, pulling her chair out of place.

"Don't move the furniture!" Brand cried fiercely.

Startled, Violetta put the chair back. She called after Ilsa, "Don't you give one little thought to me, Ilsa, sugar. You run along and rent your room and I'll be right here when you come back."

Ilsa said nothing. Holding herself very straight, she went out, followed by the dog. Brand and I watched after her. We could hear her talking at the door, her voice low and steady.

I turned, ignoring Violetta, and went out of one of the French windows into the rain.

The long grass stroked my ankles and drenched them. The rain was clean and cool on my face. Far off I heard the long beseeching whistle of the train, calling its longing cry through the wet autumn air.

ABOUT THE AUTHOR

Madeleine L'Engle (1918–2007) was an American author of more than sixty books, including novels for children and adults, poetry, and religious meditations. Her best-known work, *A Wrinkle in Time*, one of the most beloved young adult books of the twentieth century and a Newbery Medal winner, has sold more than fourteen million copies since its publication in 1962. Her other novels include *A Wind in the Door*, *A Swiftly Tilting Planet*, and *A Ring of Endless Light*. Born in New York City, L'Engle graduated from Smith College and worked in theater, where she met her husband, actor Hugh Franklin. L'Engle documented her marriage and family life in the four-book autobiographical series, the Crosswicks Journals. She also served as librarian and writer-in-residence at the Cathedral Church of Saint John the Divine in Manhattan for more than thirty years.

MADELEINE L'ENGLE

FROM OPEN ROAD MEDIA

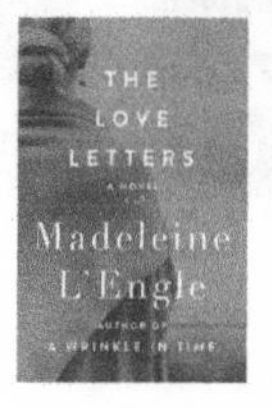

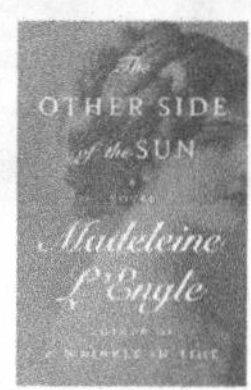

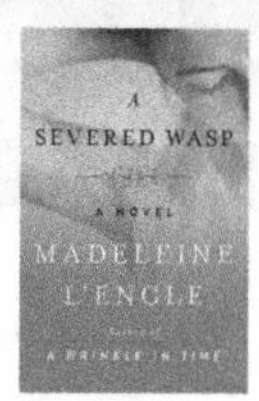

CPSIA information can be obtained
at www.ICGtesting.com
Printed in the USA
BVHW03s2150040418
512548BV00002B/5/P